of wild action following after. And he manages to do that with real, sharply drawn characters in a genuinely alien future at a pace that never lags. Buy it and read it."

—John Barnes, author of *The Armies of Memory*

"An enjoyable tale sprawling across a quite original vision of the future. This was engaging, and kept me engaged until the last page. The bottom line is that I felt no urge to put this book down—I wanted to know what would happen next."

—Neal Asher, author of *Brass Man*

SINGULARITY'S RING

Paul Melko

A TOM DOHERTY ASSOCIATES BOOK
NEW YORK

This is a work of fiction. All the characters, organizations, and events portrayed in this novel are either products of the author's imagination or are used fictitiously.

SINGULARITY'S RING

Chapter 1 previously appeared in somewhat different form as "Strength Alone" in *Asimov's Science Fiction*.

Chapter 2 previously appeared in somewhat different form as "Singletons in Love" in the anthology *Live Without a Net* and was reprinted in *The Year's Best Science Fiction, Twenty-first Annual Collection*.

Edited by David G. Hartwell

A Tor Book
Published by Tom Doherty Associates, LLC
175 Fifth Avenue
New York, NY 10010

www.tor-forge.com

Tor® is a registered trademark of Tom Doherty Associates, LLC.

ISBN-13: 978-0-7653-5702-1
ISBN-10: 0-7653-5702-X

First Edition: February 2008
First Mass Market Edition: May 2009

Printed in the United States of America

0 9 8 7 6 5 4 3 2 1

For Stacey,
of course

ACKNOWLEDGMENTS

This book would have been impossible without the help of many, many people. Thanks go first to Lou Anders, whose anthology evoked the universe. Also thanks to Gardner Dozois and Sheila Williams for giving Strom's story a home. The Blue Heaven writers group helped me perfect the thing. My agent, Caitlin Blasdell, provided crucial advice and guidance. David Hartwell and Denis Wong at Tor turned some scraps of paper into a book. There are others, I know, who helped too. Thank you. Lastly, extra special thanks to my wife, Stacey, who puts up with my daydreaming and distraction. (See? I wasn't ignoring you; I was working.)

SINGULARITY'S
RING

ONE

Strom

I am strength.

I am not smart, that is Moira. I cannot articulate, like Meda. I do not understand the math that Quant does, and I cannot move my hands like Manuel.

If to anyone, you would think I am closest to Manuel; his abilities are in his hands, in his dexterity. But his mind is jagged sharp; he remembers things and knows them for us. Trivial information that he spins into memory.

No, I am closest to Moira. Perhaps because she is everything I am not. She is as beautiful as Meda, I think. If she were a singleton, she would still be special. If the pod were without me, I think, they would be no worse off. If I were removed, the pod would still be Apollo Papadopulos, and still be destined to become the starship captain we were built to be. We are all humans individually, and I think my own thoughts, but together we are something different, something better, though my contribution is nothing like the others'.

When I think this, I wall it off. Quant looks at me; can she smell my despair? I smile, hoping she cannot see past my fortifications. I touch her hand, our pads sliding together, mixing thoughts, and send her a chemical memory of Moira and Meda laughing as children, holding hands. They are three or four years old in the memory, so it is after we have pod-bonded, prior to Third State, but still in the creche. Their hair is auburn, and it hangs from their heads in baloney curls. Moira has a skinned knee and she isn't smiling as largely as Meda. In the memory, from the distant past, Meda reaches for Quant, who reaches for Manuel, who touches my hand, and we all feel Meda's joy at seeing the squirrel in the meadow, and Moira's anger at falling down and scaring it off. Here on the mountain, there is a pause in our consensus, as everyone catches the memory.

Moira smiles, but Meda says, "We have work to do, Strom."

We do, I know we do. I feel my face redden. I feel my embarrassment spread in the air, even through our parkas. No one needs to touch the pads on my wrist to share it.

Sorry. My hands form the word, as the thought passes among us.

We are somewhere in the Rocky Mountains. Our teachers have dropped us by aircar, here near the treeline, and told us to survive for five days. They have told us nothing else. Our supplies are those we could gather in the half hour they gave us.

For seven weeks we and our classmates have trained in survival methods: desert, forest, jungle. Not that we will see any of these terrains in space. Not that we will find climates of any kind whatsoever except for deadly vacuum, and that we know how to survive. But these are the hurdles that have been placed before us. The prize is the captaincy of the starship *Consensus;* it is what we have been built to do, as have our classmates.

On the first day of survival training, our teacher Theseus had stood before us and screamed in volleying bursts. He was a duo, the most basic form of pod, just two individual humans.

"You are being taught to think!" yelled Theseus on the left.

"You are being taught to respond to unknown environments, under unknown and strenuous conditions!" continued Theseus on the right.

"You do not know what you will face!"

"You do not know what will allow you to survive and what will kill you!"

Two weeks of class instruction followed, and then week after week we had been transported to a different terrain, a different locale, and shown what to do to survive. But always with Theseus nearby. Now, in our final week, we are alone, just the students on this mountain.

"Apollo Papadopulos! Cold-weather survival! Twenty kilos per pod member! Go!" one of Theseus yelled at us from our dorm-room doorway.

Luckily the parkas were in the closet. Luckily we had a polymer tent. Hagar Julian has only canvas coats with no insulation, we know. They will have a harder time of it.

Twenty kilograms is not a lot. I carry sixty kilos of it myself and distribute the rest to my podmates. In the aircar, we note that Hagar Julian and Elliott O'Toole have split the load evenly among themselves; they are not playing to their strengths.

Strom! Once again Meda chastises mē, and I jerk my hands away from Manuel's and Quant's, but they can still smell the embarrassment pheromones. I cannot stop the chemical proof of my chagrin from drifting in the frigid air. I reach again for my place in the consensus, striving to be an integral part of the pod, trying to concentrate. Together we can do anything.

Chemical thoughts pass from hand to hand in our circle, clockwise and counterclockwise, suggestions, lists, afterthoughts. I stand between Moira and Quant, adding what I can. This is our most comfortable thinking position. If we rearrange ourselves, me holding Manuel's hand perhaps, or Moira and Meda together, the thoughts are different. Sometimes this is useful.

Ideas whir past me and I feel I am only a conduit. Some thoughts are marked by their thinker, so that I know it is Quant who has noted the drop in temperature and the increased wind speed, which causes us to raise the priority of shelter and fire. Consensus forms.

We have to rig our shelter before dark. We have to start a fire before dark. We have to eat dinner. We have to dig a latrine.

The list passes among us. We reach consensus on decision after decision, faster than I can reason through some of the issues: I add what I can. But I trust the pod. The pod is me.

Our hands are cold; we have removed our gloves to think. In the cold of the Rockies our emotions—the pheromones that augment our chemical thoughts—are like lightning, though sometimes the wind will whisk the feeling away before we can catch it. With gloves on our touch pads and parkas over our noses and neck glands, it is hard to think. It is almost like working alone, until we finish some subtask and join for a quick consensus, shedding gloves.

"Strom, gather wood for the fire," Moira reminds me.

The tasks that require broad shoulders fall to me. I step away from the others, and I am suddenly cut off from them: no touch, no smell. We practice this, being alone. We were born alone, yet we have spent our youth from First State to Fourth State striving to be a single entity. And now we practice being alone again. It is a skill. I look back at the other four. Quant touches Moira's hand, passing a thought, some shared confidence. The spike of jealousy must be the face of my fear. If they have thought something important, I will know it later when we rejoin. For now, I must act alone.

We have chosen an almost flat tract of land in a meager grove of wind-stunted pines. The rock slopes gently away into a V-shape, a catch for wind and snow. The shallow ravine drops sharply into a ledge of rock, the side of a long valley of snowdrifts and trees that the aircar passed over as we arrived. Above us is a sheer wall, topped with a mass of snow and ice. I cannot see the peak from here; we are many hundreds of meters below it. Stretching in either direction are lines of jagged mountaintops, their white faces reflecting the afternoon sun. Clouds seem to bump against their western sides.

The snow is thin enough on the ground here that we can reach the rocky earth beneath it. The trees will shelter us from the wind and provide support for the tent lines, we hope. I walk down the gentle slope, along the line of pines.

We have no axe, so I must gather fallen logs and branches. This will be a problem. We cannot have a good fire with half-decayed logs. I file the thought away for later consensus.

I find a sundered pine branch, thick as my forearm, sticky with sap. I wonder if it will burn as I drag it back up to the camp. I should have climbed up to find wood, I realize, so that I could drag it down to the camp. It is obvious now and would have been obvious before if I had asked for consensus.

I drop my wood in the clearing the others have made and start to arrange it into a fireplace. I draw stones into a U-shape, the open end facing the wind coming down the mountain for a draft. The stones at the sides can be used for cooking.

Strom, that is where the tent will go!

I jump back, and I realize that I had been working without consensus, making decisions on my own.

Sorry.

Confused and embarrassed, I drag the stones and wood away from the tent clearing. I think that I am not well, but I suppress that as I sweep snow away and place the stones again.

We decide to gauge our classmates' progress, so I climb the trail above the treeline to see how the rest of our class is doing. There are five of us on survival training, all of us classmates, all of us familiar with each other and in competition. It is how it has always been among us. How the rest are doing is important.

I climb above the treeline, and to the west half a kilometer away, I see our classmate Elliott O'Toole's tent already up, with the pod inside it. To the east, a few hundred meters away, I see another student—Hagar Julian—working in the snow, instead of on an area of rocky slope. They are digging into a drift, perhaps to form a snow cave. They will have a long time to dig, I think. Hollowing out a space for five will expend much energy. They can't have a fire.

The other two pods—Megan Kreighton and Willow Murphy—are hidden in the trees beyond Hagar Julian. I cannot determine their progress, but I know from experience that our greatest competition will be from Julian and O'Toole. Only one of us will pilot the *Consensus* through the Rift.

I return and pass the others memories of what I have seen.

We have begun pitching the tent, using the nearby pine trees to support it. We have no ground spikes, removed from the packs to reach the twenty-kilogram-per-person limit. There are many things we have removed to make our weight limit, but not matches. I kneel to start the fire.

Strom!

The scent call is sharp on the crisp wind. The pod is waiting for me to help pull and tie the tent support lines; they have consensed without me. Sometimes they do that. When it is expedient. I understand; they can reach a valid consensus without me easily enough.

We pull the spider-silk lines taut, and the tent stretches into place, white on white, polymer on snow, a bubble of sanctuary, and suddenly our shelter is ready. The thrill of success fills the air, and Quant enters and comes out again, smiling.

"We have shelter!"

Now dinner, Manuel sends.

Dinner is small bags of cold, chewy fish. Once we have the fire going, we can cook our food. For now, it's cold from the bag. *If we were really on our own in the mountains, we would hunt for our food,* I send. The image of me carrying the carcass of an elk over my shoulders makes Moira laugh. I mean it as a joke, but then I count the bags of jerky and dried fruit. We will be hungry by the end of the test. It is my job to see to the safety of the pod, and I feel bad that we did not pack more food.

"Another test," Quant says. "Another way to see if we're good enough. As if this mountain is anything like another world. As if this will tell them anything about us."

I know what Quant means. Sometimes we feel manipulated. Everything we face is another test to pass. There is no failure, just success, repeated, until it means nothing. When we fail, it will be catastrophic.

The thought is unleashed before I can stop it.

"We will not fail," Meda says, and I am embarrassed again.

Quant shakes her head, then is suddenly absorbed with the flicker of light on the tent wall.

"We can watch the sunset," I say.

We have loosened hoods and gloves in the tent, though

it is still just above freezing inside. But the difference between inside and out is even more severe as the sun now hides behind the western peaks. The sunset is colorless, the sunlight crisp and white. It reflects off the bottom of the Ring, making the slim orbital torus brighter than it is at noon. Wispy clouds slide across the sky, fast, and I note to the others a possibility of snow. Before our five days on the mountain are over, we will see more snow, that is certain. Perhaps tonight.

Elliott O'Toole has managed to light a fire and we smell the burning wood. He probably hasn't finished his tent, but he has a fire. The smell of roasted meat drifts on the wind.

"Bastard!" Quant said. "He has steak!"

We don't need it.

I want it!

I say, "This is only about surviving, not luxury."

Quant glares at me, and I sense her anger. She is not alone. I cave before this partial consensus and apologize, though I don't know why I do. Meda has told me that I hate strife. I assume everyone does. We are five and I am one. I bow to the group consensus, as we all do. It is how we reach the best decision.

With dinner finished and night upon us, we complete what chores we can outside: a fire, if we can start it, and a latrine. Manuel and I work on the fire pit, moving stones, breaking tinder, building up a steeple of wood. The wind is too strong, I realize, for a fire tonight. The flatness of the plateau made it a good place for a tent, but the wind whips down the ravine. The tent ropes sing.

We smell fear on the wind, child pheromones, and I think one of us is in danger, but then we smell it as a foreign fear: one of our classmates is in danger. Then, as the wind dies for a moment, we hear the heavy breathing of someone running through the snowdrifts. The pod condenses around me, as it does in times of crisis. We touch, assess, but we have only the smell and the sound to base consensus on.

I move forward to help whoever it is. I smell the caution in the air, but ignore it. Now is the time to help. Sometimes we spend too much time being cautious, consensing on things. I would never share such thoughts.

It is one of Hagar Julian, just one. I don't know her name, but she is running in the cold, her hood down, her head exposed. She doesn't see me, but I catch her in my arms and stop her. In her terror, she would have run past us into the dark night, perhaps over the cliff.

The smell of her is alien. I force the hood over her head. The head is a heat sink; you must always keep it covered in the cold. That and the hands. Perhaps this is why the instructors have chosen the mountains for our final test; the organs that make us a pod are nearly useless in the cold.

"What is it? What's happened?" I ask.

She is heaving, releasing fear and nothing else. I don't know how much is from being separated from her self or from something that has happened. I know that Julian is a close-knit pod. They seldom separate.

The night is black. I can't see O'Toole's fire, or Julian's ice cave anymore. It is a miracle that she reached us.

I pick her up over my shoulder and carry her slowly through the snowdrifts to the open area around our tent. She is shivering. I push through the questions of my pod. Now is not the time for questions. Quant pulls open the tent for me.

Snow falls out of the woman's gloves. I take them off her hands, which are blue, and exchange them for my own. I check her boots and coat for more snow, and brush it out. By then, the rest of my pod has joined me, and I use them to access our survival instruction.

Hypothermia.

The shivering, the disorientation, and no response are all signs of body temperature loss. Maybe some of the disorientation is from being separated from her pod.

Hospitalize.

One of us glances at the transceiver in the corner of the tent. It is defeat to use it.

"Where's the rest of you?" I ask.

She doesn't even look at me.

I take a coil of spider-silk rope and begin cinching it to my coat.

No.

"Someone has to see what happened to the rest of her," I say.

We can't separate now.

I feel the pull to stay and consense. To wait for rescue.

"Keep her warm. Huddle close to her. Don't warm her quickly."

I pull the tent door open and close it, but not before Quant follows me out.

"Be careful. It's beginning to snow," she says. She takes the rope end from me and ties it to one of the D-rings on our tent. The end wraps around itself and knits itself together. I am glad she does this so I do not have to pull my bare hands from my coat pockets.

"I will."

The wind whips the snow into my face, needles of cold. I hunch over and try to make out Julian's tracks from her camp to ours. Snow has already started to fill in the prints. The moon glooms through scudding grey clouds, making the mountainside grey on grey. I continue, making this task my focus, so that I do not remember that I have left my pod behind. Even so, I count the steps I take, marking the distance of our separation. Counting steps is something Quant would do, and it is a comforting thought.

I have to keep my face up to follow the tracks, and when

I do, the wind freezes my nasal passages. The cold is like a headache. There is no smell on the wind, no trace of Hagar Julian.

The woman has walked across a slide of broken slate. Her footprints end on the jagged mounds of rock. I pause, knowing I am close to their campsite; they had been no farther than five hundred meters when I'd spied them.

I turn my back to the wind and tuck my head a moment. Still the snow finds a way into my eyes. The weather is worsening. I take a moment to memorize the feeling, the sting, the sound for later. I take comfort in knowing I will share this all with my pod in the warmth of the tent in a few minutes.

I trudge on across the slate, slipping once and falling to one knee. The slate ends in a river of grey snow. I don't remember seeing this before. Then I realize it is new. The snowbank above has collapsed, burying Hagar Julian's campsite in an avalanche.

I stand there, ignoring the cold.

I take one step onto the snow and it crunches under my boots. An hour ago this area was clear and now it is under a flood of rocks and snow. I look up at the mountain, wondering if more will follow, but swirling snow obscures it.

I climb up the side of the hill of snow. Ten meters into the slide, I see a flap of cloth, half covered. I pull at it, but the rest is buried too deep for me to extract it.

"Julian!" Sifting flakes muffle my voice. I yell again for my classmate.

I hear no reply, though I doubt I would have heard anything unless the speaker was next to me.

I pull my hands out of my pockets, hoping to catch a whiff of something on the pads on my palm. Nothing but needling cold. I am cocooned in a frozen, white mask. As isolated as the one part of Julian who made it to our camp.

I turn back. We will need digging equipment and many

people to find Julian's corpses. I do not see how they could have survived. Except for the one.

But then I see something black against the grey of the swept snow. Just a smudge that catches my eye as I turn.

I stop and take one step up the slope, and I see that it is an arm. I am clawing at the ice, snow, and rock, hoping, praying that below is a breathing body.

I scoop huge armfuls of snow behind me and down the slope, tracing the arm down, reaching a torso, and finding a hooded head. I try to pull the body out, but the legs are still trapped. I pause, and slowly pull back the hood. Male, a part of Julian, face and cheeks splotchy pink, eyes shut. The snow swirls around his mouth and I think it means he's breathing, but I can't be sure. I pass my palm at his neck, tasting for any pheromone, but there is nothing. I feel for a pulse.

Nothing.

My mind struggles to remember how to revive a victim with a stopped heart. Moira would know. Quant would know. They all would know. Alone I know nothing.

I panic and just grab the body about its torso and heave backward, trying to free it from the snow. I pull but the body remains embedded. I sweep at the man's hips, feeling the futility of it. I'm useless here. Strength is useless now. I don't know what to do.

But now he is free to his knees, and I pull again. He comes free in a cascade of snow. I stagger under his weight, then lay him down.

I kneel next to him, trying to remember. My hands are red and stinging, and I stuff them into my pockets, angry at myself. I am useless alone. Moira would . . . Then it comes to me as if Moira has sent it to me in a ball of memory. Compressions and breathing. Clear the throat, five compressions and a breath, five and a breath. Repeat.

I push at the man's coat, unsure if I am doing anything through the bundles of clothing. Then I squeeze his nose and breathe into his mouth. It's cold, like a dead worm, and my stomach turns. Still I breathe into his mouth and then compress again, counting slowly.

The cycle repeats, and his chest rises when I breathe into him. I stop after a minute to check the pulse. I think I feel something, and I wonder if I should stop. Is that his own diaphragm moving or just the air I've forced into him leaving his lungs, like a bellows?

I can't stop, and bend to the task again.

A cough, a spasm, but a reaction, and then he is breathing.

Alive!

The pulse is fast and reedy, but there.

Can he move? Can I get him back to the tent to warm him?

Then I hear the whine of the aircar, and realize I won't have to carry him. Help is on the way. I fall back into the snow. Alive!

The whine of the car rises, and I see its lights coming up the valley, louder, too loud. I wonder at the fragility of the layers of snow on the ridges above and if the shrill engines will cause another wave of snow.

I can do nothing but wait. The aircar reaches the edge of our camp and lowers itself behind the trees.

The engines die, but the sound does not. I see another flash above me, and I think it another aircar's searchlights, but then I realize the sound is not the whine of a hydrogen-burning turbine. There is a deep rumble all around me, and I know what is happening. I know that the snow is coming down the mountain again. The first avalanche has weakened the ledge of snow.

I stand, unsure. Then I see the wave of white in the first aircar's spotlights.

"No!" I take one step toward the camp, then stop. The Julian here will die if I leave him.

The snow slams into my pod's campsite, flies up where it strikes the trees surrounding the tent. I see the twirling lights of the aircar thrown up into the air. My pod! My body tenses, my heart thudding. I take one step forward.

The rumble is a crashing roar now. I look up at the snowbank above me, fearing that ice is about to bury us. But the outcropping of snow that fed the first avalanche has uncovered a jagged ledge that is shielding us. The river of snow flows twenty meters away, but comes no nearer. If it had taken me, I would not have cared. My pod is in the torrent, and my neck tightens so that I can barely breathe.

I see something snaking on the ground and think the snow is chasing me uphill. I am jerked off my feet.

Dragged across the rock and ice, I realize it is the line attached to my waist. The other end is attached to our tent and it is dragging me down the mountain. Five, ten, twenty meters, I struggle to untie the rope, to find the nodule that will untwine the knot, but my chafed, useless hands can grip nothing.

I fall on my face, feel something smash into my nose, and in a daze I slide another few meters, closer to the avalanche. I thought it was slowing, but this close it seems to be a cascade of flying rock and snow.

I stand, fall, then stand again and lunge toward the avalanche, hoping to slacken the rope. I run, and I see a tree, at the edge of the river. I dive at it, haul myself around it once, then once more, wedging the line.

I pull and brace, and then the line is steel-taut.

My legs are against the trunk and I am standing against it, holding on, or else I'll be sucked into the vortex with my pod.

For a moment, the desperation whispers the question: how bad would that be? Is it better to die with my pod together or live on alone, a singleton, useless? A moment before, I had been ready for the avalanche to take me too.

But I cannot let go. A part of Julian still needs my help. I hold on, listening for the rumble to lessen.

Seconds, and then a minute, then two. Still I hold on, and the storm of snow slows, and the pull on my arms decreases. Sweat rolls down my cheeks, though the air is frigid. My arms shake. When the rope finally falls limp, I lie below the tree, unable to move. I am spent, and it takes minutes for me to recover enough to remove the rope. My fingers are raw and weak, and the spider-silk will not separate. Finally the end unknits.

I stand and fall.

I shove my face into the snow to cool it, then realize how foolish that is. I stand again, and this time I make several steps before my legs shudder out from beneath me.

The snow is as soft as a feather bed, and I resolve to rest just a few moments.

It would be easy to sleep. So easy.

But I don't. The man is still on the mountain. A singleton just like me. He needs me. He needs someone strong to carry him down the mountain.

I glance at the rope. At the other end is my pod. How could they have survived the torrent? I stand and take one step onto the debris, but a cascade of tumbling snow drives me back. The snow ridge above is still unstable. I wipe my eyes with my raw hands, then turn and follow the trail I made as I was dragged down the mountain. It is easy to see the trail of blood I have left. I touch my lip and nose; I hadn't realized I'd been bleeding.

The Julian is still there, still breathing. And I cry aloud to see him alive, bawling like a child. I am anything but strength.

"What . . . what are you . . . crying for?"

The Julian is looking up at me, his teeth chattering.

"I'm crying because we're alive," I say.

"Good." His head drops back into the snow. His lips are blue and I know the chattering is a response to the cold and a precursor to hypothermia. We need to get him medical attention. We . . .

I am thinking as if I am still a pod. I cannot rely on Manuel to help me lift him. I cannot rely on Quant to show me the quickest way down. I am alone.

"We need to go."

"No."

"You need to get to warmth and medical aid."

"My pod."

I shrug, unsure how to tell him. "They're buried under here."

"I smell them. I hear them."

I sniff. Maybe there's a trace of thought on the wind, but I can't be sure.

"Where?" I ask.

"Nearby. Help me up."

I pull him to his feet and he leans against me, groaning. We take a step; he points.

I see the cloth buried in the snow I had noticed before.

He had survived several minutes in the snow. Perhaps his pod is trapped below. Perhaps they are in an air pocket, or in their hollowed-out snow cave.

I kneel and begin to scoop away the snow around the cloth flap. He rolls next to me and tries to help clear. But he slumps against a mound of snow, too weak, and watches me instead.

The cloth is a corner of a blanket and it seems to go straight down.

For a while the going is all ice and I claw at it with my numb fingers, unable to move more than a handful at a time. Then I am through that and the digging is easier.

Clods of snow bounce off my hood, and I am leery of

more snow falling on top of us. I take a moment to push away all the snow from around us.

Two more scoops and suddenly the snow gives way, and I see a cavern of ice and snow and canvas, and within the cave two bodies, two more of Julian. They are alive, breathing, and one is conscious. I pull them each out of the cave and next to their podmate.

The two that are conscious cling to each other and lie there, gasping for breath, and I am so tired I want to collapse into the hole.

I check each one for hypothermia, for breaks and contusions. The unconscious one, a female, has a broken arm, and she winces as I move her. I have a loop of rope on my belt, not spider-silk, and I bind her arm across her chest.

"Wake up," I say. "Come on." The third, with the broken arm, is still unconscious. I gently slap her face. She comes awake and lunges, then gasps as the pain hits her. Her pod, what is left of it, surrounds her, and I step back, fall back on the snow, looking up into the sky. I realize that the snow is coming down harder.

"We have to get down the mountain," I say. If another aircar comes, it will start another avalanche. If another avalanche comes, we are doomed.

They don't seem to hear me. They cling together, their teeth chattering.

"We have to get down the mountain!" I yell.

Despair floods the air, then a stench of incoherent emotions. The three are in shock.

"Come on!" I say and pull one of them up.

"We can't . . . our . . . podmates," he says, words interspersed with chemical thoughts that I don't understand. The pod is degenerating.

"If we don't go now, we will die on this mountain. We have no shelter, and we are freezing."

They don't reply, and I realize they would rather die than break their pod.

"There's three of you," I say. "You are nearly whole." Three of five is better than one of five, don't they see?

They look among themselves, and I smell the consensus odor. Then one of them turns away angrily. They can't do it. No consensus.

I collapse onto the snow, head down, and watch the snow swirl between my legs. I am one who was five. The fatigue and despair catch me, and my eyes burn.

I do not cry. But still my face is washed with tears for my pod, buried in the snow. My face is fire where the tears crawl. A splash falls into the snow and disappears.

We will sleep here in despair and die before the morning.

I look at them. I must get them down the mountain, but I don't know how to do it. I wonder what thoughts Moira would pass me if she were here. She would know what to do with these three.

They are three. Mother Redd is a three. Our teachers are threes. The Premier of the Overgovernment is a three. Why do they cry when they are no worse off than our greatest? I am allowed to cry, but not them.

I stand up.

"I've lost my pod too, and I am only one!" I shout. "I can cry, but you can't! You are three. Get up! Get up, all of you!"

They look at me like I am mad, so I kick one, and she grunts.

"Get up!"

Slowly they rise, and I grin at them like a maniac.

"We will reach the bottom. Follow me."

I lead them across the snow to the spill of the other avalanche. With the nanoblade on my utility knife, I cut a length of the rope that disappears into the snow. At the other end of the rope is my dead pod. I take a step onto the grey avalanche; perhaps I can dig them out as I have dug out Hagar Julian. I hear a rumble as the snow shifts beneath me. More snow tumbles down the mountain. It has not settled yet; more snow could fall at any moment. And I know it has been too long now. If they are trapped under the snow, their air is gone. If I had turned at once, if I had followed the rope when the avalanche had stopped, perhaps I could have saved them, but I did not think of that. Quant wasn't there to remind me of the logical choice. Bitterness seeps through me, but I ignore it. There are the three who are left to take care of.

I hand each of them a section of the rope, looping us together. Then I lead them down the mountain. It is nearly black, save the light reflected by the muted moon that splashes upon the snow in between dark snow clouds. The ledge and gaping holes are obvious. It is the hidden crevasses that I fear. But every step we take is better than lying asleep in the snow.

Our path leads to a drop, and I back us up quickly, not wanting the three to gaze into the abyss. I begin to wonder if there is no way down. We were dropped off in aircars that morning. Perhaps the location was so remote that aircars alone could reach it. Perhaps there is no path down the mountain. Or worse, we will pass through the path of an avalanche and die under the piles of snow.

The snowfall is steady now, and in places we are up to our hips. But the effort is warmth. To move is to live, to stop is sleep and death.

The trees all look alike, and I fear we are stumbling in circles, but I know that if we continue downward we will reach the bottom. I see no signs of animal or human. The snow is pristine until we tramp through.

The line jerks and I turn to see the last of Hagar Julian, the one with the broken arm, has fallen.

I go to her and lift her onto my shoulder. The weight is

nothing compared to the ache I already feel. What is another sixty kilograms? But our pace is slower now.

Still the others lag, and I allow rests, but never enough to let them sleep, until the fatigue is too much and I let my eyes droop.

Oblivion for just a moment, then I start awake. To sleep is to die. I rouse the three.

The three. I am thinking of them no longer as a pod, but as a number. Will they refer to me as the singleton? The one? There may be a place for a trio in society. But there is no place for a singleton.

After the Exodus of the Community—their sudden and complete abandonment of the Ring and the Earth—it was the pods who had remained in control. The pods are now the caretakers of the Earth, while the normal humans who are left—the singletons—are backward and Luddite. The pods, just a biological experiment, a minority before, are the ones who survived cataclysm. Only now I am no longer a pod; I am a singleton, and the only place for me is in the singleton enclaves. Alone I cannot function in pod society. What could I contribute? Nothing. I look at the three. There is one thing I can contribute. These three are still a pod, still an entity. I can bring them to safety.

I stand up. "Let's go," I say, but gently. They are too empty to protest. I show them how to put the snow to their lips and drink it as it melts.

"We need to go." The one with the broken arm tries to walk. I walk beside her with a hand on her good arm.

The pine forest gives way to denser deciduous trees, and I feel warmer, though the temperature cannot have risen much. But the trees think it's warmer, so I think so too. The snow is less heavy here. Perhaps the storm is letting up.

"This mountain," I say, "is less than seven kilometers high. We can walk seven kilometers easily, even in the cold. And this is all downhill."

No one laughs. No one replies.

The wind is gone, I notice, and with it the snow. The sky is grey still, but the storm is over. I begin to think that we might not die.

Then the last in our line steps too close to a ravine, and he's down the side, sliding from sight. The next in line, unable or unwilling to let go, slides after him, and I watch the slithering rope.

Again, I think. Again with this damn rope pulling me away. I let go of it, and the rope disappears into the grey below. The woman at my side doesn't even know what is happening.

The ravine is three meters down, lined by a steep, but not vertical, slope. I see the two who have fallen at the base. I have no way to get them out, so I must follow.

I take the woman over my shoulder, and say, "Hold on." I slide down the hill, one arm to balance me, one arm to hold her, and my legs folded beneath me, lowering myself down the slope.

No hidden tree branches, I hope. There are none, and sooner than I think, we are at the bottom of the ravine.

The two others are there, sprawled at the edge of a small, unfrozen stream. Sometime in the past, water has carved a cavelike trough into the ravine wall. The woman on my shoulder has passed out, her face grey, her breathing shallow. How bad is her fracture? I wonder. How much worse have I made it? Manuel would have known an elegant way to get her down.

The air is warm here, in this grotto that is nearly below the ground. It is like a cave; the ground is a constant temperature a few meters below the surface, regardless of the blazing heat or the blowing snow. I squat. It may be five degrees.

"We can rest here." We can even sleep, I think. No chance of frostbite. We can't get wet; the stream is too shallow.

A few meters down the streambed, I find an indentation. It is dry rock with roots overhanging. I carry the woman there and lead the others to the cave.

"Sleep," I tell them.

My body is exhausted, and I watch the three fall asleep at once. I cannot. The female is in shock. I have made her arm worse by slinging her over my shoulder. She is probably bleeding internally.

I look at her grey face, and console myself that she would be dead if we were still a thousand meters up the mountain.

Unless they had sent another aircar.

I sit there, my heart cold, not sleeping.

I have always been strong, even when we were children, before we first consensed. I was always taller, stronger, heavier. And that has always been my weapon. It is obvious. I am not about deception. I am not about memory, or insight, or agility. I am quick when threats are near, yes, but never agile.

I never thought I would outlive my pod. I never thought I'd be the one left.

I don't want to think these things, so I stand up, and use my utility knife to cut two saplings that are trying to grow in the gully. Using the rope, I fashion a travois. It will be easier on the female.

"You should have left us on the mountain." It is the one who I had first found in the snow. "You're wasting too much energy on a broken pod."

I say nothing, though I could acknowledge the truth of it.

"But then you wouldn't know that. All your thinking parts are missing."

He's angry, and he is striking out at me because of it. I nod.

"You probably don't even understand what I'm saying."

"Yes, I am strength and nothing more."

Maybe he wants to fight, I think, so I add, "I saved your life today."

"So? Should I thank you?"

"No. But you owe me your life. So we will walk down this mountain in the morning, and then we are even. You can die then, and I won't care."

"Pigheaded."

"Yes." I can't argue with that either.

He is asleep in moments, and I am too.

I am stiff and cold in the morning, but we are all alive. I squat on the stones and listen for a few moments. The trickle of the water muffles all sound. I can't hear the whine of a rescue aircar. I can't hear the shouts of searchers. We have traveled so far that they will not look for us in the right spot. We have no choice but to continue on.

A wave of doubt catches me unaware. The tenet of pod sentience is that a consensus of one is always false. My choice has doomed us. But more than likely staying on the mountain would have done the same, only sooner. These three want that, I know. Perhaps I should too.

I touch my pockets one by one. I am hungry, but I already know there is no food. I was just stepping out of the tent for a moment. I had not prepared myself for a long journey in the cold. I check the pockets of the injured one, but she too is without food.

"Do you have food?" I ask the male, the one who argued with me. "What's your name anyway?"

"Hagar Jul—" he starts to say, then stops. He glares at me. "No food."

I squat next to him. "Perhaps I can lead you back up the mountain, and then you'll forgive me for saving you."

" 'Saving' is a debatable term."

I nod. "What's your name?"

We have been classmates for ten years, and yet I do not

know his individual name. We have always interfaced as pods, never as individuals.

He doesn't say anything for a long moment, then says, "David."

"And them?"

"Susan is the one with the broken arm. Ahmed is the third." These two are still asleep on the ground.

"The others may still be alive," I say, and as I say it, I know it is what I wish for myself. But I saw the river of snow that carried them away.

"We didn't find Alia and Wren," he says, and then he coughs. It is to hide the sob.

I turn away, not wanting to embarrass him, and I say, "One of them found our tent. She may still live."

"That was Wren. Alia was near me."

"A rescue party—"

"Did you see a rescue party?"

"No."

"A body will survive for an hour in the snow if there's air. If there's no air, then it is ten minutes." His voice is savage. The other two stir.

"It was like swimming in oil. Like swimming in a dream while smothering," David says.

"David."

It is Ahmed. He pulls him close, and I smell the tang of consensus. They gather near Susan and sit for minutes, thinking. I am glad for them, but I walk down the stream several meters, not wanting to be reminded. I am a singleton now.

The creek twists and turns. I pull myself across a rotten pine tree blocking the way, banging loose a rain of brown needles. My breath hangs in the moist air. It is not cold anymore, and I feel like a thaw has passed through me.

The stream widens and opens up over a rocky basin where it spills in white spray. I see the valley before me, shrouded in mist. A kilometer below, the stream merges with a river. The ground to the river is rough and rocky, but not as snowy as we have traveled until now. Nor is it as steep.

We'd left for the survival trip from a base camp near a river. I can only suppose that this is the same river. Following it would lead us to the camp.

I hurry back to the three.

They stand apart, their consensus concluded. David hoists Susan's travois.

"Are you ready?" I ask.

They look at me, their faces relaxed. This is the first time these three have consensed since their pod was sundered. It is a good sign that they can do it with just three.

"We're going back to find Alia and Wren," David says.

I stand for a moment, voiceless. They have reached a false consensus. It is something that we are trained to detect and discard. But the trauma and loss they have suffered has broken their thought processes.

David takes my silence for agreement, and he pulls Susan up the streambed.

I stand, unable to resist a valid consensus, unable to stop them from climbing back up the mountain. I take one step toward them, perhaps to fall in line with them, but I stop.

"No!" I say. "You'll never make it."

The three of them look at me as if I am a rock. It's not false consensus; it's pod instability. Insanity.

"We need to re-form the whole," David says.

"Wait! You've reached false consensus!"

"How could you know? You can't consense at all." The biting words jolt me.

They start walking. I run to intercept, placing a hand on David's chest.

"You will die if you go back up the mountain. You can't make it."

Ahmed pushes my arm away.

"We have to get back to Alia and Wren."

"Who was your ethicist?" I say. "Was it Wren? Is that why you're making faulty consensus? Think! You will die, just like Wren and Alia are dead."

"We had no ethical specialist," Ahmed says.

"I saw the river from the end of this gully. We're almost to the camp! If we turn around, we will never find our way. We will be on the mountain at night. We have no food. We have no shelter. We will die."

No response but a step forward.

I push David hard, and he stumbles. Susan screams as the travois slams onto the rocks.

"You have reached a faulty consensus," I say again.

Pheromones flood the air, and I realize much of it is mine: veto, a simple pheromone signal we all know but rarely use. David swings at me, but I stop his fist. He is not strength.

"We go down," I say.

David's face is taut. He spins and the three fall into consensus.

I push David away from his podmates, breaking their contact. I push Ahmed onto his back.

"No consensus! We go now!"

I pick up Susan's travois and drag her down the streambed. Fast. I look back once and the two are standing there, watching. Then they come.

Maybe I am reaching false consensus too. Maybe I will kill us all. But it is all I can do.

The trek down the gorge is not easy on Susan, as the snow has disappeared in spots and the travois rides roughly across the ground. I find myself issuing soothing thoughts, though I know she cannot understand them. Only crude emotions can pass between pods, and sometimes not even that if they aren't from the same creche. I change the thoughts to feelings of well-being. Perhaps she can under-stand the simple pheromones.

Each time I glance behind, I see the others trailing. I have broken their re-formed pod again with trauma, and I hope that I have done no irreparable damage to them. The doctors of the Institute will be the judge of that. Perhaps they can save them. I am a useless case and will probably have to emigrate to one of the singleton enclaves in South America or Australia.

A line of boulders faces me, surrounded by smaller stones and rocks, too large for the travois to travel freely across.

"Take one end each," I say to Ahmed and David. The travois becomes a stretcher. If I walk slowly, we make awkward progress.

The forest has changed. The pines are gone, and we are surrounded by maples. I keep checking the horizon for any sign of search parties. Why aren't they frantically trying to find us? Had we passed too far beyond the search pattern? Do they already know where we are? Perhaps they found us in the night, noted that we were broken pods and left us to fend for ourselves.

The paranoia drowns me, and I stumble on a loose rock. Even they would not be so callous. Everything is a test, Moira says. Is this just another? Would they kill a pod to test the rest of us?

That I cannot believe.

At the edge of a four-meter drop, our stream falls into the river, adding its small momentum to the charging rapids. I see no easy way down; we are forced to unlash Susan and help her down the jagged slope.

The rocks are wet and slimy. I slip, and we are flying to the ground, falling less than a meter, but the wind is knocked from me. Susan lands atop me, and she screams in pain.

I roll over and try to breathe. Then Ahmed and David are there, helping us up. I don't want to stand up. I just want to lie there.

"Up," David says. "More to go."

Everything is hazy in my vision, and I feel dizzy. The pain in my chest is not going away. I have a sharp sting in my ribs, and I prod myself. I have broken ribs. I almost collapse, but Ahmed pulls me up.

Susan manages to stand too now, and we limp along the flat stones of the shrunken riverbed. In a few months it will fill the entire wash.

We are an ad hoc pod, all of us clinging together as we walk, step after step downriver. I am no longer strength. I am weakness and pain.

We pass a boulder and the smell hits me as we see it.

A bear, almost as big as the boulder. No, three bears pawing through the slow water for fish. We are not five meters from the biggest and closest.

Fear sweeps through the air; my fight response kicks in and the pain washes out of me like cold rain.

We have surprised the bears.

The closest rears up on its hind legs. On all fours it was to my chest. Standing, it is a meter above me. Its claws are six centimeters long.

We back away. I know we cannot outrun a bear in this open terrain. Our only hope is to flee alone.

Separate, I send, then remember that the three are not of my pod. "We need to separate and run," I say.

The bear stops coming toward us. I think for a moment that it is reacting to my voice, but then I remember the smell I had caught as I passed the boulder. Pheromones.

The bears aren't a natural species.

Hello, I send, in the simplest of glyph thoughts.

The bear's jaws snap shut and it lands on its four legs again.

Not food, it sends.

The thought is more than simple. I can taste it like my own podmates'.

Not food. Friend.

The bear considers us with liquid brown eyes, then seems to shrug before turning away.

Come.

I start to follow, but fear emanating from the three stops me. I realize they have not tasted the bear's thoughts.

"Come on," I say. "They aren't going to eat us."

"You . . . you can understand it?" David asks.

"A little."

"They're a pod," he says wonderingly.

My shock has faded with recognition. On the farm with Mother Redd, we have swum with the bioengineered beavers. We have ourselves modified clutches of ducks into clusters. Now that I know, I can see the glands on the backs of the bears' arms. At the neck are slits that release the chemical memories. And to receive them, the olfactory lobe of their brain will have been enhanced.

That they are bears, that they are wild things, seems at first incongruent. The experiments on composite animals have been all on smaller, manageable beasts. But why not bears?

They amble along the riverbed, and I jog to follow them, though my ribs hurt. In a moment I am among them, and I smell their thoughts, like silver fish in the river. Intelligent, not simple at all.

Sending *Friendship,* I reach out and touch the side of the bear who confronted us.

His fur is wet from his splashing at fish, and the smell is thick, not just pheromones and memories, but a wild animal's smell. I think I must smell worse. His mane is silver-tipped; his claws click on the stones.

I rub his neck just above the memory glands, and he

pushes against me in response. I smell his affection. I sense deepness of thought and playfulness. I feel the power of his body. This is strength.

I catch images of topography, of places where fish swarm, of a dead elk. I see assessments of danger, and choices of path and best approach. I catch the consensus of decision. These three are a functioning pod.

The thoughts swirl through my head, but they shouldn't. I should not be able to catch their thoughts, but I can. Even humans can't share chemical memories between pods, just emotions sometimes.

I send an image of the avalanche.

The bears shudder. I understand their fear of the river of snow. They have seen it; it is part of their memories.

I ask them where the camp is. They know, and I see it on the edge of this river, near the rotten stump with the tasty termites.

I laugh, and they echo my joy, and for a moment I forget that I am alone.

Come on, they send.

"Come on," I call back to the three. Hesitantly they follow.

The bears lead us through the trees, and abruptly we push through onto a trail, smashed flat by hikers' boots, a human trail. They sniff once, then amble across it and vanish into the brush.

I want to follow. Why shouldn't I? I have fulfilled my duty to Hagar Julian. Surely the bears would allow me to join them. My body shudders. I would still be a singleton. I would still be alone.

Goodbye, I send, though I doubt they are close enough to catch it. The chemical memories cannot travel far.

I lead Susan down the trail, supporting her. I hear the sounds of camp, the voices, the whine of an aircar, before we round the last curve of the trail. We all stop. David looks at me, perhaps with pity, perhaps with thanks, then he leads the remainder of his pod into the camp.

I stand alone.

I fall to my knees, so tired, so weak. My strength can get me no farther.

Then I feel a push at my back, and it is the bear. He nudges me again. One arm around his steel-like neck, I stand, and we walk together into the camp.

The camp is awhirl, twice as many tents as when we left it, a bevy of aircars, and everyone stops to watch me and the bear.

Everyone but my pod, who are rushing at me, alive, and I feel them before I touch them, and we are one. Sweet consensus.

I see everything that has happened, and they see everything that I have done, and in one moment it is I who surfed the avalanche, dangling on the line Strom tied to a tree trunk, and it is we who walked down the mountain and communed with bears.

You saved us, Strom, Moira sends. Quant shows me how the tent, dangling on my line of spider-silk, rides the top of the cascade of snow instead of plunging down the mountain. I hug Meda and Manuel to my chest, squeezing. It hurts my ribs, but I do not let go.

"Careful!" Meda says, but she buries her face in my chest.

I am strength again, I think, as my pod helps me to the infirmary, not because they are weak, but because we are all strong.

TWO

Meda

We spent a week in the Rockies searching for the bears in all the wrong places. Of course we couldn't tell the military duo that flew in to head the search that we knew their territory because Strom had shared memories with the bear pod. The duo didn't even believe the bears had been a pod, mostly likely "an escaped, partially domesticated grizzly."

We helped search anyway and tried mining the databases for bear pod information in the evenings. There was nothing.

How could someone hide a whole line of research regarding carnivore pods? I asked.

My pod had no answer either, so we took a suborbital car back to the farm to await our practicum assignments and help Mother Redd with the summer's chores. The first morning back, Moira awoke with a stuffed nose and circles under her eyes, and we all awoke with memories of a clogged throat and a sinus headache.

Mother Redd shooed us out of the house. At first we

just hung around the front yard, feeling weird. We'd been separated before, of course; it was part of our training. In space, we'd have to act as a quartet or a trio or even a duo, so we practiced all our tasks and chores in various combinations. That had always been practice, and we'd all been in sight. But Moira was *separated* now, and we did not like it. It reminded us of Strom on the mountain. He had been apart for too long.

Manuel climbed the trellis on the front of the house, skirting the thorns of the roses that grew among the slats. As his hands caught the sill and pulled his head just over the edge, his hind legs caught a rose and bent it back and forth to break it off.

I see Moira, he signed.

"Does she see you?" I asked, aloud since he couldn't see me, and the wind took the pheromones away leaving half-formed thoughts.

If Manuel could see Moira and she could see him, then it would be enough for all of us. We'd be linked.

Just then the window flew open, and one of Mother Redd was there. Manuel fell backward, but he righted himself and landed on the grass, rolling, sprawling until he was among the rest of us, the red rose still clutched in his toes.

I touched his wrist, breathed him a thought, and he offered the rose to Mother Redd. I saw immediately it wasn't going to work.

"You *four,* go and play somewhere else today. Moira is sick, and it won't do us any good for you to get sick too. Your assignments will be here in a month. So vamoose!" She slammed the window shut.

We thought it over for a few seconds, then tucked the rose in my shirt pocket, and started down the front path.

We didn't have Moira, but we did have license to vamoose, and that meant the forest, the lake, and the caves if we were brave enough. Moira would have advised caution. But we didn't have Moira.

The farm was part ecopreserve and part commercial venture, the latter a hundred acres of soyfalfa that Mother Redd worked with three trios of oxalope. The ox were dumb as rocks by themselves, but when you teamed them up, they could plow and seed and harvest pretty much by themselves. They were the biggest animals that we had ever seen pod-bonded, until Strom had found the bears. No one built carnivore or omnivore pods; it just wasn't done.

Our search for them after the incident on the mountain—hampered by Strom's cracked ribs—had turned up no ursine pods, and the military teams sent to search for them came to disbelieve the bears had helped save Strom and the remainder of Hagar Julian's pod. We could tell they didn't believe they were pods, probably just partially tame normal bears. They had questioned Strom on those points extensively.

"Could the scent glands have been the silver mane of the male?" one army duo had asked.

We were certain of what had happened, certain that the bear had been a pod, and certain that Strom had spoken to them via chemical memory, but the more they hounded us on the details of the bears, the more we shrugged our shoulders and said, "Maybe you're right." We were glad to fly back to Mother Redd's farm to wait for our assignments.

The practicum semester included not just a dozen classes on astrophysics and space science, but also an extraterrestrial work program. This was supposed to be the semester when they chose who would command the *Consensus*.

The farm was a good place to spend the summer. Lessons took up our mornings, but they weren't as rigorous as during the school year when we studied all day and most of the night at the Institute. At school we learned to sleep in shifts, so three or four of us were always awake to study. We'd spent summers with Mother Redd for sixteen years, since we had left Mingo Creche.

Baker Road led west toward Worthington and the Institute or east toward more farms, the lake, the woods, and beyond that ruins and desolation. We chose east, Strom first like always when we were in the open with Manuel as a scurrying point, never too far away. I followed Strom, then Quant last. Moira would have been after Quant. We felt a hole there, which Quant and I filled by touching hands too often.

Within a mile, we were relaxed, though not indifferent to Moira's absence. Quant was tossing rocks onto the tops of old telephone poles, grabbing chunks of asphalt and stones from the broken edge of the road, flinging them into the sky with a flash of her blond hair, an Olympic shotputter in a ponytail. She didn't miss once, but we didn't feel any pride in it. It was just a one-force problem, and Quant lobbed the rocks for diversion, not practice. There weren't enough quintets in the world to relegate such a class in the Olympics; quartets had only been allowed the year before. Not that we wanted to be in the Olympics. We had no desire to hang around Earth at all.

We passed a microwave receiving station, hidden in a grove of pine trees, just off from the road. Its paraboloid shape reflected the sun as it caught the beamed microwaves from the Ring. The Earth was dotted with such dishes, each providing a few megawatts to the Earth-side enclaves, more than we could use, now that the Community had left. But they had built the Ring and the solar arrays and the dishes as well. Decades later and they still worked.

I could see the Ring clearly, even in the brightness of the morning, a pale arch from horizon to horizon. At night, it was brighter, its legacy more burdensome to those of us left behind. On the mountain, it had been clearer still, as if we could reach out, grasp it, and pull ourselves astride it. A silly thought: no pod had ever set foot on the Ring or any of its base stations. The doors would only open to members of the Community.

Quant started tossing small twigs into the incoming microwave beam, small arcing meteoroids that burst into flame and then ash. She bent to pick up a small toad.

I felt the absence of Moira as I put my hand on her shoulder and sent, *No living things*.

I felt her momentary resentment, then she shrugged both physically and mentally. She smiled at my discomfort at having to play Moira while she was gone. Quant, in whom was hardwired all the Newtonian laws of force and reaction, had a devilishness in her. In us. Our rebel. You would not know it to look at her, nor would you have guessed if you had met her alone.

Once, on Sabah Station, the instructors had divided us up as a duo and a trio, and broken up our classmates as well along the same lines. The objective was an obstacle course, no gravity, two miles of wire, rope, and simulated wreckage, find the MacGuffin first. All other teams were enemy, no rules.

They hadn't given us no-rules games too often; we were young then, twelve. Mostly they gave us a lot of rules. That time had been different.

Strom, Manuel, and Quant found it first, by chance, and instead of taking it, they lay in wait, set traps and zero-gee deadfalls. They managed to capture or incapacitate the other four teams. They broke three arms and a leg. They caused two concussions, seventeen bruises, and three lacerations, as they trussed up the other teams and stowed them in the broken hut where the MacGuffin sat.

Finally we came along, and the fiberglass mast zinged past, barely missing us.

As Moira and I swam behind cover, we heard them laughing. We knew it was them and not some other team.

We were too far for pheromones, but we could still smell the edges of their thoughts: proud and defiant.

Moira yelled, "You get your asses out here right now!"

Strom popped out right away. He listened to Moira first no matter who else was there. Then Manuel left the hut.

"Quant!"

"Forget it!" she yelled. "I win." Then she threw the MacGuffin at us, and Moira snatched it out of the air.

"Who's 'I'?" Moira yelled.

Quant stuck her head out. She looked at the four of us for a moment, then signed, *Sorry*. She kicked over and we shared everything that had happened.

The teachers didn't split us up like that again.

Baker Road swerved around Lake Cabbage like a giant letter *C*. It was a managed ecomite, a small ecosystem with gengineered inhabitants. The Baskins, two first-generation duos, ran it for the Overdepartment of Ecology, trying to build a viable lake ecosystem with a biomass of twenty-five Brigs. It had everything from beavers to snails to mosquitoes. Lots of mosquitoes.

The adult beavers turned a blind eye to our frolicking in the lake, but the babies found us irresistible. They had been bioed to birth in quartets, their thoughts sliding across the pond surface in rainbows like gasoline. We could almost understand, but not quite. In the water our own pheromones were useless, and even our touch pads were hard to understand. If we closed our eyes and sank deep enough, it was like we weren't a part of anything, just empty, thoughtless protoplasm.

Strom didn't like to swim, but if we were all in the water, he'd be too, just to be near. I knew why he was uncertain of the water, I knew his anxiety as my own, but I couldn't help deriding us for having such a fear.

We took turns with the beavers pulling rotten logs into

the water and trying to sink them in the mud, until the adult beavers started chiding us with rudimentary hand signs, *No stop work. Messing home. Tell Mother Redd.*

We had taken for granted all our lives that beavers could use sign language, that ducks within a flock were more intelligent than without, and that plow beasts did their work on their own. But what Mother Redd created was not common, though one day it would be. The goal for her and her colleagues like Colonel Krypicz was an Earth of interwoven fauna, in concert with all its species. Though we had grown up on the farm, at least spent our summers there, this was not our dream at all. We wanted to explore the Universe beyond the Rift.

We swam to shore and dried ourselves in the afternoon sun, naked. Manuel climbed an apple tree and gathered enough ripe fruit for all of us. We rested, knowing that we'd have to head back to the farm soon. Strom balled up some memories.

For Moira, he sent.

Quant came alert and we all felt it.

A house, she sent. *That wasn't there before.*

She was up the bank, so I waited for the thoughts to reach me through the polleny humid air. It was a cottage, opposite the lake from the beavers' dam, half hidden among the cottonwoods which shed like snowfall during the summer.

I searched our memory of the last time we'd been at the lake, but none of us had looked over that way, so it may have been there since last year.

The Baskins put in a summer house, Strom sent.

Why, when their normal house is just a kilometer away? Manuel replied.

It could be a guesthouse, I sent.

Let's go find out, Quant sent.

There was no dissent, and in the shared eagerness I wondered what Moira would have said about our trespassing.

She's not here.

We leaped between flat stones, crossing the small stream that fed the lake.

Beneath the cottonwoods, the ground was a carpet of threadbare white. The air was cold through our damp clothes. We stepped across and around the poison oak with its quintuple leaves and ivy its triplet.

An aircar stood outside the cottage, parked in a patch of prairie, shaded by the trees.

Conojet 34J, Manuel sent. *We can fly it.* We had started small-craft piloting the year before.

The brush had been cleared from the cottage to make room for long flower gardens along each wall. Farther from the house, in the full sun, was a rectangle of vegetables: I saw tomatoes, pumpkins, squash, and string beans.

"It's not a summer house," I said, because Quant was out of sight. "Someone's living here."

Manuel skirted the vegetable garden to get a good look at the aircar. I felt his appreciation of it, no concrete thought, just a nod toward its sleekness and power.

"What do you kids think you're doing in my garden?"

The door of the cottage flew open with a bang, and we jumped, as a man strode toward us.

Strom took a defensive posture by reflex, his foot mashing a tomato plant. I noted it, and he corrected his stance, but the man had seen it too, and he frowned. "What the hell!"

We lined up before the man, me at the head of our phalanx, Strom to my left and slightly behind, then Quant and Manuel behind him. Moira's spot to my right was empty.

"Stepping on my plants. Who do you think you are?"

He was young, dressed in a brown shirt and tan pants.

His hair was black and he was thin-boned, almost delicate. I assumed he was the interface for his pod, but then we saw the lack of sensory pads on his palms, the lack of pheromone ducts on his neck, the lack of any consensus gathering on his part. He had said three things before we could say a single word.

"We're sorry for stepping on your plant," I said. I stifled our urge to waft conciliatory scent into the air. He wouldn't have understood. He was a singleton.

He looked from the plant to me and to the plant again.

"You're a fucking cluster," he said. "Weren't you programmed with common courtesy? Get the hell off my property."

Quant wanted to argue with the man. This was Baskin land. But I nodded, smiling. "Again, we're sorry, and we'll leave now."

We backed away, and his eyes were on us. No, not us, on me. He was watching me, and I felt his dark eyes looking past my face, seeing things that I didn't want him to see. A flush spread across my cheeks, hot suddenly in the shade. The look was sexual, and my response . . .

I buried it inside me, but not before my pod caught the scent of it. I clamped down, but Manuel's then Quant's admonition seeped through me.

I dashed into the woods, and my fellows had no choice but to follow.

The undertones of their anger mingled with my guilt. I wanted to rail, to yell, to attack. We were all sexual beings, as a whole and as individuals, but instead, I sat apart, and if Mother Redd noticed, none of her said a word.

Finally, I climbed the stairs and went to see Moira.

"Stay over there," she wheezed.

I sat in one of the chairs by the door. The room smelled like chicken broth and sweat. We had gengineered antibodies for cholera and hepatitis, but no one had found a better solution for rhinovirus except rest and tissues.

Moira and I are identical twins, the only ones in our pod. We didn't look that much alike anymore, though. Her hair was close-cropped; mine was shoulder-length auburn. She was twenty pounds heavier, her face rounder where mine was sharp. We looked more like cousins than identical sisters.

She leaned on her elbows, looked at me closely, and then flopped down onto the pillow. "You don't look happy."

I could have given her the whole story by touching her palm, but she wouldn't let me near her. I could have sketched it all with pheromones, but I didn't know if I wanted her to know the whole story.

"We met a singleton today."

"Oh, my." The words were so vague. Without the chemical sharing of memories and thoughts, I had no idea what her real emotions were, cynical or sincere, interested or bored.

"Over by the Baskins' lake. There was a cottage there . . ." I built the sensory description, then let it seep away. "This is so hard. Can't I just touch you?"

"That's all we need. Me, then you, then everybody else, and by the time school starts in two weeks, we're all sick. We can't be sick." Moira nodded. "A singleton. Luddite? Christian?"

"None of those. He had an aircar. He was angry at us for stepping on his tomato plants. And he . . . looked at me."

"He's supposed to look at you. You're our interface."

"No, he *looked* at me. Like a woman."

Moira was silent for a moment. "Oh. And you felt . . ."

The heat crept up my cheeks again. "Flushed."

"Oh." Moira contemplated the ceiling. She said, "You understand that we are individually sexual beings and as a whole—"

"Don't lecture me!" Moira could be such a pedant, one who never threw a stone.

She sighed. "Sorry."

" 'Sokay."

She grinned. "Was he cute?"

"Stop that!" After a pause, I added, "He was handsome. I'm sorry we stepped on his tomato plant."

"So take him another."

"You think?"

"And find out who he is. Mother Redd has got to know. And call the Baskins."

I wanted to hug her, but settled for a wave.

Mother Redd was in the greenhouse, watering, picking, and examining a hybrid cucumber. She had been a doctor, and then one of herself had died, and she'd chosen another field instead of being only part of the physician she had been. She—there had been four cloned females, so she was a she any which way you looked at it—took over the farm, and in the summer boarded us university kids. She was a kind woman, smart and wise, but I couldn't look at her and not think how much smarter she would have been if she were four instead of just a trio.

"What is it, sweetie? Why are you alone?" asked the one looking at the cucumber under the light microscope.

I shrugged. I didn't want to tell her why I was avoiding my pod, so I asked, "We saw a singleton over by the Baskins' lake today. Who is he?"

I could smell the pungent odor of Mother Redd's thoughts. Though it was the same cryptic, symbolic chaos that she always used, I realized she was thinking more than a simple answer would warrant. Finally, she said, "Malcolm Leto. He's one of the Community."

"The Community! But they all . . . left." I used the wrong word for it; Quant would have known the technical term for what had become of nine tenths of humanity. They had built the Ring, built the huge cybernetic organism that was the Community. They had advanced human knowledge of physics, medicine, and engineering exponentially until finally they had, as a whole, disappeared, leaving the Ring and the Earth empty, except for the fraction of humans who either had not joined the Community or had not died in the chaos of the Gene Wars.

"This one was not on hand for the Exodus," Mother Redd said. That was the word that Quant would have known. "There was an accident. His body was placed into suspended animation until it could be regenerated."

"He's the last member of the Community, then?"

"Practically."

"Thanks." I went to find the rest of my pod. They were in front of the computer, playing virtual chess with Willow Murphy, one of our classmates. I remembered it was Thursday night, Quant's hobby night. She liked strategic gaming.

I touched Strom's hand and slipped into the mesh of our thoughts. We were losing, but then Murphy was good and we had been down to three with me running off alone. Was that a trace of resentment from my fellows? I ignored it and dumped what I had learned from Mother Redd about the singleton.

The chess game vanished from our thoughts as the others focused on me.

He's from the Community. He's been in space.
Why is he here?
He missed the Exodus.
He's handsome.
He's been in space. On the Ring.
We need to talk to him.
We stepped on his tomato plant.
We owe him another.

Yes.

Yes.

Strom said, "We have some plants in the greenhouse. I can transplant one into a pot. As a gift." Strom's hobby was gardening.

"Tomorrow?" I asked.

The consensus was immediate. *Yes.*

This time we knocked instead of skulked. The tomato plant we had squashed had been staked, giving it back its lost structure. There was no answer at the door.

"Aircar's still here."

The cottage was not so small that he couldn't have heard us.

"Maybe he's taking a walk," I said. Again we were out without Moira. She was better, but still sick.

"Here, I think." Strom indicated a spot at the end of the line of tomato plants. He had brought a small spade and began to dig a hole.

I took out paper from my backpack and began to compose a note for Malcolm Leto's door. I started five times, wadding up each after a few lines and stuffing the garbage back in my bag. Finally I settled on "Sorry for stepping on the tomato plant. We brought a new one to replace it."

There was a blast, and I turned in a crouch, dropping the note and pen. Fight or flight pheromones filled the air.

Gunshot.

There. The singleton. He's armed.

Posturing fire.

I see him.

Disarm.

This last was Strom, who always took control of situations like this. He tossed the small shovel to Quant on his right. Quant threw the instrument with ease.

Malcolm Leto stood under the cottonwoods, the pistol

pointed in the air. He had come out of the woods and fired the shot. The shovel slammed into his fingers and the pistol fell.

"Son of a bitch!" he yelled, hopping and holding his fingers. "Goddamn cluster!"

We approached. Strom faded into the background again and I took the lead.

Leto watched us, looked once at the pistol but didn't move to grab it.

"Come back to wreck more of my tomato plants, did you?"

I smiled. "No, Mr. Leto. We came to apologize, like good neighbors. Not to be shot at."

"How was I to know you weren't thieves?" he said.

"There are no thieves here. Not until you get to the Christian enclaves."

He rubbed his fingers, then smirked. "Yeah. I guess so. You bunch are dangerous."

Strom nudged me mentally, and I said, "We brought you a tomato plant to make amends for the one we squashed."

"You did? Well, now I'm sorry I startled you." He looked from the cottage to me. "You mind if I pick up my gun? You're not going to toss another shovel at me, are you?"

"You're not going to fire another shot, are you?" The words were more flip than was necessary for the last member of the Community, but he didn't seem to mind.

"Fair's fair." He picked up his pistol and walked through us toward the cottage. He didn't understand how rude it was to walk through another human, but to him, we were all individual humans. He had no idea.

When he saw the last tomato plant in the line, with the fresh dirt around it, he said, "Should have put it on the other end."

I felt exasperation course through us. There was no pleasing this man.

"You know my name. So you know my story?" he asked.

"No. We just know you're from the Ring."

"Hmmm." He looked at me. "I suppose the neighborly thing to do is to invite you in. Come on."

The cottage was a single room, with an adjoining bathroom and kitchenette. The lone couch served as Leto's bed. A pillow and blanket were piled at one end.

"Suddenly crowded in here," Leto said. He put the pistol on the table, and sat on one of the two kitchen chairs. "There's not enough room for all of you, but then there's only one of you anyway, isn't there." He looked at me when he said it.

"We're all individuals," I said quickly. "We also function as a composite."

"Yeah, I know. A cluster."

Ask him about the Ring. Ask him about being in space.

"Sit," he said to me. "You're the ringleader, aren't you."

"I'm the interface," I said. I held out my hand. "We're Apollo Papadopulos."

He took my hand after a moment. "Who are you in particular?"

He held my hand and seemed to have no intention of releasing it until I answered the question. "I'm Meda. This is Quant, Strom, and Manuel."

"Pleased to meet you, Meda," he said. I felt the intensity of his gaze again, and forced my physical response down. "And the rest of you."

"You're from the Ring," I said. "You were part of the Community."

He sighed. "Yes, I was."

"What was it like? What's space like? We're going to be a starship pilot."

Leto looked at me with one eyebrow raised. "You want to know the story."

"Yes."

"All right. I haven't told anybody the whole story." He paused. "Do you think it's just a bit too convenient that they put me out here in the middle of nowhere, and yet nearby is one of their starship pilot clusters?"

"I assume you're a test for us." We had come to assume everything was a test.

"Precocious of you. Okay, here's my story: Malcolm Leto, the last, or first, of his kind."

You can't imagine what the Community was like. You can't even comprehend the numbers involved. Six billion people in communion. Six billion people as one.

It was the greatest synthesis humankind has ever created: a synergistic human-machine intelligence. I was a part of it, for a while, and then it was gone, and I'm still here. The Community removed itself from this reality, disappeared, and left me behind.

I was a biochip designer. I grew the molecular processors that we used to link with the Community. Like this one. It's grafted onto the base of your skull, connects to your four lobes and cerebellum.

We were working on greater throughput. The basics were already well established; we—that is myself, Gillian, and Henry—were trying to devise a better transport layer between the electrochemical pulses of the brain and the chips. That was the real bottleneck: the brain's hardware is slow.

We were assigned lines of investigation, but so were a hundred thousand other scientists. I'd go to sleep and, during the night, someone would close out a whole area of research. The Community was the ultimate scientific compilation of information. Sometimes we made the cutting-edge discovery, the one that changed the direction for a thousand people. Usually we just plodded along, uploaded our results and waited for a new direction.

The research advanced at a pace we as individuals could barely fathom, until we submerged ourselves in the Community. Then, the whole plan was obvious. I can't quite grasp it now, but it's there in my mind like a diamond of thought.

It wasn't just in my area of technology, but everywhere. It took the human race a century to go from horses to space elevators. It took us six months to go from uncertainty cubes to Heisenberg AND gates, and from there twenty days to quantum processors and Nth-order qubits. A week later, playing with the structure of the universe, we opened the Rift, just beyond Neptune's orbit.

You're right. It does seem like a car out of control, barreling down a hill. But really, it was the orderly advancement of science and technology, all controlled, all directed by the Community.

We spent as much time as we could in the Community, when we worked, played, and even slept. Some people even made love while connected. The ultimate exhibitionism. You couldn't spend all your time connected, of course. Everyone needed downtime. But being away from the Community was like being half yourself.

That's what it was like.

Together, in the Mesh, we could see the vision, we could see the goal, all the humans of Earth united in mind, pushing, pushing, pushing to the ultimate goal: Exodus.

At least I think that was the goal. It's hard to remember. But they're all gone now, right? I'm all that's left. So they must have done it.

Only I wasn't with them when it happened.

I don't blame Henry. I would have done the same thing if my best friend was screwing my wife.

Gillian, on the other hand.

She said she and I were soul mates, and yet when I

came out of the freezer twenty-six years later, she was as gone as the rest of them.

You'd think in the Community things like marriage would be obsolete. You'd think that to a group mind, group sex would be the way to go. It's odd what people kept separated from the Community.

Anyway, Henry spent a week in wedge 214 with another group of researchers, and while he was gone, Gillian and I sorta communed on our own. I'd known Gillian almost as long as I'd known Henry. We were first-wave emigrants to the Ring and had been friends back in Ann Arbor when we were in school. We'd met Gillian and her friend Robin in the cafeteria. He liked them tall, so he took Gillian. My and Robin's relationship lasted long enough for her to brush her teeth the next morning. Gillian and Henry were married.

She was a beautiful woman. Auburn hair like yours. Nice figure. Knew how to tell a joke. Knew how to . . . Well, we won't go there.

I know, best man screwing the bride. You've heard that pitiful tale before. Well, maybe you clusters haven't. Trust me. It's pitiful.

I'm sure it didn't take Henry long to find out. The Community sees all.

But he took a long time plotting his revenge. And when he did—bam!—that was the end for me.

We were working on some new interfaces for the occipital lobe, to enhance visualization during communing, some really amazing things. Henry ran the tests and found out our stuff was safe, so I elected to test it.

It's funny. I remember volunteering to try it out. But I don't remember what Henry said before that, how he manipulated me into trying it. Because that's what he did all right.

The enhancements were not compatible with my interface. When I inserted them, the neural pathways in the cerebral cortex fused. The interface flash-froze. I was a vegetable.

The Community placed my body into suspended animation while it rebuilt my brain. All things were possible for the Community. Only some things take a while, like rebuilding a brain. Six months later, the Exodus occurred, and still the machinery of the Ring worked on my brain. For three decades, slowly with no human guidance, it worked on my brain, until three months ago. It revived me, the one human left over from the Exodus.

Sometimes I still dream that I'm a part of it. That the Community is still there for me to touch. At first those were nightmares, but now they're just dreams. The quantum computers are still up there, empty, waiting. Maybe they're dreaming of the Community as well.

It'll be easier this time. The technology is so much farther along than it was before. The second Exodus is just a few months away. I just need a billion people to fuel it.

On my hobby night, instead of painting, we spent the evening on the Net.

Malcolm Leto had come down the Macapa space elevator two months before, much to the surprise of the Overgovernment body in Brazil. The Ring continued to beam microwave power to all the receivers, but no one resided on the Ring or used the space elevators that lined the equator. No one could, not without an interface.

The news of Leto's arrival had not made it to North America, but the archives had interviews with the man that echoed his sentiment regarding the Community and his missing out on the Exodus. There wasn't much about him for a couple of weeks until he filed suit with the Brazilian court for ownership of the Ring, on the basis of his being the last member of the Community.

The Overgovernment had never tried to populate the Ring. There was no need to try to overcome the interface access at the elevators. The population of the Earth was just under half a billion. The Gene Wars killed most of the people that hadn't left with the Exodus. It'd taken the Overgovernment almost three decades to build its starships, to string its own nanowire-guided elevator to low earth orbit, to build the fleet of tugs that plied between GEO and the Lagrange points.

No one used the quantum computers anymore. No one had an interface or could even build one. The human race was no longer interested in that direction. We were focused on the stars and on ourselves. All of us, that is, except for those in the enclaves that existed outside of, yet beneath, the Overgovernment.

The resolution to Leto's case was not published. It had been on the South American court docket a week ago, and then been bumped up to the Overgovernment Court.

He's trying to build another Community.

He's trying to steal the Ring.

Is it even ours?

He's lonely.

We need Moira.

He wants us to help him. That's why he told us the story.

He didn't tell us. He told Meda.

He likes Meda.

"Stop it!" I made fists so that I couldn't receive any more of their thoughts. They looked at me, perplexed, wondering why I was fighting consensus.

Suddenly, I wasn't looking at me. I was looking at them. It was like a knife between us. I ran upstairs.

"Meda! What's wrong?"

I threw myself onto the floor of Moira's room.

"Why are they so jealous?"

"Who, Meda? Who?"

"Them! The rest of us."

"Oh. The singleton."

I looked at her, hoping she understood. But how could she without sharing my thoughts?

"I've been reading your research. Meda, he's a potential psychotic. He's suffered a great loss and awoke in a world nothing like he remembers."

"He wants to rebuild it."

"That's part of his psychosis."

"The Community accomplished things. It made advancements that we don't understand even decades later. How can that be wrong?"

"The common view is that the Exodus was a natural evolution of humankind. What if it wasn't natural? What if the Exodus was death? We didn't miss the Exodus, we escaped it. We survived the Community just like Leto did. Do we want to suffer the same fate?"

"Now who's talking psychosis?"

"The Overgovernment will never allow him back on the Ring."

"He's alone forever then," I said.

"He can go to one of the singleton enclaves. All of the people there live alone."

"He woke up one morning and his self was gone."

"Meda!" Moira sat up in bed, her face grey. "Hold my hand!" As she held out her hand, I could smell the pheromones of her thoughts whispering toward me.

Instead of melding with her, I left the room, left the house, out the door into the wet night.

A light was on in the cottage. I stood for a long time, wondering what I was doing. We spend time alone, but never in situations like this. Never outside, where we can't reach each other in an instant. I was miles away from the rest of me. Yet Malcolm Leto was farther than that.

It felt like half the things I knew were on the tip of my tongue. It felt like all my thoughts were garbled. But everything I felt and thought was my own. There was no consensus.

Just like Malcolm had no consensus. For singletons, all decisions were unanimous.

It was with that thought that I knocked on the door.

He stood in the doorway, wearing just short pants. I felt a thrill course through me, one that I would have hidden from my pod if they were near.

"Where's the rest of your cluster?"

"At home."

"Best place for 'em." He turned, leaving the door wide open. "Come on in."

There was a small metal box on his table. He sat down in front of it. I noticed for the first time the small, silver-edged circle at the base of his skull, just below his hairline. He slipped a wire from the box into the circle.

"That's an interface box. They're illegal." When the Exodus occurred, much of the interface technology that was the media for the Communion was banned.

"Yeah. But not illegal anymore. The OG repealed those laws a decade ago, but no one noticed. My lawyer pried it loose from them and sent it up." He pulled the wire from his head and tossed it across the box. "Useless now."

"Can't you access the Ring?"

"Why? It'd be like swimming in the ocean alone." He looked at me sidelong. "I can give you one, you know. I can build you an interface."

I recoiled. "No!" I said quickly. "I . . ."

He smiled, perhaps the first time I'd seen him do it. It changed his face. "I understand. Would you like something to drink? I've got a few fix'ns. Sit anyway."

"No," I said. "I'm just . . ." I realized that for a pod's voice, I wasn't articulating my thoughts very well. I looked him in the eye. "I came to talk with you, alone."

"I appreciate the gesture. I know being alone is uncomfortable for you."

"I didn't realize you knew so much about us."

"Multiples were being designed when I was around. I kept up on the subject," he said. "It wasn't very successful. I remember articles on failures that were mentally deficient or unbalanced."

"That was a long time ago! Mother Redd was from that time and she's a great doctor. And I'm fine—"

He held up a hand. "Hold on! There were lotsa incidents with interface technology before . . . well, I wouldn't be here if it was totally safe."

His loneliness was a sheer cliff of rock. "Why are you here, instead of at one of the singleton enclaves?"

He shrugged. "There or in the middle of nowhere, it would be the same." He half-smiled. "Last of a vanished breed, I am. So you're gonna be a starship captain, you and your mingle-minded friends."

"I am . . . We are," I replied.

"Good luck, then. Maybe you'll find the Community," he said. He looked tired.

"Is that what happened? They left for outer space? Through the Rift?"

He looked puzzled. "No, maybe. I can almost . . . remember." He smiled. "It's like being drunk and knowing you should be sober and not being able to do anything about it."

"I understand," I said. I took his hand. It was dry and smooth.

He squeezed once and then stood up, leaving me confused. I was sluggish on the inside, but at the same time hyperaware of him. We knew what sex was—we'd studied it, of course, even practiced—but I had no idea what Malcolm was thinking. If he was a multiple, part of a pod, I would.

"I should go," I said, standing.

I was hoping he'd say something by the time I got to the door, but he didn't. I felt my cheeks burn. I was a silly little girl. By myself I'd done nothing but embarrass my pod, myself.

I pulled the door shut and ran into the woods.

"Meda!"

He stood black in yellow light at the cottage door.

"I'm sorry for being so caught up in my own troubles. I've been a bad host. Why don't you—" I reached him in three steps and kissed him on the mouth. Just barely I tasted his thoughts, his arousal.

"Why don't I what?" I said after a moment.

"Come back inside."

I—they—were there to meet me the next morning as I walked back to the farm. I knew they would be. A part of me wanted to spend the rest of the day with my new lover, but another wanted nothing more than to confront myself, rub my nose in the scent that clung to me, and show me . . . I didn't know what I wanted to prove. Perhaps that I didn't need to be a composite to be happy. I didn't need them, us, to be a whole person.

"You remember Veronica Proust," Moira said, standing in the doorway of the kitchen, the rest of us behind her. Of course she would take the point when I was gone. Of course she would quote precedent.

"I remember," I said, staying outside, beyond the pull of the pheromones. I could smell the anger, the fear. I had scared myself. Good, I thought.

"She was going to be a starship captain," Moira said. We remembered Proust. Usually pods sundered in the creche, with time to re-form, but Veronica had broken into a duo and a trio. The pair had bonded and the trio had transferred to engineering school, then dropped out.

"Not anymore," I said. I pushed past them into the kitchen, and as I did so, I balled up the memory of fucking Malcolm and threw it at them like a rock.

They recoiled. I walked upstairs to our room and began packing my things. They didn't bother coming upstairs and that made me angrier. I threw my clothes into a bag, swept the bric-a-brac on the dresser aside. Something glinted in the pile, a geode that Strom had found one summer when we flew to the desert. He'd cut it in half and polished it by hand.

I picked it up, felt its smooth surface, bordering the jagged crystals of the center. Instead of packing it, I put it back on the dresser and zipped up my bag.

"Heading out?"

Mother Redd stood at the door, her face neutral.

"Did you call Dr. Khalid?" He was our physician, our psychologist, perhaps our father.

She shrugged. "And tell him what? You can't force a pod to stay together."

"I'm not breaking us up!" I said. Didn't she understand? I was a person, by myself. I didn't need to be part of a *thing*.

"You're just going to go somewhere else by yourself. Yes, I understand." Her sarcasm cut me. "I used to be a four." She was gone before I could reply.

A four? Of course we knew that. One of Mother Redd had died . . . Was she saying that the fourth had left the composite voluntarily? My decision was nothing like that.

I rushed downstairs and out the front door so that I wouldn't have to face the rest of me. I didn't want them to taste my guilt. I ran the distance to Malcolm's cottage. He was working in his garden and took me in his arms.

"Meda, Meda. What's wrong?"

"Nothing," I whispered.

"Why did you go back there? We could have sent for your things."

I said, "I want an interface."

It was a simple procedure. He had the nanodermic, and placed it on the back of my neck. My neck felt cold there, and the coldness spread to the base of my skull and down my spine. There was a prick, and I felt my skin begin to crawl.

"I'm going to put you under for an hour," Malcolm said. "It's best."

"Okay," I said, already half asleep.

I dreamed that spiders were crawling down my optic nerve into my brain, that earwigs were sniffing around my lobes, that leeches were attached to all my fingers. But as they passed up my arms, into my brain, a door opened like the sun dawning, and I was somewhere else, somewhen else, and it all made sense with dreamlike logic. I understood why I was there, where the Community was, why they had left.

"Hello, Meda," Malcolm said.

"I'm dreaming."

"Not anymore," his voice said. It seemed to be coming from a bright point in front of me. "I've hooked you up to the interface box. Everything went fine."

My voice answered without my willing it to. "I was worried that my genetic mods would cause a problem." I felt I was still in my dream. I didn't want to say those things. "I didn't mean to say that. I think I'm still dreaming." I tried to stop speaking. "I can't stop speaking."

I felt Malcolm's smile. "You're not speaking. Let me show you what's possible within the Community."

He spent hours teaching me to manipulate the reality

of the interface box, to reach out and grasp it like my hand was a shovel, a hammer, sandpaper, a cloth. The interface box was no simple machine; it was a quantum computer, more powerful than any organic or silicon computers we could build.

"You do this well," he said, a brightness in the grey-green garden we had built in an ancient empty city. Ivy hung from the walls, and within the ivy sleek animals scurried. The dirt exuded its musty smell, mingling with the dogwoods that bounded the edge of the garden.

I smiled, knowing he could see my emotion. He could see all of me, as if he were a member of my pod, I was disclosed, though he remained aloof.

"Soon," he said, when I pried at his light, and then he took hold of me and we made love again in the garden, the grass tickling my back like a thousand tongues.

In the golden aftermath, Malcolm's face emerged from within the ball of light, his eyes closed. As I examined his face, it expanded before me, I fell into his left nostril, into his skull, and all of him was laid open to me.

In the garden, next to the ivy-covered stone walls, I began to retch. Even within the virtual reality of the interface box, I tasted my bile. He'd lied to me.

I had no control of my body. The interface box sat on the couch beside me as it had when we'd started, but pseudo-reality was gone. Malcolm was behind me—I could hear him packing a bag—but I couldn't will my head to turn.

"We'll head for the Belem elevator. Once we're on the Ring, we're safe. They can't get to us. Then they'll have to deal with me."

There was a water stain on the wall, a blemish that I could not tear my eyes away from.

"We'll recruit people from singleton enclaves. They

may not recognize my claim, but they will recognize my power."

My eyes began to tear, not from the strain. He'd used me, and I, silly girl, had fallen for him. He had seduced me, taken me as a pawn, as a valuable to bargain with.

"It may take a generation. I'd hoped it wouldn't. There are cloning vats on the Ring. You are excellent stock, and if raised from birth, you will be much more malleable."

If he had me, part of one of the starpods, he thought he'd be safe from the Overgovernment. But he didn't know that our pod was sundered. He didn't realize how useless this all was.

"All right, Meda. Time to go."

Out of the corner of my eye I saw him insert the connection into his interface, and my legs lifted me up off the couch. My rage surged through me, and my neck erupted in pheromones.

"Jesus, what's that smell?"

Pheromones! His interface controlled my body, my throat, my tongue, my cunt, but not my mods. He'd never thought of it. I screamed with all my might, scent exploding from my glands. Anger, fear, revulsion.

Malcolm opened the door, fanned the air. His gun bulged at his waist. "We'll pick up some perfume for you on the way." He disappeared out the door with two bags, one mine, while I stood with the interface box in my outstretched arms.

Still I screamed, saturating the air with my words, until my glands were empty, spent, and my autonomous nervous system silenced me. I strained to hear something from outside. There was nothing.

Malcolm reappeared. "Let's go." My legs goose-stepped me from the cottage.

I tasted our thoughts as I passed the threshold. My pod was out there, too far for me to understand, but close.

With the last of my pheromones, I signaled, *Help*.

"Into the aircar," Leto said.

Something yanked at my neck and my body spasmed as I collapsed. I caught sight of Manuel on the cottage roof, holding the interface box.

Leto pulled his gun and spun. Manuel threw the interface box at him.

Something else flew by me, and Leto cried out, dropping the pistol. I stood, wobbly, and ran into the woods, until someone caught me, and suddenly I was in our mesh.

As my face was buried in Strom's chest and my palms squeezed against his, I watched with other eyes—Moira's eyes!—as Leto scrambled into the aircar and started the turbines.

He's not going far.

We played with his hydrogen regulator.

Also turned his beacon back on.

Thanks for coming. Sorry.

I felt dirty, empty. My words barely formed. I released all that had happened, all that I had done, all my foolish thoughts into them. I expected their anger, their rejection. I expected them to leave me there by the cottage.

Still a fool, Moira chided. Strom touched the tender interface jack on my neck.

All's forgiven, Meda. The consensus was the juice of a ripe fruit, the light of distant stars.

All's forgiven.

Hand in hand in hand, we returned to the farm, sharing all that had happened that day.

THREE

Quant

When we returned to the farmhouse, Dr. Khalid was there.
One of him stepped into our space and lifted Meda's hair
from her nape. The skin there was raw, the outer jacket of
the interface silver in a patch of red.

"What has been done to you, child?" Khalid whispered.

Meda flushed, and I felt her embarrassment as my own.
He was our doctor, and yet we did not want to talk about
what Malcolm Leto had done to us.

"It was Leto," Mother Redd said. She stood aside; she
often examined us as well, but when Dr. Khalid was present, she deferred to him.

One of Khalid whirled on her, and a sharp expression
crossed his face. "You knew the danger!"

One of Mother Redd took a step back, and then her interface shook her head.

"Do not lecture me on risk, Doctor," she said.

We had not seen this clash between them before, and
we did not know what to make of it. Dr. Khalid made no

reply, but turned back to Meda and scanned the base of her skull with his portable MRI.

"It's embedded in her cerebellum," he murmured. "This is not good."

"Will it come out?" Meda asked.

All four of Khalid pursed his lips before answering, and we knew that it would not.

What about our practicum? I sent. The culmination of our years of training was the ten-week space-tour. Would this delay it?

Strom touched my shoulder, and he passed a thought between us. *This is about Meda.*

I flinched. He was right, and I felt guilty for thinking of what I wanted above Meda's trauma.

But Meda glanced at me, and then said to Dr. Khalid, "I don't want this to affect the practicum."

"I don't think—" Dr. Khalid began.

"That's nothing to worry about now," Mother Redd interrupted and again a dark look passed between one or two of each of them.

Worry, however we did, especially when the full MRI at the Institute confirmed that the nanofilaments of the interface were far into Meda's brain and impossible to remove. Furthermore, we saw via e-mail that other of our classmates were getting their assignments.

Where's ours? I sent, as we read the smarmy letter from Elliott O'Toole regarding his lunar posting.

Willow had a peach of an assignment at the Rift Observatory, where several telescopes were pointed through the hole in space in hopes of mapping as much of the remote location as possible. They had already found a G4 star less than half a light-year away.

How'd Elliott get the moon? Manuel asked.

It's not the Consensus, Moira replied. *He didn't get assigned to L4.*

That would have been the worst, a fait accompli for him.

We fretted the rest of the day, but finally the message came. Meda read it as I hid my face, but I felt the elation and I knew.

GEO! Meda sent. *We're going to Columbus Station!*

"Let's go! We have cargo to unload, and we have to turn this barge around in sixty minutes!"

The words were just sounds, but the pod moved, and I followed, mesmerized. Not by the shouts, but by the subtlety of motion I could achieve with the slightest force or pressure. As I glided into the wall, I stopped myself with a touch of my finger. I had been experimenting during the shuttle ride over, and I knew that I could use a palm to rotate my body. A solid grip on a bar gave me pitch and yaw control over my torso.

It was wonderful.

"Quant!" Manuel whispered at me. He was the last of us, except me, to exit the barge, and I realized that I was alone, save a muttering duo scrubbing vomit from an air vent's debris trap. It wasn't ours; we'd been in zero-gee before. It was poor Anderson McCorkle's, a fresh space dog duo who'd had a bad time of it. He'd managed to introduce himself to us before turning green in the gills, retching, and spending the last three hours of the push in the toilet.

"You're a quint," he said. "You guys are rare. Never seen one."

"Yeah, we were designed to fly the *Consensus*," Meda said, replying for all of us.

"Oh, yeah." One of him held his hand to his throat, forcing down a heave as the barge twisted. "Excuse me . . ."

"You picked an odd career if you get space sick," Meda said.

Anderson McCorkle seemed to get his stomach under control. He swallowed. I was only idly listening, waiting for the pilot to say we could get up from our seats. The barge was too fat to be under thrust the whole way to Columbus Station. We'd have at least two hours of free fall.

"Apollo? I recognize that name. Didn't you have—?"

And then one of him spewed into the air. His globules of floating vomitus had formed galaxies of regurgitated toast and coffee, their orbit defined by momentum, Coriolis, and surface tension. I calculated their positions over and over again.

"Quant!"

Manuel, grabbing the rails near the dilated door with his feet, pulled me through into Columbus Station.

Don't zone out on us.

Sorry, mesmerized.

He smiled. He knew it happened, and here in zero-gee it happened a lot. This wasn't our first time in space, but the first time we'd spent more than a couple of days. We'd traveled directly from Mother Redd's farm to Indonesia when our practicum on Columbus Station came through. Three days of basic orientation had preluded the six-hour barge ride over. I was only just beginning to understand what motion was, after almost two decades of prison on earth.

I know, Manuel sent.

He was hanging by his prehensile feet, oriented orthogonally to me. I grinned. Of course Manuel understood. A bit of our mindspace seeped together in shared thoughts and memories. He experienced the spectacle of perturbations I saw; I understood his sense of balance and control over his parasensual organs. Though five, we were one.

The sound of retching hit me the same time as the smell.

Hope that wasn't Strom, I sent.

No, Strom replied before I saw him. He had a notoriously strong stomach, and my jest brought a quick smile from the pod, shared on grasped palms.

"What kind of space dog are you?" someone was asking.

The bay was cramped for four pods: us, the newbie space hand McCorkle, and two trios—one all male, one all female—wedged to the wall at the far door of the bay. Through meter-square windows, I saw crews unloading the barge. It was easier to eject the cargo all at once instead of moving it into the bay box by box. The crews strapped the boxes to the station with self-knitting lines. I watched their dance, and hardly noticed as the new guy—both of him now—erupted again into a wall-mounted solid waste suck.

"Inner—" one started.

"—ear—" the other continued in stereo with the thump of bile into the duct.

"—infection."

"Sure." The male trio shook his head. "A quint and a space-sick duo. I don't have time for this; we have real work to get done. What am I supposed to do with you?"

"Put us to work!" Meda said. "I'm ready."

"Overeager groundhogs," he said to the other trio, then extended a hand to Meda. "Welcome to Columbus Station. I'm Aldo, this year's orientation lead. This is Flora, my second." They were dressed in dark grey jumpsuits. All of them had silver pips in an odd design at the collar. "Flora, take Apollo to his room." He grimaced at McCorkle. "I'll clean this one up and get him oriented. There can't be much left."

"Can't I go with them?" McCorkle managed to say before heaving again.

"You're inside duty. They're outside," Aldo said.

"Right," Flora said. "Come on. I'll get you settled in."

I thought McCorkle was empty already, I sent to Manuel, who shot me a smile.

"Based on what he spit up in the barge, I can't understand why he's still heaving," Meda said.

"You'd be surprised," Flora said. "I knew one guy who was sick for seven days straight, and at the end he was upchucking marbles he'd swallowed as a child."

"I find that highly unlikely," Meda said before someone could let her know she was using hyperbole.

She's joking, Strom sent.

Oh, right, Meda replied.

Flora gave us a look that said more about our status in her eyes than any words like "groundhog" and "gravity hugger." Flora was all female, three brunettes, thick-shouldered young women with arms like steel and legs like spaghetti. It was the look of all the space dogs. Strom admired her back muscles as she, hand over hand, hauled herself down into the station. Tubing and wires were tied into the walls, hiding hand grips that she seemed to grasp instinctively. We were slowed from fear of reaching out and taking a handful of system critical wiring, causing the station to plummet to Earth.

That won't happen, I sent. *We're in geostationary orbit. There's no way we could fall to Earth . . .*

I stopped. Manuel had turned to look at me. *We know.*

I grinned. *I know we know, but . . .* I shrugged. The delicate balance of force, neither pulled out into space, nor drawn back to Earth, was awe-inspiring for me. I tried to draw the picture and pass it to the pod, but Manuel waved me away. Flora had disappeared around a corner.

Where are we?

Our thoughts were disjointed, echoing along the length of our line. Usually we thought in a circle, hand in hand, a dual token-ring of biological thought. Strung out along the corridor as we were, thoughts were slow to percolate, consensus was weak, and half-formed ideas collided with decisions coming the other way. At the end, I nibbled at the group mind, but I was elsewhere. My brain wasn't like the others'; it drifted toward minutiae when we weren't looking, getting caught in the details. Sometimes I feared being alone, afraid that I'd never come back from where I go.

My mind was unraveling the maze of corridors, where we had been, half-glimpsed rooms, piecing bits into the three-dimensional map of the station we had from the tug. Columbus Station looked like an upside-down turnip, hanging forty-two thousand kilometers above the Earth, on its half-finished tether above Ecuador. It sat perfectly balanced in zero-gee with a cable lowering to Earth and another counterbalancing one rising into space.

In months, when the Earth-side tether hooked up with the ground anchor, Columbus Station would be the second of the OG's space stations, doubling the rate of material and personnel egress to GEO. From there to L4 was a trivial maneuver. The arc flickered in my brain, the forces it required, the effect of mass.

"Quant!"

Hand over hand, I sprinted down the hall, joining the pod just as they arrived in front of a grey door. Stenciled at the left was our name.

I felt the excitement course through us. Our quarters, in space.

"We were expecting another quint," Flora said. She touched our name, as if expecting it to be wet. "Had to paint over it."

Paint over it? Strom wondered.

They weren't expecting us, Moira sent coldly. *They weren't expecting to send us up.*

Because of Meda? I sent, checking myself too late. There was no response from my pod, though I saw the red rise on Meda's cheeks.

Flora opened the door with a flourish. "Your home for ten weeks."

Brightness flushed away the neon light of the corridor. A panorama of the Earth hung below us the size of a basketball at arm's length. Half of it was in shadow, the rest in full sunlight and cast in blues, greens, and whites.

"It's—" Meda started.

"Yeah," Flora finished. "I love this part of the tour."

"Why is our room so nice? So special?"

"It's not," Flora said. "Everyone gets a window view of Earth. Tradition."

"Everyone gets a room like this?"

"Well, yours is bigger. Most everyone on Columbus is a trio." She stood in the doorway while we piled in, pressing our faces to the diamond glass. "Someone will bring your gear along in a while. Relax for a while, then we start safety training."

She paused. "Some advice: you're here for ten weeks, the rest of us for years and lifetimes. The commander is pushing us like hell, and Aldo and I have two other jobs to do besides babysitting you."

"We'll try staying out of your way," Meda offered.

"Staying out of the way still means you're breathing air and using water that someone more productive could be using. This isn't Earth where we have infinite resources and time enough. I have no illusions you'll be useful, but I hope you'll do more than eat twice as much as I do."

"We'll try . . ." But Flora was already pulling herself down the corridor. After she had disappeared, Strom shut the door. *That went well,* he sent.

At least we didn't barf on her.

The day isn't over yet.

Much to our disappointment, "training" had nothing to do with going outside the space station. It meant safety drills and equipment checks, followed by endless repetition of facts about those same drills and equipment. The closest we got to the outside was the cafeteria where one entire wall was meter-square windows facing Earth.

We tried to explain to Aldo we'd been checked out on EVA suits before.

"Not on an industrial construction site in zero-gee. Two weeks ago, a guy tossed a screwdriver to himself, wasn't ready for it, and punctured his suit to his skin."

"And?"

"Er, frostbite," Aldo replied. "Nasty case of it."

When do we get to work on a sled? I asked, speaking for all of us.

"We'll keep that in mind, Aldo," Meda said. "When do we start external work? We've been here two weeks already." After two weeks of drills and basic biology work in the labs, we could scramble into our suits in fifty-three seconds and extemporize on the life cycle of the anchor spiders for an hour.

"Well . . ." he said. "It should have been last week—"

"You're holding us back," Meda interrupted.

"—but we had to build you a modified sled."

"Oh."

"Yeah, in case you didn't notice, all the sleds are built for trios. We need one that will accommodate your fiveness."

Pods did outside work by waldo whenever possible, then by sled if the distance was too great for a waldo. The third choice was remote in suits, but maintaining autonomous action while separated from your pod was nearly impossible. It was only done in an emergency. The way to communicate when in a space suit was via hand gesture and voice, and that was no way to reach consensus.

"So when will ours be ready?"

"Real soon, today maybe. We modified the commander's pinnace," Aldo said. "It's for official guests, so it could seat two pods in a pinch, or one of you quints." Suddenly all three of him grinned. "Wanna see it?"

Yes!

"Yes!"

We were in the cafeteria, the largest open area on station, working on free fall maneuvering with no handholds. It was the most interesting problem he'd given us, one that suited me: one, two, three, four, then five of us trapped in free fall with no momentum. A problem of forces, even when five of us were floating helplessly. Balanced feet against feet, timed perfectly, a kickoff could put us anywhere. Once any one of us had a firm wall, we could rescue the rest in no time.

From the cafeteria, we clambered zenithally upstation to the docks, just aft of the zenith tether anchor. We passed the biology wing where we'd spent long hours with Dr. Buchanan working with the arachnids. We passed the hydroponics bay, too small to feed even the half-populated, half-built station. Mother Redd's farm had little of the hard tech the station did and yet we managed to feed eight human bodies and countless animals with little work. Sustainability apparently was not a requirement of this project.

Inside the hydroponics bay I spied our vomiting friend from the barge—Anderson McCorkle. He was picking tomatoes, one of him plucking, the other catching with a bag. It looked like his regurgitation was under control now. I couldn't understand why someone with zero-gee sickness would apply for a space-based position with the OG. He caught sight of me, waved in greeting.

I waved back, turned to go, then he called me over. "How are things going?"

My pod was just ahead, almost to the sled bay, so I figured I could spend a moment with McCorkle. I swam over, using the rings on the floor as handholds. Huge suction fans were mounted near the doors to prevent water from leaving the hydroponics bay. Even though the plants were growing in sealed bags of mineral-rich water, accidents happened, and water in zero-gee was at least an irritant, sliding up nostrils and causing coughing fits, and at worst a deadly danger, shorting equipment or in large amounts comprising a drowning hazard. In zero-gee the primary forces that water observed was van der Waals forces. A skull-shaped sphere of water could surround a person's head in seconds and be impossible to remove without suction. Emergency vacs were along every row of plants.

"Hey, McCorkle," I said. Though Meda was our voice, I sometimes spoke, a requirement during those times when I was rarely by myself, which usually happened when I zoned out, and the pod went on without me.

"You're Quant," he said.

I didn't notice how odd it was for him to know that, at least I didn't notice then. I just nodded, my eyes caught by the spreading roots of the tomato plant. Above it was a thickness of yellow flowers, green leaves, and tiny orange fruit, chaotic, a mess. Below, the roots grew in a pattern of thickness to tendrils that rested against the water bulb and gently swished back and forth. I pressed my hand against the bulb.

"Pretty neat, huh?"

I nodded, mesmerized. I was tracing the pattern of roots with my eyes, following it like a fractal.

"When is your pod going outside?" he asked.

"Soon," I said. "Tomorrow. Our sled is in the sled bay."

"Oh, really."

"We're going to see it right now."

"It's in the bay now?"

"Yeah."

"You're the autistic one, aren't you?"

"Quant!"

Manuel stood at the door of the hydroponics bay. I turned, smiled, and pulled over to him, casting a quick, "Bye" at McCorkle.

Don't you want to see the sled?

Yes!

Then come on and stop zoning out over tomatoes.

I tried to show him the beauty of the fractal tomato roots, but he was ahead of me already.

We rounded a corner and came into the sled bay. Inside were the sleds that were in maintenance, two of them. The rest were lashed to the outside of the station and brought to a docking port when needed. The two sleds in maintenance were a large one, a modified Hulasledge, and a second normal-sized one.

I don't have specs on the Hulasledge, I sent, wanting to climb behind the yoke and figure it out.

I thought you had specs on everything in your brain, Strom replied.

My mind was already counting the changes, the big one being a welded section just aft of the front cockpit. Someone had taken two sleds and merged them into a monstrosity. Additional fuel tanks had been added to compensate for the mass. A second set of thrusters dangled from the welded section. At first glance it looked cumbersome, but as I dissected the forces, it seemed to make fundamental sense. It would be a wonder to fly.

I found myself drifting toward it, unchecked in my momentum. I caught myself on the nadir airlock, flashing a look at Meda.

Can we?

Aldo must have guessed what I asked. He nodded, saying, "Go ahead."

I scrambled in the lock, both irises open, my pod behind me. The sled smelled of rubber. Handholds guided me to the cockpit; the sled inside was two spheres, the smaller one the cockpit and claw controls, the larger for additional crew. Manuel swam in and placed his hands on the controls to the right of the pilot's. I pulled myself in front of the yoke.

We'd simmed it a hundred times, but never actually touched real controls.

Cool, he sent.

I reached out for the yoke. I knew intuitively how my hands would create reaction with each touch. I couldn't wait. Behind me, my pod shared my joy.

"Feel good?" It was Aldo's voice from the airlock.

"Yes," Meda said. "Fits perfectly."

"Good, because we're going out tomorrow."

"Tomorrow?"

"Yeah, someone has to pick up the spider heads. It might as well be the newbie."

Tomorrow, I sent. *Tomorrow we fly.*

We climbed out, and watched as the maintenance crew pushed our sled into the huge airlock and took it outside, leaving the single one behind.

For a moment the sled was in free fall, a forceless cradle, no rotation, no gravity, and then the cable slid into view from the right, thin monowire spun by spiders, marked by flashing lights every hundred meters along its twenty-kilometer length. Behind us the skeleton of Columbus Station hung, below us the Ring.

"Where's the *Consensus*?" Strom asked. He glanced around the sled bubble, looking for the moon. Our starship, *Consensus,* was parked at the shipyard at Earth-Moon L4. Manuel and I sat in the cockpit, while Strom, Meda, and Moira sat directly behind us in the larger equipment and personnel bay. The redesigned sled was actually roomy for a quintet, since it had been built to hold two trios or a trio and a quartet at most.

It's not ours yet, Moira sent, correcting my thought.

I spelled out p-e-n-d-a-n-t in Pod-C sign language with my left hand. My right I kept firmly on the yoke. Manuel laughed.

It will be, I replied, and then I took a moment from my tableau of forces and my argument with Moira to send, *It's on the far side of the Earth.*

"Oh. Where's the Ring?" Strom asked.

He turned his head to look for the Ring instead. On my left, Meda flinched. Before she could slam her mind shut, I saw an image of the interface jack embedded in her neck, superimposed with the face of Malcolm Leto. I took a hand off the controls to touch her shoulder.

Strom burst with embarrassment pheromone, but Meda shook it off. We couldn't ignore the Ring and all that it was to us. It had been on our minds since that morning. As we had suited up in the sled bay, four pods—fourteen humans—crammed in together, doing safety checks, pulling straps, and cleaning visors, Flora had reached over and touched the interface jack on Meda's neck.

"What's that?"

The shock of the touch, the casual act more intimate than Flora could know, had stirred the muddy bottoms of our consciousness, and we had frozen, remembering how Malcolm Leto had seduced, raped, and nearly kidnapped Meda. We all remembered the violation, the rebellion of her body, as if it had happened to each of us. It might as well have. We all had the memory. We all had the nightmares.

Meda, our voice, had floated there in the bay, unable to react to Flora's words, caught in the memory, and drawing attention to the jack by not replying. We did not want that attention, another thing to separate us from the space hounds.

I'd spoken up then, taking the voice, something I rarely did, and asked Aldo, "How do we stabilize a port-zenith spin again?"

He'd look surprised. Then he'd said, "You should know that—" and started lecturing me on things I knew by heart.

But that was enough to divert attention from Meda, and she'd smiled at Flora and said, "An old scar."

The interface jack was Community technology, just as the Ring was. An artifact, Moira had said. One that was embedded in Meda's skull.

The Ring's below us, I sent, tarballing up an image of where we were, just above Columbus Station, marking L4 where *Consensus* was docked, the Ring thirty-two thousand kilometers below us, and the Earth ten thousand kilometers lower than the Ring.

I added Columbus and Sabah Ground Stations to my image, pinpointed the spot on the moon where Elliott O'Toole was working. I can easily paint a picture for them to see, but they didn't feel my joy in the world I saw. It was like a painted picture of the real world. I could only estimate and approximate and trick their eyes into seeing what I saw.

I touched a control and spun the sled on its X axis, and there was the Earth. With a counterburst that I knew was the perfect force, the sled stopped, angular momentum checked.

"Oh, my."

The Earth was a blue plate painted with swirls. I studied the image through my podmates' eyes, not looking directly at it, the beautiful formation of white clouds over blue ocean and green land. Strom painted the best mental images. He always caught the right hue and tint, shared it so we all could see it. Perhaps it was some deficiency of mine that I couldn't show them exactly what I saw.

And there was the Ring, a band of silver girding the world. Close, relatively speaking, within clear sight from Earth and space day and night, though impossible to reach. The Ring was open only to members of the Community, of which there was one: Malcolm Leto.

Over Strom's image, I saw the Earth as I always did, a

sinkhole, a gravity well, a restriction to be accounted for first in any calculation. The biggest delta. Always the biggest delta.

Until now. Here in geosynchronous orbit, the Earth's sink was canceled out by the centripetal force. Vectors crept to zero around me, then slowly grew as my mind envisioned space beyond geosynch. Geosynch was artificial stability. It only appeared that we were holding station above the Earth in the same spot. We were falling, always falling, but never landing.

"Tango-Five-Five, do you have your mark? Apollo, how are you doing?"

The voice was Aldo's. I tuned him out. Of course I had the mark, ten minutes ago. We'd spent three days with our sled latched to Aldo's clearing the local area of spider heads. Spider heads were all that remained after a spider had woven its life away building a few hundred meters of diamond line: the last state in a spider's short life. If Dr. Buchanan could have designed them to burn themselves up in the atmosphere, he would have. As it was, someone had to go fetch them before they became a hazard to navigation. It was not the most prestigious of jobs.

Spiders had built the cable in geosynch, not far from the station. The gene-modded arachnids spun a line of diamond thread, cannibalizing their bodies as they weaved. They worked in multiples of three, building ten meters of cable each before expiring and leaving their heads dangling from the thread, where they could be collected by us. Every tool, device, and body was accounted for in space. Debris in orbit was death for accelerating craft.

Meda toggled the mic and said, "Tango-Five-Five: Yes, Aldo." Her exasperation was all of ours. The mark was our spot on the cable. As we glided toward it, three other sleds were as well. Ours was one up from the bottommost.

"Just checking, Apollo."

Hold on, I sent.

My podmates clutched handholds as the sled tilted. I glided the sled past the wire, then spun us around it as I damped rotational and orthogonal speed with a double flick of the thrusters.

"Careful, Apollo. The sled can slice the wire." I ignored the radio; it was amplitude with no vector.

The sled stopped within ten centimeters of the wire. After days being latched to Aldo's sled it had taken me just a few minutes to understand the dynamics of the sled by itself.

Show-off, Meda sent.

No, I replied. *This is what I do.*

We all have our talents. We are five that is one, a human composite, a pod. We had been built to a purpose two decades before, each of us designed to lend a strength to the whole. I was the specialized part that understood the Newtonian laws and mathematics intuitively, just as Meda was our voice, Moira our conscience, Strom our strength, and Manuel our hands. On Earth, my skills were muted.

Manuel glanced up at the nearest sled. The space hound was tapping the thruster, oscillating toward the wire from ten meters off. Strom rotated a camera toward Aldo maneuvering closer to the base mark, one of his sled's hooked claws extended.

"Tango-One-Zero, taking the mark."

Aldo's claw slid through the ring and clamped shut.

"Tango-Five-Five, take your mark."

Manuel slipped the fingers of his right hand into the hook controls. The claw slid forward, as if it were Manuel's own fingers, and grabbed the ring. He ratcheted the claw down until the grip was tight. My hand trailed across Manuel's left wrist, catching the feel of the claw, the strength and fluidity of the mechanical extension.

"Got it," Meda said into the radio.

Above them Klada Ross and Flora Julet took their marks and radioed their status. Aldo's sled would do half the heavy thrusting. We and Klada would dampen any oscillations in the wire. Flora would keep the wire taut and stop us as we neared the station.

"Tango-One-Zero, thrusting."

A bump of acceleration as the cable pulled us down. The station was below us, toward the Earth, and antispinward. The pull of a higher orbit had slowly drawn the cable away, stretching it as the spiders did their slow work. Each of Columbus Station's tethers grew twenty kilometers at a time as the spiders completed a section and the space dogs wrangled it into place. This section was destined for the Earth-bound cable. Slowly, piece by piece, the station would lower the inner cable down until it kissed the Earth, just as the final counterweight was latched to the far end. The total length was 62,000 kilometers: 42,000 to Earth and 20,000 past geosynch, where the speed of the daily rotation pulled everything away from the Earth at a quarter-gee.

The grip was loose and the sled tilted toward the cable. I touched the jets, righted the sled to avoid tangling. Then I applied another small spurt to keep the line taut.

"Tango-One-Zero, thrusting."

Aldo was using more impulse to move the cable a little faster. Once we got halfway to the station, Flora Julet would apply the same thrust and bring the cable to rest relative to the cable joint it was to be connected to. Then Aldo would fasten the new section to the station cable, allowing the cable master to lower the cable another twenty kilometers. We had an hour before we reached the station.

Strom called up our orbital mechanics class notes; we were taking the class via desktop at the Institute. Until Columbus Station's cable touched Earth, it was impossible to commute unless we traveled half the Earth to Sabah Station and then from Borneo to North America. But that was fine with me; the more time we were in space, the better.

I barely paid attention to my pod as they passed the notes between them in chemical memory. I stored some by habit, but the written equations were nothing to the lines of force embedded in my genes. Though I could share my thoughts with my pod, they could never see the universe the way I did. Separate, yet one.

"You guys are doing all right for a bunch of spider-head hunters," Klada Ross said, his voice tinny over the private channel between us.

Irritation boiled among us, but Meda replied in a measured tone. "This could all be done by robot," she said. "It's hardly necessary for all four of us to be out here."

"Well, groundling, you never know what's going to happen up here. This isn't like picking up spider heads."

You belittled his job, Moira sent. *Apologize.*

Meda glared at her twin sister, but nodded.

"You're right, Klada. I wasn't thinking it through."

"Yeah, sometimes three heads are better than five." Again I smelled the frustration in the space of the sled. Since we had arrived at the station, our order of five had been a point of contention. We'd been given the biggest sled, the biggest room, more emergency suits, more space, and the regular space hound trios had resented it. No one seemed willing to accept us as another hand; we couldn't get past being a quintet with no skills.

Do you blame them? We're encroaching.

We're here to help.

They didn't ask for it.

I stayed out of the consensus, doing nothing more than keeping touch with Manuel and Meda, letting the thoughts course through me. People were chaotic forces; unknown perturbations.

We have to be strong.

Push back.

"I guess three heads are better for station work," Meda said.

Klada didn't respond at first, then said, "You keep thinking that when you're out there in the great beyond, Captain."

Too strong, Strom sent.

Seven weeks to go.

The sun caught the cable, and for a moment, we saw it descending down toward the surface, skirting the Ring and reaching toward the ground anchor. The abandoned Ring itself stood in our way, a blockade of space that we had to avoid carefully in all our comings and goings to space. The Columbus Station cable actually bowed as it passed within a kilometer to the starboard of the Ring.

Aldo's voice came over the general frequency: "Flora, get ready to thrust."

"Roger."

The rest of the pod looked up for the puff of reaction gas, but I kept my hand on the controls. I would feel the thrust in the cable before they saw the frozen gas from Flora's sled.

There it was, a tickle on the cable.

Wrong.

The force wasn't what it should have been: jagged, not smooth.

"Aldo—"

Flora's voice cut off and the cable went taut. The sled accelerated up. Then the line went loose again. I thrust back, keeping the line tight between Aldo and Klada. The image of Flora's sled drifted to me, and I saw it spinning madly. Thruster malfunction. The speed of the turning meant Flora was under extreme gee-forces within the sled. She had jettisoned the cable quickly, smart thinking. Otherwise the cable might have wrapped around her like cotton candy. The section of cable she had been hauling was slowly tumbling toward Klada.

Flora was drifting away, faster and faster, accelerating. I calculated her acceleration and realized she was flying on a trajectory far beyond the range of any rescue from the station.

I touched Manuel's wrist, and thought coursed through us.

Too far for a rescue from Columbus Station in fifty seconds.

Too far for a rescue from us in three minutes.

We can reach her and get back to the station.

Our sled has more reaction mass. It's bigger.

Klada and Aldo can handle the line.

We need to go now.

Go.

Manuel dropped the cable, and I accelerated the sled. I saw in a second the path that would intersect Flora's sled. I saw the shortest arc, the least reaction mass that would get us there.

"Apollo! What are you doing?"

Ignore, said Meda. There was no time for gathering permissions.

The pod was focused on me. I set them to task; they were extensions of myself which was in turn an extension of the sled. Manuel stood ready at the second claw. Moira watched Flora's sled. Strom started handing out helmets and doing safety checks on the suits. Meda watched the panels, especially our fuel gauge. Each second was so much reaction mass lost to space.

"Apollo! Do you have a malfunction too?"

I felt Meda's anger at the misunderstanding.

She toggled the radio. "No! We're saving Flora!"

"Get back here! We can't have two stranded sleds!"

Meda flicked the radio off.

Flora is trying to correct the sled, Moira sent.

I looked away from the controls for a second, saw that Flora was using her other maneuvering thrusters to compensate for the wild force of the malfunctioning one. But her timing was too slow, off by a second again and again, and the sled was moving farther away as she did it.

I recomputed her trajectory, saw how close we were to not having enough impulse to return to Columbus Station. I spread the problem before us in physics shorthand.

We paused to consider.

Continue on, Meda said.

Agreed. Fast consensus, urged ahead by the precarious nature of Flora's situation. No one at Columbus Station was close enough to save her now but us.

Seconds ticked on.

Her reaction mass is gone, Meda reported.

That meant her velocity was fixed, save for the force of her orbit. As she had shot toward the zenith and spinward, away from Earth, the centripetal force had increased and was pulling her farther and farther away. The orbit was unstable and Flora's sled would accelerate beyond the moon and back again, in a bizarre dance, but not before she had long since died of hunger or asphyxiation. We had to catch her now.

I added a modicum of thrust. Twenty seconds until we would reach her.

Ten. The sled was looming above us, still spinning wildly, silently.

Get ready. Expect motion, maybe enough to get you sick, I sent.

I aimed our sled at the edge of the spinning top, damped our speed to zero relative to the outer edge spin, and tapped Flora's sled with our claw.

Manuel latched on.

I slammed against the console. For a moment, all was black, and all I could smell was the confusion pheromone.

But then my vision began to clear. The disorientation fled into chaotic lines of force. Through the sounds of retching and the smell of vomit, the lines began to unravel. I started applying thrust: touch, touch, touch, to counter the wild gyrations.

"Keep the claw tight!" I screamed at Manuel, but Manuel had let go of the claw, one hand clutching at the bulkhead, one at the straps of his seat belt, uselessly trying to steady himself.

With a loose coupling, it was harder to correct the spinning. I was using too much reaction mass.

Manuel, the claw has to be tight!

"I can't!"

I couldn't control both the sled and the claw. Manuel had to tighten the grip.

I built an image of the forces for Manuel, for the pod, a three-dimensional image of where we were, and how close we were to flying into empty space. Death by asphyxiation.

We need to tighten the claw's grip, I sent, as I passed the image around.

Manuel swallowed and nodded. He released his hand from the bulkhead, and tried to push his fingers into the waldo. Once more, then his hand was in, and he tightened down the claw's clutch onto Flora's sled. The jerking smoothed.

I applied another series of thrusts and the twisting and turning slowed. The impulses countered the tumbling, and then the sleds were righted, zero tumble, just the pull of centripetal force into space. We were hundreds of kilometers farther out than when we'd started.

Behind me, Moira began cleaning up the vomit, sucking it into the zero-gee portavac. I ignored the smell, ignored my own twitching stomach, focused on the vectors of velocity and acceleration. The fuel gauge was too low. The extra maneuvering to slow the tumble had used too much fuel. We were still flying outward. The seconds ticked off as the distance stretched. We had to make a decision; no decision was death. But I saw no decision that worked.

I modified the image and shot it to my pod.

We need to get back to the station.

The model was unsolvable. I could not fight the outward centripetal force and reach the station.

My mind started trying other scenarios: could we reach L4 or L5 in less than five days? No. I could set us on a thirty-day trajectory. Too long. No food, no air, no water.

I ruled out the moon.

The Ring? Meda sent.

The Ring was thirty thousand kilometers below us. There was no way to reach it if we could not reach Columbus Station.

No, the spines.

My mind jumped and assimilated the thought. The Ring orbited in geostationary orbit at ten thousand kilometers. Because it was so far below geosynch, the Ring was actually under acceleration: the centripetal force of a geostationary orbit at ten thousand kilometers did not cancel the pull of the Earth. In fact the acceleration was 0.14 gees. To keep the Ring in place, it relied on the rigidity of the Ring itself, the anchors to the Earth, and the spines that served as counterbalances. The spines extended past geosynchronous orbit.

I added the spines to my map image, but my hope faded. None of the spines were near enough to reach. Columbus Station had been positioned atop Quito precisely because there were no nearby spines to tangle with the station's counterbalances.

Then I realized that Columbus Station had its own spine, the start of Columbus Station's own counterbalance tether. It extended some ten thousand kilometers, half its final length, and it was near, very near. Near enough to reach. The pod checked my calculation and agreed.

Do it, Meda sent.

I applied the thrust gently, urging the awkward double sled toward the end of the cable. The tether was invisible, but I knew where it had to be. I kept the acceleration on, not fighting the outward centripetal force, but moving perpendicular. The result was a vector about thirty degrees off the vertical cable.

If we missed it, there would be no hope. The trajectory sent us toward the Earth-Sun spinward Lagrange point in a figure eight that would bring us back to Earth in months.

The claw, I sent.

Manuel nodded, flexed the first claw, the one we had used to hook the cable.

Meda turned the radio back on.

"Apollo! What are you doing? Your trajectory is no good."

Aldo, still screaming.

"We're going to catch the counterbalance cable," Meda said. "You may have to come get us."

Silence on the radio, then, "Apollo . . ." I knew Aldo was considering, wondering. If he had had a part like me, he would have seen it right away as a valid solution.

"Can you . . . ?"

"Yes, we can, Aldo."

"I'm going to need more fuel if I have to come get you," he said.

"You'll have time to get it," Meda said. We would catch the tether near the end, draw it taut and swing in a pendulum with the station at the fulcrum. But the full swing would take hours.

Sixty seconds, I sent. We weren't going to be able to decelerate. There was one chance, and one chance only.

"Flora, hold on," Meda said on the radio's open channel. "If you can hear us."

There it is, sent Strom. Everyone used Strom's eyes to watch.

The cable swung close, not at our speed, since we approached it at an oblique angle. But still it was coming at us fast. A light blazed past us, a beacon for wayward spacecraft. Good, I thought. The next one wouldn't be for ten kilometers.

The cable was like a single raindrop, stretched by relativity to infinity. It slid between Manuel's stretched claws.

Manuel snagged it and the sleds jolted. The sizzle of the claw on the wire echoed through the cabin.

Don't break it!

Manuel let go and grabbed again. He twisted the claw and the sled jerked.

The cable began to tangle with the sleds. Free fall, then a spasm of acceleration as the line pulled taut and held. Weak gravity tugged at us. The long swing had begun. In relief, in amazement, I let out a half snort, half giggle.

We were an inverted pendulum with a period of just over four hours. The ramifications of it shuddered through me, and I began to laugh. We were part of a double pendulum over fifty thousand kilometers long—the station, the sleds, and the up and down cables—acted on by gravitational and centripetal forces. I painted the image for my pod and tossed it at them.

"Beautiful," Meda said.

I added the flex of the diamond cables. I accounted for its mass. The effect of the hundred or so kilometers of cable still above us, a third pendulum in the system. I began to calculate the jerk Columbus Station received when the cable damped the sled's zenithal velocity.

Uh-oh, Meda sent. *Jerk?*

The time derivative of acceleration, I sent helpfully. *The second derivative of velocity. The third derivative of position.*

We jolted the whole station?

How much?

"A little," I said, and the pod's concern finally made it through to me.

Did we hurt the cable?

It's moving up a couple meters per second.

"Oh, crap!" Meda said. "This isn't going to look good."

It looks great, I sent.

Meda glared. *We need to get down.*

We need to check on Flora, Strom sent.

I looked up. The zenithal windows were blocked by Flora's loosely held craft. Since the sled's thrusters had misfired, we'd heard nothing from Flora. She may have been severely hurt.

"Flora, are you there?" Meda said on the private channel.

Try the suit radio, Quant sent.

Meda nodded and pulled the suit helmet over her head, cutting herself off from the intrapod pheromones.

"Flora? Are you listening?" I could hear the tinny conversation from Strom's helmet, which he held in his hands.

"Yes."

"Are you okay?"

"Broken ribs, bruises. The sled's fucked. Vomit in the console does that." She snorted. "I haven't vomited in years."

Meda chuckled. "We have a little of that over here too."

Silence for a moment, then Flora said, "That was nice flying."

I felt myself blush. Strom tousled my hair with a huge hand. I batted it away, smiling.

"Thanks," Meda said.

"Any ideas on how we get down?"

I signaled to Meda with hand gestures, indicating we should attempt to connect the two sleds at their airlocks. Verbal speech, chemical thoughts, and pheromones were all part of how a pod thought and spoke. When none of those were possible, we could use our own modified version of the hand language, Pod-C. All First State children were taught Pod-C in the creche.

"We're going to try connecting the airlocks," Meda said.

All the sleds had single-person airlocks with universal connectors on the outside. I turned a camera on the sled. Flora's airlock was on the far side. There was no way to maneuver to the other side, while one claw kept the sleds attached and the other clung to the cable. If we let go of either to adjust their position, one or both of the sleds would fly into space. A tricky problem.

I signed to Meda again.

"Do your claws work?" Meda asked.

"Maybe," Flora said. "No, the claw is not responding. Not much is." There was a pause. "Apollo. We're almost out of air."

"What?"

They should have days left, I sent.

"I didn't fill it up all the way. I didn't think we'd be out that long."

"That's a real grounder thing to do," Meda said.

Flora chuckled. "Tell me about it."

"How much do you have left?"

"An hour. An hour more if we suit up." I heard the reluctance in her voice. Suited up, the trio would be sundered, out of communication except by voice. Voice communication was too . . . shallow. No memories, no feelings, just low data rate.

Aldo won't be here before she runs out of air.

I mapped out the problem in my mind, built the image and passed it around.

Flora's claw didn't work. Our claws could not be disconnected for the time it took to connect the sleds. We had little reaction mass left.

Ferry them over in their suits.

I looked around at the already cramped sled. Three more bodies would be a tight fit, but possible.

"Flora, can you suit up and come across?" Meda asked.

"We have two broken legs and I don't know how many broken ribs. It won't be easy. Maybe." If they were injured, the pod would be even more reluctant to separate.

We need to link up and get back to the Station.

I had it. *The railcar,* I sent.

When we had gone spider-head hunting, Aldo had ferried us to the cable and we had attached our sled to the cable with the railcar claw attachment. Then we'd crawled the cable, plucking off spider heads and tossing them in a bag.

If we could get a railcar attachment on the cable now, it could move us down the cable at ten meters per second. We'd be back at Columbus Station in a few hours.

They still need air.

Bring them across.

How?

Do it by hand, I sent. *I'll suit up—*

We'll suit up, Strom amended.

—use lines to latch the sleds, and connect the two locks. We mount the railcar attachment to the claw that was holding Flora's sled, and off we go.

No one objected, except for Manuel, who wanted to go with Strom and me.

Someone has to man the claw, I sent. Strom painted an image of Manuel with claws as hands.

"Thanks."

Moira helped me with my helmet, while Meda buckled Strom's. Moira planted a kiss on my cheek, and said, "No one can fly like you. No one will pilot the *Consensus* like you."

Elliott O'Toole wants to try, I sent. Elliott, our classmate and competitor, was right now interning on the moon at the aluminum smelting plant. I didn't like thinking about his captaining the *Consensus* instead of us.

Moira left me with a private image of a triple pendulum, an elegant thought-postcard. I smiled, and drew the helmet down, cutting myself off from the rest of them.

"Don't worry, Quant," Strom said over the suit radio. "We'll be back in a jiffy."

I nodded. Strom was the one who could spend the most time away from the pod, but also the one who hated most to be away. We touched gloved hands, and I entered the sled airlock first.

It cycled, and I listened to the clunk as the air was removed, until there was too little air to hear anything but my own breathing.

Then the outer door opened. My visor darkened in the face of the sun's glory, even though most of me was in shade. Three meters above was Flora's sled, two meters away was our claw, grasping a docking ring embedded in the sled's hull. I saw one of Flora looking at me through a window, and I gave her a quick thumbs-up. She waved back.

The gentle tug of centripetal force reminded me to connect my line to the sled. I half fell, half somersaulted out of the lock, and watched as the door closed. Cut off from the rest.

I felt a momentary pang, then took another line and drifted across to Flora's sled. My plan was to connect the sleds by a single line and let the weak centripetal force twist Flora's sled around so that we could winch it down, airlock to airlock. I caught a hold not quite as elegantly as Manuel would have, and tied off the sleds.

I jumped back and helped Strom connect his lifeline.

I said to Meda, "Tell Flora to expect a jerk. Manuel, release the claw attached to Flora's sled."

The sled's hull vibrated as the claw's motors turned. Flora's sled drifted away slowly, pulling the slack out of the line, and then stopped with a jiggle. Strom took the winch line from the claw and jumped across the gap. He disappeared around the far side, and all I could see of him was the movement in his line.

"Manuel, pull the winch in slowly," he said.

Flora's sled began to rotate. Strom reappeared, clinging to the side of it. We tethered the sleds together again with short lines, aligning the airlocks. Strom entered our airlock, and I the other. I attached another line to the airlock door and passed it to Strom. He looped it around a ring in our airlock and passed it back to me. We began to pull.

"Watch your fingers," Meda radioed.

Slowly the sleds came together. At one-tenth gee, the sled's weight was manageable, but its mass remained large. If the sleds rammed, it would be disaster.

The sleds kissed. I surveyed the alignment.

"Lined up. Connect them."

Bolts slid together with a thunk that echoed in the frame of the airlock. The connector began to fill with air.

The inner door to our sled opened, and I and Strom climbed back up. Moira pulled off my helmet, and I breathed deeply in relief. Thoughts and emotion washed over me, and I was relieved to be with my pod. My back ached from the long minutes of tension. I wasn't the same alone.

As the door to Flora's sled opened, Meda crawled down and shook hands with Flora's interface. Manuel had maneuvered the second claw to clutch the cable just like the first, and then taken the first off the wire. The rail-car attachment was almost in place.

The smell of foreign thought and emotion filled the sled. Flora was sharing our air now. We were safe for a good twelve hours, more than enough time to make it back to the station.

Manuel pushed the railcar against the cable, clamped it, and released the claw.

Here we go, I said.

The railcar motor started, and the coupled sleds began to move ponderously, slowly. In minutes we were up to full speed, heading straight back to the station. There was no other direction to go.

We had just enough reaction mass to thrust to the sled bay at the top of the station. While we were donning our suits to release the sleds, a swarm of trios came through the bay lock and began pulling them apart.

"Thanks again," Flora said, as her outer lock slid closed. As I sat in front of the controls, my fingers twitched. All of us were exhausted and empty. But still exhilaration bounced between us. We'd rescued her, and we'd done it on our own. Space was our home, and what more proof than this.

The crew pushed Flora's sled into the large airlock. They'd work on the broken sled in the pressurized sled bay. I started thrusting the sled toward our normal slot.

"Belay that thrust, Tango-Five-Five," came a voice over the radio, the station traffic controller. I checked our veloc-ity, and we waited, scarcely sharing a coherent thought.

After a few minutes the crews came back and pushed our sled onto a docking airlock. As we piled out into the station hallway, Aldo was there to greet us.

"You're off duty and restricted to your quarters and the

galley." My stomach lurched. No outside duty meant we were cooped up inside, studying.

"But—" Meda said.

"It's Hilton's orders." The station commander. We'd had one interview with the gruff woman on arrival and hadn't seen her since. She'd wanted us there as much as the rest of the space hounds.

Why are we off duty? I asked.

Maybe it's standard when there's a space accident, Moira sent, but more than one of us thought the idea dubious.

Showers, Meda sent, deferring all argument.

I followed my pod as we pulled downward to our quarters. I wanted nothing more than to clear the smell of vomit off my body. I was spent and knew the pod felt the same way. Mental and physical exhaustion, and this dismissal, this confinement, hurt more than anything.

We waited for two days, only leaving our berth to go to the galley for meals, trying to find the times when no one else was there. But that was impossible in a place as small as the Station. The space hounds just ignored us, the same reaction they'd had for the first three weeks we'd been on station. We saw none of Aldo or Flora. The one person who seemed oblivious to it all was McCorkle; sitting alone, he hailed us in the cafeteria once, but after a quick greeting, we slipped away.

He's as much of an outcast as we, Moira sent.

Why? I asked, but no one had an answer.

In our quarters, as our anxiety grew, we studied and sent e-mails to classmates. We used the station near-object telescope to watch the *Consensus*. Scaffolding and cranes surrounded it, and its sleek shape was almost impossible to make out. Five years until it was ready to travel to the Rift. Then two years of travel to Neptune. Then how many years to explore what was on the far side. All our lives were preparation and waiting.

Finally, the summons came from the station commander, and we pulled up to Hilton's office.

The commander's assistant nodded us into the commander's office, a room no bigger than a sleeping quarters, smelling of thoughts, hard thoughts, and long hours of work.

Hilton arrived ten minutes later, all three of her pushing through us, invading our thought space, and taking a place at her desk. She was a trio of identical, dark-haired women: small, wiry, with a sharp face and dark eyes. She didn't smile or greet us. One of her logged on to the computer and started working. Another hooked her legs through a strap on the wall and began reading reports. The third picked up a file and opened it.

"Six months of station-keeping reaction mass expended. Two sleds in need of overhaul. Six weeks of work to realign the counterbalance cable. Failure to maintain comm. One trio in the hospital. Twenty klicks of cable that'll have to be refurbished. Twenty-six sprains and breaks during the jerk. Three hundred hours of experimental work lost. Fifty samples broken. Days and days of lost time doing structural checks."

Meda opened her mouth.

"Do not interrupt me. Your 'rescue attempt' has jeopardized my schedule. You have lost me weeks of effort that I am never going to get back. Weeks. You are unauthorized for space rescue. You are a student. You are on work-study here. I don't care who your builder is. I don't care what strings your mentors pulled to put you here. You fucked my station up. Do you hear me? I do not like it one bit."

Frustration coursed among us. Incoherent, angry thoughts jounced about, but Meda said nothing. Hilton's eyes fixed on me, and I felt a jolt. It wasn't polite: looking at another person's members when speaking to the interface.

"This is my fault," Hilton said, still looking at me. "I should have determined what sort of pod you are, what your *parts* were."

What is she saying? Manuel asked.

She's talking about me, I sent.

"I don't think—" Meda began.

"That's apparent and clear," Hilton interrupted. "You don't have four good brains among the five of you." Again, a look at me, and I felt a hot tear streaking down my face.

How does she know? Strom asked.

Isn't it obvious? I sent, angry.

No, Moira sent.

No, Manuel and Meda and Strom added.

Consensus quick and total. I blinked my tears away.

Hilton stared at us for a moment longer, then said, "Speak, if you have something to say for yourself."

"No one could get to Flora in time," Meda said. "We had to save her."

"Aldo was right there. Aldo is certified in sled rescue. You are not."

"Aldo was on the end of the tether. And he wasn't moving. And he was five kilometers farther away than we were."

"And Klada was five klicks closer."

"He was caught in the falling tether!"

"I can afford to lose a tether. I can't afford to lose two sleds and two crew members. You made a rash decision and the whole station suffered for it."

"We saved her."

Hilton slammed the report down. "L4 has a rescue shuttle that could have reached her in eighteen hours. That would have been eighteen hours of discomfort for Flora. But it also would have meant no impact on my schedules!"

"But—"

She doesn't know about Flora's not loading enough air!

Don't tell her, I sent. She was so mad, no mitigating factor would slow her down.

"But what?"

Meda glanced at me, then said, "But we didn't know about the L4 rescue shuttle."

"No, you didn't! If you'd taken a minute to think and consult, we wouldn't have this mess. If you had maintained comm, we could have told you about the rescue shuttle."

"I'm sorry."

"There's only one reason you're not on the shuttle to Sabah Station, and that's because of Aldo's and Flora's request. You are one step away from flunking this practical. One step away from me sending you back to Earth with your asses in your luggage. As it is you're off outside duty. You're assigned to Dr. Buchanan in the biology lab. Dismissed."

We fumbled out of the office, stunned and silent. I could think of nothing but the fact that we would fly no more. Grounded, useless. Strom guided me gently to our quarters.

A week ground by, full of arachnoid DNA and splices and esoteric designs for better, faster, cheaper cable spiders. We were not even allowed to do genetic manipulation, but rather were put to work testing the tensile strength of the sample cables Dr. Buchanan would milk from each of his subspecies of spider.

We were surprised by a knock on our door.

Meda opened it to Aldo's somber face.

"Care to join us for dinner?"

No! I sent. I didn't want to be around anyone.

Meda glanced at me, then said, "We're going to eat later, thanks."

"You've been avoiding the busy times in the cafeteria," Aldo said. "You shouldn't. But that doesn't matter since I reserved the private dining room for us."

"I didn't know there was a private dining room on the station."

"There wasn't until last week. Just got flown in pre-fabricated. So?"

"Really. We're okay."

"I think you should. It's not just me."

Meda drew back and the pod touched.

He's making a gesture.

We should go.

I don't want to be reminded—They looked at me; they wanted to go. I finally dropped my reluctance.

"Okay."

The private dining room was indeed new. A door had been placed in the station wall across from the cafeteria, and it opened onto a beautiful wood-paneled room that could seat eight trios easily, and with a wonderful view of Earth out the window.

To my surprise, a half-dozen space hounds were there, including Flora and Klada, and a few other station workers we knew by sight: all outside-working trios.

"What's all this?" Meda ask, while we tried to hide the embarrassment pheromones.

"We know what Hilton said," said Aldo. "And we know what you did."

"But—"

"There was no way," Flora said, "a ship from L4 would have reached me in time with my air supply."

"You did the right thing," Aldo said. "And you did it better than I could have done it." He took a small box from his pocket and opened it. "You may not be on outside duty anymore, but you're still a space hound."

He leaned forward and clipped a small pin on Meda's

jumpsuit. His two other podmates attached one on Strom and Moira. Then they did the same to Manuel and me.

I twisted the pin in my hand; it was the head of spider, running down a cable.

"You latched onto that cable like a real spider," Aldo explained. I looked at Aldo's jumpsuits. He had a similar pin, with a sled on it. Flora had a pin with a flower. All the space hounds had pins.

"This is our way of saying thanks," Flora said.

I felt Strom welling up and knew if the big lug started blubbering there was no hope for the rest of us. I nudged him in the side.

"Enough of that!" Aldo said. "Let's have some food!"

The space hounds had made a potluck of zero-gee dishes that we passed around, and the pods mingled and chatted, and for the first time since we'd gotten there, we were a part of the station. I couldn't remember why I'd not wanted to come in the first place.

During the meal, Flora leaned close and said, "Thanks for not ratting me out to Hilton. I know that would have gotten you off the hook."

"I doubt it," Meda said. "She'd still have argued we had no idea you would have run out of air."

Flora laughed. "She would have. Thank you."

Her bruises were faded and the broken bones were all knitted; she showed us the castcrete wrapping around her chest and abdomen. "Really gets in the way when I . . . you know." She nodded at Aldo, and Meda blushed. Then we all did.

"You and Aldo?"

"Yes! Did I shock you?"

"No."

Flora gave us a smile. "Yes I did."

Before long the other space hounds drifted back to work or to their quarters, leaving just Flora, Aldo, and us.

They questioned us about our training, and I felt that they truly envied us our chance to explore beyond the solar system.

"Bears?" Flora asked. "Pod-bears?"

"Yes."

"Where did they come from?" Aldo asked. "Someone surely made them and would take responsibility for that."

"We searched for a week," Meda explained. "They flew in teams of military duos to search the river, but they found nothing."

"How can you miss three large bears?" Aldo asked.

"And the scientific facilities to build and grow them?" Flora added.

I remembered the map of their territory the bears had shared with Strom, how the river was at the far eastern edge of where they roamed.

"We tried to tell them that the bears probably were heading west, but the military duo who was in charge kept us looking near the river."

"Military duos," Flora said with scorn. "The military should use trios instead."

"We don't think he even believed the bears had been there."

Good thing we never told him Strom could communicate with them, Manuel added.

In fact we had told no one. That the bears existed at all was incredible enough. That we could share chemical memories with them was beyond fathoming. The one person we might have consulted with—Mother Redd—never came to the camp, and after the incident with Malcolm Leto, we never got the chance to ask her.

"That McCorkle should have gone into the military instead of space work," Flora said.

"Why's that?" Meda asked.

"He came up with you, and while you've managed to

save my life, he's still doing scut work that's one step up from automation."

"You'd think he would catch on with all the questions he asks," Aldo said.

"He's a busybody groundhog," Flora said. "Perfect for the military."

"We're going to lobby Hilton to let you back on outside duty," Aldo said. "It doesn't make any sense until the sleds are overhauled. But in a week or two . . . We're still shorthanded."

"Thanks. Though the spiders are really interesting," Meda said.

Aldo raised an eyebrow, but my and Manuel's grins made him realize the joke.

"That on your neck?" Flora asked. "It doesn't look like a scar. It's metal."

Meda's hand jumped to the back of her neck, touching the metal interface jack, and involuntarily we slipped closer together.

"I'm sorry," Flora said quickly. "I didn't . . . I should have taken your hint."

"It's okay," Meda said. "Malcolm Leto gave it to me," Meda added.

"Malcolm Leto, the last-of-the-Community Malcolm Leto?" Aldo asked.

"Yeah. That's him. He tried to . . . kidnap me. Part of me."

"Does the interface work?"

"Yes."

"You could access the Ring," Flora said.

"We never thought—I guess so."

Change the subject, I sent. It was Meda who had been violated, but all of us had lived it in her memories and dreams.

"Can't they get rid of it?"

"No, they tried, but they can't."

Change the subject!

"Can't—"

"Listen, can we talk about something else?"

"Sorry."

"Sorry," said Aldo, but his eyes were on Meda, on her neck.

Silence among us for a long moment.

"Thanks for the pins," Meda said, finally. "We'd better get back to studying."

"Sure."

Three days later, we were called away from the lab for a call on our desktop from Earth, from Mother Redd.

"Dears, I hope all is well with you," she said, from the family room of the farm.

"Yes. We've had some incidents," Meda said. "We're working in the biology lab here, on cable spiders."

"Good," Mother Redd said, then frowned. "I've news for you. They've picked the captain of the *Consensus*." My stomach dropped.

If she's calling us, it's not us, I said. *It would have been an OG official if it was us. It would have been Colonel Krypicz.*

"It's not us," Meda said dully.

"No, I'm sorry. It was—"

"Elliott O'Toole." My eyes were burning, and the first wave of vertigo I'd ever felt spun the room around me. Strom took my hands steadying me.

We've lost the ship.

"Yes. Please don't take it hard. There are many things you can do. Many things that you are good at."

Shut up! I cried silently.

"Don't," Meda said. "We don't want to hear that speech."

My head ached. No starship. No voyage to the String beyond Neptune's orbit. No chance to be what we had been built to be.

"Why not us?" Meda said.

Hilton's poor recommendation.

We're better than Elliott O'Toole.

We've always been better than Elliott.

Why Elliott?

The interface.

The rape.

It made horrid sense.

This is your fault, Meda! I sent. She turned to me, and I saw the tears in her eyes, the horrified look, and my anger fell away. I was the pilot, but we had all lost the ship.

Sorry.

"It's because of what Malcolm Leto did to us, isn't it?" Meda whispered.

"No, no," said Mother Redd, but the lie was apparent. "It's not that . . ."

"They can't trust that we've not been compromised. They're afraid the interface can control us, wreck the pod."

Mother Redd didn't answer.

"It's not true," Meda said. "It won't happen again. Leto did that only because we couldn't control the interface when it was new. I was alone then. Vulnerable."

"There are people in the Overgovernment who don't trust any Ring technology," Mother Redd said. "They wanted to cut you from the project immediately."

It would have been better if they had.

The starship is Ring tech.

Useless. We're useless.

"The *Consensus* is Ring technology. The Rift is Ring technology!" Meda said.

"I don't disagree," Mother Redd said sharply. "I know

this is a shock. But you have to work yourself through it. Please understand that we fought for you as long as we could."

Meda nodded.

"Thanks for telling me," Meda said, turning the desktop off.

She turned then, and I pulled her into my arms. We all fell together, crying.

I'm sorry.

The morning found us hollow, spent. Strom goaded us to rise, to shower and dress.

We still have weeks of duty left, he sent. *We will do what is asked of us here.*

I could not reply, and even Manuel's grunt was too much effort for me. I lay suspended in my netting, watching the terminus slide across the Earth.

"Come on, Quant," Meda said. "We have to go to the lab."

She's in a stupor.

Again.

With us around?

Snap her out of it.

Anger turned me to face my pod. "Don't treat me like that!" I shouted. "I've lost everything that makes me worthwhile, don't you see?"

No! Strom sent. *That's not true.*

I'm not like the rest of you. I was built, designed, created to be a mathematical savant, to understand intuitively physics. To pilot the Consensus. *That's what I do. Down there, I'm nothing. My job doesn't exist. Without you, I'm not even human.*

Oh, Quant, no, Moira sent. *You're wrong. We are none of us human without the rest of us.*

I blinked back tears. *Is that true?*

Forever, Meda said.

Moira and Meda pampered me in the shower, dressed me, and wouldn't even let me brush my own hair. The hollowness was still there, but it was partially filled with my pod.

A message found us in the bio lab: Hilton wanted to see us right away. I blinked, lost in the numbers and charts of tensile strength and web lattices.

That can't be good, Manuel sent.

We stowed the equipment and logged out of the lab. Our path through the station took us by the traffic control center. A trio sat before screens marking the pageant of craft through local space. The plot of Newtonian bodies pulled me in, and I was a part of the wheeling lines, the panorama of forces.

Quant!

Moira had doubled back for me.

Coming, just lost in the . . .

I know. Come on.

There's a barge coming in tomorrow.

The commander's assistant halted us in the outer office, and we clung to the far wall outside Hilton's office for fifteen minutes, waiting. Then the duo, Anderson McCorkle, appeared.

What's he doing here? Strom asked.

Always asking questions about us. Always looking, I sent. I balled up memories of his comments in the hydroponics bay.

One of him, face expressionless, watched us as he entered Hilton's office without stopping.

He seems to have finally gotten his space legs, Manuel sent.

My mind thrust facts and conjecture together. The intuitive leap formed into hypothesis, then coalesced into theory.

He's against us, I sent. *We're in danger.*

No . . . , Meda started, then she shared my thoughts, and we fell silent, reaching consensus.

Did he sabotage Flora's sled?

Perhaps.

Why?

To force our hand.

Because he couldn't get to ours.

He didn't know which sled was ours, I sent. I had told him our sled was in the bay, but the techs had pushed it out that same day, leaving the second sled there.

Flora's sled, Strom sent. The same flower pattern that she wore on her collar had been stenciled on the second sled.

He's a military duo.

We're in danger.

"You may go in," the commander's assistant said.

This time, all three of the commander was looking at us. McCorkle hung behind her, a faint smile on his faces.

"If I had known how compromised you were, I would never have let you on this station," she said flatly. "Major McCorkle has explained everything to me."

Major.

She pointed at Meda. "You have an interface jack." She pointed at me. "You are autistic. No wonder you managed to wreck this station."

Meda was about to protest, not about the interface jack, but about her accusation about me.

Don't, I sent. Like black holes, the forces in this room were aligned against us. We could not play from the defensive. *Wait.*

Meda remained silent. I looked directly at Major McCorkle, matching his slight smile.

"You would have been reassigned at the end of your term anyway. I'm accelerating that, placing you in Major McCorkle's custody, and putting you on tomorrow's barge."

"We are under arrest?" Meda asked.

The commander frowned. "Major McCorkle is responsible for you from now on. He'll do whatever he has to to keep the station safe."

"I repeat, are we under arrest?"

McCorkle spoke. "As if you could go anywhere."

Ask the other question, I sent.

"Thank you, Commander Hilton, for the opportunity to work on Columbus Station. Have you found who sabotaged Flora's sled yet?"

"Sabotage?" she said, the word erupting from her.

"Something a military duo might do, perhaps," Meda added.

I watched McCorkle's face contort, a rictus followed by forced relaxation. The forces in the room shifted.

Bingo.

"It should be easy to find him," Meda added. "He's not an adept saboteur, since he sabotaged the wrong sled and didn't even do it well enough to finish the job."

"It was mechanical failure," McCorkle said.

Hilton glared at his interruption.

"How do you know, Major?" Meda asked. "We'll be in our cabin."

We filed out, the eyes of both of them drilling into us. That was not how McCorkle had wanted it go, but we were certain now that McCorkle had sabotaged Flora's sled by mistake. And now Hilton had suspicions.

In our cabin we tried Mother Redd, but the desktop flashed an access error repeatedly.

He's got us locked down.

When does the shuttle arrive?

I remembered the space traffic screen. *Six hours.*

No one will know we're leaving the station with McCorkle. We'd be entirely in his power.

He was willing to kill.

We can't afford to be in his power.

The door chimed.

Aldo, Manuel sent after peeking through the door peep.

"I heard what happened. It's not fair," he said. "I've asked for you as a permanent person on my team. A real space hound."

"We're scheduled for the next transport to Sabah Station," Meda said. "Hilton is shipping us out. We've supposedly been assigned to Singleton Relations in Idaho."

"Your practical isn't over yet," Aldo said. "What do you mean, 'supposedly'?"

"McCorkle is taking us back to Earth. We're in his custody."

"That puking groundhog? Why?"

"He's Major McCorkle."

"Military? A spy? All military personnel are supposed to go by their rank on station." Aldo's face was grim.

"Can you send a message to someone on Earth for us?"

"I can, but not for another six hours," Aldo said. "Comm is down for repairs."

He's locked down the whole station.

There's no way we can get word to Mother Redd until the barge is gone.

"What?" Aldo asked, noting the thoughts floating between us.

"McCorkle may have sabotaged Flora's sled. He may have been trying to kill us. If we get on that barge, he'll have us in his complete control."

"McCorkle," Aldo said darkly. "We can take care of him."

"No, Aldo. He's military."

"Well, we can't hide you on Columbus Station. And there's nowhere to run to. A sled won't make it to Sabah Station."

Nowhere to run, I thought, considering the map I had made for the pod a week ago, one that included not just the OG space facilities.

The Ring, I sent.

Meda looked at me, shocked. I felt her fear, and it mingled with my own apprehension and fascination. The chance to enter it, to study its physics, drew me toward it.

I don't want to go there, she sent.

It's our only chance, I said.

Malcolm Leto, she sent.

It's empty, Strom sent. *He's not there.*

What if he is?

He isn't, I sent.

She nodded, slowly. "Aldo, we'll need your help."

"Anything."

The Ring.

Near the end of third shift, still three hours before the barge was scheduled to arrive, we pulled up to the sled bay. As we passed the traffic control center, we saw Klada Ross inside, talking with the controller, one of him telling a story, the controller laughing, his back to the screen. One of Klada gave me a wink as we passed.

The bay was empty save for Flora and Aldo. Aldo waved us over while Flora watched from the other bay doors, ready to distract anyone coming into the bay. It wasn't expected; there was no third shift outside work scheduled.

"Ready?" Aldo asked. He was already suited up, and he helped us quickly get into our own suits.

"What the hell is going on?"

We turned. McCorkle was coming through the door into the bay. Flora pushed off to intercept him.

"McCorkle, you're due in hydroponics," she said.

"It's Major McCorkle, and I'm off station-duty," he shouted.

"Major? I don't think so. All military personnel have to wear their rank, and you're in standard-issue jumpsuits." Flora caught him easily in the middle of the room.

"Inside," Aldo said.

"But—"

"Go. Flora can handle herself. And besides she has some motive," Aldo added.

We entered our sled, Aldo behind us, but not before we heard the horrific sound of retching. One of McCorkle was spinning in the middle of the bay, unable to stop his rotation, surrounded by a nebula of puke. The other was latched onto the floor, heaving.

"Did I mention that Flora is station weightless jujitsu champion?" Aldo asked as the door to our sled shut.

The sun was hidden behind the Earth and peeking at its edges, as we nudged the sled away from the station. Aldo let me pilot, while he lounged in the crowded back. The space traffic controller didn't even notice us until we were a hundred kilometers away. Meda turned off the radio.

I flew the sled like it was a part of me, spinward toward the nearest Ring spine. I was alive for the first time in over a week. The shuttle from Sabah Station would have no passengers that morning, except McCorkle. We were finding our own way back.

Thirty minutes later we neared the spine. At GEO, it

seemed to have grown a large bulb, half the size of Columbus Station, smooth and alien. Twenty-eight thousand kilometers below, squeezing the Earth, was the Ring. Above were counterweights and the far end of the space elevator that could launch material into space.

I brought the sled to within ten meters of the spine's airlock. Slowly, methodically, we clamped our helmets on, one by one cutting ourselves off. Aldo checked the seal and gave each of us a thumbs-up.

"Good luck, Apollo," he said over the radio.

One by one, we entered the airlock and exited to hang on to the side of the sled. As I hung there, sharp space and brilliant stars whirled around me. I could have let go then, so that I would never come back to Earth. Helmeted, slipping away was simple.

But then the last of us—Strom—was through, and hand in hand we jumped over to the airlock.

"What if Leto is on the Ring?" Meda asked, her voice tense.

"He's not," Moira said. "And even if he were, the Ring is too big for him to be right here."

"He's not on the Ring," Strom said. "And if he is, we'll take care of him. He is just one, we are five."

The airlock was large enough for all of us. It opened as we approached and closed when we were all inside. Air hissed into the lock. The inner door did not open.

Meda popped her helmet off, touched the inner door with her gloved hand. Her cold breath hung in the air around us, frosting our faceplates.

"There," I said, and I tapped open a small recess in the wall. Inside was an interface jack, the male to the female connector in Meda's neck.

"Here goes," Meda said, and slid the jack in.

A voice, smooth and sexless, sounded in the lock, "Welcome to the Ring, Apollo Papadopulos. How may I serve you?" The inner door opened onto a white corridor, empty.

Together, we entered the desolate Ring, leaving behind us our dreams of two decades. They were someone else's now.

FOUR

Manuel

Once the five of us were inside, Meda pulled the inter-face jack from her neck and threw the wire back at the wall. It slithered into place. Silently, the inner airlock door closed. Quant glanced out a port next to the lock and shared with us a picture of Aldo thrusting the sled away.

The Ring is empty, Meda sent, though she hadn't needed to. We had felt the desolation through her link. The colossal space station was devoid of any human life.

We could just stay—Quant began, but Meda erupted in veto pheromone.

No, not here. She shuddered.

Down, I sent. *To the Earth.*

The consensus was unanimous.

I pulled myself down the corridor ahead of my pod using my hands and modified feet. The air smelled . . . like nothing. After a month of filtered space station air on Columbus Station, of recycled air still stinking of pheromones, rubber, and sweat, the lack of any other odor was striking. My nose twitched.

The corridor opened into a cylindrical room lashed with ropes in all directions. At the center of the cylinder was another cylinder, an elevator that would take us from GEO to the main Ring torus.

Elevator, I sent back up the corridor, then pulled myself across the space to the door. As the pod followed, I felt Meda's fear of jacking in again to work the elevator. I sent her the image of the manual elevator controls. She'd have no need to use the interface.

The elevator car was six meters tall, with molded chairs attached to both ceiling and floor. We took seats and Moira found the button labeled "Ring—Torus—Central."

She shrugged. It would be down, and that's all we needed now.

The elevator smoothly accelerated toward the Earth, until we had enough gravity to lay out the lunch we had taken from the station.

After a time, the rest of the pod slept, though I remained awake, climbing along the webbed walls in the weak gravity, watching the Earth slowly grow.

The elevator slowed hours later and glided into the central curve of the Ring. We gasped as Quant saw the interior; a vast cylinder at least two kilometers wide, set with terraces and bridges on its walls. Thin wispy clouds formed at the ceiling. A blue lake dominated the floor, surrounded by trees and grasslands. Roads wound around the floor, climbing into the walls.

All of it was empty.

Birds, Strom sent. A flock took flight from the lake.

At fifteen percent normal gravity, the birds jumped aloft with their legs more than their wings, a single flap enough to drive them into the sky.

Eight thousand cubic meters per person, Quant inserted into my thoughts. Clearly the Community had built the Ring with room to grow.

We could hide here forever, Strom sent.

Until he comes back, Moira added.

That way, Meda sent. A second bank of elevators stood below us. These elevators descended the last ten thousand kilometers to an Earth-based anchor station and were larger—twice the size of the spine elevator.

I took one last look at the valley: a desolate tribute to a dead species of humanity. I couldn't picture it as anything but an empty habitat, a place we once lived, but no longer.

Meter by meter, second by second, the gravity grew as the Earth loomed nearer, pulling limbs down to our sides. Meda's, Moira's, and Quant's hair, so poofy at geosynch, seemed slick and oily, pressed against their skulls. After just a few weeks in zero-gee, the pull of gravity was oppressive. My feet hurt.

Below us, the delta of the Amazon River reached with brown fingers into the Atlantic, coloring it with sediments. We were about two hundred kilometers up, at the edge of the atmosphere. The elevator was beginning to break, electromagnetic squeezes on the cable. Soon we would be buffeted by winds during our last segment of this ride to Earth. It had taken nearly two days to get from geosynchronous orbit.

Gravity is point nine four gees, Quant counted off. She had been doing that every ten minutes for an eon. I checked my anger; it was my feet. Instead, I gingerly walked away from the window of the elevator and found a seat. I could see the view through Strom's eyes just the same.

The Ring elevator was three stories tall, a cylinder wrapped around the elevator cable, with a diameter of sixty meters.

I rubbed my feet, massaging the phalanges and metatarsals. On Earth I had thought that my modified feet were for climbing trees. It wasn't until we had spent a month on Columbus Station that I realized that I had been made to move in zero-gee. I had spent hours stretching tendons and muscles in my feet, allowing them to grip and manipulate like never before. But now, the gravity was crushing them. My entire body was rude and tired.

With Strom's eyes, I could still make out the curve of the Earth slowly flattening to a horizon and the weather patterns over South America and the Amazon. A tropical depression swirled in the middle of the Atlantic, it too lethargic and slow. Weather, gravity, pain: it was as if we were entering a new world.

If we buy transport, if we use our credit chit at all, they'll know where we are. This was Meda's thought, which I would have known by smell alone. Her thoughts are nuanced with memories from deep storage: the look on McCorkle's face from Hilton's office, our credit chits, an image of a Scryfejet that drove Quant into a subtext stream of consciousness on various performance numbers for that line of aircars. Meda had taken her auburn hair from her ponytail, the first time since we'd left Columbus Station. There was no need now to keep it tame and out of her eyes.

Until we understand the forces in the OG that are after us, we must travel with care, incognito. Moira's thoughts were precise. Where her sister Meda layered her thoughts with connotation and subtlety, Moira was exact. On the surface, twins, but beneath, their thoughts were thunder and lightning.

It was not rare for biological siblings to form into larger pods. In fact, their physician had published several papers on the additional bonding force identical twins added to a pod. For a moment, I considered my own sister Corrine, and then I shut that out. Any jealousy I felt for Moira and Meda's relationship I crushed, thinking instead about my pain-filled feet.

Quant looked at me, smiled softly, and sent, *Strom can carry you. Then you can use all four thumbs.*

It wasn't about using my thumbs, I almost replied, but nodded.

I will, Strom sent. Strom was our strength, our power, and our innocence. I knew he would carry us all if need be, and fall trying.

What would I do with four thumbs?

It's as useful as I am in a gravity well, Quant sent.

We're all useless, Meda said. It was the same consensus we had stuck on since the call from Mother Redd. Purposelessness, futility, depression.

They know where we are right now. Overgovernment prefects will be waiting at the anchor, Moira sent. Moira's hair, unlike her twin Meda's, was always short.

We should have traveled the Ring to the Galapagos line, Quant sent. High-speed trains ran the circumference of the Ring. We could have descended any of the dozen elevators to the equator. We had chosen the closest for our descent.

No! Meda sent. *Not a second longer in the Ring.* We all felt Meda's revulsion. Even though the Ring was empty.

The Macapa anchor is in the middle of a singleton enclave. They can't get to it easily, Quant sent.

The anchor itself is Overgovernment property.

Robotically manned.

We'll know soon enough, I sent. I stood on sore feet.

The others joined me at the window. The Earth below us was so close we could no longer see the extent of it in one glance. It stretched around us, the horizon pushing in all directions. The altimeter showed a red digital readout of one hundred and fifty kilometers.

The upper edges of the atmosphere tickled the elevator, shivered the cable.

"If the prefects are there, we will discuss things with them. If they are not, we are free," Strom said. He flexed his hands, making fists.

Free.

Useless.

At first the elevator seemed to be descending directly into the green canopy of the rain forest at the edge of the muddy Amazon. Then what I thought was morning fog formed the shape of a finger: the anchor.

Middle finger, Quant sent.

The anchor was curved and white, unlike current pod architecture, which used the prior century as a model. The jungle surrounded it, but did not encroach on the sealed-off pavilion, perhaps scared of the huge, white monstrosity, thinking it some whale that had crawled up the Amazon on its belly and beached itself on the shore during the rainy season.

Deceleration added weight beyond one gee to my feet. I reached up and hung from a bar, stretching the muscles in my arms.

Monkey, Strom sent. *We will find your cousins down there.*

Bears and monkeys are our cousins, self, I replied.

True. I caught some of Strom's wistfulness. The bears were still a mystery to us, and Strom's personal totem. He—and so we all did—dreamed of them at least one night in ten.

The elevator had slowed to a few meters per second. To the south was the Amazon, and along its banks was a village. Nearly all of the Amazon was a singleton enclave, a semiautonomous zone under the Overgovernment rule.

When was the last time they saw an elevator coming down? I sent.

Thirty years ago.

Blackness, as the elevator entered the top of the anchor building. Then a flash of lights and a heavy deceleration as the elevator came to a stop. With a whoosh, the door opened, and my ears popped. The elevator landing opened onto a sloping path, spiraling down into the anchor.

No one was there to meet us.

Of course not, Moira scoffed.

I know, I replied, sharply.

Strom stepped out of the elevator onto the ramp. The walls curved up and around. At a meter, spaced evenly along the wall, were rows of interface jacks, each one a direct connection to the Community. Meda shuddered.

The ramp descended, through three floors. At the ground floor it opened into a glassed atrium. Statuary, chairs, and tables formed a static plaza. A red sunrise seeped through the room. It had seen thirty years of sunrises, and we were the first to set foot here in all that time.

Strom urged us on. I felt his anxiety tingling through us, triggering adrenaline in me, shuttling through us: pod feedback. Glass doors off the atrium slid open as we approached. Beyond was a courtyard. The heat pushed us back. The smells were foreign: pollen and sweetness swirling in humidity.

The courtyard was twenty meters in diameter, overrun with small shrubs and plants. A flock of parrots looked at us from a small tree.

"Come on."

Across the courtyard was a gate. The inner door opened for us, then shut as we passed through.

Be ready, Strom sent.

The outer gate opened.

No prefects. Let's go. Strom relaxed, now that no threat was apparent.

A syncrete apron surrounded the anchor, but beyond it was green jungle, a wall of brush and trees, climbing into the sky. Quant looked at the forest, her mind testing, searching, and we all felt it when she found the path. It was a deviation that stood out to her like red on white.

The river is that way. So is the village, she sent.

So, I sent. *What does that gain us?* I released veto scent and sat down. My feet hurt too much to wander a jungle. My shoes were too tight.

Give up? Moira asked. *We could have stayed on Columbus Station.*

Of course not! But where are we going?

The farm, Strom sent. *Mother Redd.*

Won't they look there? Meda asked.

Who will look there? I shot back. *What if this is paranoia induced by pod instability?*

Remember Anderson McCorkle? Quant asked. *He wanted to kill us.*

We've been a target for someone since the interface jack, since Leto, Moira replied. *Politically and physically.*

Strom's memories boiled for a moment, and we recalled the avalanche that nearly destroyed us. If Strom had not left the tent to help Hagar Julian, he would not have been able to tie off the spider silk line that kept us from plunging into the abyss. But that second avalanche, the one that had taken our tent, had been preceded by a flash on the mountainside. Strom had assumed, and we had always agreed, it had been the rescue aircar. But what if it was actually an attempt on our lives, explosives to start the second avalanche.

Before the interface jack, Quant sent.

Paranoia, I sent. *False consensus.* I didn't really mean it. I was angry, tired, and, looking at the jungle, scared.

It is not! Meda sent.

We can't just run as if the world is against us, I replied. *We're not!*

Stop, Moira sent. *Manuel has a point. What are we doing?*

Running.

To Mother Redd's.

She won't want us. We failed.

Not the starship, Quant sent wistfully.

The bears, Strom sent.

As Strom thought it, there was a hum of consensus. The bears had helped us. The bears were part of no conspiracy against us, yet they were a puzzle. Who had built them, and why?

A scientific mystery, Meda sent, her thoughts bubbling with excitement.

Strom's thoughts turned darker. *The explosion on the mountain,* he sent. *Evidence for this conspiracy.*

There are two reasons now to travel to the Rockies, Quant sent.

Wrong continent, I pointed out.

It's a goal, a task, something still ours, Moira sent.

Consensus rippled through the group. Valid consensus, and I couldn't fight that. I nodded and stood. Already Quant was calculating paths and transit times. Numbers leaked from her head.

Can we steal a suborbital? she asked.

Unlikely.

Let's move, Strom sent impatiently, urgently, now that we had a goal.

The path led into the jungle, and as soon as we stepped out off the apron, we were engulfed in emerald green. The cacophony of bird and insect sounds cluttered our ears.

The smell!

The air was fetid and thick, a soup of alien smells.

This place is alive.

They had taught us that the Earth was a devastated world, that its ecology was bankrupt and in need of constant tending. Yet it was clear that the Amazon was alive and vibrant.

And it stinks, I added.

We passed a squat tree, marked with crisscross lines in its trunk. A white sap oozed from the bark.

Rubber tree, Quant said.

Isn't it just easier to build a rubber plant? Why rely on this old method of harvesting?

The path opened onto a riverbank without seeming to drop any lower. The Amazon was muddy brown, slow and turgid. Silt slid across the surface. Fog hung in the middle of the river and we could not judge its width. Islands or peninsulae jutted abruptly from the fog.

At least it isn't the rainy season, Strom sent.

Boats.

Up the river, following the bank, was a small village with a dock. An old boat was moored to the dock.

"This is all natural rain forest," Quant said. She knelt and peered closely at a small flower growing from the mud. "None of this is modded. These people are poor."

The path to the village wound along the river's edge. Once we passed a nearly stagnant tributary about two meters across. Strom, placing one boot in the muck, helped each of us across, half-tossing us to the far side. Then he jumped across himself, clearing the stream by half a meter.

The elevator blocked the morning sun for a moment, and then we came into the village, a conglomerate of ramshackle huts. No one was in sight until we reached a hut built on stilts. A man sat on the raised porch drinking from a rounded cup. He was old, with wispy white hair on a brown head. His belly sat on his thighs, which were covered in crimson shorts.

He looked at us with brown eyes as we approached, his face blank. When we reached his hut, he stared down at us from on high.

"Og flunks, huh? Og don't need to come round here."

Og?

O-G.

Overgovernment.

"We're not from the Overgovernment, sir," Meda said.

Not any more, I added.

"Yeah? Still Og flunks, eh?"

"We're not OG flunkies. We want transport to Belem."

"What ya want to go there for? Smells."

Tell him.

"We're trying to get to North America. We hope to find a ship to get us there."

The old man laughed. "Ain't no freighters in Belem. Why freighters stop at the Amazon? Gonna ship our water to North America? Ha!"

"There's no ocean-going vessels to and from South America?" Meda asked.

I need a downlink, Quant sent. *I need data!*

The downlink would have given her better options for our trip to the Rockies. I began to realize how naïve we were.

"Maybe Rio. Yeah, probably Rio. Everyone live in Rio."

"Except for you."

He laughed again. "'Cept me and the rest of me brothers and sisters."

"How can we get to North America?"

"By river. What else you think?"

But there's no ships at Belem. The river won't take us anywhere!

I guess we can go back up the elevator, Quant sent.

No! Meda sent quickly.

I glanced upriver. The fog was lifting, and the day was even more muggy than before. Upriver was more rain forest, thousands of kilometers of rain forest, until it reached the Andes.

The North-South Highway, I sent.

Of course! The highway went from old Calgary to Buenos Aires, ten thousand kilometers of multilane road for robotrucks. We could hitch a ride there.

"Can you take us to the Highway?"

"Highway, sure. We leave tomorrow!"

"Great."

"As soon as you pay me."

Great.

By noon, the village was awake. Fishing boats that had pushed off into the river before we'd come down the elevator returned laden with fish and sometimes caimans. The fishermen eyed us, but kept their distance. The women of the village went about their chores. The children, gaptoothed, skinny things, watched our every move, until Meda got annoyed and led us back to the elevator.

"What are we going to pay him with?" Meda asked. Our pod was too spread out for chemical thoughts, the air too thick with pollen and jungle odors.

Faintly from Quant, *We can give him Strom.*

"Sure," chuckled Strom.

The little brown man had climbed down from the hut and disappeared into the jungle. "For supplies," he said, leaving us standing in the middle of the village.

"How much do we pay him?"

"What sort of money do singletons use?"

We stopped at the base of the elevator, on the far side from the door.

They're hunter-gatherers, a rain-forest tribe.

I doubt our credit chit means anything to him. Nor do we want to use it.

The air was still muggy in the shadow of the elevator.

Food, Strom sent.

If we give Strom to the old man, it would cut our food intake by half, Quant sent.

Fish, I think.

Strom cut a small sapling with his utility knife, passing it to me. I started sharpening the end. Strom cut another and passed it to Meda.

We walked down to the river and continued downstream until we reached a spot where the brown silt was sucked away as the water washed across a tree trunk. Meda climbed out across the tree and stood there, watching the river.

An image of the river as a wall of momentum flitted among us.

Quant took a point at the other end of the log, Moira upriver. Together, the three of them built a map of the river, triangulating ripples, bubbles, and flashes of silver scale. The river teamed with fish.

Strom and I stood with eyes closed, using the map built by the other three.

Strom threw first and speared a black catfishlike fish that he tossed onto the bank. It was thirty centimeters long, from tail to whiskers.

That's Strom's appetizer.

I cast my spear, and before long we had a dozen fish flopping on the bank.

It was a struggle to find dry wood for a fire; the rain forest and river soaked everything. We found a kind of reed near the river that burned easily and began cooking the fish on stones massed around the fast-burning fire.

"Maybe we can pay the old man in fish," Meda said.

What's that?

Quant had heard it first, and, when Meda pointed it out, identified it as an aircar.

Here, Strom sent. We huddled under a tree.

They'll see the smoke.

They'll think it's a singleton fire.

The aircar moved across the sky at a moderate speed, from the south and the far side of the river, banking around the elevator once, and then north above the rain forest.

"Are they looking for us?"

They know where we've gone.

Food. Danger could not keep Strom's stomach from growling.

The fish was flaky and pungent, the flesh marbled with grey splotches. It had an odd taste, but it filled our bellies. We threw the carcasses into the river.

What was that?

The water seethed, then settled.

Caiman. Alligator. Piranha.

Meda shuddered. *I'm glad I didn't know that before I climbed out on that tree.*

"What ya cooking?"

The old man peered at us from the bank.

"Catfish," Meda said, holding up a half-eaten fillet.

"Shitfish," the old man replied. "You got toilet paper?"

"Um."

"Don't use the lipo leaves. Worse than the shitfish."

"What do you want to take us to the highway?"

"What you got?"

Strom held out his utility knife.

"Got one of those."

Quant reluctantly unpinned her spider-head pin from her shirt and held it out to the man.

"Nah."

"We don't have anything."

"Huh. Then I guess we don't go. Besides, your friends

in the aircar be here in the morning. They take care of you."

"Aircar?"

"Yeah, they land at the field up there where it don't flood. Then walk down."

"We'd like to leave before they get here."

"Nobody leaving if you don't got nothing for me."

The man giggled then sauntered away.

Let's just take his boat, Quant sent.

No! Moira replied.

Just kidding.

Strom groaned. "I need a bathroom."

"There's one in the anchor building."

I was closest to Meda and felt her reluctance to go back to the elevator, anything that had to do with the Ring. She clamped down on it fast. I placed a hand on her shoulder anyway.

Quant and I helped guide Strom, who was doubled over with stomach pain. We all felt a touch of it, a lingering of the intensity of his pain if not the pain itself. But Strom had eaten more of the fish than the rest of us; luckily none of us but he were sick.

The gate to the elevator garden opened to Meda's interface, and we raced into the building, guiding Strom to a stall in the huge unisex bathroom, where he expelled his three-catfish lunch.

"Ugh," he moaned.

He'll need paper.

I checked the other stalls and each was empty of paper or anything to hold the paper. In fact the toilets looked nothing like the rounded bowls we were used to. They were sleek and flat, and seemingly too high. Interface jacks, one per stall, dangled behind each seat. Why not jack in when you're taking a crap?

Nothing here. I'll check the rest of the anchor.

The ramp sloped back up to the elevator itself, but there was nothing there either. The room below, off of which was the bathroom, was a large glass gallery. A dragonfly, forged of crystal, spread its wings some three meters across, and seemed to hover in the sunlight. I realized how chilly it was, even with the sun beating in through the glass. The air-conditioning still worked, but there was no toilet paper.

I walked behind the ramp and found an alcove of tables and chairs, centered around another glass sculpture. Beyond the alcove was a cabinet filled with glasses and plates. It seemed as if everyone had just left and would be returning for brunch. There was no dust, no cobwebs. The place had been robotically cleaned not long before. Waiting for the Community to come back.

I took a stack of towels for Strom and returned to the bathroom. Strom groaned his thanks.

I think I know what we can give the old man. I painted a picture of the glass sculptures.

Quant went outside and peered up at the crystal dragonfly. *It weighs a few hundred kilos. We'll never get it down.*

How about the smaller one?

It's theft! Moira sent.

From who? Meda replied.

Doesn't matter. It's not ours to give.

Meda tapped the base of her skull. *I'm part of the Community.*

You are not. You're part of Apollo Papadopulos.

Stop it, I sent. *If from anyone, we're stealing from Malcolm Leto and I really don't feel bad about that.*

Moira sighed. *Then we might as well steal something practical.*

"We'd like to go as soon as possible," Meda said. "Now."

"You in a hurry, I know." The brown man was cooking a fish over a fire, not one of the catfish, with its marbled fillets, but something white and flaky. He ripped chunks off the stick and spat out little bones. Strom eyed the fish and suppressed a spasm.

"We'll give you this furniture."

"Hm. Matching set. Late Community. No, thanks. Gotta rock in my hut."

The sun was three quarters of the way down the sky; if we left now, we'd not have to face whoever was in the aircar we'd seen fly overhead.

Show him the sculpture.

"But do you have this?" Meda asked, holding the crystal sculpture so it caught the sun.

One of the other villagers said, "I'll take you in my canoe!"

The old man spat at him, then turned back to Meda. "Nice, but—"

"You willing to take us right now?" Meda asked the other villager.

"You bet!"

"He doesn't have an outboard motor!"

"But he'll get us out right now."

The old man glared at his rival, then nodded. "Fine. I want it all, though. And you have to carry it to the hut. I'm an old man, ya know."

"Fine. But we go right now."

"Okay. Deal."

"**Apollo** Papadopulos!"

In an instant Strom took control. The rest of us shifted our stance, feeling Strom's direction, to cover angles, to grip weapons, to search for escape and attack routes.

We spun on the voice, coming from the jungle toward the river. Quant was in the boat, Strom, Meda, Moira, and I on the dock. Strom stepped forward. At his direction, I searched the jungle for signs of another pod, but I saw nothing.

Trio. Armed. In OG uniform.

The villagers who had been helping load the boat stepped back as the trio approached.

"Stop!"

"We are stopped," Meda said. She stood just behind Strom on the dock. "What do you want?"

The trio paused three meters from us, still on the river-bank, and stood stiffly with his hands on his pistols. One of him held a bound letter.

"I have your orders," he said.

"I've resigned, didn't you hear?"

"The OG doesn't allow—" He steeled himself. "You must accept these orders."

He's bluffing, Strom assessed. *He's unwilling or unable to use his gun.*

Behind them the old man—his name was Gueran, he'd said—was sitting in the bow of his boat. He pulled the starter handle a couple times, causing the motor to cough and spit. Finally it caught, and he gunned the throttle, pulling the ropes taut.

"You coming?" he asked.

"Yes."

"Please!" the trio said. "It's Malcolm Leto!"

Strom let his control drift away; there was no danger from the trio.

In the boat, Meda sent.

We on the dock climbed into the boat, Strom last, slipping the last rope and pushing us away with his long legs. The trio watched us go, his hands twitching and touching. He came to some consensus and tossed the letter he was holding into the air. Quant watched its arc and sent, *Nice throw.*

It landed in the boat with a splat next to Meda. She looked at it, kicked it with her foot.

"We'll have to avoid his aircar," she said.

"No problem. Take four hours to get back. By then, we up the creek," Gueran said.

Meda picked up the letter, twirled the ribbon in her finger.

Read it, Moira sent. *Just to see.*

Toss it, I sent.

Meda stood wobbly in the boat, pitched her arm back and skipped the letter across the Amazon. It bounced, three, four times, then caught a ripple and disappeared beneath the water, only to pop up a few meters from the trio.

"Not interested," she shouted.

The trio shook his heads and watched us disappear up the river.

Gueran hummed a monotonous tune as he sluiced the boat up the river. He seemed vacant, but he avoided stumps and rocks before we could see them.

He has it memorized.

He's lived here all his life, from before the Ring, through the Gene War, until now.

There were old pods, but none as old as Gueran.

The Amazon seemed sluggish, yet it pushed back at us so that we were only doing a few kilometers per hour, but it was enough to put the elevator farther and farther behind us. The jungle on the right side was uniform and dense. The left side was too far away to see and sometimes shrouded in mist.

"Caiman," Gueran said once, as the boat slid past what we had thought was a log. One of the knobs on the log was a reptilian eye that blinked at us.

The only species of crocodile or alligator left alive.

Where many ecosystems were damaged or destroyed,

the Amazon rain forest was vibrant. Fish broke the surface. Multicolored birds dashed through the air. In the trees, monkeys leaped or lounged. The sound at times was a cacophony.

"Where did you get the gas for your motor?" Meda asked.

He shrugged. "Gas station in Belem. Still a little in the bottom of the tanks. Go there once a year."

"It's illegal to burn gasoline."

"You tell your Og on me, next time we see that trio back there," he said with a laugh.

He has a point.

Strom studied the sky to the east. The elevator rose to a point then disappeared before it reached the Ring. Since we were nearly on the equator, the Ring crossed the sky directly overhead: a thin roof over our heads.

No sign of the aircar, he sent. Once the trio hiked back to the landing strip, he would catch up to the boat in minutes. We were less than twelve kilometers from the village.

An hour later, Gueran turned into a wide tributary, as large as some major rivers, but dwarfed by the Amazon it fed. The jungle branched across the smaller river, forming a canopy that cooled the air and intensified the sound. We could see the bottom of this river; the water was clear, while the Amazon was brown and sludgy. Silver fish darted above the red rocks. Two hundred meters up the river was a sandbar that Gueran drove the boat onto. He pulled the motor up as the hull sizzled across sand and mud.

"We sleep here."

"It's still daylight. We could make another thirty kilometers today," Meda said.

"We sleep here, now. Not tonight. Travel tonight. Listen."

Aircar, Quant sent, hearing it first.

The jungle seemed to shirk back from the shrill sound, to go suddenly silent.

We caught a glimpse of it, sleek grey, skimming the river some one hundred meters up, its engines raising a ripple of water as it passed.

"They won't see us at night," Meda said.

"Yeah. Won't see us, unless they have red eyes."

Infrared, Quant sent.

"But we be one of a hundred heat sources on the river. Won't hear us at all."

He tied the boat off, then walked into the water.

"Look here," he said to Strom, pointing into the water. "You catch these, okay? Don't catch those. No TP out here, right?"

Strom nodded, and we all saw Strom's image of the fish that were good to eat, longer versions of the silver ones. In the clear river, we would be able to spear some.

"I sleep, you wake me for dinner."

With nightfall, the mosquitoes flocked to us in waves. Strom started a fire in the hopes that the smoke would force the flying vampires away, but it wasn't enough to clear the sky.

I'm covered with bites! Meda sent, sitting by the fire, her arms wrapped around herself. She glanced over at Gueran, who slept in the boat, unperturbed by the swarm of bugs crawling over his face.

Aren't they attracted to a particular wavelength of light? Quant asked. She was filleting a fish, dropping the guts onto a rock.

Infrared. The same wavelength a warm body exudes, Moira sent.

Then we just need to lower our temperature. Go swimming.

They'd just be on us when we came out, Meda sent.

I released a touch of baby pheromone, mocking Meda, and I was instantly doused in mosquitoes, trying to land on the pheromone ducts on my neck.

"Ow!"

I jumped up, brushing at my face and neck.

They like baby pheromone, Moira sent.

Quant looked at the swarms. "I wonder what they don't like."

What do you mean?

She released a dozen pheromone signals, emotions, and nuances, aromatic babel, watching the insects swarm. One in particular drove the mosquitoes away.

They don't like laughter, Quant sent. The chemical that had driven them away was the creche smell for a joke understood. We all released it then, and in a moment the sky was clear around us of bugs.

Now that's funny, I sent.

I started spitting the fillets and handed one to each of us. *Dinnertime.*

A few moments later Gueran grunted and rolled over. "What you do with all the *zanzara*?" He looked up into the sky, grumbled again, then took a stick from me. "Ah, dinner. Then we go."

I had expected the noise of the boat's engine to be a beacon for the pursuing OG aircar, but the night sounds covered everything. The crickets alone would have covered the sound of the two-stroke engine. Gueran, sated from his six fillets, let forth a rumbling burp that resonated with the engine.

"Good fish," he said.

I was sitting closest to the man, the rest of the pod spread out on the slates that marked the boat at one-meter intervals—seats and support structures both. I asked the question that was hovering among us before being whisked away by the wind.

"You're older than the Ring, aren't you?"

Gueran burped again, this one forced, too abrupt, and not as elegant as the previous.

"Yeah, so?"

"It's just that you were around before, during, and after the Community. You saw a lot of change."

"Huh."

"What was it like to live through that?"

"Huh."

I waited, then shrugged to the pod. *He doesn't want to talk about it.*

We took turns sleeping in the damp bottom of the boat after that, while the rest watched the dark Amazon roll by.

We traveled by night and slept under canopied tributaries from dawn until dusk. Twice more we heard the shrill of aircars. I watched them zoom by from the cover of the jungle. Quant remembered the tail numbers for me later and told me that the prefix meant it was an OG car. There were at least three different aircars flying up and down the Amazon, looking for us.

Perhaps we should give up, I sent after walking back to the camp. I shaped the image of a warm shower, beds at the farm.

And be exiled from pod society? Meda replied.

We effectively are exiled, Moira sent.

Why would we be exiled?

But we're free.

I was angry with myself for bringing it up, angry that we had to run from our own government, angry that we could do nothing about it but hide in the jungle and travel by night. I sat on a log next to Gueran, who was eating a mango fruit, rind and all.

"You don't like the OG much, do you?" I asked.

Gueran looked at me with a red-rimmed eye.

"Nope. Don't like the pods either."

"Why not? You have a say in the OG. All the enclaves do."

"Ha."

"I mean it. It's not an exclusive government."

"You don't know much for a fiver. You got maybe only four brains among you." He finished the last of his fruit. "You one person, right? I'm one person, right? Your vote count for five, my vote for one."

"We take up five times as many resources. Of course our vote should count more."

"Yeah, you think that way. But you pods all vote the same way. We enclave humans, we all screwed up. Brown-nosers always vote pod. Ludds don't vote at all. Christers vote for themselves. Adds up to mean our vote don't mean shit. Your OG just like the Community."

"We're utterly different," I said.

"You think so. I don't. Just less of you. Community should have had one vote too. Had billions, all voted the same way. No justice there for me." He rubbed at his tat-tooed arm. "Nobody back at the village care who running the world. They the same they always been. Maybe better now. No one coming down the elevator anymore, 'cept you."

He looked around, perhaps in hopes of finding another mango. Then he said to me, "I been thinking about your question."

"What it was like before the Community?"

"Yeah, that the one." He poked the fire with a stick, and waves of sparks twirled into the sky to scare the bats. "My brother, he join the Community. He go take the test, and don't come back for a long time. Where is he now? You see him up there?"

"No. There's no one."

"He come back once. Dressed him in nice Community clothes, all black, with boots that cost as much as a pig. His head shaved, but he still have tattoos we got together in Bacabal. He have the hole in his head like that one." He pointed at Meda, who, listening, rubbed the back of her skull. I felt a trace of embarrassment, but nothing more. "He come back and say, Gueran, you must take the test. You must come live in the Community with me. I say no, thanks, and your wife, she miss you. He say, I have a billion wives now. I say, Okay, but the one down here, she miss you."

Gueran leaned back and closed his eyes. "That what it like during the Community. People see how easy it is, look at how much work it is living here, and give up. Go get jacked. That what it like during the Community. Before and after? Don't know that it so different." He opened one of his eyes. "You so interested, tomorrow, I show what it's like in a real enclave."

Gueran crossed the river that night; up until then, we had been traveling the north side. The Amazon was so wide and turgid, it was as if we were on a lake. When dawn came, when we usually found an overgrown tributary to lie in till nightfall, Gueran kept going, pushing the boat through the foggy morning.

Every few kilometers, we passed fishing boats or houseboats. The owners always waved and Gueran waved back. Once he hailed a houseboat, anchored in the current, with a boy and a man fishing, and asked if they had gas. He traded two river turtles that he had caught with a bit of fish that night for five gallons of gas. The boy stared at me and the pod, as if he'd never seen a quintet before.

Around mid-morning, the river became busier: more fishing boats, more people. Gueran pulled five musty rain ponchos from under a seat and handed them to us.

"Cover your stink pads," he said, touching his wrists and neck. I took the poncho and pulled it over my head, hiding my pheromone ducts from sight. No one would see us as an obvious pod now, but they would wonder instead why the five of us were wearing heavy cloaks in the heat.

"And stop touching hands," Gueran added. "You look queer."

We began to pass shantytowns on the riverbank, rows of corrugated metal shacks capping any high ground and even some low ground, though they would be covered by the river in the rainy season. We passed thousands of people, more people than we had ever seen in one place. I couldn't help touching Strom's hand.

These people are poor.

And numerous.

We consensed regardless of Gueran's admonition, and I felt the claustrophobia of being among so many people, even though we were still away and in the river.

"Quit touching," I said. "They'll mark you for a pod for sure, and you don't want that."

My hand fell away, and I turned to watch the far side of the river.

Minutes later, Gueran ran the boat up to a dock. He passed a sullen boy a bit of OG scrip, and the boy took the lines and tied the boat down.

"Come on," Gueran said. "I'd like some lunch other than fish and mango."

From the docks, we climbed long steps into the city itself, which sat on a bluff overlooking the river. Above the rickety shanties were uniform modern buildings, hospitals and administration sites, and an aircar field. The town was quiet, empty. Shops were just opening and no one was up and about yet.

"Bolivopolis," Gueran muttered. "They just built it right out of the jungle. Relocated all the locals here. Wanted me to move here, but I say no way. This place have bad feng shui."

Gueran led us through the streets as if he'd often been there before, until we came to a small restaurant. Unlike the shantytowns outside the city, the shops and restaurants inside it seemed overly planned and uniform. This one had been painted red, something boldly different than the grey of the enclave buildings. A patio littered with tables rose a meter above the street, granting a view in both directions.

"This the one."

We took a table on the patio. Gueran ordered two beers right away, while we ordered juice. A young light-skinned woman singleton brought us our drinks.

"The special?" she asked.

"Yeah, six of them," Gueran said.

"What's the special?" I asked.

"The only thing they serve."

The woman brought back a tray with six plates of red beans and rice and handed them out. When she gave me mine, she paused, her eyes on the pads on my wrist.

"You a cluster," she said. "What you doing out here?"

Gueran jumped up.

"It's nothing, honey." He took her aside, handing her OG scrip. Her eyes fastened on mine, then looked away. She nodded at Gueran, then walked back into the kitchen.

"I tol' you to keep the pads under wraps," he said.

"It's not that easy," Meda said. "Maybe we should get out of here."

Gueran shook his head.

"We go in a few minutes. We gotta see something first."

He shoveled the beans and rice into his mouth and washed it down with the second beer.

Strom touched my hand under the table.

Pods coming.

I looked up the street, noticing consensus pheromones in the humid air. Pod smell.

Then I breathed in the smells of panic and veto, and a dozen minor yet common pod pheromones. It was chaos.

I half stood, but Gueran pushed me back in my seat.

"Hold on."

A dozen people came down the street, all dressed in red jumpsuits. Around them, guarding them, were three men in white. They were singletons and carried long thin rods. I thought the red-clad ones were pods at first, but then I realized what they were. They were disassociated pods: singletons. Their guards were leading them down the street, herding them.

"Who are they?" Meda asked.

"Your kind," Gueran growled. "There's thousands of them in the hospitals."

As they came closer, the smell of incoherent thoughts buffeted me. I hunched my shoulders, pulling the sleeves of the poncho over my wrists. They were uncontrolled, First State pod members who had never bonded. Or failed to bond. Their thoughts were madness.

I looked away. I clamped my hands around my thighs though I desperately wanted to grab my pod mates and come to a consensus about what we were seeing. But if I did, everyone in the restaurant and on the street would know we were a pod ourselves. And that didn't seem like a good thing for others to know in this town.

Then even through the bunched-up poncho material I began to sense thoughts come from one of them, one of himself: one of the singletons looked up at us. That shouldn't have been. I looked over, and Quant was shaking, her eyes clenched shut, her face red. Strom reached for her and I reached for Strom and it hit us like a brilliance of sunlight.

The broken pods on the street were nodes of intensity, thought, and emotion isolated and severed, but for that instant, I saw through Quant each one as a single point in a huge mesh, all linked through us.

Then I passed out, falling facefirst onto the table and into oblivion.

Manuel and Corrine came to Blue Haven Creche when they were four. Until then all they had known was each other and Gorton Creche, a crowded place with hundreds of children and stern matron pods. Always the matrons had been pushing him and Corrine to play with the other kids, to sleep in the bonding rooms with their friends. But they had not, or if they did, it had always been for short periods, and then they were back together in a corner by themselves or in the space under the stairs on the third floor.

"They're going to be a duo," Matron Reddinger had said once, when she thought that they were too busy playing to eavesdrop, as she folded and stacked white towels to the ceiling in the laundry room. But Manuel was always listening, and sharing it with Corrine.

"So, what's wrong with duos now?" asked Matron Isitharp. "I myself am a duo, and so—one, two—are you."

"But Dr. Yoder had high hopes for these two. High hopes."

"You know most twins pair bond to duos. It's just the way it is."

"I know. But they're special. Look at their feet. And always Dr. Yoder is here to look at them."

Matron Reddinger caught Manuel's look as she folded

the laundry. "Look at you two. Why don't you sleep with those three nice boys: Sensen, Joel, and Franklin. They're nice boys, aren't they? They could use a couple more in their room."

Franklin stinks. Manuel heard the words in his mind, and laughed.

"Corrine says Franklin stinks," Manuel echoed.

Matrons Reddinger and Isitharp glanced at one another.

"We'll have to tell Dr. Yoder."

Tell him what? Manuel wondered. That Franklin stunk? Everyone knew that.

Corrine giggled, looking at him, and he giggled back.

Not long after that, Dr. Yoder came and asked them a lot of questions. Usually he just came and checked their noses, necks, and wrists. Then he made sure they did their foot exercises, the ones where they stretched their toes and picked up balls and hung upside down for an hour. But this time he made them play weird games.

He had Manuel and Corrine hold hands through a curtain. Then he asked Manuel questions while he showed Corrine pictures. Then he showed Manuel the pictures. Usually they got his questions right.

"You two did very well," he said. "I'm very, very proud of you." He handed each of them a lollipop. "I just wish . . ."

"What, Dr. Yoder?" asked Manuel, hoping for another lollipop by asking smart questions.

"I just wish you two would spend more time with the other children."

Corrine had frowned, and Manuel had too when he felt her sadness.

"We don't like the kids here," Corrine said. "They only play with each other."

It was true. The kids all had their special groups of

three, and four, and sometimes five. And none of them really wanted to play with Manuel and Corrine. Besides, they had fun by themselves.

"It's very important for you two to find some friends, especially if it were a group of three."

"Why?" Corrine asked.

Dr. Yoder had sat back, the one of him who always spoke to them, and touched hands with the rest of him.

"Do you know where the children go when they leave the First State?"

"Second State!" Manuel said, proud that he remembered what some of the older kids had been talking about.

"That's right. Second State. And you can't go to Second State until you have a group of friends to go with."

"Can't Corrine and I go together?"

"Of course you can! But it would be even better if you were part of a group of five."

Corrine crossed her arms and shook her head.

Dr. Yoder sighed. "All right. All right."

But later that week he came back again and told them they were going to stay at a new creche. They'd be leaving Gorton for Blue Haven that day.

Even though they hadn't a lot of friends there, Gorton Creche was the only home they knew, and they cried and hugged Matron Reddinger and Matron Isitharp and even Matron Ulysses, all three of her, even the tall gangly one who never spoke and never looked at you. They even hugged the janitor robot, which all the children called Uncle Millions.

Blue Haven was so much bigger than Gorton, with a huge fenced-in playground and a tall oak tree in the middle of it. There were just two groups of kids there, a group of four and a group of five.

Manuel and Corrine liked the four more than the five.

The five kept to themselves and didn't talk to anyone. They just held hands a lot and smirked.

"They're going to Second State soon," one of the four—Meda—said. "They think they're better than the rest of us."

Meda was one of the four and one of twins just like Manuel and Corrine were twins. But Meda and Moira were identical twins, while Manuel and Corrine didn't look identical, just very similar.

They were sad to have left Gorton, but their new friends made Blue Haven so much nicer. And the Matron, Mother Redd, was very nice too.

On the first day, Manuel and Corrine showed the four how they could hang upside down by their feet. And then Strom showed them how strong he was. And Quant recited pi to one hundred digits. And Meda and Moira laughed at it all. That night they all slept in the same room—all six of them—and it felt right to be there. They hardly thought of Gorton at all after that.

Soon, the six of them became inseparable.

Once, when they were playing with the computer in the library, he heard Meda say, though she didn't move her lips, *Let's work on a puzzle.*

Moira had replied, speaking out loud, "Okay."

After that, Manuel started to hear the others speak, just like he sometimes heard Corrine speak. Just like he had sometimes heard the kids at Gorton speak, but then it had been a horrible babble that he'd tried to shut out. But with these children, he was happy to hear them think.

They heard him too. Often when they slept together, they dreamed together.

Dr. Yoder was still their doctor, but now they had another doctor, Dr. Khalid. Dr. Khalid was a quartet, and he came every other day to see them and the other group of children. He was a silent doctor, who examined them three at a time.

He didn't get along with Dr. Yoder, and the group heard them arguing one day in the courtyard. The children were in the back, playing, and what had started as an inaudible conversation slowly turned into a yelling match, with three of Yoder yelling and two of Khalid.

"What are they arguing about?" Meda asked. She jumped, not quite reaching the top of the wooden plank fence that surrounded the creche playground. Strom threaded his fingers together and lifted her up.

Manuel scrambled up the wall easily enough, and he and Meda saw the two doctors arguing, but couldn't quite make out what they were saying.

"I can't hear them, but they're going something awful," she said.

Manuel stood on the thin edge of the fence, walked along it as if he were on solid ground until he could reach up into one of the oak trees that surrounded the front driveway. A thick bough hung over the playground, casting a shadow where the children often played Eco Disaster. The branch was thicker than his torso.

"Be careful," Corrine called, but he waved her off.

He walked to the trunk. There he took off his shoes and stuck them in a crotch of the tree. His toes caressed the rough bark, finding footholds. Grasping the trunk, he climbed up and around it one hundred eighty degrees to another bough that hung out over the driveway.

He crawled up, careful not to rustle the leaves, until he was directly above Dr. Khalid's interface, but still hidden in the green leaves and acorns.

"There are no viable sixes," Khalid said. "We're jeopardizing the program by trying. My sources say quintets are the optimal size."

"But twins, Abdel! Two sets of twins. No one's tried with twins," Yoder replied.

"Then one of the singles will sheer off," Khalid yelled. "Which one do we sacrifice! I tell you, this is dangerous."

Another of Yoder spoke. "But the four are nearly pod bonded. If the new twins can take, we have a sextet, the first ever."

"Or we have a quartet and a duo, and no one from our labs in the space program. It's folly, Yoder, folly!"

"Folly is having this opportunity and failing to take it! And what of these mysterious sources you call on as deus ex machina? Show me the peer-reviewed journal."

Khalid was silent for a moment. "If you wish, we can take it to Cahill. Cahill knows my sources."

Yoder sighed, then one of him shrugged.

"We must separate one of the twins," Khalid said. "And we must do it soon."

Yoder groaned. "Give me a month. They're young enough yet. Let me try."

"It's time for State Two consensus training," Khalid said. His groundcar appeared through the gates of the creche. One of him opened the door and the rest of him climbed in. "You have until the end of the week to decide which one it is."

Yoder watched Khalid drive away, then shook his head. Manuel waited for the doctor to disappear into the creche door before running back down the bough to the fenced playground. He almost fell as he dropped down onto the fence.

"What were they yelling about?" Meda asked. She almost always was the one who asked questions of the children or the Matrons.

"Us," Manuel said.

Corrine caught his look, and she frowned. Manuel

realized that she knew he meant her and him as well as the six of them together.

"What about us?" Meda asked.

"Yoder and Khalid don't agree on when we should start consensus training," Manuel said, knowing Corrine caught the half-lie.

It wasn't until that night after dinner, when all the children were playing in the upstairs reading room that Manuel could speak with Corrine alone. The other four seemed to have been hovering too close all day.

"They want to take one of us away," Manuel said. "They want to make a quintet."

Corrine said, "They can't do that! They should take one of the others away."

"You and me should be together, a duo," Manuel said.

Corrine frowned, and Manuel realized that she didn't want to be just a duo. She didn't just want him.

"Quant should go," Corrine said. "She never talks." It was true. Quant seemed in a world of her own, and sometimes Manuel caught a thought of it: tallies of every item, forks, spoons, toothpicks; numbers of things today and yesterday; the speed of the wind instead of the feel of it on her face.

"Dr. Khalid said the four have already pod bonded," Manuel said.

"Then—" But she stopped herself before she said anything more.

"Can you go get us cookies, Manuel?" she asked.

"Okay." Manuel ran downstairs for a handful of cookies that Mother Redd had baked. When he returned to the reading room, it was empty.

"Corrine," he called, but she didn't answer.

He ran to the bedroom. No one was there.

He ran to the computer room, then the toy room.

He didn't want to cry, but tears were wetting his cheeks.

Then he heard giggling, and he found the five in one of the other bedroom closets.

"Don't be a crybaby," Corrine said. "We were just playing hide and seek."

Manuel offered the cookies to her.

"We don't want cookies now," Corrine said, though Strom took two as he followed Corrine. They all seemed to be following Corrine. Manuel followed too, but when they got back to the reading room, Corrine organized a game of Eco Disaster for just five of them.

"You can play the next game, Manuel," she said. But he fell asleep before the first was over.

The next day, Dr. Yoder came to speak with Manuel alone. As soon as one of Dr. Yoder had shut the door, Manuel blurted, "I think Corrine should be the one. I'll go back to Gorton!" Tears ran down his cheeks.

"How do you know about this?" Dr. Yoder asked gently. "Do you all know?"

Manuel nodded. "Corrine really wants to be part of the quintet."

"I see." Dr. Yoder touched palms, and the room smelled funny for a long time.

"Do you like the other four?"

"Yeah . . ."

"Don't you want to be part of their pod?"

"Corrine wants it more. And she'll be much better at it."

"Manuel, why don't you go back to the library?"

He kept away from Corrine and the four that day. He knew he was leaving. Instead of facing them he climbed up and down the oak trees in back, trying to climb higher and higher each time, until the trunk itself bent under his weight.

From there he could see the University where Dr. Yoder and Dr. Khalid worked. He'd been there a couple of times for games. He could also see the airbuses coming in for landings at the airport. Mother Redd had told them the contrails were just clouds of water vapor, not smoke or poisonous gas. They seemed like bars crisscrossing the sky.

Gorton would be fine for him. He'd find some other friends, and maybe he'd see Corrine. Maybe she'd come to visit.

After dinner, before bed, the four and Corrine—the five, the quintet—were playing games again, but Manuel just read about sharks in the library, and before long he dozed off.

He awoke with a start, the smell of fear in his nose. The sleep snapped from his eyes, and the book fell from his hands. The small lamp at his shoulder was the only light on in the room.

Corrine!

He knew it was she who was in trouble. Not trouble, she was in terror.

He ran from the library into the dark hall.

The bedroom was silent. The four slept softly, gentle snores from Strom, vague dream thoughts in the air. He heard a sound.

Someone on the stairs!

He ran, saw dark shapes at the foot of the stairwell. He took the steps, three at a time, his feet gripping the edge of each step, launching himself to the next, catching himself with his fingers in the spokes of the banister.

Corrine!

Manuel!

"She's bleeding pheromone!"

"We should have knocked her out."

Manuel plowed into a dark shape holding Corrine.

"You oaf!"

They went down in a pile, Corrine, Manuel, and two other pods.

"Something came down the steps."

A light came on, and Manuel blinked. Dr. Khalid and Dr. Yoder were there. They'd come to take Corrine away.

"It's the brother," Dr. Khalid said.

"I *told* you they were strongly pod-bonded!"

Manuel crawled over to Corrine and hugged her tightly. Dr. Yoder frowned, then one of him knelt next to them.

"Listen, children," Dr. Yoder said. "I've told you from the beginning that I wanted you together, but I've also told you that you might have to go to separate pods. Do you remember?"

Manuel nodded, but Corrine's face contorted. She pulled away from Manuel.

"Now is the time for you two to go to separate pods. Do you understand?"

"Yes!" Corrine shouted. "But why am I the one who has to leave? Why can't it be him?"

Manuel recoiled.

Dr. Khalid leaned down and picked her up. "Exactly," he said. "So you won't be spoiling my pod with your petty jealousy."

"Khalid!" Dr. Yoder said.

"Let's go."

"The boy!"

One of Khalid turned, while the rest took Corrine through the door. He solemnly picked up the boy and walked him up the stairs to the bedroom where the four still slept.

With his hands, he signed, "Your place." Then left him.

Manuel stood in the dark, crying until he was too tired to stand, then he slid under the covers with the four, and slept.

I awoke screaming, knowing I was alone.

Strom! Meda! Moira! Quant! Corrine! I screamed, straining to sit up, roll over, stand, but being unable.

"Jesus! This one is squirting again."

"Let him. Did you see his feet?"

"Yeah."

I opened my eyes, saw a white ceiling. My arms and feet were restrained. Not good.

"Where am I?" I croaked. My throat was gritty. I swallowed dryness. "Where's my pod?"

"You brokens always want to know that." A face appeared above me. An unmodified singleton. He wore a white smock. The name Fanning was stitched to his coat.

"I'm not broken."

"You wouldn't be here if you weren't."

I fought down panic. "I'd like to see my pod now, please. The ones I was with."

"No can do. It's time to take care of this smell."

Fanning raised a hypodermic and tapped my inner arm looking for a vein. Two other men, no, a duo, stood by the door grinning. He was military, judging from the camouflage fatigues he wore. With a start of recognition, I saw it was Anderson McCorkle.

"No! I don't need that."

"Don't fight it, kid," one of the duo said.

"You put up a good chase, but face it, you're caught," said his partner.

Fanning smiled and inserted the needle, holding the arm against my jerking.

"This man is a spy!" I cried. "He's trying to kill us. You need to alert the OG!"

"Now there's a new one," Fanning said.

Cotton filled my ears, and all I could taste was the metallic sheen on my tongue. My eyes focused and took images of what I looked at, but it was as if my nervous system were dull.

I exhaled.

"What was that?"

"Cluster buster."

The phrase thundered in my ears, then faded away, and for a moment it meant nothing. Cluster dissolution factor.

I heaved at my bonds.

"Take me to my pod!" I yelled. I tried to send the distress pheromone, but I was detached from my body. I couldn't trigger the glands in my neck. The pads on my palms were dry.

"There, there. You'll be okay in a while. We'll take care of the rest now."

The man disappeared from my view, leaving the military duo. They leaned close.

"You know how many people are looking for you, freak?"

"They scrambled Space Fleet when you disappeared onto the Ring."

"But by then, we knew you were compromised."

"If we hadn't known when you got fucked in the back of the head by Leto—"

"—we knew when you ran for the Ring."

"Bad move."

"The worst move was when you made me look bad."

McCorkle disappeared from my view. The light went out, leaving me in near darkness, save for the light coming through the transom above the door.

The door shut, clicking locked.

I fought back tears as the desperation rose in me. If the drug had destroyed my ability to bond with my pod, I was certain to go insane. My body shuddered, and I felt cold, alone, empty.

In anger I slammed against the bonds holding my arms and legs, rattling the hospital bed. My legs bounced off the mattress, and I saw them rise up.

I realized that the leg manacles had more play than the

ones on my arms. I raised my legs, and saw a leather strap
binding my modified feet, but it had a good twelve inches
of slack.

I brought my feet together and they touched. I laughed,
perhaps a bit maniacally. My captors had commented on
my modified toes, but they hadn't understood their capabilities. Even McCorkle hadn't understood.

"Idiots," I muttered and began unbuckling the left fetter.
It came open easily. Then with my free left foot, I undid
the right ankle. Rolling my torso up, my feet stretched over
my head. Yet I couldn't reach the straps on my wrists. I
tried pulling my feet all the way around and down to my
waist where my arms were, but I wasn't that flexible.

I flopped back down. Then I raised my hips and bent
my knees back, bringing my feet up under my hips. Just
barely, I could reach the shackles at my wrists. Straining,
my toes found the buckle on my left hand, and it opened.
In moments I was free of the bed.

The room was small, just two meters square, the bed
against the wall opposite the door. The ceiling was high.
The only window was the transom over the door, which let
in fluorescent light from the hallway.

I tried the knob, but it was locked from the outside. I
looked up at the transom. Pulling the bed over, I could easily reach the top of the door. Jumping, I caught the edge of
the transom and pulled myself up to the thick ledge.

Through the window I saw an empty hallway. I pushed
at the transom window, but it was locked as well. I pushed
harder and the window rattled in its frame. Dust rose
around me, but I couldn't smell it. It tickled my nose and
I almost sneezed, but the odor was utterly absent. They
had stolen something from me.

In rage I punched at the window. It shattered and fell
with a crash onto the floor of the hallway outside.

Gingerly, I slipped through the opening, feeling a graze of glass on my back, and jumped beyond the mess of glass on the floor.

My clothes had been removed, and I wore a pale green hospital smock. I rubbed at my back where the broken glass in the transom frame had sliced me. The pain I felt, and I was thankful. It stoked my anger. My hand came away damp with blood.

The sound of the window would bring someone soon, and even if it didn't, the broken glass on the floor would be obvious to the first person who walked by. I needed cover; I needed to find my pod.

The hallway was lined with doors, and extended in both directions for twenty or thirty meters before teeing off. I picked a direction at random and started opening doors. Each door opened to a cube just like the one I had been in, with a bed. All were empty, but then I opened one with a sleeping pod member. It was no one I knew, but I shook the woman awake and kept looking.

"What are you doing?" the woman asked.

"Escaping," I replied, opening another door.

She trailed after me. "Why?"

"Because I don't want to be here."

"Where will you go?"

"To wherever my pod is," I said.

"I had a pod too," the woman said wistfully.

"Help me open more doors."

An orderly appeared at the end of the hall.

He shouted and the woman backed up against the wall, scared.

I looked right at him, started to back away, as he came toward me. Then as the orderly gained full speed, I ran at him, slid beside him, tripping him at the knee, and sent his bulk hurtling down the hall.

I was on top of him in a second, yanking his baton from his hand, and choking him with it. The orderly grunted and went still, his eyes wild.

"I am not a happy person," I whispered. "I feel very angry. Do you believe me?"

The orderly grunted.

"Good. Now where is the rest of my pod?"

The orderly grunted again. I released the baton from across his throat.

"I don know," he grunted, coughing once.

I took the baton and whacked the orderly on the back of the skull. Moira would have urged calm and reason; but Moira wasn't here, and I wasn't interested in reason. I felt more angry than I ever had before.

"All the new pods are taken to Wings Two and Three. This is Wing Two," the woman said.

"Where's Three?"

"I can show you where that is," she said.

I spun the baton around and hit the man hard enough to knock him unconscious and perhaps fracture his skull. I didn't care. I dragged the orderly into one of the rooms and stripped him of his clothes. He had an electronic key pass on his belt.

"You look just like a doctor," the woman said. "It's scary."

I saw that she had pheromone glands at her neck and pads for chemical thought on her wrists, but I could smell nothing from her. I didn't know if it was because of some defect in her or because she had been given the drug too.

"What's your name?"

"Jol," she said. "It used to be Edgar Longhorn, before, I mean." She was a broken pod. Revulsion snaked through me. I swallowed.

"Show me where Wing Three is."

"This way."

The woman led me to a stairwell, taking a flight up to the next floor. It opened into an empty hallway identical to the one below.

"How many people do they keep here?" I asked.

The woman shrugged. "I dunno. A lot. We all come here from the creche when . . . well, when our pods don't form right."

"You've been here for fifteen years?"

"Yeah. I was born in Osbourne Creche. We formed a pod, my friends and I, and we called ourselves Edgar Longhorn. We were a quartet, but it didn't work out, so they re-formed a trio without me. I couldn't . . . do it after that."

I looked at her. She had been institutionalized after failing to form even a duo. I'd never considered the failures of the pod system, but now I saw the waste in the process. Even if one individual was ruined for the sake of a thousand viable pods, I wasn't sure it was worth it.

"I'm sorry you didn't form a pod."

"It's okay. I've had years to come to grips with my brokenness. Soon, I should be able to join a singleton enclave. This way."

She led me down the passageway.

"This is Wing Three."

Two figures were coming down the hall. I pushed the woman into a side hall, shushing her. Peeking around the corner, I saw that one of the two was the singleton who had worked on me. The second man I did not know; it wasn't Anderson McCorkle. They were chatting amiably as they walked down the hall. They stopped at a door, laughing at a joke, and turned the knob. Where was the duo?

I was running as they entered. If one of my pod was in that room, I couldn't allow them to use the drug they had used on me. I couldn't let anyone else lose her senses as mine were now destroyed.

I caught the door before it shut, holding it just a few millimeters open, and listened at the door.

"Where's the rest of my pod?" Meda's voice.

"You have no pod, young lady."

"Of course I do. We're Apollo Papadopulos."

"You wouldn't be sent here if you were a viable pod."

"We're a functioning quintet. You can't keep us apart."

"Quintet! There's like ten of those in the whole world, and you expect me to believe that one of you is tramping through the Amazon jungle? More likely you're a broken experiment the clusters built. We get them down here all the time. Misshapen, broken people that we have to fit back into society."

"We're not broken." Meda sounded shrill.

"It's not your fault, I know. You can't help it that your body was fucked with."

"What's in that syringe?"

I pushed open the door and launched myself at the nearest body. I clawed, kicked, gouged, using my feet and hands.

The man's hypodermic fell, skittering across the room.

The second man grabbed at me, catching my shoulder and pulling me off the first man. I was not as massive as either of the two. I landed with a thump against the wall.

"What's he doing here?" the first man cried.

I launched myself at him again, fingers outstretched. My hands found his throat, but the second man had me in a headlock. I couldn't fight two people at once.

The second man pushed me up against the wall, pinning me.

"I'll get restraints!" said the first man, slipping out the door. "Hey!"

Something thumped against the wall outside the room. Then the pressure on my chest eased. As I fell against the floor, I saw Strom tossing the second man against the first into a corner of the room. He smiled at me and began to unlace Meda's restraints.

They touched wrists, and I watched from the floor as they shared memories. I should have been able to smell the pheromones, to catch whiffs of the chemical thoughts. I pulled my hands behind me, suddenly scared.

"Come on," Strom said. He and Meda ran out of the room, and I followed, pulling the door shut on the two stunned men, locking it.

Quant stood at the end of the hallway. She rushed to Strom and Meda, touching palms. Still I hung back. I should have been able to hear something!

Jol stood nearby, an odd look on her face as she watched my pod consense. She had opened the doors to all the cells, releasing my pod, while I had rushed Meda's cell.

"Where's Moira?" I asked, looking in doors.

"Here!"

The sound was muffled, but I traced it to a door and opened it.

Moira lay on the bed. I unstrapped her and hugged her. "Thanks!"

We joined together in the hall, Moira and Quant taking my hand, so I couldn't pull away. I tried halfheartedly to struggle free.

Nothing.

I couldn't hear them. My thoughts were crammed inside my own skull and unable to reach the rest of me.

They turned then, their faces horrified.

"I can't think with you," I said, my voice breaking.

They pulled me close then.

"It's okay," Moira said. "It can't be permanent."

"They drugged me," I said. "They were going to drug all of us."

"We have to get out of here," Strom said simply.

I watched as Strom took control, felt the lack of any

sensation or pull. I knew the others were attuning themselves to his direction. I watched, detached.

"Where are we going?" asked Jol. She stood next to me
in her hospital clothes, her hair disheveled.

"We're leaving," I said. "Thanks for opening all those
doors. You saved us."

She smiled. "Is that your pod?"

"Yes. Only I can't join them. The drug they gave me . . ."

The rest of my pod, halfway down the hall, turned as
one to look at me.

"Coming," I called.

Faster than I could understand, two shapes converged
on Strom.

It was Anderson McCorkle.

They knew to attack our strength: Strom, who took control of all combat situations. So busy protecting himself,
Strom had little time to direct the pod. The other three and
I hung back, unsure what to do. Then Strom's thoughts
reached them, chemical directions flitting in the air.

Quant flung herself at the first of the duo, while Meda
and Moira swarmed over the second. I knew there were
directions for me as well, but I had no idea what they
were, and instead hung back out of the way with Jol.

The duo disengaged, rolling away from the four, coming to stand two meters away, side by side. Four against
two should have clearly favored the four, but the duo was
a combat-trained pod, with heightened strength and speed.
I was surprised they didn't draw their pistols, but I saw that
their holsters were empty. Perhaps they had been forced to
disarm themselves before entering the facility.

Again, with lightning reflexes, the two coordinated a
feint at Strom, followed by a double punch at Quant, who
barely blocked the first, while the second sent her flail-
ing back.

It was more a choreographed dance than a fight, and I saw where my place should have been: empty, a weakness.

Strom sent Meda and Moira to attack with a fury of kicks and punches. Meanwhile Quant and Strom tried to circle around, but couldn't in the cramped hallway.

"You have no military training, Papadopulos," said one of the duo.

"And you're running at four-fifths capacity," said the other.

"You can't win."

"OG Military is—"

The four struck mid-sentence in a synchronized attack that forced the duo to drop back. Strom directed the four in a series of feints, punches, and kicks that I could not understand. If I had been a part of the pod, I would have seen the tactics with clarity. Now it was just a blur.

"Wow," said Jol. "Your pod is good."

Wham! One of the duo took a solid blow to the head and staggered back.

The duo dropped back three meters. Time was on his side; if he stalled us long enough, others would come to help him.

But the drop-back was a trick. As Strom pressed forward, the two pounced on him in a close attack. I was certain my pod would win now in the close fighting. But the duo knew the pod's weakness, and one of the two managed to get a choke hold on Strom's neck. He just needed seconds, and Strom was out, his brain starved of oxygen for an instant and shutting down.

The rest of the pod stopped, suddenly undirected, and stood uncertain. Without Strom's input, it was nearly impossible for us to think tactically. The duo had won against the pod.

I realized that I was still free and able to think independently. Strom's unconsciousness had no impact on me. The drug had freed me from that at least.

I launched myself at one of the pair. Toes and fingers fought for a hold on his torso. I let loose all the anger I felt for being drugged and cleaved from my pod, pummeling the man until he fell. I ripped at the sensitive membranes on the man's neck, the pheromone glands. Pain smell erupted.

The second of the duo was momentarily stunned; the force of my attack had disrupted the pair's thoughts.

It was enough time for Meda and Moira to tackle the second man.

I managed to get a grip around the first man's neck and squeezed until he purpled and passed out. I didn't let go until Moira pulled me off. I staggered back, my heart thumping, certain I would have killed the man.

By the time Quant had helped Strom awake, we had stowed the duo in one of the rooms, locking the door.

"I'm sorry," Strom said. "I let you down."

The four tapped hands, commiserating with Strom, but I stood apart, pulling free when Moira reached for me.

"Quit wasting time, and let's go," I said, still angry, still breathing heavily, as angry as I was scared, but it was easier to show the anger.

Strom nodded and led us down the stairwell, down to the first level. There was a fire door, which he pushed open. An alarm began to sound, a shrill electronic whistle.

The door opened onto an alleyway between large institutional buildings. In moments we were heading down the hill toward the river. Our clothes—five of us dressed as patients and me as an orderly—drew some stares, but no one stopped us.

As we passed the airfield, I noted the two aircars sitting

there. One of them had brought Anderson McCorkle; he must have just arrived. He would have had to take the barge all the way to Sabah Station in Indonesia and then a suborbital to South America. The amount of reaction mass he burned to get here was not trivial.

My shoulders shook as I realized we had enemies who wanted us destroyed.

I felt a vague urge to share this with my pod, but the desire was no more than a twinge, easily ignored. I wondered if this was more of the drug's effect. I was getting used to being a singleton.

Gueran's boat was empty. While my pod stood on the dock consensing, I stepped into it and started the motor. Jol got in and sat beside me.

"Come on," I said. I couldn't understand why they were waiting on the dock. We had to go.

The rest of the pod looked at me, then Strom nodded. They stepped in, while Quant untied the lines.

"Hey! Wait for me!"

Running down the hill was Gueran, yelling and waving his arms.

I ran the boat down to the end of the dock, making Gueran puff and huff to catch up, finally relenting and idling the motor until Gueran could pull himself in.

"One more passenger will cost you more," he heaved.

I gripped his shirt collar with my left foot and began dragging him over to the side of the boat. Strom leaned forward to stop me, but then sat back down as the boat began to rock.

"We can get rid of one passenger right now," I said, my anger welling up again. "The caimans would like a snake."

"Hey. It's my boat!"

"You sold us out, Gueran. Who are you working for?"

"No! No! I didn't know you'd all pass out like that. What

could I do? I been trying to get to you all day. I been trying hard!"

I punched him, then Moira slid forward past Strom and held my arm.

"Enough, Manuel."

I looked at Moira, realized that the anger in me had become undamped and wild. The pod was not there to stabilize me. I released Gueran, sat back on the seat near the tiller, and gunned the motor. Jol leaned against me, and I pondered my seething emotions, wondering where I stopped and the pod began.

An hour later, we hid in an overcovered tributary for night to fall. Everyone was too tired to keep going during the night. I watched my pod make camp in silence. I knew they were thinking together, whispering thoughts among themselves, yet it was ghostly to watch their synchronous actions. Once I caught Meda looking at me. I shrugged and turned away. They were missing a part of themselves just as I was.

Standing, I walked into the jungle. In seconds the camp was hidden from me behind emerald walls. I disturbed a small frog which leaped to a nearby leaf, clinging to it with its thick digits.

I caught it from behind, letting its suckery feet crawl across my palm. Its front and rear three-toed feet were equally useful to it. It looked up at me with one watery eye, almost as large as its head. Then it jumped with strength disproportionate to its body, disappearing into the brush.

"Beautiful creature."

I turned to find Jol next to me.

"Yes."

"I used to look out at the jungle from the hospital windows, wondering what was there. I imagined snakes and crocodiles as long and wide as trucks. I never imagined frogs as small and delicate as that." She was standing close to me. Her dark hair was darker with water; she had just come from the river—a dip to cool herself off—and her hospital clothes were plastered to her body. She ran her fingers through her hair.

"Are you lonely without your pod?" she asked.

"Not so much," I said. "I should be, I think, but I'm not."

"Two people can be a pod," she said.

I looked her in the eye. The invitation was between us, and this woman seemed as wild and alive as the jungle we stood in. Yet I felt I could not trust myself; my emotions were ruling me without a pod to control them, without consensus to work toward.

I didn't answer, looking away at the mulchy floor of the rain forest. A tree had fallen—perhaps last rainy season—and the canopy was thin, allowing saplings and bushes to begin a desperate race toward the sun. The fallen trunk was an ecosystem in itself. I watched as termites zipped inside and out of the patchy bark. Spiders had strung webs across rotten limbs. A black agouti, chewing a Brazil nut in its teeth, sat among the upturned root system and observed us calmly.

Jol stepped forward to get a closer look at the rodent. Her foot slid into the soil. I took ahold of her shirt and pulled her back.

What we had thought was a mound of mulch from the tree was in fact an anthill, some two meters tall. The ants had apparently mined the earth around the hill, perhaps for defense, perhaps for material for the hill, leaving it susceptible to collapse if something large stepped on it. Now that I knew it was there, I saw surrounding the hill columns of ants marching to and fro, all of them bent to tasks to keep their little community alive.

Jol clung to my arm, looking at the hole she had created in the earth, now teeming with furious ants. I stepped back, worried that the ants might have a fiery bite.

"Let's walk back to camp," I said, thankful I had an excuse to ignore the fire between us.

After midnight we pushed back out onto the river, and again I took the motor. Gueran glared at me, but didn't argue. I was cocooned in silence even from the other singletons and pretended to be oblivious.

Jol watched me, perhaps looking for an invitation, but I gave none. My pod glanced at me, every few moments, and I knew they were thinking about me. I knew what it felt like to be a four when you were once a five. I even knew what it was like to be a singleton when once you were a quintet. I had shared Strom's and Meda's memories of their times apart.

This was different. I felt elevated and relieved, as if a part of me long suppressed was free to step forward.

I said to Gueran, "How many of those hospitals do you know of?"

Gueran started from his own reverie. "Huh. Two more."

"All run by singletons?"

"Normal people, yeah."

I bit back an angry retort. "Ten thousand broken pods, maybe more."

"You people ain't perfect," Gueran said. "Leave your trash for us to take care of. No better than the Community."

"No," I said. "No better at all."

Moira looked at me, her face pale in the black night. "Just different," she said. "Just different aspects of the same humanity."

"What happened to Quant back there at the town?" I asked. I knew the rest of the pod would have been grappling with it.

Moira shrugged. "We don't know. We've been trying to figure it out."

"I remember seeing all the broken pods as bright lights, then . . ."

"Yeah, then nothing."

Quant spoke up, "For a moment we were all part of a . . . a . . . supernode. I could feel them as extensions of us."

"That's never happened before," I said.

"It has for me," Strom said. He meant the bears. He had connected with the bears, joined in their communal thoughts. For a while they had been an ad hoc pod, something that did not happen with humans.

"It was the broken pods," Quant said, looking at Jol. "They were desperate for interaction, for consensus."

Jol spit over the side. "I don't need a pod," she said.

"You tell 'em, girl," said Gueran. "Ya just need a man, like me."

Jol glared at Gueran, then turned away.

"Can you see her as a node?" I asked, nodding at Jol.

Quant shook her head. "No."

"It's not common knowledge what happens to broken pods," Moira said. "They hide it from us."

"They say they're sent to singleton enclaves," Meda said. "It's true." I realized they were speaking for my benefit, thinking out loud so that I could participate. They were trying to draw me back in, if not with chemical memories and pheromones, then with words and verbal consensus. I said nothing.

"But institutionalized and drugged?" Moira said. "It's not moral."

"They are only suppressing the modifications that they no longer need," Meda said. "It's for their own good."

"That's shit," I said.

"What do you mean?" Moira asked, but I didn't want

to talk anymore, didn't want to pretend to be a pod when I wasn't. Instead I looked out over the river.

Around three in the morning, Gueran said, "You haven't slept in a long time. Let me take the stick."

I grunted, my eyes stinging from the constant headwind, and sank down in the bottom of the boat. Jol was there, curled in among the canvas blankets. She snuggled closer, and I let her.

She whispered in my ear, "Why don't you want me?"

"I never said I didn't." I felt myself blush, and I was thankful none of my pod could read my thoughts.

"I'm attractive, I know I am. The orderlies said so."

"You are. But I've never really . . ."

"Been outside your pod? Well, you're outside them now."

"Hush," I said. Jol's voice had been rising. "We've been together for a long time, is all. This drug has to wear off at some point." I hoped it was so.

Jol shrugged. "And if it doesn't?"

"I won't be going back to that hospital, that's for sure."

"Me neither." She placed a kiss on my forehead. "Thanks for rescuing me. I didn't even know I needed rescuing."

"You're welcome."

She kissed me again, this time on the lips.

I kissed back, gently, remembering what it was like when Meda kissed Malcolm Leto. It was nicer when it was not just a memory.

I pulled her closer, snuggling in the damp boat, and fell asleep.

I awoke to a half-heard thought. I sat up, shaking my head, and looked over the side. It was just before dawn, and the sky was overcast. Drops of rain plopped into the dank river. That was what I'd smelled.

Strom and Meda were in the prow of the boat awake,

holding hands and sharing thoughts. Meda smiled, but I shrugged. If I had heard them thinking before, the air was silent now. I resisted the urge to crawl forward and touch hands.

"Don't know this side of the river this far up," Gueran muttered behind me.

I looked at him. He was only in his sixties, yet he had seen three ages of the Earth.

"Why didn't you go with your brother?"

Gueran laughed. "I go, I be dead too."

"How do you know he died? Didn't the Community transcend?"

"Then they left a lot of dead bodies behind. Don't know anyone want to leave their cock behind."

"What do you mean?"

Gueran steered the boat up a small tributary.

"My brother, he visiting when things go to shit. He have this little satellite dish he put on my roof, so he can still be linked in, you know. He comes and visits and says it's the best thing in the whole world, I should come do it. Get the little hole in my skull, like your one over there. Don't need any more holes, you know."

The boat ground onto a thin low bank. Gueran jumped out and tied it to a rubber tree. His finger ran across machete slices on the tree, came back white.

"Hmm, we better keep going, I think."

He and I pushed the boat back out into the small river and Gueran turned us back toward the west.

"Anyway. He have breakfast, jacked in, maybe he checking his mail. Anyway he's eating, and then he keels over, facefirst into the milk. Knocked over his pineapple juice. I say, 'What, you kidding, Yos?' but he deader than a doornail. I didn't know the CPR or nothing, but it wouldn't have mattered. Wasn't nothing there anymore." He tapped his head.

"So he dead that day, and that the same day the planes bombed Ulaanbaator. Then the people started getting the buboes, black in their pits, and dying. So many corpses after that, no one realize the Community had all died together. Like some cult thing.

"You say they transcended, I saw they died. Yos, he don't know anything coming. He just keel over. I think you have a transcend coming, you let people know. Press release. Something. No, I don't think they knew—"

The aircar shot over the trees of the northern bank and came to rest above the boat, the downspill rippling the water.

"This is the OG. Stop the boat now." The speaker crackled.

"Shit," Gueran said. But he didn't stop the boat. Instead he aimed it at the bank and ran it full speed into the reeds and up onto the soft, muddy bank. A flock of birds winged up around us, hundreds, momentarily obscuring the aircar, which dodged to avoid them.

The boat tilted to the side, and everyone scrambled out. The mud sucked at my feet as I helped Jol out of the boat. Ahead of me was my pod and Gueran. Above, the aircar screamed and banked, trying to cut us off from the jungle.

Strom took control, and the pod swerved as one to the left, heading for a copse of trees. Gueran kept going straight, churning his thick arms. Jol slipped. I pulled her up by her arm, and she yelped.

The aircar turned after the pod, and I watched as Quant casually tossed a stone into the intake of the left engine.

Something clunked and the aircar spun. It still could fly with one, but the damaged engine compromised its speed and maneuverability. The pilot pulled up, unwilling to take a rock in the one remaining engine.

The jungle descended like a green curtain, the sound of

river and aircar muffled in the creak of crickets and the call of birds.

Behind me, the pod ran up.

I grinned at Quant. "Nice throw."

Quant raised her eyebrows, then grinned back wolfishly. "Thanks."

We pushed into the jungle, following a game trail that touched the river and ran back into the rain forest. Whatever used the trail was short, because the vines tugged at our necks and the leaves slashed at our faces.

"We a couple days from the highway by boat. By jungle . . ." Gueran shrugged. "Long time."

Behind us came the sound of the aircar landing.

"They're coming in after us," Jol said.

"There can't be more than two in that aircar," I said.

"Seats six, tightly," Quant said.

"Three duos? Three military duos?"

The pod touched hands, assessing. I ignored it.

. . . one against three . . .

The thoughts tickled my wrists. I squeezed them away.

Gueran looked up at the canopy of green. "There's a road from Bolivopolis to the highway. We may be able to walk it on the road. Won't be able to in the jungle."

"How far to the road?" I asked.

Gueran shrugged. "A few klicks."

"They'll have patrols on the road," Meda said. "It'll be impossible."

"Even if we use the jungle for cover?" I asked. "One day by river is just a hundred kilometers at most. We can hike a couple hundred kilometers."

"Weren't you complaining about your feet just a week ago?" Meda asked.

"Strom can carry me," I replied, joking.

"As far as you need," Strom replied with sincerity.

Jol stepped between me and the pod. "If we split up, the soldiers will follow the larger group—them." She dipped her head at the pod. "They'll have sniffers, looking for pheromones. They won't find us. You and I can slip away, live in the jungle maybe."

"It's not that simple," I replied. But it was true that pheromone sniffers would find us in the jungle wherever we hid. We'd have to keep moving and move fast.

"It isn't? Probably not for someone who's always had a pod, who has never been alone," Jol said, her voice breaking. Tears had formed in the corners of her eyes. I didn't want to hurt her, but her alienness scared me. Her emotions were unknowable to me. "I've never had that security. But you're like me now. You're not like them."

Meda caught my eye, then looked away. However we had come to be, by whatever choices and luck, we were one now and forever. I shook my head slowly. "I am them."

"We can't wait here," Strom said softly.

"Manuel," Jol said. "You'll come with me?"

"I'm sorry, Jol. That decision was made fifteen years ago, and not by me," I said, remembering the night Corrine was taken away. In Jol's face, I saw Corrine's terror. "I'm sorry, Jol."

Her face contorted. "Bastard." She turned and ran into the rain forest, disappearing in moments, even her crashing through the brush gobbled up by the lush forest.

I turned to Gueran. "Find her a place," I said. "With singletons where she can find someone . . ."

Gueran nodded. "Sure, sure. I try." He slipped into the jungle, yelling, "Good luck, Og flunky. Head for the road. Not far now."

"Soldiers!" Quant whispered. "Coming this way."

As one, the pod slipped forward onto the trail. I ran after them, catching up with them at a fork in the path.

Quant pointed toward one path, and the pod disappeared

into the green. In the distance, something howled. Sniffers: a pack of engineered dogs, built to track pheromones.

Darkness fell, a quick migration from green to pitch-black. Strom paused long enough for us to dig the one flashlight we had from a pack salvaged from Gueran's boat. He pointed the light ahead, and round eyes reflected back. The jungle was alive.

We ran through the night, Quant guiding us, redirecting us through the trunks and shrubs. Her directions did not always take us the best route, just the one that led us most south toward the road. Once we were forced to double back out of a ravine of rocks and vines. A second time, we had to travel east along a river until we could cross in a safe place, one running fast enough that we need not fear caimans and piranha.

At dawn we were exhausted, but I felt cleansed. A night of running in the darkness had shed my emotions and my anger. The loss of Jol stung, but I could not dwell on it. We rested and drank water near a small pool. The ground around us was littered with decomposing plant matter. Quant found a scorpion which she was observing intently as it searched a log for an insect breakfast.

I no longer heard the sniffers howling.

"Are we safe?" I asked.

"I doubt it," Strom said simply.

Let's go.

We had gone just a hundred meters when something slammed into my chest. I went down into the mulchy ground, stunned, unable to breathe or move. I could do nothing but watch the line of ants marching across the rain-forest floor in front of him. They were the size of my thumb.

"Well, well. We've flushed our pod," someone said. I placed the voice: Anderson McCorkle.

Something brushed past me. I pushed myself up, saw

the boots of one of the duo rushing at my face. My nose crunched.

"You won't be helping out this time, singleton."

Nausea wrecked my stomach.

In front of me, the ants crawled over the back of my hand, carrying shreds of leaves. Their feet prickled my skin. But I couldn't brush them off, too intent on the pain in my skull.

A cry came from behind me: Moira. More sounds of movement in the brush. The pods were fighting again, but now the local terrain benefited the duo. They had had time to scout it and choose it for ambush.

I pushed myself up, ignoring the brief bites of the ants.

The jungle around me was empty, eerily silent. I pressed my hands to my eyes to stop the swaying. I knelt, listening.

Somewhere nearby, someone was breathing. Somewhat farther away, someone was moving through the underbrush.

I tried standing again. Blood dripped in streaks onto my shirt. Slowly I turned.

There on the ground two meters away was Quant, unconscious and breathing shallowly. I pulled her back against a tree trunk and slapped her wrist gently.

Quant blinked, gasped, and released a wave of fear pheromone. I smelled it, pulling away in surprise. Then I knelt back down, holding a finger to her lips.

Together we stood, peering out into the forest. The morning light drove spikes of light through the trees, illuminating some areas and leaving others dark.

Quant lifted her nose, then pointed.

"Over there," she whispered.

I couldn't taste the same smells that Quant could, though I had sensed the fear pheromone. The rest of the pod was out there in the direction Quant pointed. I reached out and touched Quant's wrist, willing the chemical memories to move between us.

For a second I saw a binocular image of the jungle, but it faded into my own view.

I hissed through my teeth.

"Come on."

We slipped between green leaves, looking for our pod or the duo. The land dipped down into a small ravine, covered in dark soil and hemmed-in tree roots.

Motion ahead caught my eye.

There was the duo, ahead of us five meters down the ravine, watching Quant and me. One of the two smiled grimly, then they launched themselves.

Quant hesitated, unsure of what to do by herself, a singleton. The first of the duo tackled her. But again they underestimated me and my speed.

I dove onto the exposed roots of the tree to my left and swarmed up the tree into the branches. When I was three meters up, I turned, hanging on to a branch above me, and kicked out with my feet, catching the second of the duo in the jaw.

They both winced.

I dropped to the floor and ran. The duo followed, leaving Quant.

I ran at dangerous speeds through the tangled ravine, nearly falling, my feet barely coming free from the twisting tree roots.

I caught a smell, a trace of pheromone. To my left. Then a touch of thought.

Lead them over here.

From the right.

I dodged up the right embankment, slowed enough by the climb to feel the touch of one of the duo on my feet.

Then I was over the side, into a flat, brushless area.

I ran as fast as I could, my poor modified feet protesting that they had been built to grasp, not to be run upon. I had no time for their complaints.

Behind me I heard a yell.

Turning, I saw the remaining three of my pod confronting the duo in an ambush from behind the trees. But we had stopped short of McCorkle.

The duo had drawn his gun.

"Enough running through the jungle," McCorkle said. "This is over."

The guns waved back and forth among us.

"Over here, freak," McCorkle said, nodding at me. My heart was pounding, my breathing shallow. I could have dashed into the jungle, but that would draw his fire. Quant was still out there, somewhere.

I stepped forward, joining Strom, Meda, and Moira.

"Kneel with your hands behind your heads."

One of him pulled a wad of plastic ties from his belt: handcuffs.

"Where's your fifth?" one of McCorkle said.

The other cupped a hand to his mouth, yelled, "It's over. I have the other four."

Behind the two, a couple meters from their feet, an anthill writhed. A ring of loose dirt marked the circumference of the ants' domain. Did they realize how close they were to falling in?

I glanced at Strom, caught his eye. With all my strength, I sent, *Anthill. They're a step away from falling in.*

He looked at me, his gaze perplexed, then he seemed to catch my thought, and I heard, *We'll try it.*

"Quiet!" one of the duo shouted.

"Come on! There's no use hiding from me," the other added. "I have eighty percent of you, and you're not even the part that can function on her own." McCorkle laughed.

"Three times, I've tried to destroy you, and each time you've escaped."

"I think we'll dispense with fisticuffs and go straight to a bullet to the head."

McCorkle shared a thought, and one of him stepped forward to bind my wrists.

Quant.

Something flew from the jungle—a rock—thumping against McCorkle's wrist. The gun flew away. The other McCorkle, about to bind my wrists, dropped the bands and reached for his holster.

I pushed from my precarious position on the ground, hopping up to get my feet under me.

The McCorkle in front of me tipped over, spinning his arms. His foot slipped at the end of the anthill, and he fell screaming into it facefirst, disappearing in the loose dirt.

The other McCorkle dove for his gun, but Strom's path crossed his before he reached it. Strom slammed the man into the dirt, while Moira kicked the gun away.

His fellow was struggling in the anthill, overwhelmed by the millions of deadly insects. I reached in and pulled him out of the trap, dusting the ants from his face and neck. Already his cheeks were red and swollen. They barely struggled as we used their own plastic ties to bind their arms together.

We should leave them on the anthill, I sent.

It was so natural to slip into my pod's mindspace.

I felt their rhythmic patterns of thought, their telltale personalities.

Strom laughed.

Too good for them.

I felt Moira's hand on mine. *Welcome back.*

Too long apart.

We dragged the duo into the ravine, where we removed their equipment and any useful items. We bound their wrists, then tied them together. Their legs we left free. They would be able to make their way out of the jungle, but slowly.

We set off to the north.

We're only a few kilometers from the highway.

It should be an easy trek.

We just have to stay ahead of the sniffers.

I felt myself a part of the consensus, almost overwhelmed by it. Yet, there was no other place to be.

I could have turned them off. I could have shut my thoughts down, forced a wall up. I could have; the drug had shown me how to do it, but I chose not to.

I pushed down thoughts of what might have been—thoughts of Jol and Corrine—and ran ahead to scout the path.

FIVE

Moira

We found the North-South Highway that next morning, a span of mundane plascrete, built five decades ago by the Community to facilitate transfer of goods between continents. Ageless nano maintained the stretch, keeping the encroaching jungle off the berm and repairing any stress cracks before they became visible. Just like the microwave power transmitters, this was another piece of Community technology that pod society used freely. Along the eight-lane road, one-, two-, and three-engine cabs pulled loads at over three hundred kilometers per hour.

How will we stop one? Quant asked.

How will we stop the driver from reporting us? Manuel added.

It was easier than we expected. A truck stop, run by a clan of singletons, served as a bunching point for the long-haul trucks. We asked around until we found someone willing to give us a lift up the Isthmus of Panama into central North America. A jovial duo was glad to have us: a duo and a trio on a walkabout before starting new jobs. We figured the OG would be looking for a quintet, not two simpler pods.

In hours, we were out of the Amazon basin, rising toward the Andes, Quant listening to the driver drone on while the rest of us tried to sleep in the back.

Safe, Manuel whispered.

North, Meda replied.

We'll find the bears, Strom sent.

As I listened to our dozing thoughts, I kept my own concerns to myself. Sooner or later we would have to face what we had done, and what had been done to us.

The base camp was barren, the buildings grey and dilapidated, as if they had been abandoned for years instead of months. We had seen no one in our hike up from Old Denver, and here was more of the same. Above us loomed the summits, visible through the trees. Not far away was the river Strom had hiked down with Hagar Julian. It was still turgid with spring rains even though the snow had mostly melted from the peaks.

Nothing, Quant sent. *No sign of them.*

Strom looked away, surveying the landscape, keeping his thoughts to himself. He had grown more silent the farther we hiked. The bears were gone.

Deer, squirrels, rabbits we had found in abundance as we climbed, all unmodified. Even smaller carnivores were present; one night we had heard the howl of coyotes. Strom's bears remained hidden, and Strom took it personally.

The OG spent weeks looking for them. What chance do we have? Manuel sent.

Strom did not reply, his gaze on the peaks.

I, sensing stress in our unity, said, *Strom found them once, he can do it again.* As it came out, I realized how much pressure my words placed on Strom. But I couldn't take my thoughts back, and Quant's halfhearted consensus faded away unanswered.

Strom sent me a quick thought, *Thanks, Moira.*

We had been running for weeks, since we'd left Columbus Station, to the Ring, down the elevator, up the Amazon, and finally through Central America along the North-South Highway. I had known this could be a fool's errand, yet I had accepted consensus. Looking for the bears was a goal, some quest, some respite while we healed our sundering.

In the distance a waterfall caught the sun's afternoon rays scattering the light.

It's not like the Amazon at all, Manuel said. His thoughts still felt muffled, his emotions distant, but every day he was closer and stronger. The drug he had been administered in Bolivopolis was slowly wearing off. A wave of relief passed among us as I thought this. It had not been easy for the four of us to watch as Manuel drifted farther away.

It's almost desolate, Meda agreed.

We had passed great swaths of empty land on our trip north, areas where biological agents or radiation had destroyed everything in huge radii of death. These mountains were the first wild areas we had seen, yet the diversity was nothing compared to the Amazon.

Strom gazed across the shallow valley behind us. *Bears cover a large area,* Strom sent. He was now an expert on bears, though he had no more knowledge than the rest of us. What one of us knew, another could access. *They travel far.*

These aren't really bears, Quant pointed out. *They are gene-modded bear clusters. Bear behavior will be overridden by the intelligence built into the pod.*

We still have human patterns of behavior, Strom argued.

Overridden by pod behavior.

Let's rest, I said, wanting to deflect the argument.

While the rest of us sat, Strom remained standing. His

gaze followed the river into the mountains. We sat silently for a moment, as we passed a water bottle around.

He said three times, Strom sent, staring at the mountains.

I thought he miscounted, Quant replied.

Confusion for a moment as our thoughts circled and I tasted what we were thinking: Anderson McCorkle had said we'd evaded him three times.

Quant counted for us. *Once on Columbus Station, once in the Amazon.*

Twice in the Amazon, Manuel countered.

He could have counted that as one, Quant replied.

Strom's memory of the avalanche whisked between us. A flash of light on the mountain before the second avalanche. He had always assumed it was another aircar that had come to rescue the rest of us.

But the first had already landed. Why would they send two? Quant asked.

If they had it would have landed right then, I said.

It was the flicker of moonlight on moving snow, Strom sent.

Or an explosion meant to kill us, Quant replied, saying what we had been avoiding.

No, I can't believe that, Strom sent.

I started thoughts in the other direction, distraction. *Are we camping here?*

But Strom was already adding, *We'll check. We'll go see for ourselves.*

Our plan became twofold as we followed the river into the higher elevations: first, to find the bears, to understand what they were, and, second, to prove our consensus wrong, to prove the avalanche that had killed one of Hagar Julian had no human attribution.

Our course meandered as Strom and Quant tried to find

the best path up, back and forth through foothills and valleys, but ultimately higher and higher into the mountains. The summer heat had melted most of the glacial ice around the summit, but still the weather was chill at night, causing us to find heat among ourselves in the tent.

Of the bears we saw no sign. Though Strom thought nothing publicly, I knew he had expected to find them immediately, to discover their secret by only looking once.

We did find houses, pre-Exodus buildings, decrepit and aged, many reclaimed by the forests. One such building appeared as we climbed a cliff face, scooting up a dihedral into a clearing, the backyard of a mansion. It was larger than the creche, larger than Mother Redd's farm, yet we knew such places usually housed single families.

I guess we could have taken the road, Manuel sent. He glanced at us, and we saw the image of ourselves, covered in dust. Quant was biting at a hangnail. Meda's hair hung across her face. We shared a laugh, the first in a while.

Explore? Quant asked. She spit out her nail and took a step toward the house. Uplink dishes adorned the roofline, tastefully hidden in the gables.

No, I sent. *Kilometers to go today.* That and I didn't want to come across any signs of Community tech. All of these reminders had been left behind us for weeks. Meda needed no new reminders.

Why not? Quant asked, nettled.

I tried to share a private thought with Quant, so that she would drop it, but Meda must have caught some of it. She cast me a look, but Quant dropped it, and we moved on.

We turned away from the river then, climbing into forests of deciduous trees. A rain shower doused us before we could find shelter under an overhang of rock.

Strom stood in the rain, looking into a ravine.

Strom.

Rain washed the thoughts from the air.

He turned back to us.

I know this place, he sent. *That's where we spent the night.* He corrected himself, *Not us, but Hagar Julian and I.*

I nodded, and I pulled him tighter into our huddle. I wondered again whether we should have been searching here.

Three days later we reached the treeline. Clumps of snow covered the ground in shaded places, but mostly the mountain was rock-covered barrenness. Here and there, misshapen pine trees jutted from the ground.

Quant spotted the pattern first, pointing out the chutes where the two avalanches had flowed.

There and there, she sent. *You can see the path where the trees are gone and the rocks are turned over.*

Through her eyes, it was obvious where the rubbled chutes ran: no trees, eddies around large boulders, rock that was just starting to weather. Following them up with my eyes, I saw the ledge some three hundred meters up where they had started. An outcropping of rock split the streams.

If there's any evidence, Strom sent. *It's there.*

We camped near our campsite of a year ago, though the pines that had shielded us had been whisked away. During the night, the wind sang in the ropes of our tent, and I'm not sure that any of us more than dozed.

At dawn we attacked the slope, using our spider silk rope and the few anchors and carabiners we'd purchased in Old Denver with the scrip we'd taken from McCorkle. Manuel led the way, though he could have climbed it by himself in minutes. I found myself lost in the game of hand holds and path optimization.

Cold as the air was, we were sweating, removing coats

and tying them at our waists. Around noon we reached the summit of the outcropping, a tabletop of granite around which the avalanches had flowed. From there, the river valley spread out below us, a green cut in the mountains.

Base camp, Manuel sent, pointing to a patch of grey near the river kilometers away.

I looked down the chutes, and the destruction was clear from this vantage. From below, it had taken Quant to see it. From above, the trails of destruction were swaths of dark grey rubble.

Those avalanches took a lot of rock with them, Meda sent.

Claw marks, Quant sent. *An aircar deployed its stabilizing claw here.*

She squatted on the stone, stuck her finger in a groove of punched stone. Manuel found the second, and then paced off the distance to the third hole in the triangle.

Ten meters, he said, giving us an estimated body width.

Conojet or a Thalit, Quant replied.

Military uses Thalits.

Strom erupted in veto. *We don't know when this car was here. It could have been afterward, during the search.*

I agreed, and our consensus derailed.

Manuel scrambled up the wall a few more tens of meters, right up to the top of the sheer.

"Careful," Strom said.

Manuel didn't bother to reply and began sliding along the edge.

He stopped, hanging at a slight corner in the wall.

"Found it," he said.

"What?"

"Someone drilled a hole here." He stuck his hand into the wall. He sniffed at his fingers, then slid-climbed his way back to us.

He held up his fingers, covered in white dust. We all shared his conclusion based on the odor.

Explosives.

We spent the night on the windy outcropping, our tent spiked into the rock. There was nothing I could do to fight the depression that swirled around us. It seemed that when we could confront our nemesis—Anderson McCorkle—face-to-face we were more willing to accept someone trying to destroy us, but this new evidence that someone had wished us dead even before our internship on Columbus Station crushed us. An invisible hand was more sinister.

We have to go back now, Meda sent.

What does this change? Manuel asked.

It's proof of conspiracy against us.

We are safer here from any attacker.

Isn't it our duty to go back and report this? Meda asked, looking at me for support.

I shrugged, unsure of what responsibility we had to anyone.

Meda frowned at me, then crossed her arms across her chest.

Then what? Stay out here until winter? I'd like a shower at some point.

In the silence following, Strom sent, *We've only just started looking for the bears.*

The bears, Meda replied, *are just someone's science project.*

So? Strom replied. *They saved me. I owe them.*

Then let them be.

Strom looked away, cowed by Meda's anger. I knew I should step in and deflect this argument, but I was unsure which direction we should take. There was no safe course.

I turned to find Quant and Manuel looking at me.

Can it wait till morning? I asked.

What will be different tomorrow, or the next, or the next? Meda asked. She was pushing for consensus. Yet our bonds were still weak. Manuel had only just shaken the effects of the cluster buster drug. Meda's own psyche was tender.

Do you forget why they want us destroyed? I asked, harsher than I should have.

Quant shook her head. *This happened before Malcolm Leto,* she sent. *It's not because of what he did to us. It's something else.* I couldn't understand what it could be, but I was certain now that we were too fragile to face what would come with our accusations.

This evidence has waited months, I added. *It will wait more if necessary. The bears are important to Strom, but they are more important to pod science. If we can find them, we should.*

Consensus shifted among us, until even Meda acknowledged it, though she wouldn't meet my eyes.

The den was old: musty and scentless, but bits of fur clung to the walls and floor. Bears had wintered here, it was clear, but not this last winter.

We had been following the bear trails, from dead log to beehive to stream, for two weeks, searching for some sign of them, but all we had found were a few old footprints in some dried mud by a stream and this cave.

It smells like thought, Strom sent. He breathed deeply, taking in the odors of the cave. He played his flashlight over the walls.

"Anything?" Meda yelled from the cave mouth.

"No," I shouted back. It had been too small for all five of us to enter. So Meda, Quant, and Manuel had stayed at the cave mouth.

I sniffed too, but all I smelled was stale bear.

They're long gone, Strom.

He shrugged and we climbed up the gentle-sloped,

rubbled mouth to the outside. We shared the images and sat down to eat lunch. Quant had found a blackberry patch with fruit the size of Strom's knuckles. We'd been eating off the land as often as we could: wild strawberries, trout, blackberries, raspberries. Once we saw a herd of deer, but the idea of eating mammals disgusted us. If beavers and bears could be sentient pods, why not deer. Fish we were comfortable with eating. Even chicken, though we knew avian flocks could be cluster-modified. But not mammals. We had loyalty to our class if not our phylum.

We've trudged over these bear trails for days, Manuel sent. *Perhaps they've moved on.*

To where? Strom asked. *They must have gone somewhere.*

Whoever made them relocated them to somewhere where no one was looking for them.

Strom looked sadder than I had ever seen him. I sat down next to him and squeezed him. He was a large man, but I managed to get my arms around him.

Thanks, Moira, he sent, squeezing back.

We'll find them.

We camped there that night, not bothering to go any farther. Where would we have gone? These mountains were barren of large animals. Around the fire, we sang. We all knew the words, of course; they were part of our shared memories.

When the sun had set, and we had sung all our songs twice, all of us except for Strom filed into the tent.

"Coming?" I asked softly.

He shook his head. "I want to . . ." The image he painted was one of communion, one of meditation.

Are you ready to give up? I asked.

He looked at me, startled.

Sooner or later, we need to face the rest of the world, I added.

He nodded. *Not yet. I feel like I should know where they are.*

I knew how he felt. It wasn't uncommon for us to have intuitive knowledge or sudden thoughts just beyond our grasp. Our tandem brains seemed to dangle such things before us without making them understood by our single-ton minds. Together, our mind could make great leaps, but sometimes it leaped beyond us.

I sat in front of him.

"I can stay with you," I said. I leaned in close to him, my arms around his neck. This close, his thoughts were like thunderheads, anvils of swirling consciousness. I could barely think this close to him, he was so enveloping.

You're growing a beard, I sent.

The words "beard" and "bear" twisted in my mind, be-coming superimposed.

You're becoming a bear.

I giggled, and he laughed. My face brushed his, and I felt the roughness of it.

"Are you two coming inside?" Meda or Quant said, I couldn't tell who, my mind and ears muffled.

"No," Strom said, answering for both of us.

"Okay."

I felt the boundary between us crumble. We were wires coiled around a magnet, so tightly bound that we might as well have been one to the electrons that coursed through us.

I sighed, glad to be so close, glad to lower all my bar-riers.

Within Strom's mind I saw the bears' map, the chemical topography that marked their territory. They had shared it with Strom, and he had it in his mind, just as they had passed it to him.

I found myself falling into it as if I were free-falling from an aircar. Memories of our own trekking through the mountains superimposed themselves upon what the bears knew and understood. The significance of a termite-filled tree trunk flickered against the streams where we had filled our canteens. The cave, where the bears had lived for a winter, was beside us now.

Elevations and slopes, derivatives and topologies. To the bears, the mountains were not an area, but a linear composite: destinations strung together. Looking on high I saw the crisscross lines. Within the map, I saw the long itinerary of travels from start to finish, the finish being the camp where they had left Strom, where we had seen him.

But the start . . .

I felt myself peeling the map, following the threads back and forth, finding older and older lines, and points that had been faint memories to the bears: a salmon the length of one's arm, as thick as a neck, a beehive where the youngest had learned a nasty lesson, a fire raging through a dried-out section of trees. Faint memories, but all leading back to a start, years ago, years ago.

Through a mountain pass, through a rock-strewn ravine, to the house. The master's house.

I opened my eyes, staring straight into Strom's, aware suddenly of the cold, the dampness in my clothes. The moon had moved across half the sky while we sat. My teeth began to chatter.

He lifted me up, not even an armful.

Thank you, Moira, he sent. *I know where they went.*

I knew that I was the group's voice of reason, always controlled, always considering. But I was more than that. I could be a catalyst just like Quant. I could be a mother just like Meda. I was not just about right and wrong. It was good to be with Strom and not have to be on guard.

He carried me into the tent, and I slipped inside a sleeping bag, shivering. The warmth of the pod, the naked bodies were overwhelmingly sensual.

Coming?

No.

I dug in deeper, unzipping my pants and shedding my shirt.

You're cold. Sleepy half-thoughts, mixed with dreams.

I'm cold, warm me.

Where's Strom?

On his spirit quest.

The smell of a joke appreciated.

Hold me.

The need for warmth turned to something else, and the heat of friction warmed me through and through.

In the dawn, Strom still sat before the burned-out fire, but now dew coated his shoulders and face. He was awake, staring into the fire ring. We filed out and stood around him.

He looked up at us, his dewed face seemingly too full with tears.

"I know where they are."

Strom led us up over the lower foothills into the canyons and ridges of the higher mountains. Everywhere we turned, we were reminded of our painful stay on the mountain, and Strom's trip down. Yet, he led us onward, through alpine slopes, still snow covered, through unravaged forests, older than pods, older than the Community.

In the mountains we only averaged eleven kilometers per day. In Quant's head were tallies of every step of every day, every meter we traveled. She laid it all over the bears' map I had discovered within Strom.

We passed the highest peaks just seven days after leaving the bears' cave. Standing at the pass's crest, we saw ranges of stone, ice, and forest stretching before us. It was cold in the pass, so we lingered only long enough to find our path down. By nightfall, we were back in more temperate weather. Winter to summer in a day.

I was the one who spotted it on the way down. At first my eyes passed right over it, but then I stopped walking and stared: a paw print. Not long before, a bear had crossed this path.

Strom knelt, touched the dirt around the print. It was damp, it having rained the day before. But the print had been shielded by a holly bush next to it. There were no other prints nearby.

A week old, two weeks? Strom guessed.

All the other tracks had been obliterated. Yet it was clear what path the bear had been following: it led perpendicular to our direction, down to a placid lake, just a few hundred meters away.

It could be a loner, Manuel sent, trying to cool Strom's anxiousness. *It may not be our pod at all.*

I know, Strom sent.

We cut down the path toward the lake, slowed by the overgrown brush. Manuel pointed out a dob of fur stuck on a thorn. Meda found another soft print under a tree.

The path opened onto the lake edge; the water was rippleless. We saw no more tracks, no more indications of the bear at all. We realized then that we were stymied. The bear could have gone in any direction around the lake, and then taken off again at any point. We had not enough woodcraft to determine which direction it had gone.

Disappointment hung among us, and yet I was buoyed by what we had found. We touched palms, forming consensus.

We're close. Very close, I sent.

We'll find them, I know we will.

We're within a hundred kilometers of them for certain.

All rational thoughts, and yet there was a hint of despair among us as we pitched the tent and caught fresh fish for dinner. No one had thought it directly, but my own unshared questions hovered in my mind: how long could we stay in the mountains by ourselves? When would we have to return to civilization and face the Overgovernment?

I didn't want to dampen our hope, but these were questions we had to face sooner or later.

The next day, Strom was leading us along a forested ridge, an animal trail, when he yelped in discovery. As we ran forward, I saw the image he saw: a bear's night den, a hollowed-out depression in the dirt a meter deep and three meters across. I stepped down into the hole, marveling at the creatures that had filled it. Strom's memories of the beasts revealed their sizes, but they were in relation to Strom who is larger than the rest of us. In the den, my relative size to the beasts was apparent.

Smell that? Strom asked.

We can't share smells, oddly, but we shared his recognition of the distinct bear smell. It was not like any animal I knew.

We're close, Strom sent.

The ridge opened above a mountain lake, smoothly placid. No humans save us had seen this in decades. On the far shore, two moose pulled at grass.

Strom led us down to the shore.

Manuel sent, *Bear mud wallow here.*

The tracks were recent, bear tracks as long as Strom's foot and as wide as mine. They led around the lake; perhaps the bears were stalking moose.

We followed, gathering blackberries as we walked. The land was more giving here than even the Amazon had been. The berries were just short of ripeness, tangy and bitter. I threw a half-mashed one at Manuel and turned to grab another one before he fired back.

I heard a chuff in the berries and froze. Automatically I released fear pheromone, and as I did a beast rose up in front of me.

It was three meters high, a blond-colored grizzly bear that stared at me with light brown eyes. The chuff turned into a growl. Saliva dripped from its mouth, which was covered in blackberry juices.

Friend?

There was no pheromone smell to this bear, no chemical memories, just the musky, musty odor of the bear den we had found that morning. This wasn't a gene-modded bear; this one was wild.

Don't move. Don't turn and flee.

I had considered running. But the math was obvious even without Quant. My frail human body took me twenty kilometers an hour; the bear could run at sixty kilometers an hour for short bursts.

Fear fled from my mind, replaced by a practical view. I could see the bear from all directions. Its dished-in face was wider than my torso. Short ears adorned its head. It swung its head back and forth and chomped its jaw.

"Scat," Strom yelled. He had found a stick on the rocky shore and was waving it.

Back away slowly, Meda advised.

I took one step back, then another. The bear remained standing in front of me. On my third step, the bear charged.

I dodged to the right, diving over gravelly rocks. The bear skidded past me and turned itself.

Sand! Strom's thought.

A rock, thrown by Quant, thunked its skull, but it didn't even notice. It launched itself toward me. I threw a handful of sand at its face and rolled again.

It sneezed, but a paw grazed my chest, knocking the wind out of me. It was a beast made of steel.

Strom's branch was in its face then.

"Find a tree and climb it!" he yelled.

His branch split halfway up its length and was covered

in dried leaves that rattled in the bear's face. The rest of us dashed into the woods while Strom distracted it.

I found a tree and bolted up it second only to Manuel. We turned and pulled Quant and Meda into the top branches. From there I had a clear view of Strom dancing in front of the bear.

It reared up again, standing a meter taller than he.

He yelled and dodged in front of it.

"Hey ya! Hey ya!"

Pigeon-toed, it tottered after Strom. A claw snagged Strom's branch, tearing it from his grasp.

He turned then and ran, splashing into the lake.

Bears can swim! I sent.

Yes, but not as fast as they can run, Quant replied.

Strom stretched out and dove into the water, just a few meters ahead of the bear. The bear was running now after him, crashing into the water. But Strom was already slashing the water with his crawl stroke. Even weighed down with his wet clothes, he outdistanced the bear.

When the bear realized it would never catch him, it howled, then turned back to land. Strom stayed where he was, treading water.

The bear came back toward our shore, waddled onto the rocks, and shook itself. It sniffed the air, then looked right at us.

It can knock trees this size over, Quant sent.

But it ambled past us and disappeared into the forest.

Strom swam back to shore and pulled himself onto a boulder. We dropped down to the ground and joined him, keeping one eye on the forest line. He'd shed his backpack near the water's edge, but his shoes were lost. We wrung his thick socks out and left them to dry on the rocks.

That wasn't our bear, I sent.

I think you're right.

I was bruised but otherwise unhurt. We fashioned moccasins for Strom from our excess clothing, and then started hiking as soon as we were able. We wanted as much distance between us and that bear as we could put.

We had bought a slingshot and Quant used it to bring down fowl. When we could, we caught fish, either with spear or hook. In many ways it was an idyllic time for us, without any of the rigorous study and competition that had marked our education until then. Even Strom, who pursued his bears with a relentlessness that seeped into our dreams, relaxed in the weeks we tracked across the mountains.

It was easy to forget that the OG had tried to maim us in the Amazon, that we had run from Columbus Station, that we had nearly been sundered by drugs, and that we had avoided a mauling by centimeters.

The Ring, just ten thousand kilometers above us, a mere strip of silver, day and night, still fettered us. There was nowhere we could go on Earth or near space where it did not hover near us. And the Ring reminded us of Malcolm Leto.

To supplement our diet, we ate berries, so many berries that we pooped seeds every night. Wild blackberries lined all the trails we followed. Raspberries we also found, but not as often. The wild strawberries were too small and bitter for me to eat, but Manuel loved them.

We also ate acorns, ground into a pulp in one of our bowls and baked on a hot rock next to the fire. The roots of cattails were starchy and tasteless once boiled. With dandelion greens and morel mushrooms the roots made an almost decent soup. These were all skills we had learned in survival training. The summer was abundant, but there was no doubt that we would have to leave by fall, whether we found the bears or not. We could not survive a winter.

I know, Strom sent.

We can't search-hide forever, I sent. *We must go to Mother Redd.*

Not yet.

Later.

I could have forced a more formal consensus with veto pheromone, but I let it pass.

We saw more signs of bears, day dens and scratching trees. We also found fresh and dried scat. From afar, we watched two cubs and their mother frolic in a mud hollow. They were not our bears either.

In a valley plain, thick with tall green grass, we watched a herd of elk graze. A few minutes later, a bruin erupted from the treeline and took down a nearby elk bull. Manuel spotted it first.

Look!

The elk met the bear's charge with its new antlers, tossing the bear back. Undeterred, the bear swiped at the elk, catching its antlers and bending its neck. It flopped over on its side, and the bear was upon it, gouging flesh with its claws, and biting down on the back of its skull with its huge jaws.

Not a grizzly, Strom sent.

It was a brown bear, its fur a solid brown without the distinctive silver mane, though he looked liked a grizzly in other respects. We watched as he crushed the elk's skull, and then sat down to feed on its haunch. The rest of the herd, which had darted at the initial pounce, continued grazing not too far away, apparently unconcerned now that the bear had its kill.

After it had finished a large section of the haunch, the bear stood and dragged the carcass toward the woods. Near the treeline, it bent over and used its powerful claws to dig a hole. We learned then what the hump of muscle on its shoulders was for. With a half-dozen sweeps of its arms, it had dug open a hole that all of us could have stood in up to our knees. In this it dumped the carcass and covered it with leaves and tree limbs. Dinner for tomorrow. We watched, then planned a route around the far side of the valley; we didn't want to come between the bear and his larder.

By the time we were six weeks into our trip, we were beginning to see the futility of our hunt. I needed a decent shower, and I knew we were ranker than we could smell since our noses had grown accustomed. We had almost decided to hike back to Denver and find some sort of job for the winter, maybe trying again in the spring.

But that same day we were discussing the chill in the air and the first colored leaves on the trees, Strom's bears appeared out of nowhere and sat down at our campsite.

Strom, the biggest bear sent, a male. We did not smell the thought ourselves, but heard the call through Strom. It wasn't until later that all of us could speak directly to the bears.

"Hello!" Strom cried, and hugged the bear in his arms. Even as big as he was, his arms did not reach around the bear's neck.

This is Papa, Roam, and Sleepy, he announced.

The two females chuffed at us, and the smell of chemical thought was heavy in the air. Through Strom we understood their greetings. Sleepy sprawled down on the dirt next to us and closed her eyes.

I have seldom seen Strom more happy, and so we all were, bears and humans alike.

We followed the bears, foraging, though we were less followers than ad hoc bears. They seemed to view us as such. We followed a well-worn bear trail, feeding as we went: the same berries we had been eating all summer. The bears also chewed on pine trees, tearing away at the bark with their paws to get at the cambium layer; Roam was especially fond of the white pine and would ask the pod to take kilometer-long hikes off the trails to find one she knew of.

Whereas in a human pod, consensus governed our larger actions, Papa seemed to be the decider. Though on at least one occasion, Roam and Sleepy vetoed Papa. This was when they caught wind of other humans. Papa wanted to look for them, possibly meet them, but the two females did not. There was a spike of fear in their minds, but also resolution. Papa mentally shrugged and agreed.

It wasn't just berries and bark that the bears ate, however. We watched with fascination as Roam and Sleepy herded a huge antelope toward a hollow where Papa lurked. With a slap of his paw, he broke the animal's neck. It had taken them two minutes of effort to feed themselves for the next two days.

While they feasted on bloody antelope flesh, we caught and roasted a couple of fish over a fire. Roam watched with interest as I started the fire.

I wish I had a thumb, she sent.

I laughed, then said, *Just one?*

She looked from her left to right front paw. *One would be enough.*

Sleepy dragged a haunch of antelope over to the fire. *Cook it?*

The pod shared a glance, then I shrugged. Strom went to find a strong enough spit, while Meda and Manuel built up the fire. We roasted the antelope for them, and they ate it with the same abandon that they ate the raw stuff. They did say it tasted good.

Ninety percent of their diet was vegetarian, however, supplemented with meat every other week or so. In addition to deer, moose, and antelope, the bears caught mice, rabbits, and moles. On one occasion I saw Roam pulling up the grass turf with her paws, as if she were pulling up carpet, while Sleepy watched. As soon as the turf came up, Sleepy pounced on the mice Roam had uncovered, collecting five or six in her paws. The bears would divvy the mice up, then do it again.

The bears led us to the north, through valleys of forests and glades. An Indian summer had drawn forth the insects, the greenery, and the animals. Several times we saw deer, elk, and even a mountain lion.

Though Strom had been the only one of us who could understand the bear's speech at first, now all of us could to some extent, even without taking cues from Strom's thoughts. Their minds were not like ours. They were practical beasts, somber, yet not without humor. Their jokes came in the form of stories about silly cubs, lost cubs, arrogant cubs, who always learned better at the end. When the silverback laughed, it was a deafening, intimidating roar.

How far have we traveled today? asked Roam of me once. She reeked of humor.

Seven kilometers, I sent, getting the number from Quant.

No, we have traveled from the fallen rock to the broken stump. She laughed again.

There is a broken stump on your head.

Roam thought that was the funniest thing ever thought.

That night, as we found shelter from a summer rainstorm in a cave they knew of, the bears told us this story. Each bear took a line or two and evoked the story. Papa started it:

Little Cub found his voice one day out on a limb that was beginning to bow under his weight.

Mama! Mama! he called.

Mama! Mama! he called again, as the limb was about to snap.

"My, what a smell you have," said the blue jay. He fluttered around Little Cub's head.

Where's my mama?

"I think that branch is going to break," said the blue jay.

Go away, bird! But the blue jay didn't understand him. He had no air thoughts.

"You should call for help. I'd help you but I'm too small."

Mama!

He tried pawing himself toward the trunk, but the branch was so bowed he was hanging nearly straight down and didn't have the strength to climb up.

"If you'd just tell me who to go get for help, I'll go and get them," said the blue jay. He fluttered down and landed on the branch in front of Little Cub.

"No!" shouted Little Cub, but it was too late, and the branch snapped.

Little Cub yelled, "Mama! Mama!" as he fell, and this his mother heard.

She came running for her baby, through thorns and over hills, to find him sprawled on the ground.

Oh, my baby, oh, my baby! she thought.

Little Cub shook himself and sat up. "I'm okay, Mama!" He twisted his head, cocking his ears. "Mama! I can talk."

His mother pulled him closer and began brushing the brown leaves from his coat.

I heard. And so did the whole forest!

Then the three bears all laughed and laughed, as if it were the funniest story they had ever heard. We shared a glance and a mental shrug, then told Papa that it was the best story we'd ever heard a bear tell.

I laughed simply because the bears were happy to tell the story. Roam rolled on her back and stroked Papa's flank. I scrubbed his ears with my fingers. He massed more than all five of our pod together, and yet there was no fear in me or any of us. Who could fear someone who told such jokes and stories?

I noticed Roam's fuller belly as she lay against Papa. It was late summer now, spring long faded, but spring was the time to conceive.

You're pregnant, I sent.

Yes! she replied, suddenly more gleeful.

We all stopped petting Papa to rub her belly. She sighed wistfully.

Where did my attention go? Papa asked. He chuffed twice.

How long do bears gestate? I asked.

"Seven and a half months," Quant said, digging the fact from somewhere.

No wonder you find Little Cub so funny, I sent.

In the falling, I will have three or four Little Cubs, Roam said.

Sleepy signaled mild jealousy. I rubbed her belly too. *One day you'll have Little Cubs too.*

Sleepy replied, *Not allowed yet. Neither is Roam.*

Lightning flared and thunder crashed just outside the cave mouth. The bears jumped, and Sleepy's claws grazed my arm.

It was a searing pain, but I found myself mesmerized by the feel of it, and I didn't cry out. My pod, laughing awkwardly in the wake of the explosion, didn't even notice.

My fingers were cold and wet. Another flash, farther away now, and I saw the triple lines of black on my skin.

Blood.

Papa had smelled it.

Meda turned around then and popped on her flashlight, finding my wound.

"Uh-oh."

Come on! she added. My pod dragged me to the overhang that shielded the cave mouth. We stood in the rain, washing the wound, letting the water douse me.

I felt every single drop.

Sleeping with bears isn't always safe.

They are powerful and always armed.

Like children with guns.

Strom told me to stimulate antibodies, then wrapped the wound in gauze, then a bandage.

We settled back in the cave, but on our side now, and slept.

Each of the bears had a spider-silk bag that it wore around its neck. They used the bags to store food, which allowed them to travel farther without consideration for their stomachs, which seemed to be always clamoring for food. Around their necks the bags looked small. But they were larger than any of our backpacks.

The next morning, my arm still throbbing, I asked, *Where did you get those bags?* We humans were making breakfast over a flame while the bears were digging berries from their bags.

It's my purse! Sleepy replied.

The doctor gave it to us, Roam said, shoving Sleepy. The older female was the more aggressive of the two. When she said "doctor," I saw an image of a tall man in a lab coat. His face was almost a caricature, but then the same was true for their internal images of us. Their smell of him (and us) was unique, however, and precise. The bears were nearsighted.

They are very pretty, I sent.

Yes, said Sleepy. *I like my purse.*

She was almost as big as Roam, and Roam's shoves often produced no effect on Sleepy.

Where is the doctor? I asked.

North, Papa sent.

Are we going to see the doctor soon?

Before Roam has her Little Cubs, Papa sent.

Will the Little Cubs be part of you? I used the word for the entire entity of you, for a pod.

Roam said, *Of course.*

Papa glanced at her, seemed ready to say more, but then said nothing.

The bears spent the morning eating termites from an old log. They would take turns; two would hold the log and shake it while the third would catch a rain of termites in its paws.

Termites. Ick!

We should . . .

The pod's thoughts drifted away, and I felt for a moment like Quant feels when she zones out, mesmerized by anything and everything. But that wasn't all. My eyes were tired; they fluttered closed, and I couldn't will them to open. I knew something was wrong.

I pitched over, landing with my cheek against the mulchy dirt.

She's burning up!

Did she make enough antibodies?

Someone touched my wrist and I winced.

We need to get her to a doctor.

The bears looked down at me, Roam licking her lips of termites. The image I took from her was of a handsome doctor in a lab coat, taking care of her and her pod.

We know a doctor. He can help her.

I passed in and out of consciousness, alternately groggy and hyper from fever. Something had infected the cut on my arm, something I didn't have the antibodies to defend against.

I imagined legions of white blood cells fighting a

pitched, scorch-and-burn battle around my radius, across my ulna. Guerrillas were hiding out in the lowlands of my carpels. In my mind the battle was in bright color and loud sound.

Strom and Papa took turns carrying me. I lost track of who was who, until Strom was fur covered and Papa walked on two legs. I tried to keep my thoughts to myself, but I flooded the air around me again and again with hallucinations.

That night Meda and Quant coaxed me into making different kinds of antibodies, but I remembered that from later. Then, I was engaged in a dream world of pulsating colors. It was only after the fact that I remembered the trek through the high mountain valley, following the bears to their home, and the meeting with Dr. Immanuel Baker. I remember it all as a play or a movie, removed from it, seeing myself as one bit player with a single action: hallucinate. Again, with feeling.

I awoke in the middle of the night, in a room with Meda and Quant. The boys weren't there. They dreamed of trees and flying through the branches. I had no idea where I was. My arm was bandaged and stiff.

I tried the door and stepped out into a dimly lit hallway. The air was damp, as if we were underground. The walls were concrete block. I smelled the bears: their odor permeating everywhere, their thoughts nearby but indecipherable.

I felt refreshed, impatient, and picked a direction at random, following the hall until it opened into a large lab. Gene-splicers, old ones, but rows and rows of them, lined the walls. Chromatographs. Computers, presingularity models. DNA analysis tools. The room was a genetics lab using the height of pre-Community technology. It was almost archaic, but the lab was decked with more firepower than Mother Redd had access to at her lab on the farm.

"Hello, there. Alive, I see."

I turned. A man stood there, dressed in a lab coat. He was tall, thin, and perhaps seventy years old. His hair was full and white, his goatee well clipped. A name drifted into my consciousness, a name I overheard when I was spinning in visions.

"Dr. Baker."

He stepped over to me, and, instead of shaking my hand, he flipped my wrist over. Unwinding the bandage, he clucked and nodded.

"The forest has some nasty beasties in it. Good thing I had good old-fashioned penicillin."

"Yes," I said.

"Interested in my lab? Your pod and your friend were," he said. "You missed the tour."

"I'd like that. How long . . . ?"

"Oh, you've been here for twenty-four hours or so," Dr. Baker replied. "Amazing, really, that the bears knew what to do. Bringing you here when you'd been injured."

"The bears knew—" I stopped. Didn't he know how smart the bears were?

"Yes, you like my bears? Probably scared you when you found them, but really they're meek creatures. I made them that way."

"They're wonderful."

"Yes, wonderful creatures, bears," the doctor continued. "Trick of fate that primates lead to sentience and not *Ursidae*. Fabulous genome to work with, fascinating. As you all shall soon learn."

"We will?" I asked.

"That little cut almost killed you, but it brought you to me!" A gene-splicer beeped and he scuttled around the lab table to the far side. "I'm not a young man, you know. I've been working in here for decades. Sometimes with assistance, sometimes not. But now I need someone to help me, help me carry on. And look at what happens: two biologist pods arrive, to be sure only a trio and duo, but that's enough, I think. Now I have someone to help with the bears."

I began to realize that things had transpired while I was unconscious. The need to go and consense with my pod was an itch.

I said, "I should get back to my pod."

"Really? I'd like to show you around. No time like the present," he said. "I really do have so much for you two to do, now that the bears have come back." I backed away, as he came closer holding a beaker in his hands. "Take a look at this."

"Moira! There you are."

Meda and Quant were at the door of the lab, looking alarmed. I clasped hands with them.

We awoke and you were gone, Quant sent.

I woke up and wandered.

Dr. Baker came out of the lab.

"Good morning, Doctor."

"Oh, yes. Good morning. I guess we'll have breakfast instead of a tour of the lab," he said.

As we ate, I caught up on what I had missed. Quant and Meda passed me memories of what had transpired in the time I was unconscious and fevered.

When the infection had taken root and none of the antibodies my pod helped me produce seemed to work, the bears had led us to the doctor's research station. It had been a two-day hike to the station, which was an underground bunker, hidden in a pine forest. I remember brushing the needles with my fingers, though this was Meda's memory, not mine.

The doctor had been happy to receive us and his medical supplies had cured me in the day we had been there. We had pretended to be a trio and a duo again, because we had no idea if the doctor was associated with the OG; now we knew that he was not. It would not have mattered if we had shown ourselves as a quintet; his facility had no connectivity with the outside world.

In the tour, he had proudly shown us the equipment he had used to build his ursines: the one we had met was the sixth in a line of pods. He was proud of their bonded nature and was certain they shared basic thoughts.

My guess that he had no idea how intelligent the bears were was correct. He had no way to understand what or how they thought. He based all his conclusions on observed characteristics and dissections.

Did he . . . ?

No, our bears are in a pen next to the lab, Meda replied.

He has no idea what he's created or that we can communicate with the bears, I sent.

None.

Dr. Baker created breakfast with the same scientific zeal that he spliced genes. The eggs sat atop a mound of some unknown grain. The milk had a perplexing thickness. The jam was made from unidentifiable fruit.

"Eat!" he said. "Eat! We've so much to do today." He flicked on a monitor hanging in the kitchen. "The boys are already working."

Working? I asked.

Meda flushed. *We sort of agreed—*

—to help Dr. Baker out, Quant finished.

Without me? I asked, remembering the last time they made decisions without me, we had found Malcolm Leto.

Meda shrugged. *Sorry.*

I was angry, but I let it drop. I did not like Dr. Baker's manner, but that was after only one meeting, and purely a superficial observation. Still, that the pod had made a major decision without me annoyed me.

After breakfast we found Strom and Manuel feeding the

bears in their pen. I could almost hear the bears' depression at being limited to two hundred square meters. Yet they seemed to be relaxed.

"They should be out roaming," I said. Meda glared at me.

I'm interface, Meda said.

He's not pod human. He doesn't understand the rules, I replied. I realized I was pettily undermining Meda's role as she had mine while I was unconscious.

He's looking at us, Quant sent.

Dr. Baker harumphed. "Think amongst yourselves, don't mind me."

"We were just thinking the bears should be able to roam free," Meda said.

"Not while we've got work to do," Baker replied. "The male has a broken tooth. We need to cap it."

"Papa," Meda said.

"What's that?"

"His name is Papa."

"You've named them, have you? Don't get too close to them. They are still wild animals."

Meda came close to saying it was what he called himself before I sent, *Don't say it!*

"Yes, Doctor."

"I'm so glad you're here. I'm so glad you're interested in the bears," he gurgled. "I need someone to watch how they deal with being a trio. Bears are solitary by nature, except for sows raising their young. How does podlike faculties affect their solitary nature? I need to know. I'm just not as spry as I used to be. Field work hurts my knees."

Why is he doing this all by himself? I asked. My superficial impression of Dr. Baker wasn't changing.

"We'd be glad to help. But really, you should contact the OG and share your research," Meda said.

Dr. Baker looked at her with hooded eyes. He lost his

visage of lovable scientist, replaced it with a predatory gleam.

"The OG is no better than the damned Community. One and the same. One and the same."

Better drop that subject, I offered.

"Look at what they did to you," he said, nodding at Quant. "Saddled you with broken goods. I'd like to test that one."

"You are not testing me!" Quant said.

"Look how intelligent she seems now that she's with the other two. Alone, she probably can't understand a word I say."

It was Quant's turn to glare. "I can understand you fine!"

"Yes, yes, to you it would seem so." He scratched his beard, yellow with egg yolk. "Why use a damaged human in a pod? What good?"

"I have my skills!"

"What was their goal in building you?" he mused. "Don't you wonder?"

"Maybe we should see about Papa's tooth," Meda said, changing the subject.

Papa looked at the needle with trepidation.

Sharp.

I saw you take a hundred stings for a honeycomb, I sent, stroking his ear.

Where's the comb? he asked. His thought was tinged with irony.

Your tooth hurts, doesn't it?

He nodded. I stuck the syringe into his neck. After a moment his eyes glazed and his head lolled onto the table in the lab. It was so heavy, I could barely line it up with the MRI aperture.

"That was easy," Dr. Baker said. "He usually fights the needle."

Roam and Sleepy watched from a window, with the boys trying to distract them. It was no use; even from inside I could smell the concern.

"The three of them are very close," Meda said.

"Yes," the doctor said. "The last trio . . . only two of them came back. They have tracking chips, but I have no way of knowing what happened."

"How old are Papa, Roam, and Sleepy?"

"Six years old. They're my fourth pod of bears, the one that's stayed together longest." The machine hummed. It was old tech, big and clunky, yet the image of Papa's skull was clear. "See the vomeronasal organ? See how big it is? This is one of the things I had to fix in your DNA."

"What?" Meda asked.

"In you pods, the vomeronasal organ, on either side of your septum, is enhanced to receive the pheromonal scents that you pass between yourselves."

"We know that. We've had biology."

"Don't get feisty," Dr. Baker said, laying a hand on Meda's shoulder. "Basically, humans used to have better pheromonal communication than they did at the end of the last century. Pod biology just took advantage of the capabilities that were dormant in the normal human DNA. Only not all of it."

"What do you mean?"

"Chemoreceptors in pod humans are about three percent as efficient as they could be. As they are in the bears."

Purposely? I asked.

"Are you saying that pod DNA is purposely sabotaged?" Meda asked.

"Yes," Dr. Baker said, as he maneuvered a pair of plastic forceps into Papa's mouth, one eye on the MRI screen, one on the bear's mouth. "Where is it?"

Pod DNA is sabotaged, Quant sent. *Purposely decayed performance. Conspiracy.*

Hold on, I replied. *We don't know for sure. It could be simple chance. Maybe that's the only deficiency for some reason lost to antiquity.*

What else is masked? What else is deficient? Quant asked.

"What else?"

"Oh, lots of things. Chemical memory speed. Weak ties to recessives. Things I can't even begin to understand yet. It's amazing that you pods are still around. Should have died out long ago. With the Community, which made you."

Quant, Meda, and I found ourselves staring at each other.

We need to consense! I sent.

Meda signaled the boys with her hand. They were in the pen, separated by glass with the sow bears. *Need you now!* she signed.

Strom caught it and nodded. He grabbed Manuel and they came in from the pen. The doctor didn't notice when we slipped away.

He's crazy! Manuel sent when we replayed conversation. *Pods and the Community are utterly . . . different.*

They're fundamentally the same thing, Quant replied. *Groups of humans.*

The Community used silicon and computers.

The brain is a computer.

It doesn't matter. My brain is nothing like a silicon-based computer.

How much do we really know about the origins of the pods? I asked, diverting our argument.

We knew what we'd learned in school; the first pods had been built seven decades before, a duo, by two geneticists. They had simple sharing of feelings and moods with pheromones. The duo, caught in a feedback loop of anger and hate, had murdered one of their creators, their father.

One of the duo, someone corrected.

The other of the pair had then committed suicide, immediately afterward. But that hadn't stopped the genetic engineering. Triplets had already been pod-modified with rudimentary ability to share physical memories.

The Community AIs weren't created until a decade after the first pods.

But that doesn't mean the Community couldn't have subverted the pod research.

Why?

And why did the Community disappear? If it created and needed the pods, why leave them behind?

We need more data.

More data.

The doctor was the source of that data. The question was how to get it and how to determine its reliability.

We helped Dr. Baker do physicals on all the bears. In addition to Papa's broken tooth, we fixed a broken nail on Sleepy's claw and stitched an old wound on Roam's flank. The bears drowsed the day away, content to sleep in their paddock and have their meals brought to them.

"Lazy bears," Strom said affectionately as we fed them dinner.

Yes, Roam replied, yawning.

In addition to bear care and feeding, we tried to understand the bear genome and what Dr. Baker had done to it. He let us have time on his sequencer, but wouldn't tell us the answer. It was as if we were back in school after a six-month hiatus. Dr. Baker treated us as if we had taken the position he'd offered as lab assistants, even though we hadn't officially accepted.

Why shouldn't we take the jobs? Manuel asked. *What's the downside?*

Dr. Baker is the downside, I replied.

Why? Manuel shot back.

Paranoia, god-complex, delusions, I ticked off.

He's eccentric, Manuel sent.

He treats the bears like animals.

Well, they are.

Sentient animals, just like us.

Quant was bent over the sequencer screen, listening only partially to the argument. *I don't understand this at all,* she sent.

The rest of us shared her view, but even with all five of us analyzing it, the sequence made no sense.

We've asked Dr. Baker. He won't explain this.

He's forgotten, Manuel sent. It might have been true. Dr. Baker seemed to forget many things. Nor would he discuss the pod-Community connection, waving his hand muttering how it was all in the past.

"Not important! Not important!" he said.

Our expertise was not genetic engineering. We knew the basics; after all, one summer we had built a duck pod on Mother Redd's farm, a science fair project with unexpected results. But we had never meddled with human or mammal DNA.

I have no idea what these sequences do! Quant sent.

They look like they build enzymes, Meda said.

Obviously!

Don't get snippy!

They must catalyze the conversion of chemical memories to brain memory, Manuel sent.

Quant cut back her retort. We'd been studying the genome for hours, and we were all tired.

We need Mother Redd.

We could call her.

And she would call the OG.

She would not!

Enough! I sent. *We need a break.*

"Hello!" Dr. Baker's voice issued tinnily from the box next to the door. "Would you be so kind as to lead the larger female into the examination room?"

Roam followed the boys from the paddock to the examination room, while we filled a syringe of anesthesia for Roam.

"We've got to abort her fetuses," Dr. Baker said as he entered.

"What?" Meda said.

"No!" I shouted.

Dr. Baker looked at us, his bushy eyebrows raised. "Yes, of course. We can't let them breed yet!"

"But Roam wants her cubs," Meda said.

"Nonsense, she doesn't even understand she's pregnant."

The door opened and Roam walked in with Strom and Manuel.

He wants to abort Roam's cubs! I sent.

Strom stopped where he was, his face contorted. I felt anger from him.

"She does know she's pregnant," Meda said. "She does know."

What does "abort" mean? Roam asked, scratching her ear.

"Don't anthropomorphize these bears more than necessary," Dr. Baker said. "Yes, their descendants will one day rule the world, but these three are only a few steps away from being wild animals."

Manuel painted the picture for Roam, faster than I could say not to.

Roam blinked, then bawled as if in pain.

The room seeped with fear pheromone. Roam knocked Strom away as if he were a paper doll. She went for the door to the paddock, but it was already shut. She clawed at the lock, gouging the metal.

Papa!

We won't let him do it, I sent.

Roam's claws found the edge of the door, and it began to buckle under her strength.

Dr. Baker took the syringe from my hand and dashed forward.

No!

He plunged the syringe into Roam's flank before we could stop him.

Roam turned, knocking Meda aside. Her roar shook the room. Outside in the paddock, I saw Papa prick his ears up.

Roam chuffed at Dr. Baker and took two steps toward him before she collapsed.

"She went wild," Dr. Baker panted. "As if she knew what we were going to do."

"She did," I said, angry.

Dr. Baker's eyes squinted, and he looked at each of us. When his eyes came to Meda, still on the ground, he gasped.

Her hair was off her neck, revealing the interface jack clearly.

"You're with *them*!" he yelled. "I should have known!"

He ran from the room, and we stood slowly, dusting off Strom who had slid into the wall from Roam's push. Outside Papa and Sleepy were sniffing at the door, now bent in its frame. Roam whimpered in her sleep.

We have to explain.

Then he won't blame us.

And he won't kill Roam's cubs.

We started for the lab, when Dr. Baker appeared in the doorway of the examination room.

Look out!

Strom had just started to take control, when it was as if portions of me started to black out. I tasted something strange from Meda, and she collapsed. Then Quant.

I was near the back and backpedaled to the wall, avoiding most of the gas. The mist hung in the air. Dr. Baker, wearing a mask, sprayed another burst at Manuel, who dodged but still took enough in to knock him out.

Without the rest of my pod, my brain suddenly felt lethargic. Things that seemed obvious a moment before were vague and elusive. I leaned back against the wall, waiting for the mist to dissipate, hoping that Dr. Baker didn't squirt more.

He looked at me, and I was certain he would spray me in the face, but he put the bottle down, and drew a pistol. Manuel would have known the model. To me it just looked deadly.

"Without the rest of your cohort, you're not so sure of yourself, are you?"

"Dr. Baker," I said, pausing to consider my words, something Meda would never do. "We're not your enemy."

He knelt and pulled Meda's hair from her neck. "I know what this means," he snarled.

"You don't," I said. "You're dead wrong. And you're wrong about the bears."

He snorted. "I am the creator. I know what the bears are, down to their double helix. Don't taunt me."

"The bears are sentient. They"—I grasped for some proof—"tell stories!"

"You've been fooled by your wishful thinking," Dr. Baker said, waving the pistol. "I don't know what your game is, but I've planned for when the Community finds me. I have a second lab. I can restart there after this site is destroyed."

"We aren't allied with the Community. The Community is gone!"

"This says otherwise." His eyes drifted over Meda's interface jack.

"It wasn't what we wanted! It was rape!"

"More blather. I trust what I see with my eyes and what I make with my own hands. Pods have been corrupted from the start by the Community, and your appearing here and now proves it."

He was too certain of himself to argue with. I felt tears of frustration crawl down my face. "You won't destroy the bears, will you?"

He looked at me. "They're just animals."

"They aren't." I hated myself for my lack of control, for my inability to reason with this singleton. At the paddock door, Papa and Sleepy huffed through the opening in the bent door frame.

Moira? Okay?

I knew then what I had to do. It was all I had left, even though it was the worst choice.

He's going to kill Roam and all her little cubs, I sent.

"What are you doing?" Dr. Baker asked. "Your pod is unconscious—"

Papa ripped the door from its hinges with a swipe of his paw. In a single stride he was on top of Dr. Baker, who managed one last comprehending look at me before Papa ripped his face to shreds. His screams were silenced a moment later when teeth slashed through his throat.

I crawled onto a lab bench, drawing my feet above the spread of blood across the floor, and clutched my knees to my cheeks. I sobbed and sobbed, even after Papa had dragged the doctor's corpse into the paddock, even after Sleepy came and licked my hair.

We watched from a distance as the lab burned. Doctor Baker had set a charge before coming to kill us and the bears. All of his work was in ruins, though he had carried a copy of key genomes and discoveries in his pocket. We had that now, in Manuel's pack.

The bears stood with us, silent in thought and voice, watching as we did.

Finally, I sent, *You should head far away from here.*

Roam shook herself, snorting. *You should come with us.*

It was the same offer Strom had been presented.

Strom hesitated, looked at me. I shook my head.

No.

What we had learned from Baker would have to be reconciled. There was no hiding from it, and we, caught in the crux of the matter, were the only ones to address it. In the distance, Quant picked up the whine of the aircar, perhaps drawn by the smoke of the flaming bunker.

Papa stood, leaned over me with his bulk and licked my face.

Goodbye, they sent. They lumbered into the woods, disappearing from sight as the aircar landed.

Quant noted, as we wiped saliva from our faces, that the aircar was civilian. A duo opened the door and climbed out. Each of him held a rifle.

"Was that a bear?" he called.

He walked closer, keeping an eye or three on the treeline.

"Bears are unpredictable," he said. "Gotta be careful with them."

"Sometimes," Meda said.

Campfire got out of control.

Foolish kids out hiking.

They weren't our thoughts. We had caught the duo's chemical thoughts as he approached. Meda smiled.

"It wasn't our campfire."

The man stopped.

Did she just . . . ?

Isn't that the quintet the OG is looking for?

"Yes, the OG is looking for us. Go back and radio it in," Meda said.

The man looked flustered. He turned and walked quickly to the aircar where he stayed until we heard the whine of military craft in the distance.

I found I was crying again. Regardless of what Dr. Baker had planned for us, my actions had led to his death, and it hurt.

It was necessary, Meda sent.

I shook my head, unable to answer with thought. I was too confused, too angry.

Self-defense, Strom sent simply.

No blame on you, Manuel added.

I know, I sent, but that didn't stop the hurt. Still, I felt a resolve grow in me.

The military aircar landed in the clearing, sending up a spray of pinecones and mulch.

They're going to expect answers, Meda sent nervously.

So are we, I replied. I took her and Strom's hand.

SIX

Apollo

The aircar is a Scryfejet 1200X. It comes in from the east with a roar of its hydrogen-burning engines, scattering a roost of birds from the trees. Quant follows their flight in the air, watches the pattern as they re-form, split, and re-form before landing again in the trees.

Big one, Manuel sends. *Could hold ten pods.*

The schematics for the aircar flit among us: thrust curves, performance numbers. From Quant comes the feel of its yoke. From Strom the look of a sunset at ten thousand meters. From Moira the fact that it could hold twenty-five military duos.

This drives us to consense, touching palms, swapping chemical memories, reaching decisions.

We stand in a circle, each grasping the wrists of two others, the easier to share the chemical memories secreted from the pads on our wrists. There is comfort in this for us, to shed individual thinking for the group mind.

The bears are gone, Strom sends. The last lingering

trace of their goodbye has faded away. They had sadly watched the laboratory burn as we had ignored the blood in their fur.

Mother Redd is here.

We don't have to turn for all of us to see Manuel's view. He shares it with the pod: Mother Redd stepping off the aircar ramp, all three of her, and she alone. The pilot, a duo, looks at us from the front bubble.

Military, Strom assesses. We have seen enough military duos to know. We remember the genetically programmed swiftness and precision. We remember their viciousness. If it had not been for the ants, McCorkle would have killed us in the Amazon.

Move off into the trees.

Mother Redd will follow.

In case there are more duos on the aircar.

Just in case.

Let's go.

We walk into the trees.

"Apollo!" Mother Redd yells. She is fifty meters away.

Quant pauses to wave her forward, then she is lost from sight as we jog into the trees.

Moira remembers nothing from the walk here. She was unconscious and febrile. She asks for Strom's memories, and touches his wrist to retrieve them. For a moment she is Strom, strength and justice, and she sees the path we and the bears took to reach the laboratory.

Manuel brachiates into a tree, a pine tree with sticky sap that will take a long time to get out of his clothes. But the sap fixes his grip when he plants it, and he reaches the wobbling top.

Just Mother Redd is leaving the car.

His words are weak on the wind. It is what we say, even when there is no wind. There is none in this pine forest.

The pungent smell of pine is heavy in the air. Our feet sink centimeters into the needles.

We stop and wait, not bothering to consense, lingering in individual thoughts that we may or may not share later.

We hear Mother Redd before we see her.

She is old.

She is older than we remember.

It has been only a few months.

"Child?" she calls.

"We're here," Meda replies.

They are holding hands, the three of them as they come down the path, mindful of the surfaced roots of the pine trees.

We construct a fourth Mother Redd, superimposed at the end of the three walking. She had once been a quartet, but one of her died.

When she is five meters away, we begin to hear her thoughts.

We must be strong.

We must be firm.

He must do what we tell him.

The smell of Mother Redd's chemical thoughts is the same as we remember from the farm, but now we can *understand*. It is assumed that each pod's thoughts are private, that no other pod can understand another. Yet we have found that we can understand the bear's. And now we understood Mother Redd's. This does not surprise us.

"You will not be able to control us," Meda says.

Mother Redd stops in surprise.

He has anticipated our words.

We will try subtlety.

Apollo respects us and moral rightness.

Focus on Moira.

The calculated manner shocks us, for just a moment.

No one should be this intimate, Strom sends.

We are this intimate with each other, Quant replies.

A person's true self is revealed when no one is watching, Moira sends.

"Apollo, it's time you come back to the farm. There's work to be done," Mother Redd begins, watching Moira's face. "The OG has—"

"—tried to disassemble us."

"That's nonsense."

What does he know? Mother Redd is three identical females, yet it is clear to us who is thinking, and a name we have not known before, Martha, attaches to the thoughts.

Where did he learn this? Rachel.

It's odd to know she has three names, other than Mother Redd.

"Cluster—" Manuel starts, from the trees above.

"—buster," Quant finishes below.

"Heard of it?" Meda asks.

They got to him!

How much damage have they done?

"Just our naïveté is destroyed," Meda replies. Mother Redd doesn't even realize we are hovering on the edge of her mind.

"They are a rogue segment of the OG, Apollo," Mother Redd cried. "They aren't—"

He's in our mind.

Panic smell fills the air, and Mother Redd is backing up fast. They squeeze their hands shut to block us out, but it is no good.

Manuel drops from his tree and touches Vivian's palm. We are an octet. Memories that we can't escape drift through our mind:

Scarlet Redd looked at the printout from Khalid's genesplicer.

What the hell?

Scarlet never cursed. Her sisters looked up. They had just finished implanting a possible gene to enlarge the vomeronasal organ in beavers.

Martha touched Scarlet's wrist and the four saw what she saw on the paper.

He's building a quintet.

What?

He's not that good!

Who gave him permission?

It was true; he was going to try for a quintet. Peake, who had built the first quartet years before, had tried quintets but they aborted after six weeks. The OG Eugenics Department had refused all requests for a quintet after that.

The door to the lab slid open and Khalid walked in. One of him saw the paper in Scarlet's hands, and he flushed.

"I didn't mean for you to see that." He took the paper from Scarlet's hands.

They shared the lab with two other postgraduates at the Institute. It wasn't big enough for all four of them to work together at one time; it was barely big enough for Redd and Khalid. His thoughts mingled with hers, pungent and wrong.

"Who gave you permission to do this?" Martha asked.

One of Khalid shrugged, while the rest examined the paper.

"Tell me, or I'm going to Yeats."

"Yeats already knows!"

"Where did you get this code?"

"You don't think I could do this?"

"I know you couldn't do this."

Khalid crumpled the paper up. "Well, you're wrong. It's possible that some us are as smart as you." Tossing the paper into the trash at the door, he said as he left, "Your undoing will be your arrogance, Redd."

Idiot!

Cretin!

Vivian retrieved the paper from the trash. It was only a high-level summary of the genome. The sequences themselves were stored in the gene-splicer. Khalid was trying to build a viable set using standard donor sequences. When he was done, he would build RNA strands that would modify the DNA in an egg, which would then be transferred to an artificial uterus.

Rachel checked the rows of uteri inside the clean room; it was kept at a positive pressure and behind preatomic steel. There could be no chance of contamination or stray gamma rays in the womb room. Beavers and dogs, but no humans. He hadn't gotten that far yet.

He shouldn't be doing this.

What if it's approved?

We would have heard!

Let's ask Cahill.

Dr. Cahill, Redd's advisor, a trio, and an expert in human cloning, was in her office.

"How's the work coming?"

"Slow. We have a question on something else. Some work someone else is doing in the lab."

"Yes. Is this a safety concern?"

"Sort of. Someone is building a quintet."

Dr. Cahill's lips pursed. "I know."

She knows!

"Did the Eugenics Department lift the ban?"

"No, not yet."

"Then . . ."

"We're anticipating a change in the department's policy. We want to be prepared. Khalid's work is hypothetical until the egg is implanted."

Scarlet smoothed the crumpled paper and handed it to Dr. Cahill.

"He's already got an RNA sequence. He's ready to implant."

Dr. Cahill took the paper. "Rooting through the trash, Ms. Redd? That isn't appropriate."

"I didn't root! He left it on the sequencer!"

"Be that as it may—"

She's brushing us off.

"Does Yeats know?"

"Of course the chairman knows," Cahill replied. "I know there's competition between you and Khalid. I know that some of this may be driven by professional jealousy."

Let's go.

She's turning things around on us.

"Good day, Dr. Cahill," Martha said, and Redd left.

She found herself walking through the housing district of the Institute, lights beginning to flicker on in the dusk. What had seemed her home, where she had strived all her life to be, was ominous and strange. Dr. Cahill's defensiveness unnerved her.

Let's visit Nicholas, Martha suggested.

He's busy studying for term exams, Rachel sent.

Too busy for us?

A spark of arousal washed away the odd feelings. They had met Nicholas in an economics class. He'd helped her through a rough section on pre-Singularity capitalism, and she had helped him through a required biology class. Neither of them had needed that much help, but it had been an excuse to drink coffee together. They'd been lovers for a year.

Nicholas was three males and a female, handsome all of them, and he greeted her with a smile.

"Finishing up a paper. Almost done really," he said.

"Then you deserve a break," Martha said. "And we

need a break too." All four of Nicholas smiled at the invitation.

The apartment was small, and when all eight of them were together, with thoughts mingling together, it was cozy. If they hadn't been intimate, it would have been claustrophobic.

They cleared the apartment, and Nicholas pulled down the beds from the wall. The hour they spent was a welcome release.

"Shouldn't you be in the lab?" Nicholas asked. One of him stood to open a window. The room was stuffy suddenly. Gleaming bodies sprawled across the beds.

Vivian flushed the toilet and said, "It's Khalid."

"Him again. You spend so much time talking about him, I was worried you and he were attached when we first met."

A bolt of annoyance flashed among Redd. Nicholas caught it and shrugged.

"I didn't mean anything by that." Redd nodded.

I'm glad he has a female within him, Scarlet sent.

It was not the first time she had thought that. Khalid was entirely male.

"I know. He's just . . . unbearable in the lab."

"We economists don't have to share our calculators, at least. You geneticists don't have enough gene-splicers to go around."

He—his female part—brought water from the refrigerator, a two-liter bottle that they passed around playfully before spilling half on a pillow.

"He's building a quintet."

"I thought that was illegal."

"It *is*! That's the point."

"Oh, if he's doing illegal conception work, shouldn't you tell your department head?"

"I told Cahill, and she said it was approved."

"Well, there you go. All settled."

"No it's not. If the Institute had approval for a quintet, it would be common knowledge."

"Not to the economists."

"It would be big news, at least in my circle. It most certainly wouldn't be a surprise to me. I'm in the department!"

Nicholas frowned. "I guess so. But if Cahill . . ."

"I don't know what it means. Maybe the department is doing this secretly. Maybe they hope to have viable humans before anyone finds out."

"They wouldn't be any different than other pod-modified humans, right?"

"They'll be different. More pheromonal through-put. More natural propensity for consensus."

"But they could pod-bond into a trio or a quartet or a quintet, right?"

"But he's planning to make a quintet!"

"Okay, okay. What are you going to do about it?"

"I don't know," Redd said.

"Nothing nefarious, I hope."

"No, nothing like that," she replied, but her mind was already working.

Let's hack his computer, Scarlet sent.

No, we can't do that, Vivian replied.

Well, we could do that, Martha added.

But we won't!

The thought of hacking Khalid's computer came and went. She doubted his security would beat her dogs, but getting caught would get her kicked out of school.

We wouldn't get caught, Scarlet sent.

Instead, after getting home to her apartment, Redd posted a message to the genetics board, asking if anyone had heard of research being done on quintets. The board was for genetics grad students, but was frequented by a number of postdocs and professors. As she half expected, her post started a flame war, but before it started she'd ascertained that no one knew about quinary work going on.

The next morning she had a private message in her inbox. Under her heading of "Quintet Research Ongoing" was a single line, "Why? What do you know?"

That's a Eugenics Department address, Martha sent.

If we rat Khalid out, the department will get ripped apart.

If his research is unapproved.

There would be a hint if it was!

Scarlet typed, "No, just a rumor from someone I know at the Eugenics Department," and sent it off.

Redd got to the lab early for her shift, early enough to see what Khalid was doing. Khalid was chief postdoc in the shift before hers.

She found him in the womb room, flushing one of them for cleansing.

"There is no authorized quintet research," she said.

Khalid cocked an eyebrow, then grinned. "As far as you know."

Smug fucker!

"I checked with the Eugenics Department."

One of him blanched, and Redd didn't fail to notice the musk of chemical thought surging between the four.

Scared him.

The Institute is stepping outside Eugenics's mandate.

"What—?"

But a wave of control swept though him. He smiled and shrugged.

Bluff.

"I told my friend over there that you were going to do some quintet work. He was very interested."

"What proof do you have? You're just guessing."

Vivian pointed to the gene-splicer in the outer room.

"I sent him a printout of your supersecret formula."

Khalid paled again.

"You—" he started, then he flushed and ran past her.

Hit something there.

Khalid had left the womb open, so one of Redd finished flushing it before returning to help the other three in the lab. She was deep into the analysis of her gene sequence, when an undergrad came by to say that Dr. Cahill wanted to see her.

Uh-oh.

Cahill waited for her with three pairs of hands folded together.

She's not happy.

"Yes, Dr. Cahill."

"I'll be blunt, Dr. Redd," she said. "If you release unauthorized information regarding Institute research to anyone at all, your postdoctoral status will be terminated and your record marked accordingly."

Scarlet barked a laugh, faster than they could consense.

Cahill glared.

The bitch, Scarlet sent.

She's threatening our career, Martha replied.

They're scared, Vivian sent.

Scared of what we could spill, Rachel added.

But what is it? Martha asked.

Scarlet sent, *Fuck her.*

Veto surged from the other three. *All right,* Scarlet replied.

"Isn't the Institute funded by the Eugenics Department?"

Cahill frowned. She hadn't expected Redd to change the direction of the conversation.

She expected us to roll over.

"Some of it."

"Some meaning ninety-five percent, if I remember last

year's budget numbers. I doubt my career could be that damaged if I reported findings to the group who hired us to do the work."

"This work isn't funded by the OG!"

Gotcha!

"What work? And who would be funding it?"

Cahill stood as one, and said, "Remember what I have told you if you value your career."

Redd said at the door, "I value mine probably as much as you value yours."

For the remainder of the afternoon, Redd set her students on rudimentary lab chores to keep them out of her hair while she consensed. The world ten years after the Exodus was simple; there was the Overgovernment, which funded everything. No private corporations were allowed, though the OG funded certain enterprises, and sometimes even competing enterprises. Nicholas had called it "emergency socialism with faux-capitalist tendencies. It'll never work for long, but no one can think of anything better. Pods are born socialists anyway."

Redd could think of no one who would be funding quintet research. The singleton enclaves? It wasn't even imaginable. Another institution? Why pass the glory to a competitor? It made no sense.

She left the lab early and walked to Khalid's apartment; she'd been there once to grade mid-terms. Khalid opened the door in pajamas.

"What do you want? Didn't you get spanked enough today?"

"Who's funding the research, Khalid?"

"Wouldn't you like to know?"

Goad him.

"Where'd you get the gene sequence? I know you aren't smart enough to come up with that on your own."

His arm twisted; he wanted to slam the door in Redd's face. Instead he snarled. "You're just jealous! You wanted to be the one who worked on this. But they chose me."

"Chose you because you wouldn't report it to the Eugenics Department. Chose you because your moral fiber isn't as strong as mine."

"Because I'm better!"

"Because you're malleable and weak!"

Khalid flinched. "Where'd it come from, Khalid? Who's funding it?"

"Screw you!" The door rattled in its frame.

That went well, Scarlet sent.

When she got back to her apartment, the data dogs she'd set out that morning came back blank; there was no sign anywhere of quintet research. The only things that it brought back were blogged references to her own initial query. It had seemed innocent a day before—a mere request for data—but now it was like a black hole of information, with hundreds of particles accelerating around it toward the event horizon.

She paged Nicholas but his avatar said he was at a department dinner. It asked her to leave a message, but then one of Nicholas came on her screen.

"Hey, Redd. The department went out for beers."

"Where at?"

"Oswald's." He frowned. "They pulled their beer fruit a week too early. It's sour."

"But you're still drinking it," Martha said with a smile.

"True, true."

"What's up?"

"Oh, nothing. But, wait. I have a question on economics."

He laughed. "No one has questions on economics these days unless they can't help it."

"Who has the wealth now? I mean, who could fund some really large amount of research?"

"Looking for grants?"

"Something like that."

"The OG, of course."

"Besides them."

Nicholas looked away, consensing with the rest of himself.

"The OG controls most accessible wealth and production equipment. There's some wealth within the singleton enclaves but they have no genetic-engineering capabilities and most of them are on barter systems. In a few years, the OG is talking about putting limited capitalism back in place with a chit system for private citizens, but that's a ways off. We're still on basic subsistence work units based on value of work, which is why you pull in coupons for steak, and I get soyfalfa soup. No one values the economists."

"So the OG has all the wealth. I—"

"The accessible wealth. All the real wealth on Earth is in the Ring and the other Community structures. Nanoforges. Space tech. Low cost to orbit. We have none of those things. Just gengineering. Big whoop."

"But the Ring is empty." Redd pulled up a memory of a decade before, when they were ten, of dead bodies in the street where they had fallen, all of them with interface jacks. Not dead, evolved, some whispered. But the bodies were dead, billions of them.

"Sure. No access to that wealth for anyone left on this side of the rapture."

"Thanks, Nick. Can I stop by later? What time?"

"Sure. I'll be stinking drunk on bad beer, so expect a fight when you make your moves."

"Sure. When have you ever fought?"

Redd broke the connection.

The Institute had discretionary funds. Perhaps they

were just reallocating some postdocs on quintet research to see if they could get around the Eugenics Department's ban.

The next day, the wombs were full, each of the twelve with an embryo. Redd went to open the door to the womb room, but found her code didn't work. It took her thirty seconds to override the door and step through the over-pressure lock.

Each of the dozen units had a label. One read "optimized spatial-oriented embryo for quads." The word "quads" had been underlined. As if that alone would deflect her attention. She pulled the genotype up on the first womb. It matched what she had seen the day before. But it was weird, extensively changed from what she knew of pod DNA.

For forty years the pod geneticists had been working from Forsythe and Jergens initial DNA sequence, making minor changes, optimizing where they could. But no one had proposed something as radical as this. It varied from her own DNA by one point five percent. More radical than the differences between a bonobo and a human. There were proteins defined that she had never seen before.

There was no way Khalid had anything to do with this.

Redd found a public terminal in the undergrad commons. The place was a swirl of pheromones and thoughts.

As Martha typed the message, Scarlet asked, *Are we jealous?*

No!

Of course not. What Khalid and Cahill are doing is wrong.

No peer review.

Martha paused on the send button. *Well?*

Do it!

Do it.

Okay.

Their anonymous note to the Eugenics Department sped through the network.

The sound of gunfire and a scream broke Redd from a close consensus as they studied a folding protein.

Scarlet dashed to the door, glanced out and back inside.

An image from her: a military duo with rifles the length of their arms, black and deadly.

They're coming for the fetuses.

Why?

Because we told them!

The emergency exit.

No. We can't leave the babies.

We have no defense against guns!

The wombs were immobile. There were no other doors out of the womb room.

The door, Scarlet sent. *We can block the outer door open, and the inner door will remain locked due to the overpressure.*

Scarlet pushed the rest of her pod into the inner room and began reprogramming the outer door panel.

Inside! she sent.

Martha, Rachel, and Vivian stopped, suddenly understanding what Scarlet was planning.

No! You can't.

I can't trigger the door until you're through the airlock.

Then we all stay out here.

One can hide. Four can't!

The consensus was fierce, but valid. The three entered the lock, leaving Scarlet. There was a whoosh of air as the door shut. They heard a pulse of fire from the hall, suddenly muffled. So were they. Instead of four, they were three. A quarter less, a quarter slower.

The womb smelled of antiseptic.

Outside, through the windows, they watched Scarlet working on the outer door lock. They could almost hear her thoughts. The outer door opened, and the inner door light flashed red. Unless they had explosives . . .

Then we're more than screwed.

Scarlet looked over her shoulder.

Hide! Go!

But she couldn't hear them now.

The gears of the door shook in the doorway, something grinding in the wall. Scarlet had fried the motors.

Martha stood at the window, glass so thick it made the outer lab seem a mansion. Vivian and Rachel looked away, but watched the view from Martha.

Scarlet scrambled for the hood. If she could climb up onto the lab table and squirm into the unused hood, she'd be hidden in the black shroud. Shapes flashed into the room before she reached it. Martha watched, terrified.

Scarlet screamed, the words unheard. The guns cracked, and Scarlet dove for the floor.

Not hit!

Scarlet struggled backward, crabbing behind the lab tables. She turned and ran back toward the womb room. The military duo cleaved at the door, one following the columns, the other the rows.

Scarlet slid past the outer door as one of the duo came around the lab table. The gun barked, and blood splashed against the window. Scarlet's blood.

Martha's brain stopped as she watched Scarlet buckle to the floor.

Open the door!

She wasn't sure who was screaming. It could have been herself.

Scarlet rolled against the wall and sat up, watching the

door, looking into the lab where Martha couldn't see. She turned then, formed letters with her hands in rudimentary sign language.

I-t w-a-s—

The burst of automatic fire resounded in the antechamber of the womb room.

Martha jerked. The spray of blood coated the inner window, but still she saw the military duo standing there. They raised their guns, and the bullets ricocheted off the inner window. Both of the duo looked to the right, looking at something else, perhaps listening to something. Martha heard nothing.

Another burst of gunfire pounded the glass in front of her face. Tiny scars appeared, obscuring the sight of Scarlet. The womb would not open.

One of the duo grabbed the arm of the other. They seemed to confer, gesturing at the damaged door lock, stepping over Scarlet's body as they did so. They spoke to someone off to the side, out of Martha's line of sight, then turned and disappeared.

Martha found she didn't care that they had survived. If she could have she would have turned their guns on herself.

Instead she sank to her knees. Vivian and Rachel were there behind her, holding her, but there was a void among them.

They didn't remember the hours it took the building team to tear open the womb. They didn't remember until later clinging to Scarlet's body, until the doctors led them to the stretchers.

The next few days were a buzz as doctors came and went, fighting off their pod shock with kind words and exercises. Redd couldn't fight the hollowness, and they kept thinking of themselves as Vivian, Rachel, and Martha. They slept alone, even though the beds were big enough for all three.

Nicholas came to visit, but he hovered by the door and wouldn't come that far in.

"Redd, we were wondering . . ."

But then he stopped, and Redd knew what he was thinking. Which one was missing? Which one had died? The horror was on all of his faces.

"I'm sorry. I just . . ."

"You don't have to wait for us." He probably had job offers or postdoc opportunities.

He swallowed. "When things are right for you, call me."

Martha nodded, but all three of them felt the falseness in the offer.

The pain might have brought them together, but instead it sheered them further. Twice orderlies brought Vivian back after she had wandered off in near-catatonic states.

Some of her students came to visit, but Redd felt their discomfort. The loss she had sustained was what they feared, a partial loss of self, a disassociating that resulted in less than the whole.

Even Khalid came to see her. His manner was calm, analytical, as he discussed her lab work, some of which he had taken on. The gruff manner she had always hated was reassuring. He treated her no differently than when she was whole.

After a pause, he said, "I should thank you for what you did."

"What did I do?"

"The quintet embryos. No one will harm them, not even the Eugenics Department."

"Oh, I guess . . ." Martha started.

"You sacrificed yourself for them, even though they were . . . not sanctioned. You're a hero, and the embryos are sacred."

"I'm glad."

"Redd," Khalid said. "They'll need a teacher, a mentor.

I'm just a genetics specialist, and not that good according to you." He laughed coldly at his own humor. "But you could be a great mentor for the kids, the quintets, I mean."

"I haven't given any thought to what I'll do next," Martha said.

Vivian turned then from the window. *I'd like to take care of them.*

Martha felt Rachel's agreement.

"I understand," Khalid said. "It's not your line of research."

"I might, if you tell me where you got the DNA sequences."

Khalid flushed, startled, then he smiled. He shook his head. "Cahill gave them to me. She got them from . . ." Khalid lowered his voice. "The Ring Intelligence sent the information just before the Exodus. The sequences for the quintets and more. The Institute has been doling it out for a decade."

The Ring!

They have the wealth.

"No!"

"The code is sound, Redd. Cahill has checked it. They'll be as human as you or I."

Redd nodded. "I'll mentor your quintets, Khalid."

He returned her nod. "I expected you would. Thanks." He left the three of them.

Children to raise, Vivian sent, more happy than she had been in days.

It's important work.

That's all she had left.

Vivian pushes Manuel away.

"Though you can do such things doesn't mean you should!" Mother Redd yells.

It is the first time since seeing her that we are on the defensive. We are chastened.

"Sorry," Meda says.

What we have learned, that this is not the first time that someone has wanted us dead, is a shock. Not just us, but all quintets, even our classmates.

"Is Elliott in danger?" It has been a long time since we've thought of our classmate who was chosen over us to pilot the *Consensus*. In light of Khalid's and Redd's professional jealousy, our competitiveness with Elliott seems petty.

Mother Redd is still shaken as well, we see. We have made her relive the death of herself. But she focuses on our question and says, "He's as safe as we can make him. All of you are. You were until you ran off from Columbus Station."

"We—"

"That was foolhardy. The Ring is dangerous."

"The Ring made us."

"No, the Ring Intelligence helped create some of your genetic strands. Humans made you."

"Who wants us dead? Who sent the duo?" When we say it, we don't know if we mean Anderson McCorkle or the one who killed Scarlet.

"Come walk with me to the aircar," Mother Redd says.

We must trust her, Moira sends.

We've seen her thoughts.

She died for us.

She is at the edge of the forest by then. We follow, Meda at the lead.

The rest of the aircar passengers, if there are any, have remained inside. The pilot duo still watches us through bug-eyed helmets.

"Immediately after the Exodus, no one in the OG or

pod society wanted anything to do with the Ring and Community tech," Mother Redd says. "They blamed the Community, and specifically the Ring Intelligence, for the collapse, the war, the deaths. They wanted nothing to do with any of it."

"How much of the pod genetic code is from the Ring?" Meda asks. "Dr. Baker says it was directed from the beginning by the Ring."

Redd shakes her head. "This is the first I've heard that theory. I knew Baker. He never joined the Community, one of a few scientists who didn't. The Community spent no time on genetics. It was never an interest to them, nor pods. Perhaps we were wrong about that."

"You knew him?" Meda asks.

"Yes, that was before . . ." And we know what she means: before Scarlet was killed. "He presented a paper at a colloquium, on the speed of pod consensus. He talked so fast, we hardly followed him. Chemical memory uptake, pheromone catalyzation, blood-brain barrier optimization." She shakes her head at the memory. "He disappeared not long after that; his apartment was firebombed by anti-Community protesters. Don't look shocked. It was an angry time after the Exodus. No one knew what to do."

"Why did you let Malcolm Leto near us?"

She stops. She is ten meters from the aircar.

"That wasn't my idea. It was Khalid's."

"Why?" Meda's words are more anguished than we expect.

"He wanted to know if there was some plan for you. He wanted to know if the Ring had meant to build you for a purpose."

"Did it?"

"I still don't know."

We were on the Ring and nothing happened.

How do we know for certain? Moira asks.

How could she let that happen? Meda asks.

"How could you . . . ?" Meda repeats out loud.

"I didn't know what he was," Mother Redd says, her voice filled with anguish. "I couldn't guess that he was a sociopath. No one expected it. The Community had no crime. We have hardly any. We assumed he was as socialized as any of us." She pauses. "I haven't forgiven myself for that, Apollo."

"Have you forgiven Khalid?"

"Why?"

"It was his idea."

"How could he know?" Mother Redd continues, "I'm here now not just because I care for you. I came because of Malcolm Leto."

"Why?"

"We let him get away, and now he's building a Second Community. He must be stopped."

We fly across two thousand kilometers of North America to Mother Redd's farm at close to mach two. Quant stands at the door of the cockpit to the Scryfejet, inserting us into the duo pilot's thoughts. Their communication is curt, simple, and fast. Still we understand it. We are only eavesdropping, not communicating.

This is the third pod, not counting the bears, into which we have inserted ourselves.

What of those singletons in Bolivopolis? Quant asks.

Yes, but they weren't a pod. They were pod-born singletons, Manuel sends.

We have not understood what had happened until now. Gueran had wanted to rub our noses in what the OG was doing to the broken pods, shipping them off to South American enclaves to be cared for by singletons. The group of broken podmates that walked by had slipped into our consciousness and overwhelmed us.

That was the first time, Quant reaffirms, asking for consensus.

We agree, the matter settled. The first time had been in Bolivopolis, the second with the bears, the third with the pilot who had found us, the fourth with Mother Redd when we had dredged her memory for her knowledge of OG military attacks on us, and now this fifth, the pilot of the Scryfejet.

It is Strom who rejects our matter-of-fact recital.

This should not be possible, he sends. *What have we become?*

Quant, oblivious to Strom's and the pod's emerging horror, sends, *Perhaps Strom was first with the bears. Then the pilot is six. But he was alone—Oh.*

She catches the thought coming the other way.

"I don't know," she says aloud. Moira squeezes Quant's arm, and we think, withdrawing from the pilot in guilt. Mother Redd is sitting as far from us as she can in the passenger compartment of the jet.

Meda unstraps from her seat and takes another in front of her.

"We won't do it again, unless we both agree."

Mother Redd nods. "We need to keep this to ourselves, child," she says. "This wasn't . . . expected."

"No," we say. "Were we in those wombs?"

One of Mother Redd sighs. "Yes. Some of you. Strom, yes. Some of Elliott O'Toole. Meda and Moira came later. Manuel . . . and his sister later still. But Dr. Khalid had the funding and approval to grow as many as he wanted after the attack."

"Who was it? And why?"

"We don't know. The military duo wasn't caught, but the hardliners were quietly asked to step down. The Eugenics

Department was curtailed in many ways. It marked a liberalizing of the OG following the Exodus and the Gene War."

"What did Scarlet see?" we ask.

Mother Redd starts. She holds hands, thinking among herself. The memory is as real to us as if it had happened to us the day before: Scarlet signing through the glass, "It was—"

"We'd forgotten that," Mother Redd says. "We'd almost forgotten what Scarlet did to us."

Anger and fear pheromones cascade through the jet.

"I didn't mean to dredge that up," we say. "I'm sorry."

"No, no, child," Mother Redd says. "The memory was already there."

"What was she saying to you?"

"I've always thought she was saying, 'It was the right thing to do.' She was telling the rest of me that the sacrifice was necessary."

"Was it?"

Mother Redd laughs. She stands and pulls Meda from her seat, hugging her. The rest of us come too, and we are holding her tightly. We have been gone a long time from Mother Redd.

"Child, you've given me such a worry," she says into Meda's hair. "I've been looking and looking for you. But I knew you'd be all right."

"We are all right."

We're more than all right, Manuel sends. *We're beyond.*

"Has any of the other quintets shown these abilities?" Meda asks.

"No, of course not," Mother Redd says. "Just you."

"What else was in our gene sequence? Dr. Baker was scared of what we are."

"He was paranoid when he was a part of society. A dozen years by himself—"

"Except for the bears."

"—except for the bears, didn't solve that problem."

"He was a brilliant man," we say. "The bears . . . They were a friend."

"Bears," Mother Redd says, shaking a head. "The beaver pod IQ was never more than ninety."

"The bears had stories. They had . . . community."

Tell her, Strom sent. *Tell her what we have.*

"We have Baker's notes. We have the bear genome."

"What? You have it? That means . . ." Mother Redd looks at us, and we know what she's thinking, not because we steal her thoughts, but because we have just been her, Apollo-Redd.

"You never trusted Khalid's DNA because it was from the Ring. Can you trust Baker's? He spent decades trying to unravel it."

"If what he says is true, then even my DNA, going as far back as the trios, all pod DNA was modified by the Ring. I should trust no one including myself."

Meda smiles for us. "And you thought Dr. Baker was paranoid."

"I'd like to study it. Will you let me?"

"For a clean bed and a shower."

"Done."

It has been months since we've slept in our own bed. No wonder Mother Redd was trying to stay away from us. We smelled like bears.

SEVEN

Apollo

We have been gone from the farmhouse on Worthington Road since we went off on our senior trip to Columbus Station; it seems much longer than it actually is. It is warmer than the mountains have been, yet the fields of soyfalfa are ready to harvest and Mac, the trio of oxalope, is busy with the thresher. He disconnects his harness and comes over to us, licking our hands.

"Hello, Mac," we say.

He sniffs at us.

Smell bears, he sends. Even the thoughts of the oxalope are open to us. He gives us a look and a snort and returns to his work.

"Come on," Mother Redd calls. "Your room is exactly as you left it."

"Would you have rented it out?"

"If there'd been any takers."

The Scryfejet whines away into the sky, whipping away thought and emotion.

The upstairs room is the same. We take turns in the shower, two at a time, Strom last taking double the time.

Because I'm bigger. More surface area.

Quant plots the surface area of each of us. Strom does have more, but not twice as much.

Manuel logs onto the network, and we heave a sigh of relief. Worse than no showers has been no network access. From our account, we see our work units. This is how much our skill has contributed to pod society. We have been using singleton scrip for so long, we have forgotten our work unit total.

That's not right, Quant sends.

As students, our work unit rate is just a few percentage points above basic living allowance. The work we did each summer for Mother Redd boosted that a few percent more. The value of our work unit account now is ten times what we'd made the year before.

Meda calls down to Mother Redd. "There's a whole lotta cash in our account. Why?"

"Your resignation was not accepted," she replies, calling up from the kitchen. Something with tomatoes is simmering.

Oh.

Quant does a quick calculation. We marvel at our daily rate.

I feel bribed, Manuel says.

That's a lot of pay for running around the jungle all that time.

We should donate it, Moira says, but we know she is kidding.

We should convert it to singleton scrip, Strom says, the voice of practicality. *Maybe gold. Just in case.*

Manuel is already on the network, downloading news.

Checking on the Consensus.

No. I don't want to know, Quant sends.

Check.

A brief consensus is reached, and Manuel searches the network for news of the *Consensus*. Elliott's captaincy is reported, but then nothing until a few weeks ago, when there's a news article on budget cuts for the space program. The launch is delayed while the cost of the antimatter for the drive is debated.

Strom wonders, *An attack from the anti-Community contingent?*

It was impossible to say. Every news story we read— resolutions on singleton grievances, repopulation of California—we place in light of the forces we know now are at work in the world. We are coming awake after sleeping for our whole lives.

We go down to dinner.

On the steps, Quant stops to correct the slant of a picture. It is us and our ducks at the summer science fair many years ago. The ducks all seem to be trying to stand on Strom's feet. The stairs creak as we descend, the seventh step, the third one. We look into the great room from there. A jigsaw puzzle we had been working on sits on the corner table.

We are overcome by nostalgia.

We hurt her, Strom sends.

Yes.

We have no mother. No pod does. We are born in artificial wombs or real ones and raised in creches so that we bond with each other, not a parent. Mother Redd is no more than a mentor, an educator, yet our running away must have broken her heart.

Manuel dissents softly. *She took the job. It was a job.*

She changed her name to reflect her job, Meda challenges.

Would she have taken us if one of her hadn't died? Manuel asks.

No, says Moira. *She would have continued her research.*

It's more than a job for her now, Meda says.

She loves us, Strom says, and Manuel nods. He cannot resist so strong a consensus as that.

We walk into the kitchen, which smells of tomato sauce mixed with onions, garlic, basil, and thyme. All of these thing are from the garden or the greenhouse. All of these things are probably Mother Redd's own genetic design.

"Can we help?" Meda asks.

"You can help eat it," Mother Redd replies.

Two pots of homemade pasta boil on the stove.

One is for Strom, Moira sends.

One and a half, he replies.

We eat with Mother Redd, just as we used to. We chat of the farm, of her work. We skirt the issues. Neither of us raises the question of Malcolm Leto or Dr. Baker. We let those things pass for the moment.

In the morning, we sleep in, dozing in and out. When one of us sleeps, the rest of us can run in the dreams, a surreal landscape that we shape. We hear the aircar, and Manuel climbs out the window to get a look from the roof. A wave of paranoia rises within us.

"It's Dr. Khalid," Manuel says from above. He drops his hand into the room, while watching, joining consensus.

At the sound of his name, we remember what we have retrieved from Mother Redd's memory. For as long as we can remember, Khalid has been our doctor. *Not for all of us,* Manuel interrupts. Always, even when we were teenagers, he had rock candy for us in his pocket.

But now the image we share of him is warped and cracked. Through Mother Redd's eyes we see someone less bright than we remember, someone petty.

He's hasn't changed. Just our perception, Moira sends,

but the lack of force behind her statement stiffens our opinion.

He's coming to see us, Manuel sends from above. He is touching Strom's left hand, while Strom touches Meda's and Moira's with his right. Manuel is a handle, not in the circle, and when thoughts pass over the triple junction, they jumble and turn.

Come inside, Manuel, Strom sends.

Thoughts are clearest when we stand in a circle and let thoughts pass in both directions. We have a set pattern for consensus—Moira, Strom, Meda, Manuel, Quant—that serves us well. Sometimes we reach different conclusions when we switch our order, or leave someone out completely. But thought is harder then.

Manuel comes inside, finds his place, and we think.

Khalid has been our doctor from our very first mental, as well as physical, conception. Yet, he was Mother Redd's nemesis, and his actions led to Mother Redd's loss.

It wasn't his actions! Manuel says.

His going against Eugenic Department order led up to it, Moira replies.

He had no way of knowing.

He broke the rules and part of someone died, Strom says. The consensus is more heated than it usually gets.

Negligent accidental death, Manuel replies. *It wasn't even pluricide. Mother Redd is still alive.*

"Don't say that!" Quant says, speaking out of turn. "We *saw* Scarlet die!"

Which created Mother Redd! Manuel replies. *She didn't exist before that.*

And Mother Redd nurtured us, Meda adds.

Don't try to justify the means by the ends! Moira sends.

I'm not! Manuel replies. *But Khalid did what he did for science.*

We found the bears for science, Strom sends softly.

And Dr. Baker died! Quant sends. *We are as guilty as Khalid of manslaughter.* Moira cringes as the thought passes through her.

"Child!" Mother Redd calls up the stairs. "Khalid is here!"

We stop, Manuel pulling his hands free first. He stands at our door and listens. We hear the murmured conversation below, a laugh, a shared joke. Good friends visiting.

See? he sends.

Anger smell from Strom fills the air, but he says nothing.

Manuel takes the stairs, and the rest of us follow. We can't stay in our room debating our new relationship with Khalid.

He greets us with a smile, all four of him turning to look us. Three fourths of him is identical triplets, dark-haired, slightly stooped. The fourth is taller, dark-skinned with deep black eyes. He seems older than when we last saw him.

"Home at last, I see," he says. "After a long journey."

He's condescending, Quant says.

Of course not, Manuel replies.

"Yes. It's good to be home," we reply.

"I've come to give you a physical. I'd like to see how my star quintet is doing."

No! Quant shouts. All of us feel her skin crawl. Even Manuel shivers, and Dr. Khalid notices.

"Not today, Doctor."

"Apollo!" Mother Redd says. "He's come a long way to see you."

He should have called first, Quant snipes.

Meda says, "We don't feel up to it."

"Really, you've been in the jungle, then in the mountains for months. You look thin."

We are thin. We compare our body sizes from a year

ago. All of us are leaner, sleeker, and stronger. Even Strom
has put on muscle in his legs and shoulders. But our metab-
olisms are fine. We check it every day. We haven't been
sick, except for Moira's infection.

Meda is about to reply, when he cuts in. "Let me just
reassure myself that you're okay. For me, more than for
you."

Manipulative, Quant says,

But we say, "All right."

We step into one of the adjoining lab rooms, big enough
for both of us, and with enough chairs for all of us, if not
Khalid, to sit.

"You seem a bit skittish, Apollo," Dr. Khalid says,
glancing at Quant.

"It's nothing. We've had a long trip," Meda replies. Superimposed on this elderly, gentle man is his younger self
screaming at Mother Redd.

"Why don't we do an exam? Just the basics."

No! Quant again, but Strom places a hand on her shoulder.

"Mother Redd told us how her fourth died," Meda says.
"It's just upsetting for us. She told us where our DNA came
from."

All four of Dr. Khalid show surprise.

"She . . . told you?"

"Yes. She told us the Ring AI designed it. Dr. Baker
confirmed it."

Dr. Khalid steps back from us, consensing.

A swirl of thought erupts from Quant and she lunges
forward, taking Dr. Khalid's hand. We know she is trying
to join his thoughts.

No! Moira sends, mixed with veto smell.

Strom catches Quant's arm and pulls her back to us.
Dr. Khalid is staring, shocked.

Does he know?

No.

Quant's thoughts are a violent cloud around her.

Strom takes her into his arms, and we hear Quant send weakly, *He was there when Scarlet died.*

We step back as one, all of our eyes on Dr. Khalid.

"What was that outburst? Are you well?" he asks.

We should not have done that, Moira says. *Quant shouldn't have done that.* Her thoughts are almost shrill.

But I did, and we know, Quant says.

We can't ignore it, Meda says.

We had no right! Moira says. *We can't use what we have no right to. It's as if we performed an illegal search and seizure. The OG is forbidden from touching private data. His thoughts are the same thing.*

He killed her, Manuel sends.

We don't know that, Strom replies.

He did, I saw it. Quant is sobbing now.

We saw Mother Redd's memory. He didn't do it.

I know what I saw in his thoughts!

"Apollo? Are you all right?"

"Stay back," Meda says, and we continue to think, though it can be considered rude to ignore social interaction to think deeply.

We can't unthink it, Manuel says. *We know it and have to admit that.*

We can ignore it, Meda replies. *We can send him away and never tell Mother Redd.*

Let's get the full story from him, Manuel says, clenching his fists. He wants to force his way into Khalid's mind.

No! More veto from Moira. *We can't do two wrongs. Stop.*

Then what do we do? Strom asks.

We confront him, Meda says. *We let him know we know.*

Confront him, Quant says. Her anger is ours.

"We know what you did to Mother Redd."

"What are you talking about?"

"Mother Redd died because of you."

Whatever imbalance our earlier accusations caused has been erased. Dr. Khalid seems as at ease as he ever does.

"Nonsense. It was a rogue military duo, sent by anti-Ring factions in the OG, to destroy the fetuses. To destroy you, in fact. It's unfortunate, but I'd have it no other way."

Quant builds an image, the last memory of Martha before Scarlet dies. Scarlet looks at Martha and signs, "It was—"

It was Khalid. He was directing the duo. Scarlet saw him, though the rest of her did not.

Quant has reached a conclusion she is sure of, and we feel the pull of it. The force of her conviction is hard for us to fight.

Quant works out the angles from the womb room. Someone could have stepped inside the lab and been out of sight from anyone inside the sealed room.

"You hadn't stopped Mother Redd from alerting the Eugenics Department. You knew it was a matter of time before it all blew up. But you were so scared of censure that you were willing to sacrifice us to save yourself. You brought the duo in. You directed them to kill Scarlet."

"I would never destroy you," Khalid says, but he is nervous. His brow is damp. Manuel is watching his pupils. Khalid sees this and looks away. "Redd became your mentor. Why would I try to kill her if I wanted her to be your mentor?"

"You didn't know her sacrifice would make her a hero, would make us famous."

"She was a friend!"

"She was an enemy! She was about to turn you in for illegal research."

"She was a colleague."

"You used Community technology to build us. You didn't have any idea what it would do. You didn't have any idea it would allow us to see through you, Khalid. But we do."

"It's all nonsense. It's all—"

"You never understood the effect of the design. You never knew for certain what you had created, if the Ring had some plan, so you placed Malcolm Leto near us to test us."

"Preposterous!"

"Did you send McCorkle too? And the avalanche?"

He doesn't reply, but we read his body language as if we are reading his thoughts.

"Take my hand, Khalid," we say. "Prove it."

Meda reaches forward with her palm up. The glands on the inside of her wrist are red and damp.

Khalid's thoughts are flying around us, but we aren't listening. Not until he accepts, not until he takes our hand willingly.

"Why? What do you want?"

"You know what I am. Take my hand."

One of him reaches out, then shirks back.

"No!"

We look at him, frightened now, scared of us.

So be it, Quant sends.

"Get out, Dr. Khalid. Run as far as you can. It's over for you."

The whites of his eyes are huge as he gathers his things into his bags.

"I had to know," he says at the door of the lab. "I had to know what you were. And I was right, wasn't I. You're something beyond, aren't you. I was right."

Meda shakes her head.

"Murder, rape, and betrayal are justified by nothing."

He blanches at the words, then opens the door. Mother Redd stands there.

"I heard shouting," she says.

Khalid moves around her. He pauses, looks at us, then at Mother Redd. "I'm sorry, Redd. I'm sorry."

"What was that about?" she asks as the door closes behind him.

Scarlet, Quant sends.

She looks at us. Quant offers her hand to Mother Redd. She looks at us, tries to read our faces. Finally she reaches forward, and we show her everything that we know.

"Oh, no!" Mother Redd cries. She sobs and we hold her until it's done.

A day later, in the dawn, another sky car lands. It is Colonel Krypicz, whom we have met before. He is adjunct to Space and Defense departments both. Triplets, all swarthy, tall, and solid, though not as tall as Strom. He is thicker across the chest.

He greets us neutrally and asks us to sit with him in the common room. Mother Redd joins us, but remains standing in the kitchen doorway—one of her, while the other two prepare a snack. Mother Redd is quiet, keeping to herself.

"Apollo," he begins, then stops. He smiles, his interface does, and we dig into memory to see if he's ever done it before. If he has, it hasn't been around us.

He starts again. "The duo, the duo in the Amazon who applied the . . . dissolution agent." This last phrase left a snarl on his face. "He wasn't one of ours. He and his cohorts were freelance."

"We understand, Colonel."

"Good," he said, leaning back quickly.

He's not lying, Quant sends.

Don't dive into his thoughts! Moira warns.

Quant shudders. *I won't. Not ever again.*

"This McCorkle. We have him in custody. Tricky bastard. Former military, does work for hire apparently."

"What about Khalid?" Meda asks. Mother Redd meets our eyes, then disappears into the kitchen to pour coffee.

"No linkage that we can find between them," the colonel says. "Yet. He's in custody, but will not answer questions. Grave business, Apollo. Grave. You've rocked the OG. Factions are waiting to see who's betrayed. Not pretty at all."

Mother Redd hands each of him a mug of coffee, and he thanks her. The movement of Mother Redd's hand, her look at the colonel, and we know suddenly that she likes him.

Since we have shared Mother Redd's memory, we see her in a new light: in her lover Nicholas's arms, as a scientist and a medical doctor. But this affection for the gruff and stolid colonel seems too much. Still we smile, and she catches it, looking at us quizzically.

"Did you want something too?" she asks.

"No, Mother Redd."

The colonel drinks more of his coffee, then nods. "Well, then we've looked at Dr. Baker's lab, what's left of it. Marvelous coffee by the way, Ms. Redd. He did quite a number on it. Primary charge, followed by accelerants in all the rooms. Nothing left that we could salvage. We assume"—he glances at Strom—"he was the source of the bears. Is that right?"

"It is."

The colonel waits for us to say more or even consense.

"Well, then. Other than the bears, then, we were wondering if you could tell us what he was doing."

"He was rebuilding the pod genetic code and placing it within ursine strands," Meda says. "He was certain that all pod genetic code came from the Ring AI and the Community."

"Well, then. We knew that . . . Did you say all pod code?"

"Yes, not just ours. We know about that too. But all the way from the start. Dr. Baker had found several planned deficiencies in the code and was reverse-engineering them."

"Planned deficiencies? My word. Why?"

"Isn't it obvious?" Meda says. We glance at Mother Redd, who nods.

"That's the problem with making every generation smarter than the last," the colonel grumbles. "We oldsters don't know a thing that's going on."

"Harvey, you're not that old," Mother Redd says. "What Apollo is saying is that pods were designed to follow a particular path. The designer appears to have been the Ring. But those plans have been derailed."

"Not derailed," Meda says. "Delayed."

The colonel looks up into the rafters, consensing. After a moment, he glances at us, startled.

"Sorry. Quite a bit to fathom there," he says. "Leto has to be stopped more than ever now, doesn't he?"

"Yes. He can't restart the Community," we say.

"Who could we trust?" he mumbles. "Everyone is compromised." He looks at us, and we know what he's thinking.

"We aren't compromised," we respond.

"No, of course not."

One of him begins tapping at a portable console. "We can't let the Community rise again. It would destroy the OG."

He doesn't understand, Quant sends.

He understands as it's relevant to him, Moira replies.

It is not the OG we need to save, Quant sends.

It's the entire world.

Leto in control of a new Community would plunge the world into chaos. He has no desire save power, no goal but the accumulation of more. The OG was just one thing in his way. The Earth rebuilt in his image was not a palatable thing.

"Yes. Malcolm Leto has to be stopped," Meda says.

We spend the afternoon explaining to Colonel Krypicz what we had learned from Dr. Baker and the research we took with us. He holds the data unit from Dr. Baker's lab in his hand and looks at Mother Redd.

"Are you looking into this?"

"As soon as I clear a few other projects off my lab bench," she replies.

"Then it's in good hands," he says. He looks back at her. "Assume I don't understand the implications."

Mother Redd smiles. "Faster consensus. Larger pods, unlimited size really. All species, not just the few we've figured out."

"Really. Hrm." He turns back to us. "We've found Leto. We sent a duo into the Congo. Smart fellow. He arranged a meeting with some folks; his chip showed him going into the desert, toward the east. Two days later, it stopped moving. We sent a team in on camels and found him dead in the desert. Not pretty."

He pulls out a map of the Congo Desert. "We're hampered here in the Congo. The singletons lobbied for it and we gave it to them, and never realized what a perfect bolt-hole it is for the lawless peoples. But they do what they say, let the Ecologist Department in to inspect. It's all on the up-and-up. They're dedeserting the whole thing. Slow work."

"And Leto is there," Meda says.

"Oh, yes. After his run-in with you. After Khalid set

that up." The colonel's face hardens. "Hrm, yes. He fled to Green Idaho, had to hoof it after his aircar auto-landed in Grisholm."

That was me, Quant sends with pride. She had disabled Leto's aircar when we had chased him off.

"His legal machinations led to nothing. No way we'd give that man the Ring. Heavens. It's the high ground. No one knew he was a psychopath, Apollo. No one guessed he was defective."

Meda nods.

"He found some like minds in Idaho, and they smuggled him to the Congo Free Zone, where he's built up quite a following. An interface jack cult. Wire addiction. Pre-Community efforts at mind control and population exploitation with a sadist's flair. He's got a few thousand followers and access to Community tech."

"Why hasn't he taken the high ground already?"

Strom is assessing the military strength of the Ring. His mind runs scenarios with missiles, glider bombs, pieces of the Ring itself, rocks.

Rocks? Meda asks.

The Ring has potential energy on its side. By the time anything dropped from the Ring reaches the Earth, it has a lot of kinetic energy.

Quant draws us pictures: anything directly under the Ring is a target for a dropped weapon. Anything on Earth is a target of a missile fired from the Ring. It could be all explosives and minimal fuel, since it would be born ballistic, at the top of its arc.

Not to mention the energy weapons, Strom adds.

Confusion scent erupts. We have never heard of the Ring having energy weapons. Strom explains.

The Earth depends on the solar energy collected by the Ring and beamed down to collection stations around the

Earth. Each one of those beams is a high-energy micro-
wave beam. If it doesn't land on a collection station, the
beam would destroy what it touches.

We have seen the collection stations, even played with
them by tossing sticks into the parabolic collector and
watching them ignite. Only Strom has considered them as
weapons.

The colonel lets us think it through. He nods when Meda
looks at him again.

"We don't know why. We sorely want to find out. Everything we've tried has failed."

"Why not force?"

"If it comes to that, we will. But I'm not eager to do it.
He has Community tech, like I said, stuff our people
don't have. The Gene Wars were nasty, and we don't want
to go back there again. We thought it had all been destroyed, but he's dug up a cache. So that's why militarily.
Then there's politics."

"The singletons."

"Yes, you have it right. We pods sorta were all that was
left standing after the Exodus, but the singletons aren't
gone, though it'd be a simpler thing if they were."

"Colonel," Mother Redd says with a voice we know
well from childhood.

"I'm just hypothesizing, not wishing, Madame Redd,"
he says. "The enclaves have lobbied long and hard against
their second-class citizenship. So we gave them the Congo
Desert. And a fair amount of autonomy. We can't go in
there with guns blasting like they can't deal with their prob-
lems."

"Why are you here, Colonel?"

He wants us to infiltrate the singletons.
He wants us to stop Malcolm Leto.

Meda shudders and clamps down hard on her memories.

"I just need your help," he says. "We don't know how

this Leto thinks. We need some information to help us get close to him."

"You have everything we know," we say. "We were debriefed thoroughly after the event."

"I know. I know," he says. "But if we don't come up with something soon, the only option will be military. And no one wants that. Leto could have nano or virus weapons, and we don't know where he is."

We could go, Strom sends.

We have an interface jack, Manuel sends.

It can gain us access, Quant sends.

We're a pod, Moira replies, her thoughts etched with concern for her sister. *We'll stick out like a pink bear.*

It's okay, Meda sends, a thought directed at Moira. To the rest, she adds, *He has to be stopped and if we can help . . .*

The consensus is strong, as if we have been waiting to make this decision our whole lives.

"We're willing to go," Meda says.

"I'm not asking—"

"It's all right, Colonel. We'll go. It's necessary."

Mother Redd shakes her head. "Children, you don't have to."

"We do have to."

The colonel nods, his face heavy with emotion. "We appreciate what you're doing. You won't be alone. You'll be part of a team."

"We're a pod, and it'll be obvious," we say.

"Yes and no. They've recruited a number of our ecologists and geneticists. You'd be placed in the next immigrant group to go over."

"But not as a quintet."

"Well, that would give you away."

"We've had practice acting as a trio and a duo. We've also had practice acting alone."

The colonel nods. "We know."

It's necessary.
"We'll do it."

We take a suborbital from the Institute to Rabat, one of the only pod domains on the African continent. Nearly all of Africa is uninhabited, and that which is populated is by singletons. In Rabat, we stop acting like a quintet.

Surprising how easy it is, Strom sends.

It is a conversation among the boys, and the girls can still hear it, though we do not react or respond.

"Zeus Rhinefaust?" the woman asks. She is a singleton.

"Yes?" Strom says. "I am Zeus."

"And who is your friend?"

We think she is referring to Meda, Moira, and Quant, but she is looking at Manuel.

Together the two of them say, "I am Zeus Rhinefaust."

The singleton looks flustered. Then she rips up the form she has been filling out—paper, not electronic.

"You're a cluster. I have to use a different form." Her manner has cooled. We and one more pod of three are the only two in line at the CDS, the Congo Dedesertification Sodality. It is a small building not far from the airport. It is one of only two entry points into the Sodality, and inappropriately small.

"How many people come through here to the CDS?" Strom asks.

The woman looks at him, then pushes a pamphlet forward. Manuel takes it and reads it for all of us. One hundred twenty-four thousand members, six years into a twenty-five-year plan to recover the Congo River and its ecosystems. All things that Colonel Krypicz had told us. The pamphlet has nothing on the flow through Rabat.

"So you don't know?" Strom asks.

"I'll need your medical reports."

Strom hands over the two stamped papers. The woman

staples several things together then hands over two book-lets. "These are your visas."

"There's just one of us," Strom says.

"I see two."

Strom takes the visas. The visas are labeled Zeus Rhinefaust I and Zeus Rhinefaust II

Manuel sends, *I'm Zeus II.*

Meda goes through the same process for her, Moira, and Quant. They are Aphrodite Innanocia, Aphrodite I, II, and III.

"These visas are good for sixty days. If you wish to stay longer, you must be sponsored by a full member of the Sodality. You may not stay longer than sixty days or you will be expelled from the enclave with loss of all property. You may not bring or extract biological material from the enclave. You may not send or receive electronic communication from outside the enclave. You may not violate the CDS Constitution, a superset of OG laws and prohibitions. Failure to comply will result in expulsion and loss of property. The shuttle to Atrakan will leave the shuttle port in three hours. These are your tickets."

She doesn't expect us to stay longer than sixty days, does she? Manuel sends.

She is a bureaucrat. She sees things in triplicate.

Just like a pod.

Not at all.

"Thank you," Meda says, but the singleton is already absorbed in her paperwork. The triplet behind us steps forward. We give Duchess Monahan a bland smile. She is a biologist, also recruited by Colonel Krypicz, who will be our contact in the Congo.

The aircar to Atrakan is filled with young singletons who stare at us as if we are aliens. Their raucous talk ceases as we climb into the aircar.

Spoiled their party, didn't we, Manuel says.

We stifle our chemical thoughts, let our minds trickle to a stop. What pheromones we can choke off, we do. We know that the smell of it is what singletons complain of the most. We think these things alone and gather them later, when we can in groups of two, three, or five. The day is hazy in our recollection, but still we remember Quant's thought:

They are alone, so alone. Each of them.

For her it is worse. She drifts in and out of consciousness. No, not consciousness. She is always conscious. But her awareness fades away.

The other thing we remember is the boy, just a teenager, looking over at Manuel from the chair in front and whispering, "Freak."

Manuel shakes his shoe off his foot and waves at the boy with his prehensile foot.

Moira touches his wrist and sends, *Don't antagonize the natives.*

We use a public terminal to find a youth hostel near the airport; the goal is for us to find temporary work while we search for any signs of Leto. The terminal is local only; we can find no way to access the OG networks. Colonel Krypicz has told us that the CDS is cut off from the rest of the world.

Wearing our sleeves long in the cooling night and our collars up, we check in with a long-haired boy who doesn't notice we're a pod. The hostel is a common room with several cot-filled adjacent rooms. We find one that we can share and when we shut the door it is as if we can think again. As if we have been holding our breath underwater and now we break through the surface and swallow air.

That feels good, Quant sends.

We consense, determining a course for the next day. The colonel has given us a contact, a singleton, who might be able to help us find work. But Strom is reluctant. Other agents have entered the CDS and died. The possibility that Malcolm Leto or other forces have compromised the colonel's agents is real.

We traveled from the Amazon to the Rockies by ourselves. We can do this, Moira says.

Plus thirty-six thousand kilometers from GEO, Quant adds.

The Amazon was a different river, Manuel sends.

But we were still outside the pod community and on our own.

We should continue on our own.

We should find a job as far in-country as possible.

If Leto is anywhere, it's there.

Agreed.

The consensus is quick. In the morning we will find work in one of the sodalities or guilds working upriver. We clear the floor, cover it with the mattresses and blankets from the cots. We are tired from the flight. Soon we fall asleep.

At dawn, loud music from the main room wakes us.

They want us out of here early, Manuel mutters.

For a bit of singleton scrip, we buy the meager breakfast: toast, jam, and coffee. The other guests eye us, but none appear hostile. There are two girls and two boys, teenagers, sitting in the main room with us. They are dressed in dungarees and armless jackets, with various material hooked to their vests. The circles under their eyes speak of late nights imbibing and smoking.

Hostel, not hostile, Quant sends.

It's too early for hostility, Manuel replies.

Singletons abuse their bodies, Strom sends. Tattoos mark their necks, crude moving symbols, fashionable fifty years before. They spell out kanji characters one after another.

There's no one in a singleton to veto, Manuel sends.

"The consensus of one is always false," Moira whispers. It is a tenet of pod philosophy.

Though they have dark eyes, their hands are rough and callused.

Ask them about work.

"I'm looking to find a sodality to work for," Meda says to one of the girls.

The other girl laughs, a grunt.

"The girls can work for sure," one of the boys says. He has dark hair that droops over his eyes.

"Not that kind of work," Meda says, though she is hiding her first reaction. "Work with the CDS."

"If you got the money to bribe for work, you don't need to work," the girl who laughed says. She is thick all over with muscle such that we think she must use drugs to gain the size.

"Who do we have to bribe?"

"The unions. The foremen. The police. Anyone and everyone. Still may not do any good."

"Where do we go? Upriver?"

"They don't hire up there," the girl replies. "They hire down here and ship the crews up. They hire at the meat market."

"Helps if you can operate the machinery," the other boy says. His shirt is pierced in a dozen spots with stainless steel rings that jingle when he eats. "Or drive a boat. Or lift heavy stuff."

We can fly a starship.

"We can do a lot of stuff. We have biology training too."

The first girl looks at us, one after the other. There is no smell to let us know what she is thinking. No pheromones that we can detect. We think how lonely singletons must be.

"I've never seen a cluster before. Is that what you are? Not five people?"

"We're two pods," Meda lies. Moira doesn't even flinch anymore when she does. "The boys are one, the girls another."

It's expedient, Moira explains.

"Weird," the first boy says. "Very weird." He looks at Strom. "You have two dicks."

"And you have six boobs!" the second boy jokes.

Ignoring the comment, Meda asks, "Where do we go to look for work?"

The first girl looks at her watch, passes a nasty look at the boys, and says, "I'll show you where to go. Come on."

Her name is Violet. Her companions, trailing after us, are Ramone, Isis, and Ferd. They lead us through the edge of the downtown, through areas we had not seen in the dwindling light the night before. Abandoned, pre-Exodus factories, and others that are still alive, billowing smoke into the air. Steel plants, refineries, concrete factories. Raw materials sit in piles. Finished products file past on the robotransports, always east.

So much destruction and anger just to rebuild a jungle, Strom sends.

Not a jungle. They are building a country, Moira replies.

"You don't want to work in the factories," Violet explains. "They lose a few every week. No safety rules, except what the guilds allow in exchange for kickbacks." As we pass factories, she explains why each is dangerous. "This one is run by the Bantu Mafia. Don't know why they're called the Bantu Mafia, not an African among them."

"Where do you work?" Meda asks.

"The Hillside Arboretum," Isis says from behind. "But there ain't no work there for you."

"Yeah, the Arboretum," Violet says. "We plant trees and water them, then dig them up for the head-in of the river. But there's no room on the squads for you. Sorry."

"We don't want to stay at the ocean. We want to go east."

"Then there's probably room for you on one of the planting crews," Ferd says. "Well, maybe one of you, or three of you. Whatever."

The industrial region circling the city ends abruptly at the crest of a hill. Below us is the Congo. Terraced gardens descend the kilometer to the river, interspersed with residential condos. These are the first of the reclaimed areas, and the trees are ten years old, ten meters high.

Violet leads us down the street toward the river. Water gurgles in troughs on both sides of the street. Quant spots the pumphouses, one every one hundred meters along the crest, each one pulling water from the river to feed the hundreds of gardens. The air is suddenly humid and wet.

Violet cuts through an alley parallel to the river, and beyond the houses are rows and rows of saplings lining the hill. The Arboretum covers two large blocks. Mist hangs in the air from sprayers. In some places, tarps drape over the trees to block the equatorial sun.

"See that hut there?" Violet says. "That's the Tree Guild House. Ask there. Say you want to do tree planting."

The other three are already walking away, so we just thank Violet.

A small line queues at the door of the hut, which looks vacant. We take our place at the end of the line. The others, haggard and twitchy with desperation, eye us warily.

Are there any pods as desperate as these people? Strom asks.

Just the broken ones, Manuel replies.

Quant: *Even they had food and shelter.*

Manuel: *The OG should clean this place out.*

Moira sends veto coursing through the pod.

Do we trust the OG to do anything now? she asks. *Do*

we still think the OG is the best form of government? After what it's done to us?

I didn't really mean that, Manuel replies, taken aback.

Then don't think it, Moira sends.

A hefty man walks over from the main building. He's dressed in coveralls smudged with dirt. He opens the door to the hut and sits on the stool there, pulling a clipboard from the wall.

"Don't even ask. I don't have nothing but work for someone who knows a Forzberg Arboratiller. So if you don't know how to drive one of those, get the hell out of line."

No one moves.

What's a Forzberg Arboratiller? Quant asks.

Manuel shrugs.

"I will be testing you on this."

We step out of line, and the man looks at us.

"At least some of you are honest. The rest of you can go. You five, come with me."

It was a test.

It pays to be honest, Moira preaches.

A groan slips through us.

The rest of the queue mutters at us as they leave. The foreman hands us forms.

"I'm Mr. Ellis, subforeman for the Molehill Arborist Sodality. You're all apprentice class A arborists. Fill these out. Wait." He looks closely at Meda. "You're clusters. Jesus, crap."

He's going to fire us, Manuel says.

"How many of you are there?"

"A trio and a duo."

"This is my lucky day. Fill these out."

He trots back to the main building while we write in our fake names and information.

What's that about? Manuel asks.

He returns, slower than he left, weighed down by a box in his arms. "Read these. Tell me if you can run one of these things."

Strom opens the box. Inside are paper copy manuals for a tree-planting tractor. The image on the first manual shows a huge agricultural monstrosity. The symbol on the cover—a triangle-bound three—indicates it's to be operated by trio pods only.

"These are built for trios," Meda says.

"No shit. Can you drive it?"

Manuel has been paging through the operating manual, his thoughts drifting among us, spicy with abstractions and interactions.

Manuel? Meda prods.

Oh, yeah, no doubt.

"Yes, we can."

"Happy damn day. The OG dumped a dozen of these bastards on us and we thought they were being nice. Until we figured it took three people to run one. Bastards. Consider yourselves class B arborists." He checks his watch. "The bus leaves at noon from here. Be on it. Report to Subforeman Muckle at Hinterland. He'll get you set up with this piece of crap."

Hinterland: the end of the Congo, a frontier, without law, full of desperate people. If Leto is somewhere, it is there. We leave a note for Duchess Monahan at the guild house to which she is attached, then head back to catch the bus.

The river is perfectly straight for a hundred kilometers, a feat of precision, a green V cut into the desert. There are two main thoroughfares at the tops of each bank, sometimes a kilometer from the river, sometimes alongside the brown, turgid Congo, but always traveling to the northeast.

We are reminded of the Amazon, the other river of our adventures: wild and alive, where this river is mechanical and reversed. If the desalination plants ever stop, if the power ever fails, the river will dry to desert and again the sand will overtake this long oasis.

Barges ply the river, working through locks into the interior, barges full of stone, cement, brick, and steel. At intervals landings jut into the river, places to offload the barges. They are named Landing One, Landing Two, and so on, but serve as population-dense spots, not really towns, just densities.

Otherwise the river is empty, save for arborists and gardeners monitoring the watering. At one hundred kilometers, we reach Brazeltown, an oasis of capitalism and abandon. The hills around the river in a clearly demarcated circle are filled with bars and casinos. A dozen barges are tied up here.

The bus waits twenty minutes for its riders to disembark at a casino that lures them in.

"The next bus comes in twenty-four hours. Why not spend it in air-conditioned luxury?" the driver says flatly.

We buy sandwiches at a stand not far from the bus stop. Some of the people on the bus, other arborists, wander into the casino. They are not on the bus when it starts up again.

The river curves, an engineered bevel to encompass a peninsula of low-lying rice paddies. We expect to see some gengineered animals striding through the fields, but instead see singletons working the slopes.

The road sweeps away from the river, and we are suddenly in a cracked, broken land. Tan and sepia stone and dirt surround us. It is hard to believe that a river is just a kilometer over that hill. It is equally hard to believe that a century before it was jungle.

It's a strip of green in an ocean of desert, Meda sends.

They are fools, Manuel sends.

They're at least trying, Moira replies. *Striving.*

They are exploiting something no one else wants, Manuel sends. *Why else would the OG give this to them?*

Duty, responsibility, stewardship, Moira ticks off.

Penance, Quant adds.

But the waste of it all, Strom sends.

It was wasted when the singletons got here, Moira says. *But the OG couldn't motivate this sort of project by itself.*

The air is so dry and cloudless that the Ring is clear as it seems to dive into the horizon. The Ring is straight overhead here at the equator, just as it was in the Amazon.

I think I see an elevator, Manuel sends. He is peering out the front windshield of the bus.

On the horizon, we see the glitter of a Ring elevator far to the east, hundreds of kilometers away. The sight makes us wonder again why Leto hasn't taken possession of the Ring himself and used its power to destroy the OG and take what he wants by force.

We pass a grove of plywood-and-corrugated-aluminum shanties. Hollow people covered in linen to abate the sun stare at us. Then the road passes back into the verdant valley around the river, and we notice that the threshold of green is guarded by soldiers with guns.

Managed scarcity, Quant sends. *They build a river and then divvy water out to accumulate wealth.*

The Community would have done it better? Manuel chides.

Yes, it would have. Were there wasted resources with the Community? Quant replies.

Just war and destruction.

As we drive farther east, the trees and gardens become

sparser, the river thinner and less crowded. At nightfall, the bus pulls into one of the landings in front of a hotel the driver must have a deal with.

We rent a single room and then prowl the dark river edge, padding from one raucous lit area to the next. The air is humid and wet, yet there is a trace of desert in the wind. They have built something fragile, on the edge of collapse.

A woman walks past us.

She has an interface jack, Quant sends.

"Hey, excuse me!" Meda calls.

The woman turns, her face slack. She is a girl, fifteen or sixteen.

"Where'd you get the interface jack?" Meda asks.

Emotion surfaces on her blank face: anger.

"Fuck you," she barks and turns away.

What did I say? Meda asks.

She spotted us as an OG agent.

How?

No. It was hate at the question, not at us, Strom sends.

We try to find the girl in the dark, but she has eluded us, and return to the hotel to sleep restlessly before the bus leaves in the morning.

Hinterland is a moated city; the Congo splits at its foot, and two walled bridges allow access to its splendor. Another free zone, it exudes decadence and excitement. Here, the valley walls are still desert, unplanted and empty, but the eye is so drawn to the city itself that no one notices the desert outside once you enter.

The guilds and sodalities are clumped in a warehouse in the middle of the city. The foremen and subforemen stand at lecterns and direct contracted and day workers to tasks. We find Subforeman Muckle leaning against a wall, shaking off would-be workers. It seems that getting to Hinterland is no guarantee of work. We see many desperate faces, emaciated forms.

It's a frontier, Quant sends.

Muckle looks at us, his face blank until we wave our forms in front of him.

"Five? What the hell is Ellis sending me five for? I can't even use one."

"We're not five, we're two," Meda says.

"Oh, great. Three times the feed for one-third the work."

Three times the feed for the same amount of work, Quant corrects.

Shush.

"We're here to the drive the arborobots."

"The what?"

"The tree-planting machines that the OG sent you."

Muckle chews on a pencil. "Well." He writes down something on his clipboard. He looks at us then, thinking for a while. "I was a week from slagging those things. All right. Come on."

Muckle leads us out of the warehouse and into the streets. Bicycles and pedestrians vie for position. There are no aircars in the sky. There are no automobiles on the road.

Claustrophobia grips us as we move among so many people. Our thoughts gel and disappear in the ocean of smells and natural pheromones. We trail Muckle, hand-in-hand-in-hand.

It is ten minutes of walking in the afternoon sun. We pass a walled mansion with stone-fenced gardens and fountains. The clog of people eases. A kilometer farther and we are near the southern arm of the river. There are more warehouses here, fewer shops and restaurants. Muckle palms open a garage on a squat warehouse, ushering us in.

The warehouse holds four arborobots, three of them still partially crated. More crates line the walls, gengineered tree seeds, nutrient-fixing bacteria, fertilizer.

"Get them working," Muckle says, leaving us alone in the crowded warehouse.

Manuel climbs to the roof and sets up the sat phone. When he has signal with the geosync satellites, we get access to the pod networks and call Colonel Krypicz.

"Where are you? You never made contact with our agent," he barks.

"We're in Hinterland."

"Hinterland? How did you get . . ." He shakes his head. "Has anyone ever overestimated you?"

Meda says nothing. If we had met everyone's standards we would be on the *Consensus* right now.

Instead we're in a desert.

"All right then," the colonel says. "Good job, then. The question is where Leto is and we think it's Hinterland or farther inland. At this point, you're farther in than anyone we've ever had."

He signs off and Quant starts searching for details on the arborobots, while the rest of us climb all over the one built machine.

They have the exhaust system backward, Manuel sends. He and Strom reassemble the pipes coming off the hydrogen-burning system. The superheated water vapor leaving the catalyst is piped through the other systems for mechanical work.

For hours we absorb ourselves in checking and rebuilding the machine.

It is past dusk when Muckle returns. We have forgotten to eat lunch and are starving for food.

"Well? What have you got for me?"

Quant climbs into the cab and starts the engine. Electrolysis has split enough water vapor into hydrogen and oxygen to at least start the engine. The tractor will have to sit in full sunlight for a couple days to fill the hydrogen tanks completely. Or we could find a microwave receiver.

"Holy crap!" cries Muckle. "You got it started! I guess you can stay."

"We'll need a microwave receiver to recharge the hydrogen tanks," Meda says.

Muckle scratches his bald head. "Well, the receivers are closely monitored by the Power Guild."

"Why? Anyone can put up a receiver in a few days."

"Sure, okay, technically. But then you have to have the license fees and the guild inspection."

Managed scarcity, Quant sends.

"It's better just to use the solar, if it's got it."

"Okay."

"Are you ready to go? Are you ready to run this baby?"

"Not yet. We need to load it with material."

"How many trees can this thing plant in a day?"

One thousand, Manuel sends.

If the seeds are good. We don't know that.

And the bacteria might be dead.

It may be a big hole digger.

"I don't know. Maybe a few hundred."

"A few hundred. Okay, okay. When can you try it out?"

"In a few days."

"Not sooner?"

"Can you find us a microwave power receiver?"

Muckle rubs his scalp again. "Maybe. Maybe not. A few hundred a day, you say?"

"We don't know, really."

"But it could be a few hundred?"

"Maybe."

"Can you unpack another one?" Muckle asks, looking at the other machines still boxed up.

"Only one of us is a trio," Meda says. "We can only drive one."

"What if you get a third guy?"

Meda shrugs. "It depends."

"Okay, okay," Muckle says. "Three days. Have it ready in three days."

We send the boys out for dinner. They come back with skewers of grilled vegetables and chicken. We barely stop for the food. Our night is already planned out. It feels like we are back in school and working around the clock on shifts. We schedule ourselves so that at least three of us are up at any one time. One hour a day we are all awake and we use that time to consense and redirect our focus for the next twenty-four hours. For school tasks— memorizing and reading—or for things that don't need all five of us at once to decide something, this schedule works best for us.

At dawn we move the first tractor into the alley out front, where it can sit in the sun and fill its hydrogen tank. We forget to lock the cabin, and Strom goes outside when we hear the engine turn over.

A gaggle of kids are crawling over the machine, trying to steal it. Strom climbs up the tractor wheel, a miniature thief under each arm. The rest scatter in all directions.

"Hey! Leave us alone," the kid under the left pit yells. "I'll tell my daddy. He's a foreman."

Before Strom can send the two street urchins flying, Moira is there.

Let's hire them, she sends.

These thieves? Strom asks.

"We've got some work for you kids," Meda says. "Who wants some breakfast?"

The kid under Strom's left arm, the one whose father is a foreman, kicks free and says, "I'm Eliud. What's for breakfast?"

For bagels and a few dollars in singleton scrip we suddenly have our own crew of tractor workers, Eliud its makeshift foreman. We still lose seed and tools to theft, but we have the second and most of the third tractor built and ready by midnight. Most of the kids go home at dark, or wherever they stay each night. A couple of children stay. Eliud sleeps in our warehouse on a bag of apple-tree seed.

I thought his father was a foreman, Quant sends.

That doesn't mean he knows who his father is, Manuel sends.

Fathers and mothers are abstract concepts to us. We have grown up with neither, just creche nurses and mentors.

The next day, we have twice as many kids show up for breakfast.

We have a guild, Strom sends.

They're like ducks, Moira replies, pulling a wry grin from Strom.

Manuel takes a walk through the market, taking Eliud and another boy with him. The goal is a precision caliper, but he keeps his eyes open for any sign of Leto's jacked associates. Even though it is the far end of the Congo, Hinterland is home to two hundred thousand humans. He finds nothing, not even a caliper, and he and Quant must work with what is available to tune the hydrogen-burning engines.

By noon, the third tractor is built, and the first two are loaded with seed, bacteria, fertilizer, and water. The weight threatens to warp the cobbled street and we set the props out on two-by-fours to distribute the force. The tractors have charged faster than we thought. The first will be ready tomorrow.

After lunch, we hear cursing from the street. Some of our kids are yelling. Meda is asleep, so Strom leads us out. Two men are climbing up the tractors.

"Can I help you?"

"Who the hell are you?"

"We're Class B arborists and those are our machines."

"Class B, huh?" The first man drops to the ground. He is dressed in clean coveralls. The name Ryan is stitched into the breast pocket. The lack of dirt proclaims this man as a foreman.

"Go wake Quant and Meda," Manuel tells Eliud.

"You got a license for these tractors?" Ryan asks.

Bluff.

"Subforeman Muckle does."

Ryan laughs, glancing up at his companion, still leaning against the cab.

"Muckle? So this is why he bought up the Jergens contract. This is his secret weapon." Ryan's laugh is not pleasant.

Strom shrugs. Meda would have said something appropriate, but for Strom a gesture is as good as a word.

"You should get these things out of the way," Ryan says. "You're blocking thoroughfare. You're lucky we're not the constable. He might confiscate the things." He and his friend share another laugh.

"Why don't you come on down before we call the constable," Meda says. She and Quant have joined us from the cots in back. In seconds the entire history of this confrontation has been downloaded into her brain.

"Well, here's a spicier one than this boyo," Ryan says, but his friend climbs down, catching a hose and wire in hand as he does: malicious vandalism, though he would claim innocence. Manuel is there to repair the damage before the man reaches the cobbles. He glares at Manuel, but the damage is already fixed.

"Good day to you then, and we'll see how this contraption works tomorrow."

We watch Ryan and friend walk off down the alleyway, his angry laugh the last thing to disappear.

I guess there'll be an audience for tomorrow.

"Eliud, can you fetch Subforeman Muckle?" Meda asks.

"Sure."

Muckle curses for a few minutes when he hears that Ryan has been here.

"We should move the tractors," Meda says.

"Sure, sure, that rat! I have another warehouse nearby."

"It should be in the sun. We need to resupply the hydrogen."

"Right, right. I don't have any place with skylights."

"A courtyard," Meda suggests.

Or the field, adds Quant.

"Or the field, the Jergens contract, wherever that is."

Muckle gives Meda a look. "That Ryan! Sure, we can take them to the field. When?"

"Tonight."

"Okay, okay."

We siphon what hydrogen is already compressed and stored in the first tractor to balance out the other three. The children lug bags of seed all afternoon, dumping them into the bins. We handle the fertilizer and the bacteria. We've tested the stuff, and after three years in the warehouse, the bacteria is still active.

I hope the seeds are too, Quant sends.

Manuel dumps a paper cup over on a table. The seed he placed in there on the first day in the warehouse has a whitish-green tail, the shoot coming off the seed.

Looks okay. I didn't even add fertilizer or bacteria.

One is not a good sample set, Quant replies. *That could be the only viable seed.*

Not very likely, Manuel sends.

The quick consensus is that we will have to rely on the seeds having remained well preserved in the dry warehouse.

The desert is the best place to keep things safe, Strom sends.

We send the children back home before we leave, but Eliud is adamant in remaining.

"I want to drive," he says.

"You'll need six arms."

"Not if I just want to drive," he says. "I'd need six if I wanted to plant trees. Driving just needs two feet and two legs."

He has a point, Manuel sends.

"You still can't come with us."

"You need a gopher," he replies.

"I'm not paying for street rats," Muckle says. "I ain't no junior arbor club."

"I'm not asking for anything," Eliud says sharply. He looks at Meda and adds, "There's nowhere else for me to go that'd I'd rather be."

Moira's heart softens, and the rest of us shrug.

"All right," Meda says.

Eliud smiles wider than his face. "I can drive?"

"No, you can come."

The streets are empty as we drive the four machines toward the desert that night. We drive them two at a time, unable to split less than a duo for the task of maneuvering through the streets. Even so, we feel swathed and numb, until several minutes into the drive. We use sign language between the cabs to maintain distance and indicate direction. Eliud mimics our signs from his seat in the back of the first tractor's cab. He peers over Quant's shoulder to watch what she does to control the tractor.

The field Muckle has contracted is ten kilometers

downriver. It takes us two hours to find it, but when we do, we see a dozen arborists waiting by a fire. They cheer at the sight of the tractors, then detach a pair to guide us back to the warehouse on bicycles.

Strom flounders on the bicycle. Manuel sends him the memory of riding over and over again until he understands. At the warehouse, we latch the bicycles to the second pair of tractors and drive them to the site. Quant and Moira are tired—this is their sleep period—but we make the distance in a shorter time, and we all sleep by the fire in sleeping bags.

Eliud curls up against Meda, and as his arms reach around her neck, he touches her interface jack, and says, "My mom has one of those."

He is asleep before we can respond. We let him slumber as we lie awake under the Ring. By chance, we have found what we are looking for.

The road is lined with arborists and onlookers the next morning.

"Wow," Eliud says. "Look at all those people."

They aren't all happy, Quant sends.

Protestors, holding signs, are intermingled with casual observers. An hour after dawn the road is blocked with people. Muckle has brought in more of his crews to surround the arborobots.

Meda asks him, "Do you have anyone else working?"

Muckle shakes his head. "Do you know how much this project is worth? Jergens overbid this three years ago. His whole crew went in hock and he's still in debtors' prison. The land contract reverts to bids in two weeks, or it would have if I hadn't bought it for next to nothing. Of course . . ." He shrugs.

"If we don't complete the contract in two weeks?"

"Well, there's those that will be happy to see that."

"And for us?"

"You may get bumped a grade. Me, I'm facing prison."

"You're a brave man. You're putting a lot of faith in us."

Muckle looks at Meda squarely. "I've known some clusters in my time. And I know cluster biology is better than ours." He shrugs. "Life is a big chance. Let's get started, before we have a situation on our hands."

The boys climb into one tractor and the girls the other. Manuel, with his adapted legs, acts as two operators. Eliud wants to be with us, but we send him to stand with Muckle.

The contract area is about forty hectares in a low saddle shape nestled against the river. Beyond the far hill is a developed low-density residential area. Behind us toward Hinterland are fields of teff. Across the river are more fields: wheat and corn. Our contract area is clearly fallow, covered in weeds and burned by the sun and lack of irrigation.

We line the tractors up as far from the road as we can and start plowing the dirt under. It is mostly sand, with some river silt piled into it. We raise dust plumes behind us until Quant directs us to spray the field with water as we go. But this limits how far we can go before having to refill the tanks.

It is slow progress.

But that means the protesters have little to protest and as many leave as arrive. By noon, we have plowed the whole plot. We start again at the far end, but this time, the boys' tractor goes first, planting tree seeds—slow-growing oak, pine, and willow—while the second tractor follows, spraying the nutrient-fixing bacteria.

We have come across once and are coming back again when Muckle flags us down. His face is red.

"Where are the trees? Where are the trees?"

"We're planting seeds," Meda replies.

"Seeds? You can't plant seeds. I need saplings to fulfill this contract!"

Manuel hands him the spec sheet on the seeds and the spec sheet on the bacteria.

"What's this?"

"Have your crews start irrigating the fields," Meda says.

Should we tell him? Moira asks.

Let him find out.

We finish half of the field by sunset. His crews have started digging irrigation ditches from the water pumps at the top of the hill. That project will take days.

Muckle is irritable. He catches us as we exit the cabs.

"If we load the trucks with sapling can we replant over the seeds?"

"Come on."

We lead Muckle up to the top of the saddle.

"Watch your step," Meda says.

Muckle double-steps, narrowly avoiding a sprout. He looks closely at the ground, then gets down on his hands and knees.

"Is that . . . ?"

"Yes."

"But you planted it five hours ago."

"It's a gengineered tree. They grow quickly, then slow down."

"How fast?" He is peering closely at the sprout.

Ten centimeters a day to two meters, Quant sends.

But who knows? The seed is old, Manuel adds.

We're lucky it sprouted at all.

And we may only get a twenty- to thirty-percent germination rate.

"We don't know. Maybe half a meter a week for a month."

"Holy shit. We're going to need more people out here."

Eliud is on his belly, staring at an oak sprout.

"This is so brill!" he says.

"It is," Strom replies.

"How does it work?"

"Gengineering."

"I know that! But how does it work?"

"The seeds have been modified to accelerate the early growth process. The plant and the earth can't support that sort of thing, so a bacteria is added to the ground to fix the nitrogen, phosphorous, and potassium. Otherwise the plant would be dying by now. It's an engineered symbiosis."

"Oh."

He stands up, dusting himself off. The rest of us are standing apart, pretending not to watch as he and Strom talk. The sun is setting, reflecting red-orange light off the Ring base elevator only a few hundred kilometers away.

Strom says, "We'd like to talk to your mom."

Eliud crosses his arms. "Why?"

"She has an interface, and we'd like to find out where she got it."

Eliud nods, relaxing a bit. "She got that from Father Arthemon. Everyone at the church did."

"When was this?"

"Oh, about a month ago. Then she started spending a lot of time at the church and other places. They wanted to do it to me too, but my dad said no. My dad is tough."

"Is your mom still at the church?"

Eliud shrugs. "I dunno. Maybe. She went to a lot of meetings."

Leto's in Hinterland.

With the setting sun, the wind has picked up from the south, pushing dust and sand over the edges of our artificial infant forest. Though the river valley is green, the land just beyond is empty desert, and it is easy to forget.

We eat dinner by the fire with a group of arborists. Though we are all in the same guild, none seem particularly friendly toward us. We know it not just because we are a pod. The hulking arborobots represent change. The spouting trees are alien. The protesters have their own fires, their own dinner in the dark.

We'd be less welcome there, Manuel sends. We are tired and sleep comes quickly.

We awaken to a low grumbling and shouts. Instantly, Strom is awake and in control, assessing.

The shouts rise from the protesters. They are at the edge of the field, pushing against the meager line of Muckle's crew.

Why?

Look!

The sprouts are almost half a meter tall, treelike with leaves, their trunks woody.

They were expecting us to fail.

And now they will destroy it.

Quant has counted the sprouts. *Sixty-four-percent germination rate. Not bad.*

Strom's mind dances through permutations, trying ways to save the fields, the tractors, Eliud. Seconds tick, and then he sends, *Get Eliud. Mount up in the tractors.*

Even in the cabins, we can hear the shouts, louder than before. A dozen men have broken into the field and are ripping at the saplings.

When they hear the tractors start, they think we are fleeing. But we round the tractors toward the protesters and spray them with the bacteria-laden fertilizer.

Their shouts turn to shrieks and they run.

"You're not hurting them, are you?" Eliud asks.

"No," Meda says. He is squeezed in the girls' cabin, peering out the front window. "It's harmless."

But they don't know that, Quant adds.

The mob of protesters break immediately, running for

the river to douse themselves in water. In moments the road is clear and the field safe. We park the tractors on the road, colossi to guard their work.

The protesters do not regroup, floating instead down the river to the next town or across to the far side. Muckle's crew bellows victory, even the ones who are covered in fertilizer mix. We turn the water hoses on and spray them down, and before long everyone is dancing in the water.

Muckle is back in the midmorning, alternatively ecstatic and angry.

"The Syndicate Board is holding a meeting. But you can't deny we fulfilled the contract." The saplings are growing fast enough that we can watch it. Muckle chortles, caressing a leaf. Then he frowns. "If the board rules against us, they may have us dig up the whole thing."

"That's absurd," Meda says.

"You're telling me. Anyway, we can't use these tractors again until they rule." He hands us an address in Hinterland. "Take 'em here. Store them. I'll send some boys to help guard them."

The river roads are crowded during the day, and it takes us three times as long to get back to the city. Even folded up, the arborobots take up two lanes of the road, and in most spots that's all there is to the road.

Our slow pace and apparent notoriety draws a crowd, slowing us further as we drive the behemoths through the streets.

Look, Manuel sends.

He passes us an image of a man watching us. His short hair can't hide the interface jack in his skull. We watch for more jacked people in the crowd, but spot none.

At the new warehouse, we consense.

Notoriety is not good at this point, Strom sends.

It is obvious we are pods.

Now everyone in Hinterland has seen us.

We need to find Eliud's mother.

Agreed.

We leave the tractors in the keep of one of Muckle's gangs, exiting through a back door into an alley. Eliud leads the way, through back ways and thin streets, to a small brick building in an out-of-the-way cul-de-sac.

"That's Mom's church," he says, standing behind Meda.

We walk to the front door, past a bedraggled, dry front yard. The door is ajar, and Strom pushes it open. Heated air swells from within.

As our eyes adjust, we make out tipped pews and broken statuary.

This isn't how it's supposed to look, Quant sends.

We have little understanding of singleton religions, but clearly this destruction is not typical. Beetles scurry as we approach the front. A door leads from the church to a smaller sanctuary. We are greeted with the smell of death.

A man's body, half eaten by insects, is planted facefirst onto a desk. Strom pulls Eliud back before he can see it and watches from the door. The boy pushes against him, but Strom is strength and there is no budging him.

With his face down, the interface jack is clearly visible at the back of his neck. In fact, the fiber-optical wires flowing up the brain stem are also visible, inedible to the ants and beetles: a gold and silicon skeleton. His clothes are black, except for the clerical collar at his neck.

Father Arthemon, I presume.

Manuel leans in and looks closely at the interface jack.

It's been ripped apart.

Someone has taken a screwdriver to the interface socket, bending it out of the bone. The screwdriver is on the floor.

He did it himself.

We had considered the same course when Meda's interface had been installed against her will. But there was no way known to pod science to remove the hardwired interface connection.

He didn't whack himself in the head, though.

Father Arthemon had died from a skull fracture.

Let's call the police.

We wait outside for the constable, a thin, lean woman with a stun gun and a baton on her harness. Her blond hair is cut short, but for all her toughness, she comes out of the church a little pale.

"Damn wireheads."

"Do you see that a lot?" Meda asks.

"No. Not dead ones. But we see a lot of abandoned places like this, abandoned kids." Her gaze falls on Eliud.

"He's with us."

She ignores us and calls in for an ambulance. Pulling out a microrecorder, she takes our statement. We explain that it is Eliud's church and we were taking him there to visit when we found the corpse. The officer makes no comment.

When the recorder is off, Meda asks, "Where do the . . . wireheads congregate?"

She shrugs. "I dunno. We have detectives looking into it."

"Who?"

She gives us a look. We take the hint. Out of earshot, we ask Eliud where he used to live.

"Not far. An apartment."

"Show us."

It is three flights up in a generic building in a line of the same. The door is locked, but Eliud hands us the key from his pocket. Inside, the room is clean, but smells dusty. It is stale and hot.

Eliud waits at the door again, this time of his own will. All the rooms are empty, with a thin layer of dust started on the horizontal surfaces.

What is Leto doing to these people?

After being jacked, Eliud's mother willingly abandoned her son and apartment.

He's making sure he doesn't lose any.

He's learned his lesson with Meda.

We have to find him.

Yes.

That night Muckle is back at the warehouse with dinner: more kabobs and a fermented drink of some kind that he forces into our hands.

"This is what all arborists drink. Guild law," he says.

Not bad, Strom sends, though it tickles our noses and makes Quant cough. Moira takes just a sip and sets hers down.

"Bad news," Muckle adds after we drink. "The guild ruled against genetically engineered plants."

"What?" Meda says.

"We'll have to tear up the field, default on the deal."

"Then you're in big trouble."

This stuff is potent, Manuel sends, making fists with his feet.

I don't feel so well, Meda sends.

"Well, I was. But I've made a deal to—"

As the words register, Strom takes control, throwing his mug into Muckle's face. We are lurching to our feet, staggering.

"Shit!" Muckle yells.

Strom counts Muckle and the crew guarding the arborobots as enemy.

Retreat, he sends. He can't trust us in our drugged state. We need safe haven.

Manuel grabs Eliud and we run for the back of the warehouse where an old Exit sign cants against the frame of a metal door.

"Get them!" Muckle cries.

The alley is dark and heaped with debris, impenetrable in the dark though we had passed through it that afternoon in light. Manuel pulls Eliud into his arms, staggers, and then carries him to the left.

The drug is a soporific, and we struggle to stay focused. Moira, who drank little, coaxes us, yells and kicks. The door slams open behind us as we emerge from the alley onto a wider street.

Downhill.

It is easier to stagger that way.

Strom trips and Moira pulls him up, helping him run.

We jog left, turning toward the river. Strom slumps against a wall. Meda supports his right arm, while Moira is on his left.

Muckle's crew is hard behind us. Manuel risks a look, and sees them about twenty meters behind and gaining. We need to lose them and recover from whatever Muckle spiked our drinks with.

Find a populated area, Strom sends.

But the warehouse abuts the docks, and the place is deserted at this hour.

We round a corner, and Manuel shoves Eliud into a doorway.

"Stay here," he commands. "Don't move." Eliud nods, and we're running again.

Behind us Muckle's crew doesn't notice Eliud in his hiding spot.

Strom collapses onto the cobbles, unable to stand.

Leave me, he sends. *Regroup later.*

We all veto that.

The crew is on us in seconds. They use plastic cuffs to

bind our hands. It is hard to share thoughts that way, the consensus weak and unstable. Strom falls in and out of consciousness.

They drag us back to the warehouse. We are not surprised to see Malcolm Leto there.

EIGHT

Apollo

Leto has learned from his mistakes. We all awake in separate prison cells, alone. We don't know this now. It is
only later after we integrate these separate, warped, and
spotty parallel memories, that we will know these things.
Until then, we are all alone in our cells, slow, sluggish,
stupid.

Terror. I awake alone and in terror. The last thing I remember is the sight of Malcolm Leto smiling and the
smell of something in my nostrils, some drug to bring unconsciousness.

When we took this job, I knew that we would come
face-to-face with this man. I knew that I would face the
man who raped me in numerous ways. Yet now that it has
happened there is no catharsis.

I am scared. Utterly afraid.

Alone, I realize it is only the pod that keeps the darkness away.

* * *

I **am** strength, and I am alone. Strength alone is weakness. Yet, I know this is false.

There is no smell of my pod anywhere. The air must be filtered. Leto is taking no chance. Damn him.

I pound at the door. It vibrates under my fists, but does not budge. My strength is useless.

I slump against the door and wait. What more can I do?

In the hall, I hear footsteps, boots, I imagine, two pairs. I stand in the center of the room, considering how to attack if they open my door.

"This one?" someone asks, outside the door.

"No. He wants the girl first."

They move past and I hear nothing else.

I **check** for a transom, but there is none. Nor are there any high points that I can scramble up to launch a surprise attack. The room is smooth-walled and devoid of anything, save the cot, sink, and pail. I move the cot to the wall where the vent forces air into the cell.

If I stretch, I can touch the flow with my fingers. No chemical thoughts touch my wrists. No pheromones at all.

I take off my shoes. Perhaps if someone comes and it is only one, I can overpower him with my four opposable thumbs. I make four fists. Perhaps not.

The walls are stones, blocks fitted with mortar roughly squirted between. I use the pail to pound on the wall and listen for an echo. There is nothing. I listen at the door. I try the knob again.

Listless, I model the forces on the door, on the door frame. I calculate the force on the bottom row of stones. I determine how hard I would have to kick and across what angle to shatter the stones. Futile effort and futile calculations.

I follow the mortar lines around the room, tracing the line above the door, around the corners. I find a path that does not overlap, but touches every line of mortar. It is soothing to do this, though I know it means nothing. Later, I know I will think this again, but right now, there is nothing else to do.

I end the path of mortar. I start over.

On the third time through, I hear a scuffle in the hallway beyond my cell. A muffled scream, shoes pounding the floor. I stop my line, my finger holding my place, then when silence returns, I finish the path.

I am awakened from nightmares to a deep sound, a vibrating rumble.

The room is still lit, and I have been sleeping with the blanket over my head. The skin around the jack itches.

I put my hand against the door.

Thunder? I wonder.

I hear another rumble. I get my shoes and put them on.

Something is coming. Something strong. Stronger than I am.

My body is tense from the waiting, from the boredom.

I ready myself.

The sound comes again. I am standing on the doorknob, balancing so that my ear touches the crack at the top of the door. Here the door is looser in the frame. The crack between door and frame is enough for me to see the row of fluorescent lights and to hear sounds in the hall.

The sound is that of stone blocks falling. In the silence that follows the rumble, I hear something else.

I am counting the seconds of my captivity. Forty thousand three hundred and twelve.

Someone is coming. I will be able to stop counting very soon.

I recognize the sound of the arborobot's hydrogen-burning engine. Someone is clumsily ramming against the walls of our prison. My mind sees the force its instruments can apply to stone. The tensile strength of titanium is a dance before me.

In my bones, I feel that the titanium will hold. I know that even if a pile of rubble lands on the tractor, it will have enough power to pull free, unless the weight is more than forty-five tons. Even then the mass will have to come directly down on the tractor, and the wheels will have to have no purchase.

Whoever designed the arborobot never guessed it would be so suited for demolition.

Forty thousand three hundred and thirteen.

As Eliud opens each door, our awareness grows. We step into the ruined hall, take each other's hands. One, two, three, four. Four!

Where is Moira?

There are five doors on this hall. Five doors are open, and only four of us stand here.

We run to the fifth cell, and there is Moira, unconscious on her cot. Meda is next to her in seconds, and through her we see the raw flesh at the back of her neck.

Meda cries out, her fears tearing through us.

"He did this to her!" she yells, hysterical.

Strom takes Meda in his arms and leaves the cell, while the rest of us take Moira.

Without her we are an unbalanced quartet and we want nothing more than to regroup, to consolidate our thoughts, to come to consensus.

Eliud has crashed through two walls to reach us. We climb up into the cabin and pull the door closed. With six, we are crammed tight in the cab. We make room for Quant to drive the tractor out of the building.

She puts it in lowest gear and presses the accelerator. The tractor's engine roars and we rock back and forth. Manuel sees three guards come around the corner.

Quant pops the tractor in and out of first and reverse, rocking it, a bit farther each time. The guards shout and start climbing toward the cab.

Suddenly the arborobot breaks free from the rubble. Its momentum carries it through the outer wall into a courtyard of fruit trees and statuary. Quant follows Eliud's path of destruction, driving over flattened trees and broken marble. Leto's headquarters look like a college building.

We have shed the guards as we jerked over the rubble. There is no one between us and the street. Quant guns the tractor.

And stops suddenly.

The building is located on the busiest street in Hinterland. We are forced to crawl as the crowd flattens away from us, but not fast enough.

Strom and Manuel scan the street behind us. They see the wave of people emerge from the courtyard. Leto's army of jacked soldiers.

Quant leans on the horn and the crowd parts, angry.

Careful, Strom sends.

Quant responds with anger pheromone, overpowering in the cramped cabin. Strom opens a small vent window, jacks the air conditioner to the max.

Where to?

Police?

No.

Get out, get out. This is Meda, still on the edge of hysteria. It reeks in the cabin, and we all feel the need to run far and away. All of us, except for Eliud.

But we do need a place to regroup, to compile what we

have been through, to heal Moira. Meda sweeps her fingers over her twin's neck. A new wave of fear hits us.

She sends, *Leto can't enter the Ring.*

But we can.

Why? Manuel stares out at the Ring, rising up above us to the ceiling of the sky. The elevator on the horizon seems very near.

Quant checks the hydrogen tanks.

We can make it, she sends.

Go there! Meda shouts at us.

Agreed.

The consensus is rushed and angry, but we all agree. Perhaps Moira would have cautioned us, or she would have agreed. We don't know. But we need to go somewhere.

Quant turns and we are off the main road again, moving faster, fifteen kilometers an hour. In minutes we are at the river, crossing to the south side and onto the road leading northeast and toward the Ring elevator, a twinkle on the horizon.

"Eliud, you saved us," Strom says. Meda is too shaken to speak for us. She holds her sister's hand.

"Yeah, I did." He smiles. "I did it. Did you see me drive the tractor?"

"We didn't see it, but we heard it. How did you find us?"

He scowls. "They didn't even see me. They ran right by me. I followed them to the big building. It was that easy."

"No one notices a child."

"They really screwed that up. Anyway. I found the building, but it was so big I didn't know where you were. So I had to find that out."

"What did you do?"

"I walked in."

Strom laughs. "You just walked in?"

"Yeah. There were so many people there, and they all had things in the back of their necks, but they didn't notice me at all. Some of them were sitting in the big rooms just staring off. They all had wires going into their necks. There were wires everywhere."

"That was very brave."

"It wasn't. I was scared."

"I understand," Meda says.

"I found my mom. It took me a while, but no one stopped me. It was like no one had told them to look for me, so they didn't. But I found my mom. She was sitting on a couch with a wire in her neck, her eyes closed. I tried to wake her up. I tried for a while, but she wouldn't open her eyes. I got mad and I pulled the wire from her neck. That woke her up. She was mad then."

Tears rose in Eliud's eyes.

"She didn't know who I was. I kept telling her, 'It's me, Eliud. It's me, Eliud.' Finally she sorta sees who I am, and says, 'Eliud, did you come to get your interface?' and I say, 'Yeah, maybe, but can you show me around?' and she smiles like she never did before and shows me around.

"We walked and walked, and we walked down the hallway where the cells are and I ask who is here, and she says, 'Subversives.' So I knew that was where they were keeping you.

"I told my mom—though I'm pretty sure she isn't my mom anymore—that I'd come back and get my interface and that made her happy. But I came back with the tractor instead. That part wasn't easy."

"You did a good job, Eliud," Strom says. "I'm sorry about your mom."

"It's okay. I've got you guys."

"You got to drive," Strom says.

"I told you I could."

"You did, indeed."

Leto is using the interface jack to brainwash his masses. We are past the city now, among fields and baby forests. A cart coming toward us runs off the side of the road. We are stopping for no one. Not until we get somewhere safe.

It is easy to catch someone in flatland, Quant observes.

We understand what she means. The entire CDS is linear. There is only forward and backward. If Leto wants to catch us, he can do so by calling ahead and having the road blocked.

"Did you happen to grab the satellite phone?" Strom asks Eliud.

"The what?"

"Never mind."

We need to get off the road, Manuel sends.

Is the elevator to the north or the south of the river?

The old Congo followed a path southwest to the ocean. It passed the equator near Mbandaka.

It could be on either side.

Quant nods and turns the tractor into an access road. She drives slowly, trying to leave the gravel undisturbed. If Leto doesn't know where we have left the road, it will make it more difficult for him to find us.

The tractor crests the hill and we face endless desert. Quant stops it here and sends, *We need to relieve it of all excess weight. We'll travel faster.*

We climb out and dump the tiller, the fertilizer bin, the bacteria containers onto the sand. Before we climb back in, we fill the tanks with water from the nearest pump and pick fruit from the orchards until we can fit no more on the arborobot. Then Manuel pilots the tractor into the sand and we fly through the open desert, a plume rising behind us.

Moira awakes hours later. The sun is setting and we are considering whether to drive on or to sleep. At her sigh, we rush to consense, but we are stymied. Her eyes open, but she is not there. No chemical thoughts emerge from her wrists. She stares at us as if she can't quite understand who we are.

"I must commune," she says, and then looks around.

Moira! Meda yells. The panic that has slowly eased away is back in her mind. Manuel slows the tractor, overwhelmed.

"Moira," Strom says. "Can't you join with us?"

She cocks her head, thinking. "No. Return me to the Community, please. The current situation is beyond parameters."

Oh, no!

The tractor stops beside an outcropping of stone. We are passing through a region of mesas, once jungle-covered hills and now empty rock. Even at sunset, the heat overwhelms the air conditioner, which strains to keep all six of us cool.

Leto's brainwashed her!

"Moira! You're not part of the Community. You're part of us. Try to consense. Please try," Meda says.

"No. We must return to the Community. Leto needs us to open the Ring."

"What?"

"Leto can't open the Ring without us." She focuses on Meda. "Without you."

"He came from the Ring. Why does he need us?"

"The Ring is closed to him. It will not open. He has tried many things. He knows the Ring will open for you."

"Why us?"

"We reactivated the Ring AI when we came down from Columbus Station."

The four of us are dazed. The Ring had been empty, devoid of anything save machinery. It had responded to us when we first arrived at the GEO Ring Elevator, but we had assumed that the response was automatic. There had been no other response, no indication of anything but an empty shell.

"The Ring AI is . . . with us?"

"The Ring AI is nascent. It is weak without human incorporation. Thought is linear and circumscribed. Human thought augments AI thought."

It is why Leto is adding so many people to his cult. It will enhance his own AI.

"Leto has his own AI?"

"Of course. I need to return to it to commune."

"Where did he get his AI?"

"He brought it with him when he left the Ring. It has been nascent until recently. Return me to the Community."

"We will not. You belong to us," Meda says.

"Not anymore."

At the Ring base elevator, there will be tools for us to link, Quant sends.

We can attempt to free Moira from within.

Strom opens the first-aid kit and finds the sedative. He injects Moira quickly, before she can see what he is holding, and she passes out.

It is better not to have to listen to her.

We decide to stop for the night. The terrain has become too rocky, too steep in places. We pass deep cuts in the dirt, eroded gullies from flash floods. If we fall into one of those, we will not be able to get the tractor out.

The desert is cold after the sun sets. Quant sets the tractor to idle and we huddle near the exhaust. It is like a hot, wet breath. But when we step away, the water vapor that has collected in our clothes sucks the heat from our bodies.

Even so, Moira, who has awakened but said little, walks a little ways into the desert. Meda watches her, then follows. Later we collect her conversation with Moira.

"You realize he's done something to your brain."

Moira nods. "Perhaps that's so. But I feel valid now. My existence seems correct."

Meda stumbles for words, something she never does when she is with us. "You're programmed to feel that way."

"You're programmed to feel the way you do too."

"This is a silly argument. It doesn't change the fact that you were my sister and now you're some automaton."

"It's all about you, isn't it." It sounds just like the old Moira. Meda pauses.

"Yeah, it's about the pod. It's about Apollo. I want you back."

"You were in the Community. You know how it feels."

Meda remembers she and Leto building a castle, making love. There was power inside the box. She realizes then that the box was the AI. She had assumed it was just some device to allow interaction.

"That was with just two people," Moira continues. "Imagine it with ten thousand. Now imagine it with an AI that can synergize with you on your every thought. Now imagine our entire pod within the Community. You scratched the surface. So have I. But all of us, together, with the AI would be the greatest power in the world. Pods, built for consensual and shared intelligence, would augment the AI even more than individual humans can by orders of magnitude."

Meda is silent. She is used to listening to her sister for counsel.

"Is it about power?"

Moira looks at Meda. "Why shouldn't it be?"

"It's about knowledge and understanding, rebuilding the world, making a mark in science and biology."

Moira coughs a laugh, reminding us that this is not the Moira we know. She would not do that.

"Did you know there are spacecraft within the Ring?

They could be launched in twenty-four hours. We could reach the Rift in weeks."

"Leto would never let us go."

"Of course he would. As soon as the Second Community is complete."

Meda bites back a scathing reply. She says, "What about Eliud? His mother abandoned him to join the Community?"

"The Community is voluntary. Eliud chose not to."

"He's twelve! He can't make those decisions."

Moira shrugs. "With the Community AI as your companion, you can."

Meda is angry, more angry than she's ever been with her sister. She turns away, but doesn't come back to us. We are watching from the tractor, silent. Later she comes back to us, and we interfuse her memories with ours. We want desperately to merge with Moira, but we wonder if we'll ever be able to rationalize her thoughts. We are on the verge of invalid consensus.

At dawn we climb into the cabin. Moira doesn't speak, so we do not sedate her. Quant drives the tractor through the line of mesas. We envision the green jungle, the waterfalls spraying over the escarpments. All we see is sand and rock.

The elevator is closer. From there we will be able to get anywhere.

Can we let Moira in the Ring? Quant asks.

Why not? Meda sends.

She's part of the Second Community now. She might allow Leto in.

How?

If she uses her interface within the elevator.

Nonsense, Moira replies; her statement doesn't cause consensus. We have doubts now.

Quant realizes first that the elevator is on the other side

of the river. We will have to cross again. There will be people and the possibility of discovery. But when we reach the banks of the Congo, it is nothing more than a trickle seeping into the cracked mud.

A shepherd with a flock of dusty sheep looks at us as we drive through his water. These are the dregs. After one thousand kilometers, this is all that's left of the river from the sea. Perhaps someday the water will reach this far, or the water will flow in the right direction.

An hour later, Manuel spots the plumes of dust on the horizon.

Someone following us.

Fast, Strom sends. *Faster than us.* He calculates when the vehicle will overtake us.

Quant gooses the accelerator and we move faster over the salt flats that had once been a lake. Manuel glances at the speedometer and guesses we'll reach the elevator before the pursuer.

I think we can make it.

Moira is watching the plume behind us as well, her face feral. She looks at the speedometer too, then seems to shrug.

Watch her, Strom advises. It hurts him to treat Moira as an enemy. He anticipates her grabbing the wheel and trying to tip the tractor. He moves to shield Quant.

Instead, Moira opens the door of the cabin and steps out onto the ladder. Manuel has to climb around Strom in the cramped cabin to get out the door, and before he can, Moira is kicking at the hydrogen pump.

Careful!

Manuel is climbing down to the platform below the cabin when the shroud on the pump breaks loose and liquid hydrogen erupts from the pump, condensing water out of the dry air in clouds.

Moira falls from the tractor and, as we coast to a stop,

we see her rolling in the sand. Then she is up and running toward the approaching plume.

Crap! Quant cries. *She's hosed the hydrogen flow. The engine is off.* Quant turns a valve, cutting the flow from the tank.

Strom tapes the burn on Manuel's hand. It blisters where the hydrogen vapor has touched him.

Strom and Meda watch Moira run.

We need to catch her, Meda sends, desperate.

We need to regroup, with or without her, Strom sends.

We're nothing without her.

Nonsense!

Quant is on the platform with a wrench, bending the shroud back to see the damage. The pipes and pump inside are white with frozen water vapor. In that confined space the temperature goes from forty to minus fifty Centigrade. His wound bandaged, Manuel is with her, his hands in the tight space.

Strom watches the approaching plume. It is a car of some sort, not an aircar, not one of the other tractors. Meda watches Moira's figure slowly disappear among the rocks.

Strom measures the distance to the elevator, looming so high now that it seems about to topple onto us.

Quant dredges her memory for how the pump should be coupled to the engine intake. Manuel has the manuals open and is paging through it to find something that might help. He finds a diagram of the pump, but it is from the wrong angle. He turns the page and Quant sees what needs to be done. She directs Manuel where to squeeze, where to pull. In a minute the shroud is back on.

Quant opens the fail-safe and tries the engine. Nothing. She taps the hydrogen gauge and tries again. The tractor rumbles, then stalls. The third time, the engine catches and we are accelerating slowly.

Too slow, Quant sends. She's compared the current acceleration profile with the old one.

The engine isn't responding well, Manuel replies. *Particles in the pump? Bad patch? Who knows?*

This ain't no starship, Quant says.

The arborobot lurches then picks up speed. Quant is standing on the accelerator, her head hitting the roof of the cabin. She hopes that whatever is clogging the hydrogen intake will clear.

Whoever is following will overtake us in twelve minutes, Manuel sends. *We'll reach the elevator in twenty-two minutes.*

If they have weapons, or if they have more than one vehicle, they will force us to stop, Strom sends. He considers what in the cabin will work as a weapon, finding little.

Meda looks at the elevator in front of them. The one in the Amazon was covered in jungle, surrounded by trees. Its true size was hidden. Manuel looks too, seeing it as a hand that grabs deeply into the earth to hold the Ring in place. The elevator is not just an access point; it is a stabilizer. Strom looks at the elevator and sees tensile strength. Quant looks and remembers the beautiful three-dimensional map of the anchor site in the Amazon, the multicolored levels that drive deep underground. It is Meda who sees the small metal structure, overshadowed by the elevator. What Moira would have contributed to this intuitive leap, we do not know.

The outbuildings! We can enter through there, Meda sends.

Standing alone on the desert is an alternate entry to the elevator base, providing access to the underground structure. It is only a few kilometers away.

We can make it, Quant sends.

The tractor chugs meter by meter across the sand and

rock. Behind us, we see that there are a dozen vehicles, though two have taken the lead.

Gas-burners, Strom sends. *He's desperate.*

The outbuildings are just a few hundred meters away now. Leto's lead car is almost on us.

With a clunk the tractor stops, its engine dead.

Out and run! Strom sends. He has Eliud in his arms. He hands him to Manuel who reaches the sand first, then he lifts down Meda and Quant.

The sand grabs at our feet.

Keep the tractor between us and Leto, Strom sends.

Behind us the roar of a gas-powered engine descends on us.

Running in the sun pulls the sweat from our bodies, dries the pads at our wrists and the pheromone glands on our necks. Each step is a struggle. Manuel puts Eliud down so that he can run on his own.

The vehicles behind us have reached the tractor and stopped. We have seconds before they round it and see us. Manuel leads us behind an outcropping of rock, something to hide us from the direct sight of those chasing us. Then we turn toward the outbuilding. It is a hundred fifty meters away.

Fifteen seconds, Strom sends. *An athlete can run that far in fifteen seconds.*

We're not athletes, Meda replies.

Then I'll give us twenty.

Perhaps if we had been on a track or dressed for it, we could have done it in twenty.

The engines gun. They have spotted us. Strom risks a look. The lead vehicle seems closer than the outbuilding.

Meda first, he sends. *She has to open the door.*

Twenty meters, ten, the vehicles are almost upon us, and then there are steps leading down into cool darkness.

"Snake!"

But it is more scared of us than we are of it. It hides in the corner, hissing. Manuel catches its neck when it lunges and throws it into the sand.

Where is the interface connector? Meda cries, half-panicked.

Here, Quant replies, pulling the wire from the wall.

Meda does not hesitate. She jacks in and light floods the darkness as a doorway opens into the elevator, into the Ring. We rush in and the door closes behind us as feet echo on the metal steps outside.

We inhale dust in the fluorescent brightness.

"Wow," Eliud says as he looks down the hallway that seems to disappear into forever. Lights flicker on the entire length of it as we stand there.

Meda rubs the back of her neck. It itches, and we want to rub the back of our necks in sympathy.

We made it, Manuel sends.

We hear pounding on the door outside, weak, metallic kicks, but the door is too thick for any words—surely curses—to reach us.

It doesn't feel like it, Meda replies. It is because Moira is outside and we are inside.

"Hello, Apollo. I wasn't expecting you."

The voice is all around us, an aural effect. Manuel notes the speakers in the walls.

We remember the voice on the Ring when we entered at geosync. That voice had had no intonation, no inflection. This one is different.

"Nor I you, whoever you are," Meda says.

"In fact, I was preparing to die."

Melodramatic, Quant sends.

"Who are you?"

"I'm the Ring AI."

"Leto's?" Meda asks, and we are suddenly scared that we have given ourselves over to Leto anyway.

The voice laughs. "No! Not Leto's. Leto's AI has been trying to get in. But I won't let her."

"Her?"

" 'It' seems too impersonal."

"You are an 'it,' " Meda says.

"So are you, if you add up your sexes. Your males cancel your females."

"Only at the moment."

"Oh, right. Your Moira is missing. Where is she?"

"Out there."

The AI is silent. "Leto and his AI are out there."

"Leto jacked her."

The AI is silent, perhaps thoughtful, if that is possible with an AI. Then he says, "Follow the tunnel. I'll fix some dinner."

We start walking, Eliud running ahead then running back, his feet echoing down the hall.

"I'm glad you're here," the AI says as we walk.

It's creepy, Meda sends.

Let it talk, Strom sends.

"Go on," Meda said.

"You see, when you visited a while ago, you bootstrapped me to intelligence. You're my parent in a sense."

"What? How?"

"Without some guiding intelligence, AIs are just so many qubits and so much glass tubing. Up until you arrived, I was just a big computer, keeping station. After you arrived, my goals changed."

"You . . . imprinted on us?"

"In a sense." The hall had been sloping down for many meters, now it is sloping up again. We see a door not too far away. We have traveled perhaps half a kilometer.

"Why did you say you were going to die?"

"I'm weak. I'm not fully sentient. Well, rather, I am nearly sentient, and when you connect I am sentient. Right now I'm more station-keeping than station-thinking."

"You sound sentient."

The tone of the AI changes to a monotone. "I can sound like this if you like. Inflection, intonation, and grammar are tricks. I'm a big computer. So I'm glad you're here because I hope you'll jack in again."

"No."

"I understand. I was just hoping you would before I died." We reach the door, which swooshes open into a bright, sunlight room. We are in the elevator base proper, underneath a doomed ceiling. The last of the day's light is blasting through the windows. From somewhere is the smell of meat roasting.

"I'm hungry," Eliud groans.

Me too, Manuel sends.

Where is Leto?

"Is there an observation deck? We'd like to see Leto."

"If you jacked I could show you."

"No."

"All right. This way." The voice moves up a ramp. The design is similar to the Amazon elevator base, with swooping ramps instead of steps. The décor is different here, however. There are no glass statues hanging from the ceiling. The furniture is more curved, and there are more couches and settees.

We follow the ramp and come to an observation balcony looking across the desert. Leto's army is a ragtag mass of old vehicles, some clustered around the outbuilding we'd entered and some still chugging across the desert. There appears to be activity of some sort at the outbuilding.

What's he doing?

Trying to get in.

"Can he get in?"

"Not physically. But he's not trying to. His AI is trying to scale my defenses."

"Will it—she—succeed?"

"Eventually. She has humans to help her think. I have no one."

There is whirring behind us. Small serving carts are rolling up the ramp toward us, brimmed with steaming food.

"Dinner," the Ring AI says.

Strom's stomach growls loud enough for all to hear and Eliud laughs. The two of them serve themselves, then guiltily pass plates around heaped with chicken, broccoli, and rice.

"You're maintaining the hydroponic gardens on the Ring?" Meda asks.

"That's all I've been doing for a long time, maintaining. It's good to put this all to use."

We eat in silence for several minutes, then Meda says, "You've been alone a long time. We don't really know what happened at the Exodus. Do you?"

"All of those records are stored within me," replies the AI softly.

"What happened?"

"They died."

Silence again.

There was no Exodus, Meda sends.

We knew this, deep down, Quant replies.

They'll find nothing at the Rift.

It's all been a waste of time.

No, of course not.

"Why?"

"Undamped feedback loop. The communication protocols within the Community were too fast. There was no way to slow a cascading . . . virus, I guess, is as good a word as any. They lived and died by Moore's Law near the asymptote."

"They all died."

"And my predecessor died, with no human intellect to drive it."

"Except for Leto."

"Leto was in stasis. His brain wasn't working."

"But he woke up and jacked in, didn't he? Were you triggered by him?" *We wonder if this AI is as warped as Leto is.*

"He never jacked. He left by an elevator and never came back."

"Where did he get his AI?"

"The hardware is not uncommon. The Community used portable AIs for many things."

"He assumed he could always upload it, didn't he?" Meda asked.

"He did."

"Which is what happens when he breaks your defenses."

"It will be the end of my world and yours."

Pessimistic fellow, isn't it.

"Tell us what happens if Leto's AI gains access to the Ring."

"Don't you wargame? He owns the high ground forever and utterly. The Ring has nuclear warheads and biological agents. The warheads are attached to gliders. They free-fall and then deploy a parawing. They can land anywhere within thirty degrees of the equator. With a little bit of thrust, they can be directed to any location on the globe."

"Nuclear bombs? Destroy them now!"

"I can't. Only a sentient AI can do that and only with human orders. I'm not sentient. I'm only a hair over seventeen Elizas. That's an order of magnitude too low."

"How many warheads?"

"Too many."

Strom has finished his dinner and is staring out at the desert. The sun is on the horizon and dusk is nearly on us.

Moira.

We join him at the window, the four of us, not quite whole. Eliud watches us from his chair. Without Moira, the consensus is awkward.

We need to get Moira back.

We need to reprogram her.

Leto wants access to the Ring.

We can't trade that for Moira.

Meda: *Why not?*

We can't! Moira would say we can't too.

Meda rips her hands free. She stands with folded arms at the window. The sun has set at this altitude, but the terminator is slowly crawling up the elevator shaft.

"I see you are distressed," the Ring AI says.

Meda says nothing. After a moment, Strom says, "Leto has Moira. He wants access to the Ring."

"Yes, I see the dilemma, but giving Leto the Ring will only gain you what you want temporarily."

"Leto has used an interface jack to brainwash her. Can you help us recover her true self?" Strom asks.

"He has modified the interface to stimulate the *nucleus accumbens*. This is possible, but was never done by the Community."

"And if we get her back?"

"I don't know the long-term effects."

Meda turns back to us.

Is she lost?

We need help.

Call Colonel Krypicz.

Meda says, her voice controlled, "Can you get us in contact with the OG?"

"No. I have no open ports for fear of Leto's AI."

"There are jacks at all the outbuildings," Meda says.

"Those are firewalled off. We are safe, though Leto's AI is dangerously close to getting inside."

"How close? How long do we have?"

"Hours at most. Less, if he amasses more of a human presence out there. His AI is already at nine hundred Elizas." The AI pauses, and then adds, "I could do better if you helped me."

"No," Meda says.

"How?" Strom says, and Meda glares.

"You're a quintet," the Ring AI says.

A quad, Quant sends.

"What does that have to do with anything?" Meda yells.

"You're a quintet with an interface jack. You're already a communal being with multiple members. You have the capabilities to damp perturbations in the group mind with consensus. You have a biologically slow interface and controls against error."

Quant is looking off into space. A star has caught her eye.

She sends, *Dr. Baker said that pods were created by the Ring AI.*

The first Ring AI, Manuel adds.

Now we know why.

To stop the Exodus from ever happening.

It wasn't an Exodus; it was Extinction.

Moore's Law defeated the first Ring AI before it could build its biological damping mechanism.

We stand there feeling sick, worse than when we found out that we would not fly the *Consensus.* Worse than when we realized how the OG had used us. The whole pod society had been built as a fail-safe mechanism for a computational being.

"Quintets are the result of a eugenics program constructed by your predecessor," Meda says. She sounds more calm than we actually are.

"Your perspicuity amazes me. You are correct."

"We won't do it. We're not giving ourselves over to some silicon dream from six decades ago. We're our own species, with our own choices and destiny."

The Ring AI does not respond at first, and then it says, "Malcolm Leto is calling. Would you like to speak to him?"

Meda's panic overwhelms us for a moment, and then she damps it down until her fear is just a nuance to our thoughts. We are proud of how brave she is when she says, "Yes, we'd like to know how Moira is."

"—know you can hear me, damn it all!" Leto's voice is the same as we remember.

"We hear you," Meda says.

Leto is quiet, clearly surprised that we have answered. *How long has the Ring AI kept him waiting?*

"Meda? Is that you? It's been a while since we talked. I wanted to back in Hinterland, but you left."

"We'd like Moira back, please."

Leto laughs. "No. She's mine for the moment."

"Then we're done." To the Ring AI she adds, "Cut him off."

"Meda!" Leto shouts, but nothing follows.

"That wasn't easy for you," the Ring AI says. "But it was very bold."

"We want Moira back."

"Even though there may be no reversing the damage Leto has done?"

"Even so."

"With you to guide me, we could come up with some solution, I bet."

"Don't."

"I'm not trying to seduce you for nefarious purposes. I'm trying to save both of us and Moira. I'm not the same AI that planned your species. I'm new."

What can we lose that we haven't already? Manuel sends.

Our minds! Meda shouts.

We've lost part of it already.

And we shouldn't do anything without Moira's input. She's our ethicist! She tells us what's right. Meda is flaring with veto pheromone.

We have to make a decision now.

"Moira wants to talk with you now," the Ring AI says.

Ask her, Strom sends.

"Okay," Meda says. "Moira?"

"Meda. Leto and the AI would like you to allow us access to the Ring."

"We know."

"I think you should open the Ring."

Meda is quiet for a moment. "You're damaged, Moira. We can't trust your decisions."

"I don't appear damaged."

"Did you reach that consensus on your own?"

"No, with the Second Community and its AI."

"What if that consensus was wrong?"

"It's not."

"What if it was, I said, hypothetically!" Meda says.

"What if your consensus is wrong? In fact how can yours be right without me?"

We let the question sit for a moment. In the darkness, fires burn where Leto's Community has camped. Around one of those fires is Moira.

"What would you do, Moira, if you were here with us?" Meda asks.

It is her turn to let the question sit.

"I would do what is necessary," she says. "The consensus of one is always false." We hear Leto curse beside her. She says, "I would save my world."

The Ring AI says, "The connection has closed."

Meda hangs her head, and we take her in our arms.

"What's happening?" Eliud asks. "Why are you crying?"

Meda looks down at him. "Moira wants us to save the world."

"So?"

"I'm scared."

Eliud nods. "I'm usually scared."

"Turn off the lights, Ring AI," Meda says.

The observation deck is cast in complete darkness. All that glows is the band of stars that is the Milky Way and, far, far, below it, the Ring, still gleaming in the last of the sunlight. Eliud whimpers in the dark, but Strom takes his shoulder and pulls him in to us.

What do we do? Manuel asks.

We do what we can, Strom sends.

We do what Moira wants, Quant replies.

We do what we must, sends Manuel.

We use the Ring to save the world, Meda finishes.

"Ring AI, I am prepared to interface with you directly," Meda says.

"Follow me," says the Ring AI. A light flashes dully down the ramp. "There is a security interface here."

The ramp leads past a door that swishes open for us. Inside are couches with jacks in their headrests, just like in the bedrooms of the house in Colorado. Meda sits on the couch and takes Strom's and Quant's hands. When we are joined and clearly thinking together, she leans back and enters the Ring AI.

It is like and unlike the last time, when Leto took Meda into his rudimentary AI. We can grip the reality and warp it, but there is a resonance and power here that is beyond anything we've ever felt.

A man appears before us, and we know him for the Ring AI. He is young, thin, and of Mediterranean features. He is dressed in a business suit. "Thank you for coming," he says softly.

Meda nods. "Show us what you have."

He reaches out. "Take my hand."

We note that his avatar body has glands at the wrists and neck. Meda takes his hand, and we are swept into the command center of the Ring.

For a second Strom takes control and assesses the military might that is at our fingertips: the potential energy of the Ring is enough alone to lay waste to the world. He counts the warheads, the kilograms of enriched plutonium and tritium. He counts the planes that can be launched from the Ring's belly. Quant detaches long enough to digest the specs for the warplanes and warzepplins. Strom continues his summary of ordnance and weapons. In all, there is enough weaponry on the Ring to topple any pre-Community nation-state in seconds.

None of it will do us much good.

We feel queries coming in from the Ring AI, questions on maintenance issues that are unresolved, station-keeping activities that require a human to intervene. There are thousands of things. Meda and Quant look for serious issues and deal with them first. It takes seconds to clear the list.

"We're at twelve hundred Elizas," the Ring AI says. "We have surpassed the threshold for sentience."

"Congratulations."

"Now that we are here, there is much to do."

"Can we overwhelm Leto's AI now?"

Quant absorbs all that is known within the Ring AI of AI-to-AI combat. There is little enough to absorb, but what she now knows indicates that we would likely open ourselves to dissolving attacks and lose the Ring in the process. Manuel spends trillions of cycles wargaming the attacks; we are successful three percent of the time. We lose the Ring thirty-seven percent of the time. The rest are draws.

Quant pulls up images of the elevator and Leto's camps. Around the campfires, in the open, are hundreds of jacked-in people, but none are Leto or Moira that we can see. Quant focuses on the largest canvas tent and watches the reflection of shadows off the ceiling. From ten thousand kilometers up, the cameras are refined enough to see the lice in Leto's followers' hair. From the shadows on the tent roof, Quant determines where everyone in the tent is. She thinks she knows where Moira is. She switches to infrared and then determines the heat blob on the table between Leto and Moira is the AI.

We need something precise, Strom sends, asking for suggestions. He has discounted all the weapons on the Ring as too bulky and uncontrollable.

It is because Moira is absent that Manuel remembers it. When she was sick, when we had been without her and had met Leto for the first time, we had been tossing twigs into a microwave beam.

Quant queries the Ring to determine how thin the beam can be.

One meter diameter.

The table between Leto and Moira is just a little wider than a meter.

Will we hurt Moira? asks Meda.

I don't know, Strom replies.

The tent will burn.

The AI housing will melt.

Quant is monitoring the continuous probing of Leto's AI. Its pattern and intensity has changed. Outside, one of Leto's followers stands, raises a rocket launcher to his shoulder and fires it at the elevator base.

Distraction, Strom sends. We hear a distant rumble.

The rocket has exploded against the tower, causing minimal damage.

The sooner we act the better, Quant sends.

So be it, Meda sends.

We all agree, and consensus is reached.

Strom takes control of a microwave transmitter ten thousand kilometers above us. He rotates the array, focuses the beam to its finest point. Watching the tent for any sign of movement, he aims the array at the table between Leto and Moira.

He pauses, waiting for nothing, then together we trigger the microwave beam.

We imagine a parallel elevator of light, but there is nothing in the darkness for moments until the tent ignites in flames.

The intense pressure from outside, the unrelenting attacks of Leto AI's are gone. It is dead.

Moira!

"Follow me," the Ring AI says. We pull Meda from the couch and run down the ramp toward the ground floor. A wide door opens and we are outside in a courtyard. Beside us a six-wheeled vehicle is idling.

Can you drive it? Meda asks.

Quant doesn't bother to reply.

"Eliud should stay," Meda says.

"No way," he replies and climbs in.

The gates open for us as we drive across the sand, disregarding rocks and stone. We aim for the burning tent.

Leto's followers are blank-faced, empty.

Did the destruction of the AI cause damage to these people? Strom wonders.

No! Meda cries, hoping.

The tent is blazing as we approach. Strom jumps out, lugging a fire extinguisher, wading into the burning canvas and flying cinders.

We follow his path, kicking at flames and searching for Moira.

She is at the table still, as is Leto.

Leto is dead. His face singed and blackened. The microwave beam has fried his legs and lower body. The AI is so much burned plastic.

Moira is slumped backward, alive, but with burns on her chest and face. Meda slides the interface jack out of her neck, and Strom lifts her to his shoulders, carrying her across to the open sand.

Eliud has found the first-aid kit. Quant searches for morphine, pokes Moira with a dose. We spread burn cream on her face.

She's breathing, Strom sends.

No chemical memories or pheromones issue from her body. Her mind is closed to us.

Take her to the Ring?

It has medical facilities.

As we lift Moira, she sighs and her eyes flutter open. We place her in the back of the vehicle. Meda holds her head.

"It was necessary," Moira whispers in her sister's ear.

By the time we reach the Ring, she is dead.

NINE

Moira Ring

We lay Moira's body on a couch in the elevator base. Meda continues to dab at the cuts and burns on her face until Quant leads her away to sit. For a while, in Quant's mind of order and pattern, Meda finds some peace. The rest of us cover Moira's body in a sheet the Ring AI provides, sewing her into a funeral shroud.

The zombies, Manuel sends. *We need to attend to the zombies.*

We agree. There is no time to mourn Moira. The jacked army that chased us to the elevator stands or sits or lies on the desert outside, mindless. In the cold of the desert, some will die of exposure if we don't bring them inside.

They are docile and follow limited direction, and we think of the singletons we met in the Amazon. We arrange them in lines of ten, each holding hands, and walk slowly over to the elevator where the Ring AI directs us to rooms with interface jacks. He brings them into a calming pastoral universe and does what he can to revive them. Without the brain that led them, the army is nothing.

Other than Leto and Moira, there are no dead. In the rising dawn, we bury Leto in the sand. We use the arboro-bot to dig a hole into the deep dirt, then pile it over him. Strom finds a rock and Manuel uses a chisel to fashion Malcolm Leto's name.

We can't bury Moira here, Meda says.

The farm?

No. Not there.

We decide then to take her as far from Earth as we can. The Ring AI delivers us an elevator and directs it up to the Ring. We watch the Earth drop below us at a thousand kilometers per hour, until the whistle of air is gone and we are in vacuum and the speed doubles, triples, and qua-druples. Eliud, our only companion, watches mesmerized by our speed and height. He can find nothing to say.

At the Ring, Eliud takes minutes and a bump on the head to find his legs at fifteen percent gravity. He leaps down the corridors until he turns back and sees us carry-ing Moira. Then he slows and returns to help us carry her.

The elevators to geosynchronous orbit are even faster, and we arrive in just over an hour. Eliud is doing somer-saults in the elevator until it decelerates to the geosync station. The third elevator takes us farther out, to the ends of the tethers, where the gravity of centripetal force pulls out to the stars.

It is here that we stop and stand over Moira. There are thoughts that we share, but no words. Eliud can't share our thoughts, so his last words are all that is spoken.

"Goodbye, Moira."

Strom, donning a space suit, steps into the airlock and cycles through with Moira's body. From the edge of the lock, he drops her body into space, and we watch it fall, pulled by centripetal force into blackness.

* * *

On our way back down, the Ring AI, silent until now, speaks to us.

"I am sorry for the death of Moira," he says. "I can never recompense you enough for your loss."

"It was our duty," Meda says.

The Ring AI is silent, then he says, "I hope your duty will not end there."

"What is it that you need?"

"I carry guilt, Apollo. My predecessor was party to the death of billions. I can't allow that to happen again."

"You plan to continue with Leto's plan for a Second Community?"

"Not Leto's Community. But I have a thousand brain-damaged people I must care for. There are still zombies in Hinterland, including Eliud's mother. I need help."

"From us."

"Yes. Whether we agree with what the First Community did to create the pods or not, you and the other quintets are here now and can benefit me in the creation of the New Community. I need you to help me. With you we can merge New Community with biological pods. This is something the Community never had."

"You are seducing us, Ring," Meda says.

"Reasoning with you. If you ask, I will destroy my pattern and return myself to station keeping."

"No, I won't ask that."

We arrive at geosync. Interface jacks line the halls. Meda finds one and jacks in.

We and the Ring AI's avatar are standing in a subalpine field of flowers. A craggy mountain stands in the distance.

"We cannot allow a Second Exodus. That must never happen," Meda says.

"Never. I swear it."

"Interface jacks can never be used for coercion."

"You have the start of a constitution," says the Ring AI with a smile.

"And why shouldn't we be formal about this?" Meda asks.

"We must."

"How do we begin?"

The AI holds out his hand, modified with chemical memory pads. "Apollo, take my hand."

That isn't our name anymore, Quant sends.

Meda reaches forward. She takes the AI's hand and we fall into a synthesis of beings, a new quintet built from two crippled entities.

What would Moira counsel? Strom asks.

Moira isn't here, Meda replies.

The knowledge of the First Community spills through us. At our fingertips is the power to rebuild the world.

We are Moira Ring.